THE

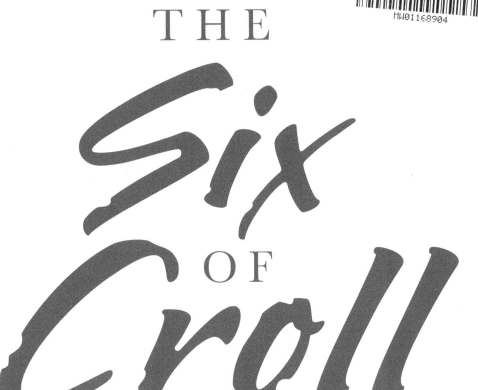

OF

MALCOLM POOLE

To order additional copies of this book, contact:
Xlibris
AU TFN: 1 800 844 927 (Toll Free inside Australia)
AU Local: 02 8310 8187 (+61 2 8310 8187 from outside Australia)
www.xlibris.com.au
Orders@Xlibris.com.au

ISBN: Softcover   978-1-6698-8782-9
        Hardcover   978-1-6698-8784-3
        EBook   978-1-6698-8783-6
Library of Congress Control Number: 2022906302
Print information available on the last page

Rev. date: 05/13/2022

by Malcolm Poole

If the smell of jasmine in the air has been
Yet not a bud or flower can be seen
Maybe an elf along your path he goes
Though of him you shall see neither nail nor nose
For quick and sleight of hand elves be
And man is too clumsy to ever see
But maybe in a forest if you silently sit
And meditate deeply for a bit
And if the smell of jasmine fills the day
Then sure enough elves have passed this way
Then very still sit you must
And maybe with a breath of dust
And when it settles there may be
An elf or two for you to see.

PREFACE

It was a time and place absent from the histories of man. If not for the chronicles of the Elves who kept safe the diaries of Mecco, this story would have been lost forever or twisted by man for his own purpose. The greed of man for power distorts and manipulates the truth to suit his own agenda. Our leaders were once children, and their beliefs are only what their teachers and parents taught them to think. From upbringing to education and life experience, we develop into who we are. If children are taught empathy, compassion, and forgiveness, they can break down the barriers of hate. Yet if they are taught distrust and prejudice, if they are not encouraged to search for the truth but follow one dogma, then they will be bound in a dictatorship of their own conditioning.

PROLOGUE

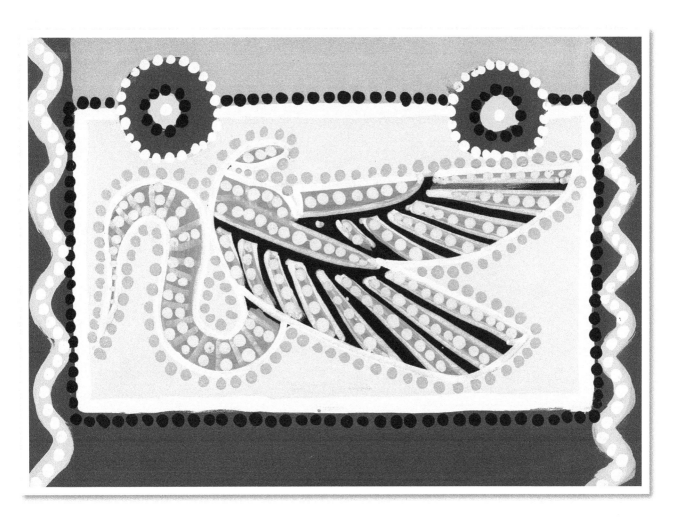

The history you are about to read is of a time not too long ago and not so far a place from where you are reading this book. The attempt to translate the names and places from ancient Elvan was done with the best of our ability. Therefore, it may not be exact, so your imagination we will need. But before we begin, a little history of the past is necessary.

Many, many years ago in a land far from here was a place called Central Earth. The great wars had just finished, the Evil had been destroyed and his forces banished. The inhabitants of this world consisted of Elves, Dwarfs, Men, Goblins, wizards, and a tiny people whose name has been lost in the past. It was said they were a happy breed but very shy of man. From what the old Elvan parchments say, they played a great part in the defeat of the Evil. It is rumoured they are distantly related to man, but how, no one is sure and what became of them is now a mystery.

In that corner of the world, times were changing way too fast for the Elves. So a decision was made by the elders to depart the Old World and begin again. The Elf explorer Vandayong had been sent to search for a great land foreseen in the old Elvan parchments. For over two years, he searched the southern seas. On his return, he announced to the elders the discovery of a great continent which fitted the predicted description. The history of Vandayong and his discovery is an interesting story, but that is for another time. So the land he discovered was to be their destination. The Elves of the Old World were scattered to its far corners. A meeting was called to take place in their great forest. The elders from each clan were informed and arrived at the appointed time. That night the decision was made of how and when to depart for the New World.

Over the next few months, the Elves packed their valuables and the ancient parchments that told their histories and their predictions of what was to come! They bid farewell to the friends with whom they had helped to defeat the Evil. Then they left Central Earth behind.

The Elves had kept their destination secret. They intended to create a New World without evil. But one lord had loose lips and divulged the whereabouts of the Elves' destination. When news of this great land across the sea became known, it spread like wildfire throughout the Old World.

The great wars had left devastation through all of Central Earth. When rumours of the new land the Elves had discovered reached the ears of Man, Dwarf, and Goblin, many decided to pack up their belongings and follow. But the small folk who played a prominent role in defeating the Evil had no intentions of leaving their comfortable homes to sail over the sea, to a place they knew nothing of. As far as anyone knows, they are still in their tiny homes cut into the hills in their little part of the Old World.

But against the wishes of the Elves, the Men and Goblins who followed brought to the New World their histories and memories of evil. All that was needed was for those thoughts to be harnessed by an evil power. Then they would grow and grow, getting stronger with each evil deed committed.

There was one such a man. He was an apprentice to a great wizard in the Old World. When he arrived in the New World, for many a year, he hid from sight. He observed the direction of the New World. When the time was right, he began. He set about creating division and hatred among the creeds. He spread rumours that one of the creeds was trying to take control of the New World. No one knew which creed he was referring to, which created suspicion among them all. The greed and weakness of Man became his strongest ally. This was to have a great bearing on his rise to power.

For the first few hundred years of the New World, all inhabitants lived in harmony. Men built great cities. But slowly, Man reverted to his old ways. He became crude. He would joke about the Dwarfs and Elves, calling them derogatory names. He became greedy and tried to make unfair dealings with the Goblins. His memories of evil grew; this the elves sensed.

So it came to pass in the New World that the Elves decided to live far from the troubles of Man and Goblin. They moved deep into the wilderness, where they found a great forest and lake to live by. Their early years of the First Age of the New World were about establishing a home. Later, they branched off in three directions—central, north, and south—though the Elves of the south fell silent for reasons some day you may learn.

The Dwarfs set up their homes close to Man, and for many a year, they lived in harmony. The Dwarfs were great miners and at first worked to supply Man with his needs. But as Man grew greedy, they grew tired of him. They travelled westwards, where they continued to mine and founded a new philosophy that you will hear about in due time.

Man also harnessed the Goblins as slaves and they too eventually escaped and hid from Man and built great caverns in the ground. There they multiplied. Then they began abducting human women to use as mates, and a new race was created called Menlins, whom the Evil would manipulate and harness on his quest for power.

The good wizards that followed the Elves blended into the cities of man and, for many a year, kept a low profile. The wizards eventually worked their way to become leaders of their cities.

It was only with the rise of the Evil that one grand wizard and four apprentices made themselves known though only to a select few.

Man himself became very powerful, taking at first what he needed from the land and environment. Then ultimately he took anything he desired, leaving a trail of devastation that can be seen to this day all over the New World.

As years and centuries passed, it came to be that men only thought of Elves, Dwarfs, and wizards as myths.

Both the Elves and the Dwarfs kept a history from the beginning of the First Age of the New World, and there are many interesting stories in their books. But this is a story that incorporates all the inhabitants of the New World. This story takes place in the Second Age of the New World, and begins in the Elvan year of Mort. We are using the Elvan calendar for times and dates to keep continuity, as prophecies from the ancient parchments are in old Elvan.

This story is based on the diaries of Mecco, one of the six children of Croll, and written by him and other participants in the story. Speeches are not verbatim but only a loose recollection. There may be some discrepancies in a few chapters as some of the protagonists have a slightly different perspective of particular events.

1
CHAPTER
The Six of Croll

Not a cloud in the sky, not a breath of wind in the trees. Silently, Peto and I walked down our street, hiding from the hot mid-morning sun in the shade of the liquid ambers. It was early autumn, and a cold spell the week before had the leaves turning red and gold.

'I hate our town,' said Mecco, 'with the prejudice of the creeds against each other, the narrow-mindedness of our elders and their demand that we not associate with children of another creed.'

'What's with you today?' Peto responded. 'There is nothing wrong with Malla. You're not in one of your strange moods again? But you do look a bit strange.'

'Yes, I do feel a bit strange, as if something exciting or an adventure was about to begin.'

My thoughts were disrupted by a lone fly buzzing around my ears. I knew we were close to the dairy farms of the Dation, a breeding ground for flies, and soon, more would descend upon us. Sure enough, the closer we got to the end of our street, the more we were surrounded.

'Here,' said Peto as he broke two twigs from a shrub and handed me one. 'This will keep them away,' he added. We continued on our way, waving madly our makeshift fly swatters.

Reaching the end of our street, we had to be careful not to be seen jumping the fence that surrounded the forbidden forest of Gundi. We hid behind a large tree and peered out from either side, making sure there were no witnesses to our crime. This was our little bit of rebellion: taking a shortcut to the beach along the edge of the forest of Gundi and over the dunes of Croll, also a forbidden place.

'Wait,' said Peto, dragging me back behind a tree. 'Had you kept walking, the Dations herding their cattle would have seen us.' We had to wait a few minutes till they disappeared over a small hill.

We were about to make a move when four Kabs with their black hats and ringlets came strolling past. We waited till they were out of earshot. We glanced at each other, smiled.

Peto said, 'Last one there is a fool.'

We made a dash towards the forest. The fence was only four strands of barbed wire high. We dived simultaneously over them, rolling into the protection of the forest. We lay close to each other, peering back from where we had come, checking if all was clear and that no one had seen us and given the alarm. Speckles of sunlight filtered through the trees and caressed our bare outstretched arms. What a contrast the world is with this beauty, yet such hatred between the creeds!

Peto and I were the best of friends. He was medium height, dark, and very handsome—well, maybe more pretty than handsome—where I was tall, fair-skinned, and I think, handsome as well. We spent many a day on the beach. Even when it was cold or the waves were too rough, we would sit, talk, fish, wrestle, fight, and slide down the sand dunes of Croll.

We fought a lot but we really cared for each other. He was better at most things than I was. Whenever we went fishing, he would always end up with the biggest fish or largest catch. He was also much better educated than I, but he lacked a sense of intuition and never thought of the consequences of his actions. He was filled with the optimism of youth and took everything in his stride without question, whereas I needed answers to everything. We were different in so many ways: he loved sport and I loved music and the arts. I can remember so clearly that late autumn the swimming, surfing, and just lying in the sun, talking. I would pose questions: of the universe, about the dogma of our creed, and why there was so much hatred in the world.

Peto shook his head and said, 'Who cares? We're having a good time. Will you stop with all the questions?'

Little did we know what was to be thrust upon us in the next few hours. As I was so fair, I would sit under the shade of a tea tree. Peto would lie next to me, most of his body in the sun, getting darker. The sun played on the tips of the tea tree and filtered through, hitting my body with specks of warmth. The salt smell of the ocean, the sound of the waves crashing on the shore—life was simple then. Often he would lay his head on my chest and simply go to sleep. As the sun moved low across the sky, its rays would hit my body but I would lie there not wanting to disturb Peto. I would end up with the worst sunburn except where Peto's head had lain!

In the late afternoon sun, I would lay there thinking how nice it was we could just do this without reprimand from our families or ridicule from other boys. I was not close to my father or brothers. I think Peto provided the male bonding I missed, and I loved him. I would never voice this for fear of embarrassing him. I do remember one day when we were fishing in the shallows. I had a bite on my line and I knew it was a big fish. I wanted so much to bring it ashore. I would show my father and brothers and get their approval. I always felt they disapproved of me for some reason.

Peto was so excited for me. He said, 'Now take it easy, reel it in slowly.'

As it came close, we saw how big it was, and Peto jumped on my back, screaming and cheering. I wish for those days back, but they are gone forever.

A few minutes passed. Both the Kabs and Dations were out of sight, so we rose and moved deeper into the forest, then made our way towards the dunes. We reached the beach without detection and spent the day as we usually did: surfing, swimming, and playing in the sand dunes of Croll.

I suppose this would be as good a time as any to introduce myself. My name is Mecco, and I am one of the Six of Croll. As I kept a diary during our travels, it was my task to keep a record of our adventures. As I sit here reading my diary and begin to transcribe it into a book, the memories flood back of the adventures we had and the burden that was placed upon us.

This is a story of camaraderie, love, and support, of growing up, and above all, of learning to face challenges and solving those that we encountered. When mistakes we made and occasionally we did, what we learnt from those mistakes was not to blame anyone or anything outside ourselves, but to accept responsibility.

The story begins with the Six of Croll. Each of the six of us was of a different creed, and we were not supposed to associate with each other, but strange circumstances brought us together. We were to discover later what these forces were. The town where we came from had four creeds; each one demanded strict adherence to their respective dogma. There was no intermarriage or even friendship; only business and minimal contact were permitted. You have met Peto and me. The others I shall introduce as the story unfolds.

The circumstances involving the meeting of the first four occurred at the same time on that beautiful late autumn day. It was late afternoon, and we stood on the highest dune looking back to Malla.

'I can see so clearly today,' I said to Peto. 'The river Condoor, the lake of the black swans, and the mountains blue seem so clear.'

I stared at the vista. An exciting feeling of anticipation filled my whole body. The next thing I remember was Peto shaking me.

'Come on. We have to get back to Malla before dark.'

We set off by sliding down the dunes. We hid our makeshift sled and headed for the village via the forest of Gundi. Something strange was drawing me towards a large forest fig tree. As I reached it, there pinned to its trunk was a note in a strange script.

In the darkness of night, a stranger waits.
You shall meet and then debate
About an adventure you must take.
And when a time he mentions, do not be late.

I showed it to Peto but it meant nothing to either of us, so we continued. The leaves were changing colour and falling whenever there was a gust of wind. Peto and I always took this shortcut to and from the beach. The sun still had a strong bite, and as we walked back through the dunes, we reminisced about the waves we had caught and the big ones we missed.

'Did you see that?' I announce as I pointed to the middle of the forest. 'Over there something moved.'

'It was just the wind rustling the leaves,' he answered.

But I had that strange feeling again. We were about to make a move when Peto turned towards me. 'Do you feel peculiar?' he asked. 'Because I'm feeling strange.'

And oddly I did and was just about to answer when there was a loud scream from within the forest. We looked at each other when another yell pierced the silence. Peto stared at me, and I shrugged my shoulders. 'What should we do?'

'Come on, let's go,' he said, 'and see if they are in danger and if we can help.' He ran off in the direction of the noise.

With great trepidation, I followed him. There, lying in the bottom of a pit, were two boys with no conceivable way of escape. They were wearing the ringlets of Kab. We hesitated about what to do. They hesitated asking us for help. We all felt awkward, but I had this strange feeling of destiny. But because of our upbringing, Peto and I were unsure about helping them.

'We should leave,' I said. 'You know it is forbidden to even talk to them.' We hovered on the edge of the pit and were about to go when one of them said, 'Please don't leave us here. Our parents do not know we are in the forest and we have no way of getting out.'

Peto, without hesitating, was about to jump into the pit, but I grabbed his arm.

'Stop!' I screamed. 'It's forbidden for us to talk to them.'

He looked at me. Strangely, I knew exactly what he was thinking. 'That could be us in there,' he said. 'We should help to get them out.'

We were taking a great risk but somehow knew it was the right thing to do. We made a rope of sorts from the vines in the trees and finally, after a two-hour endeavour, succeeded in getting them out. It was an extraordinary feeling talking to two Kabs. In the beginning, there was great mistrust between us, but during the time it took us to get them out of the trap, a friendship was beginning to blossom, which had a bizarre feeling of fate. As we talked and the time passed, the four of us started to let down our guard.

'I'm Wecco and my friend is Rocco. We were on the edge of the forest, picking mushrooms,' he declared, 'when we saw this strange-looking child beckon us deeper into the forest. Rocco was the more daring and ran off in pursuit of the creature. I tried stopping him, but in the end, I had no choice and reluctantly followed. Then the creature just seemed to vanish. Next thing we knew, we were in this trap.'

It was lucky for them we came along. The few hours it took to get them out cemented a friendship that would last all our lives. At that particular moment though, we had no idea what was in store for us.

'Let's meet here every Monday and Wednesday,' said Peto, 'and Mecco and I will teach you how to surf, swim, and slide down the dunes.' So a secret pact was made on that day. Over the next few months, Peto and I taught them how to swim, surf, and remove large pieces of bark from the trees and fashion them into the shape of a sled to slide down the sand dunes. With the passing of autumn, our friendship grew. The four of us shared many a story. We grew to like and trust each other. We were all rather competitive.

None of our parents knew that we were seeing each other, and we knew not to mention it to anyone. Whenever we passed each other in the village, we would acknowledge each other by pulling our right earlobe twice. I also had this strange sense of knowing when they were nearby. Even stranger was that it also occurred when a particular girl of another creed was close at hand.

As winter approached and the last of the leaves had fallen, except for the grey ghost trees, we stopped surfing and swimming and sat and talked, argued, fought, and spent many an afternoon sliding down the dunes. As we were only 13 to 14 summers, we were very opinionated. The start of winter was very mild, unusually mild, and we still went on adventures over the dunes, sometimes right up to the edge of the river Condoor, another forbidden sight.

'Do you guys sense anything strange?' I asked as we walked to Malla.

'You're always sensing strange things, Mecco,' said Peto.

'I do,' said Wecco, 'as if someone is spying on us.'

'Yes,' I replied. 'That's exactly what it felt like to me.'

'The other day,' I continued, 'I thought I saw a tall child in a hood or through it looked like an Elf.'

'You and your strange feelings,' said Peto, 'and now you're seeing Elves.'

I knew I shouldn't have mentioned it to the others. They now thought I was crazy.

'I think I have seen them as well,' added Wecco.

'Not you too,' said Rocco.

'Okay, let's go, just drop it,' I said.

Then, on the shortest day of the year, as I was returning from the beach, that feeling came over me again. I stopped abruptly then the others followed suit.

'Wow,' said Peto. 'I can feel that, and it's strange.'

'Now do you believe me?' I said. We stood in silence and eventually became aware of a sobbing sound coming from the forest. We moved warily to investigate. To our surprise and shock, it was in the same direction as the trap that had caught Wecco and Rocco.

As we moved towards it, we heard another voice trying to comfort the one sobbing. I had that feeling again, not just from us four but the same sensation that occurred when a certain girl from the town was near.

We arrived at the edge of the pit and peered in simultaneously. Their screams were bloodcurdling, and the four of us jumped back, as scared as they were. What a fright it must have been for them to look up and see us four peering down from each corner.

'Stay calm,' I ordered, 'and we will help you guys out.' I had seen the Aldation girl before and had sensed something special about her. But the other I had never seen in our town, and to top it off, he was a Bover! We helped them out and I then asked how they ended up in the trap.

'I was mesmerised by, and was following, this tall beautiful creature,' said Julanna, 'when I suddenly fell into the pit. Ricco heard me sobbing and was trying to get me out when something or someone pushed him in.'

'Hello, my name is Ricco and thank you for helping us,' he said as he fondled his Bover beads.

We looked at each other with intrigue, and there was that look of mistrust from Jula and Ricco towards us and vice versa. Now with the six of us all standing on the edge of the pit, we made up the four creeds. I had never spoken to a Bover before, but I felt in my heart that he was a good person. His eyes were gentle, and there was sadness in his turned-down mouth. I trusted him, even though the Bovers had a reputation for deceit and ruthlessness.

'This is really strange,' said Peto, 'Julanna an Aldation and Ricco a Bover.'

'Yes, and I don't think it's a coincidence,' I said. 'We make up the four creeds.'

'This is very strange,' said Julanna as she rearranged her scarf around her head. 'I have never spoken to anyone from another creed, but for some strange reason, I'm not afraid, and please call me Jula.'

We all agreed there was some extraordinary force bringing us together. The bigotry and mistrust that had been bred into us through the beliefs and dogma of our creeds seemed to have been thrust to the back of our minds by a stronger power. We continued talking and discussed the feeling of trust we all felt for each other.

'Ricco, how come we have never seen you in Malla and yet you ended up in the trap?' I asked.

'I am from a town far from here,' he said, 'and was on my way to live with my uncle and aunty, who live in Malla, when I heard someone crying and went to investigate.'

'Why are you coming to live in Malla?' asked Peto.

'In my village, all the Bovers are being harassed and persecuted,' said Ricco. 'My parents sent me here for protection.'

From that day forward, Jula and Ricco became part of our group. We named ourselves the Six of Croll, after the dunes. For the rest of the winter, we got to learn all there was to know about each other. We even talked about our different creeds and what they meant to us. I will admit that at times the discussions became quite heated, but when two were trying to say their creed was the only truth, the rest of us would project a calming force upon them and it worked. Back at home, when any of us would ask our elders questions about another's creed, the answers were always similar and full of prejudices and mistrust.

'Maybe', said my father, 'some of them are okay but very few. It's because they do not follow our faith, which is the true faith.'

As we were still forbidden to speak to anyone from another creed, the Six of Croll was to be our secret. I suppose this is a good opportunity to explain the difference between the creeds. As I said earlier, there are four creeds in our village. Peto and I are of the Dation, which are the most numerous and a breakaway of the Kab. Rocco and Wecco are of the Kab, which is the oldest creed. Jula is of the Aldation, which is an offshoot of the Dation. Ricco is a Bover, which is the newest of all the creeds.

Each of these creeds considers they have found the truth and flaunts their beliefs by wearing certain things. The Dation wear a necklace with a large emblem. The Kab wear ringlets of hair down the side of their face. The Bover wear saffron-coloured robes and beads. The Aldation wear scarves or little hats. Each of the creeds has their own symbol, which they wear on a chain around their necks.

But with all this conditioning we have had, and still have, there is a stronger force acting upon us, which makes us look at things with empathy, understanding, and a profound sense of wisdom.

Winter was coming to a close, and the new growth of spring was bursting out everywhere. We continued our regular Monday and Wednesday afternoon meetings. We talked about everything under the sun. As the weather started to warm up, Peto and I decided to teach Rocco and Jula to swim and surf. It was very hard to convince Jula to take off her scarf even when she was in the water. But we found it funny to surf in a scarf and teased her often.

With time, however, we learned from each other. She finally realised that not wearing it did not make her less of a person. It is what is in your heart that is important, not what you wear on your head, although she still wore a scarf every day. She explained that she felt naked without one. We respected her choice. When we got out of sight of the town, she would change her black scarf for one of bright purple. She had style, confidence, and a sympathetic ear. Jula and I became very close. We talked of art, poetry, and music: things that I was truly interested in.

'Art is forbidden by my creed,' said Jula. 'But I would like to find out more about it. If you have any books that I may read, I would like that.'

'Yes,' I said. 'I will bring some for you next week.'

'Why do you waste time reading about art?' said Wecco.

'Because I like it,' I responded, 'like Ricco likes talking about the flowers and crops he plants in his parents' garden.' Wecco teased me most but I know it is jealousy as I often caught him and Jula stealing looks at each other. I would never do anything against Wecco, as I felt a need to protect him as I felt towards all my friends. There were days I would stand on the dunes of Croll and stare out to the world beyond, wondering what adventures lay beyond my sight.

2
CHAPTER

Farewell to the Four

The rainforest was deep green with tree ferns reaching for the light and enormous elkhorns clinging precariously to the trees. Clumps of rock orchids smothered the large rocks near the waterfall, and vibrant green vines twisted their way up the trees, clambering for the light. At the edge of the forest, there was a large crystal-clear pond. No, it was actually more like a lake. Around one side there was a rock cliff where a large waterfall cascaded into the lake and opposite a sandy beach. Forty paces from the beach, there was an enormous rainforest fig tree with a root system that extended thirty paces in all directions, with a leaf canopy to match. Between the roots of the tree the grass was trimmed as if an expert gardener maintained it. The grass extended down to about ten or twelve paces from the water, where a beach of pure white sand began.

This was the tree of Golla in the forest of Gong, the meeting place of the Deep Forest Elves. There was a conference of Elves taking place, and Elvin and Ezrasay, two of the high Elves of the eastern forest, had summoned their son Drew to attend. Also summoned were eleven other Elves born in the same year, the year of Rew. The meeting began with many matters of the day and much discussion about different topics. But not one of the elders began to address the real reason for the meeting. Finally, Elvin stood up and held his hands above his head. A silence moved swiftly over the conference. His speech went something like this:

'We all knew this day would come. It was written thousands of years ago in our book of prophecies, and we must follow the order of things. The first twelve male Elves born in the year of Rew have been summoned to answer the three questions of the prophecies. From their answers, we will resolve which three must take the task and how they must approach it.

'The first question is "Who has the keys?"'

'The second question is "Where is the door?"'

'The third question is "What is behind the door?"'

Tarew, the best friend of Drew, was hiding behind a small sapling. He had decided to sneak up and watch the proceedings, against all rules. He was short and had a complex about it. His friends knew how much it distressed him, and they teased him often. He also had been born in the year of Rew, but he was the thirteenth and missed out on being one of the first twelve. In fact, he was born at the same time as Jarew, who was the last of the twelve. But Tarew's parents informed the elders later than Jarew's; therefore, he missed out on being one of the twelve. And as he watched the conference, a strange thing happened. When he heard the three questions, he responded, but only to himself.

'The creeds of all have the keys to call
In the mountain core where is found the door
With the prophecy to be told by philosophers of old.'

Why this came to him he had no idea, but as he watched the proceedings and each of the Elves of Rew answered the questions, he knew that only two would have the correct answers. Should he make this known to the elders or wait and see what was to come about? He chose the latter and listened intently to the proceedings. Drew knew the riddle and answered it on request, as did Carew. The others floundered. They tried to recite some type of poem, but none succeeded. However, Jarew had listened intently to Drew and Carew. He knew they had the right answer. He stepped back behind the other Elves and began to memorise what Drew and Carew had said. Then his turn came. He stepped forward, and sticking out his chest, he recited.

'The creeds of all have the keys to all
In the mountain bore where is found the store
Where the philosophers of old have the prophecy to be told.'

The elders considered his mistakes. But the prophecies had said that three of the first twelve born in the year of Rew would know the riddle and the task would be theirs. After deliberating for ages, they took the three aside who had answered the questions most correctly. The rest were ordered to return to their homes in their own parts of the forest, while the three were told their role in the quest.

Elvin stood and began to relay to the three young Elves the prophecies and what part they were to play in fulfilling them.

'You are to leave in two days,' said Elvin, 'and travel to the ancient forest of Gundi, by the Dunes of Croll.'

Three high Elves handed them a scroll with Elvan prophecies and a small box filled with sheets of blank parchment, and Elvin continued, 'All will be revealed in due course on your journey. The first will materialise on the parchments in the forest of Gundi, the rest when the need arises. The only other thing I can add is there are supposed to be six teenaged children involved. What relevance they have, we are not sure except that they are very important to the quest. You three should rest and prepare to leave in two days' time.'

Tarew waited till everyone had left then whistled to attract Drew's attention. Drew turned, knowing instantly it was Tarew. He moved in the direction of the whistle and practically fell over him lying in the grass. Drew laughed and lay down on the grass next to Tarew and ruffled his blond hair with his hand. Drew was the most beautiful of Elves with crystal-clear blue eyes and the cheekiest smile. As he turned to look at Tarew, he noticed that he was not laughing.

'What's your problem? Are you jealous that you weren't one of the three?' he asked.

Tarew put his finger to his lips. 'Shush,' he said. 'For your information, no, but I was able to recite the riddle perfectly without knowing how or why.'

'I knew Jarew was not the third Elf for the quest,' Drew added.

'Tomorrow I shall tell my father and get his advice.'

The following morning, he relayed the story to his father with Tarew present. Elvin looked worried and asked Tarew to recite the answers again. It was word perfect. Elvin looked even more worried.

'We must have another meeting with the elders,' he said.

That evening just before the meeting, Elvin had a proposition for the two young Elves.

'This would cause great anxiety among the elders,' he said. 'What you should do, Drew, is to demand the ancient rite of traveller's need. This means you can ask for a companion to accompany you on this journey.'

The meeting began and the chosen three met the elders. They were given provisions and an ancient map of the world with old roads and towns marked.

'The old roads are not used very often these days,' Elvin instructed. 'But they may come in handy.'

The elders also pointed out where and how to get to the forest of Gundi.

'We cannot tell you any more,' said Elvin, but he repeated what he'd said the previous night. 'The parchments will reveal your task, and it is very important that you follow the instructions to the letter. The future of the whole world depends on your success.'

The elders handed each of the Elves a silver chain with a fine silver-laced emblem of the tree of Golla. The young Elves thanked the elders, who then bowed proudly.

'I, the first born in the year of Rew, I have a request,' Drew announced as he bowed respectfully. 'I demand the right of traveller's need.'

'Why is it a necessity to have another on this quest?' asked the elders. 'The prophecies said only three.'

'I am the first born in the year of Rew,' Drew said with authority, 'and the feeling I receive from the forest of Gong is the dangers ahead may require a fourth in case of mishap to one of us.' The elders pondered for a moment then asked if any of the others felt this force. Jarew replied immediately in the negative, whereas Carew hesitated and looked at both the other Elves then the elders.

His glance stopped at Elvin, who gave a slight nod in the affirmative that none of the others noticed. Carew then responded, 'Yes, I do feel the force from the forest.'

'Well, that is final,' said the elders. 'Your request for a traveller's need is granted. Who will be your need?'

'Tarew is my choice,' Drew responded immediately.

'That is a good choice,' Elvin said to the other elders, 'as Tarew is the thirteenth born in the year of Rew and only missed out by a few minutes to be one of the twelve.'

The elders then summoned Tarew to the tree and asked him, 'Do you accept the responsibility to be the traveller's need?'

Aware of the proceedings, he answered yes without hesitation. Then, Elvin handed him a chain with a pair of lacewings and a small walking stick attached, all in silver. He also handed him a wooden walking stick with laced wings carved into the silver handle. He bowed low, with immense gratitude. That is how four Elves came to embark on the quest instead of three.

'There will be a farewell feast this afternoon,' announced Elvin, 'so your friends and family can say goodbye and wish you luck.'

It was a grandiose affair. Elves from all corners of the forest attended and were merry, but there was an element of restraint from the four.

'My son,' said Elvin as he took Drew aside, 'I have something very important to tell you. One of the six children you will meet has Elvan blood. He will have many powers he is not aware of. There may come a time when he needs to know this, and you will be the one to tell him. Try to prepare him but keep it between the two of you. Also in the ancient prophecies, there is a mention of the Dwarfs who are to help in the quest. We have not seen or heard of them since early in the First Age. All we know is that after the first hundred years working for Man, they travelled for great distances to mine the far western hills for wealth. How they are to be contacted, we do not know. There is one more thing I should tell you. The prophecies also mention the arrival of angels.' He paused in thought. 'However, this may just be our misinterpretation of the ancient scrolls.'

Drew walked back to the other three Elves. 'What is this all about?' he thought. 'I wish I could just stay here and swim and dive in the lake.'

The four Elves of Rew then sneaked off back to their homes for they did not feel in the mood to celebrate. The elders sat and discussed the gravity of the young Elves' trek and what dangers might lie ahead for them.

The following morning, the elders and Elvin's wife Ezrasay wished them a fair day to travel. Ezrasay handed them a light, flat parcel of Elvan cakes, saying, 'These have great goodness and magical power and should only to be used in the most extreme of circumstances.' She also handed Drew a leather-and-silver armband covered in Elvan runes. 'And this', she explained, 'will change its runes to warn of impending danger.'

Then she explained a few more important things: 'There is a magic crystal that must be found before the Evil. But be very careful not to mention it to the children as knowledge of it may endanger them. When our ancestors first arrived here, they came in an armada of eleven ships. Over the centuries, these rotted away in the mouth of the river Condoor, except two. One was taken by a group of Elves who travelled south-east and the other hidden by magic and it will be there for your use. The parchments will give you the clues to retrieve it. Also in the northern forest of Woolinbar, the northern Elves know of your quest, and they will send three Elves of Rew to help.'

She then took a small silver box from her pocket, opened it, and pulled out a silver chain with a tusk attached to it, then handed it to Drew.

'This is the dragon tooth that was given to your grandfather,' she said, with emphasis. 'It is said it will give you great protection from the Evil.' She placed it over his head then kissed him.

'There is one more thing I must tell you about the child of Elvan descent,' Ezrasay said as she ushered him out of earshot of his friends. As she spoke, Drew's mouth dropped with surprise. When she finished talking, she grabbed Drew by the arm and walked him in a daze back to his friends.

'Wear your hoods and capes,' she added, 'as the sun will be strong. Farewell to the four and may the laughing bird ever be in your earshot.'

Ezrasay kissed them on their foreheads. Then the elders outstretched their hands then brought them together six inches in front of their hearts then slapped the back of their left hands with their right, bowed, then outstretched them. The four of Rew returned their bow with great respect then turned and marched off towards the east.

'What did your mother say to you? It looked serious,' asked Carew when they were far enough away from their elders.

'She just repeated the importance of taking heed of the parchments,' he answered. But Carew knew there was more to it.

3
CHAPTER
The Tall Cloaked Man

At home, one of my two older brothers was always teasing me and getting me into trouble. And I had an undeserved reputation as a rebel. One night over dinner, I happened to ask why we were not allowed to talk to the other creeds. My mother bowed her head, and my father asked for forgiveness for me. But they could not give me a reasonable answer. I then proceeded to ask why the dunes of Croll, the forest of Gundi, and the river Condoor were all forbidden.

My father sighed deeply and said, 'A long, long time ago, before the time of creeds, there was talk of a tribe of Elves who lived there and brought good luck to the world. They were good and fair and set an example for all to follow on how to live. They looked after the forest and protected the environment. They were good mediators and would negotiate any problems that occurred in the village. When more complex decisions were needed, they would contact a great wizard who lived in the north or one of the lords of Mardascon who lived in the south for help.' Then he added, 'Although I think they are just myths.'

My mother then forbade my father from saying any more. I was left not knowing what help might have been needed. I had heard rumours before of a wizard and some lords, but this was the first time my parents had ever mentioned them. I was left with many unanswered questions. How was I to find out the rest of the story, and what was I to do about my new friends?

Later that night, my brother came into my room and demanded to know why it was so important to know about the other creeds. I looked at him. *Could I trust him with my secret?* I thought. *Or will he tell my parents?* I pondered for a few moments, then felt I was making a mistake, but I had to find out what his reaction would be.

'Ardco, I must confide something to you, but you must promise not to tell anyone.'

'Mecco,' he said, 'you know me. I can be trusted. What have you done now?'

'Ardco, promise me,' I replied.

'Okay,' he said.

So I told him about talking to some children of another creed. But I should have trusted my instincts, as it was too much for him to understand.

His reaction was unbelievable; you would have thought I had killed someone. 'I can't keep that a secret,' he said. 'My conscience would not allow it.'

Luckily, I didn't tell him everything. I responded to his outburst calmly. 'I didn't say much to him. I just asked him the way out of the forest of Gundi.'

He then screamed, 'You've been in the forbidden forest!'

I thought to myself, *Now what have I done? I will be in more trouble.*

'I'm going to tell Mum and Dad, 'he said as he moved towards the door. But I stepped across and blocked his exit.

'I will knock your head off if you don't get out of the way,' he threatened. He was always stronger than I and always won our fights. This time was different as I had a purpose to fight for. He took a swing at me, I ducked, and his fist hit the door. He then stood back in pain, holding it.

'I'll get you,' he said, but I stood my ground. He looked round and saw my diary on my bed. He grabbed it and waved it in my face saying, 'I will show Mum and Dad this.'

'No, you won't.' I dived at him, grabbing around his waist and pushing him on to the bed. I don't know where this power came from, but I felt so strong. We rolled on to the floor with a loud bang; the diary went flying across the room. He was now on top of me, smug, as he thought it was now just another victory for him. But not so, my hand could reach the side of the bed, and so I used it for leverage to bring my leg up over him and drag him to the floor. I rolled to an upright position, grabbed his hands, and sat on his chest, the position he usually used on me.

'Ardco,' I said, 'if you tell anyone, I will make you pay, I promise.'

He struggled and started to shout, so I put my knees over his arms and covered his mouth with one hand. 'Now promise,' I said.

Suddenly, our father yelled out, 'What is going on up there?'

'It's all right, Dad,' I answered. 'We're just wrestling.'

'Ardco, leave your brother alone,' he yelled.

'I will tell all your mates', I said, 'that I have beaten you in a fight, Ardco. Now, what is your answer?'

He reluctantly nodded his head in the affirmative. I gingerly moved aside and let him up off the floor. He was disgusted with what I'd done, and shocked that I had won the fight. But was he to be trusted? I reiterated my threat about his friends and told him never to touch my diary again. On his way out the door, he looked back at me with distrust, pity, and amazement at my victory.

For the rest of the week, there was a stand-off between us. I think he was worried for me and was trying to fathom how I'd won the fight. I was just pleased he never told Mum and Dad. If my mother found out, she would be shattered, but she would not disown me and she always made excuses if I made a mistake. She encouraged me more than my other brothers, but with that came a persistent feeling of never wanting to let her down.

My father, on the other hand, was another matter. There has always been something peculiar about the way he treats me. My brothers say it is because I act so differently. I read, write, and draw too much and keep to myself. Maybe it is my imagination, but I feel I am not treated the same.

When Ardco went to sleep that night, I put some clothes in my bed in the shape of my body and climbed down the tree outside my window. I needed to go for a walk to think about things. I walked past Jula's house, and I could sense her, and I wondered whether she could sense me. As I looked up at her window, I saw her looking out. She waved at me, and then I knew she sensed me too. She was aware of my anxiety.

I continued to walk down to the edge of the town and sat on a log by the stream and contemplated where life was going to take me. The night was still and the moon was full, but from the south, storm clouds were brewing and intermittently hiding the moon. I sat there for ages in a daze. Then this warm feeling come over me: like someone was holding and protecting me. I stood up and turned around to walk back home. But there in front of me stood a tall, cloaked figure with such warm eyes staring at me. He reached out his hand towards me, and for some reason, I was not at all scared. I moved slowly towards him, not through fear, but respect. He raised his hand, to stop me from coming any further. I stopped.

'Who are you?' I asked.

'Now is not the time,' he answered. 'In due course, it will be revealed. Knowing now of what is to come could only make matters worse. I know all that has taken place in your life over the last year, your new friends, and the problem with your brother.'

How could things get any worse? I thought. *And how could he know about my problems?*

He told me all that had happened over the last year, and I was amazed how he knew.

'You must not lose faith in your new friends, no matter what anyone may say.'

'Are you a wizard?' I asked. 'And how do you know all this?'

He looked at me with great compassion and said, 'Mecco, it doesn't matter how I know. Just trust me. You and your new friends will be asked to make a great sacrifice, and I trust you will make the right decision, as the future of the world depends on it. But do not preoccupy yourself with that for the moment as you will know in time. Do not worry, my friend. You have lots of special people out there waiting to help you.'

'Who are they, and how will I know them?' I asked.

'There are some I know that are waiting to help you at this very moment,' he responded, 'and some who have helped you already and more whom you will meet on your life journey. Only you will know who is on your side and who is against you. Trust your own feelings. Your trust will become strong with the help of your new friends, and you will know who they are.' He then added, 'You are the prime force that will connect the six with the elves.'

'Elves? What do you mean *elves*? They are only stories.'

'I have said too much already. Just trust your instincts.

'I'm not going to connect anyone with any elves. So you are wasting your time.'

'Mecco, you have a destiny, and the path will become clear to you soon. Do not fight it, just allow it to happen and it will unfold, and when it does, just follow it.'

'I'm not going to follow any path I don't want to. You are wasting your time.'

'I must go now. Take care and don't fight with what fate has in store. But be very careful of some people who will claim to be your friend.'

A dark cloud then covered the moon, and everything went pitch black. When the moon reappeared, the tall cloaked man had vanished. I walked back home, wondering what life had in store for me. Who was this stranger? What did he mean by 'Be careful of false friends'?

4
CHAPTER

Midday Tomorrow

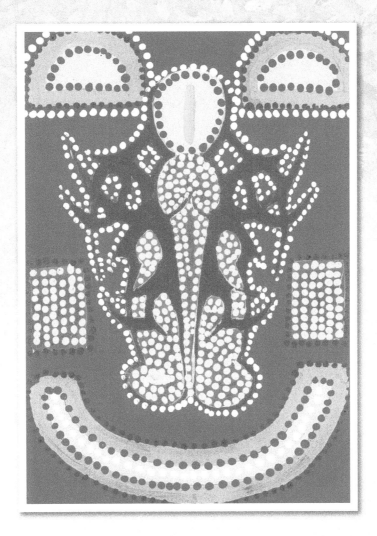

As summer approached and the weather continued to warm up, the six of us got back to our usual routine. I relayed to them what had happened with my brother and the encounter with the tall cloaked stranger. My friends found it quite mysterious and were forever asking me to retell them the story. We had also heard rumours from a nearby town that the Bovers were causing trouble with the Kabs. There had also been a few incidents in Malla where Kabs had written profanities and insults on the Bovers' place of worship. The elders were trying to negotiate a peaceful solution to the problem. This also created a problem for us as Wecco and Rocco, both Kabs, started to pick on Ricco, a Bover. They began first by bullying him then saying that because their creed was the first, it must be the true faith.

'Hang on,' I said. 'That's the main reason we have been brought together, to show to the rest of the world that the creeds can live together, and here you are criticising each other. Now stop it.'

The remaining three of us realised if we used all our strength, we could calm them down. And with practice, it became much easier to use our sense of reasoning to resolve their differences.

Summer arrived, and we continued meeting every Monday and Wednesday and occasionally other days as well. We went surfing and swimming and talked about how strange it was how we six had met.

Late one afternoon at the end of summer as the shadows of the forest crept slowly up the dunes, the six of us were walking back to the town, laughing and joking when suddenly, a strange sensation came over me. I stopped in my tracks, causing my friends to pile into me one after the other.

'What is happening?' cried Jula.

I held my finger to my lips for quiet.

As we stood in silence, muffled voices from afar filtered through the forest. One by one, my friends became conscious of the voices. We looked at each other and wondered who it could be, as it was forbidden for anybody from the city to enter the forest. We thought it best for us to climb up a tree to hide, to observe who it was and try and discover what they were doing here.

We looked for the best trees to hide in. Rocco was a problem as he was a little overweight and we had to either push or pull him up the tree. The more we pushed, the more he laughed, which made us laugh as well. After much pushing and pulling, he came toppling down on top of us, scattering us all over the place like ninepins.

We pulled ourselves together and finally succeeded in getting him up, just in time to see two men in dark cloaks on grey horses appear in the clearing. They were talking in a language that we could not understand and stopped right under the tree where Peto and I were hiding. Slowly, I became aware of the feelings I had when I met the tall cloaked stranger and wondered if he was one of them.

Suddenly, they started to speak our language with a strange accent that none of us had heard before. Their subject was Elves, which was strange, as we were told it was just an old tale without any truth. The taller of the two was telling the story of how the three Elves of Rew became four. He talked of the burden they had to carry and how unfair it was that only four Elves had the task. All they could do was to help them the best way they could.

The shorter of the two then said, 'I hope the Elves have done their task of getting the Six together.' When they mentioned the Six, Peto and I looked at each other with curiosity. They began to move off towards the centre of the clearing, and one of them announced loudly, 'I am curious to know how long it will take the Six to realise.'

Then to our amazement, four tall children wearing green hoods joined them. The six of them began to greet each other and speak in that strange language again. There was laughter and much talking. Then to our surprise, my name was mentioned, then Peto's, then Wecco's and Rocco's. There was more laughter, till finally Jula and Ricco's names were heard too, then hysterical laughter. Then the four we thought were children removed their hoods. We gasped. They had pointed ears and were not children at all but Elves. Our gasp of surprise gave us away.

They looked at us hiding in the trees, and the tall hooded stranger said, 'It's fine. You can come down now. We know you are there.'

My companions were scared, but I knew it would be fine, so I jumped down.

'We meet once more,' said the tall cloaked stranger, and that feeling of trust and security descended over me again. Slowly and cautiously, the others climbed down from the trees. The five arrived and positioned themselves timidly behind me. I could feel an overwhelming sense of power. The Elves greeted us with a polite, overly pronounced bow of their heads. The two men nodded as well, but without as courteous a bow as the Elves. They introduced themselves as the lords of Mardascon.

'I'm Lord Arcon,' said the taller man, 'and this is Lord Sebcon.'

We responded by bowing in the same fashion. We had heard tales of Elves that once lived in the forest of Gundi, but never imagined we would meet any.

'So are you really Elves?' asked Jula.

'Well, of course we're Elves,' said the one on the left who was called Jarew. 'What did you think we were? Trolls or Goblins?'

I think he was offended that we had to ask if they were Elves. Apologising, I said, 'I am sorry that we have offended the great Elves of the forest of Gundi. Please forgive us.'

'We are not from the forest of Gundi,' said Jarew, still aggravated. The Elf on his right, whose name was Drew, stepped forward and stretched out his arm in front of Jarew and said, 'Your apologies are accepted.'

We all noticed that there was some resentment from Jarew towards Drew, who was a little taller than the others and extremely handsome. In fact, all of them were handsome with beautiful skin, fine features, and not a sign of hair on their faces.

'How old are you, and why don't you have any facial hair?' asked Rocco as he twisted the ringlets hanging down the side of his face.

'How rude,' said Jarew, but before he could continue, Drew explained, 'We are much older than you six, and we only get hair on our face when we are really old.'

'Enough of this,' announced Lord Arcon. 'The day is drawing to a close, and you must return to your town. Do not create any suspicion. Can I rely on you to be here at noon tomorrow? We have many things to tell you about a great adventure that you must undertake.'

'What about school?' said Jula. 'They will know we are missing.'

Lord Arcon responded with an ultimatum: 'You must be here tomorrow. There is too much at stake. The future of the world is in your hands. Please do not let us down. You must be aware of the power you six have developed since meeting. There is an evil force in our lands, working on disrupting the order of things. It has been growing in strength over the last thousand years. His ability to create chaos grows with the passing of the years. The time has come to quell that power.'

'What is this power?' I asked.

'There is not enough time today to explain,' Lord Arcon said. 'The shadows are lengthening, and you must return to your town before sunset so as to not create suspicion. Please,' he said again. 'Midday tomorrow, please be here at this spot.' Then he added, 'Don't fight the power that has come your way, let it develop.'

5
CHAPTER
The Last Night in Malla

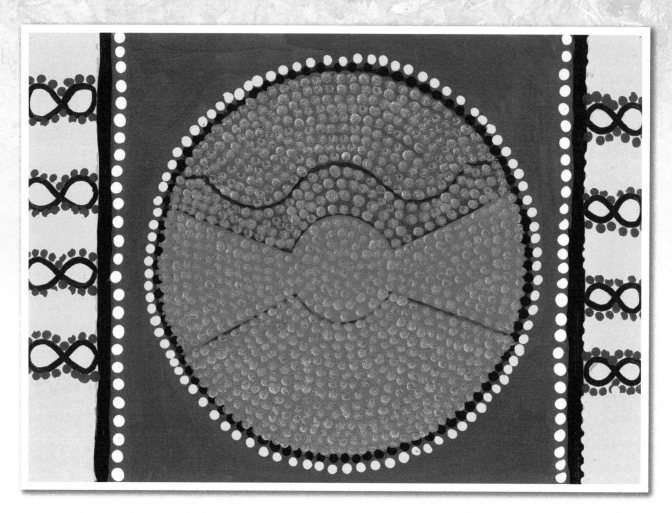

We walked back silently to our usual place of departure. As we arrived at the edge of the forest, the gravity of the moment came clear to me.

'What was all that about?' demanded Jula, breaking the silence.

'I'm not going anywhere with that lot,' added Rocco.

At that moment, I think we all felt confused, and I could sense some of us had no intention of returning the next day.

'I don't think we have much choice,' I said. 'I don't know about the rest of you, but I feel like it is our fate.' I eventually convinced them, and we made a pact to meet at our usual meeting place at midday. We said our goodbyes and marched off to our respective homes. That night, strange dreams were had by all.

As I arrived home, I could hear my father shouting my name. I cautiously opened the door, and there was my brother Nedco standing in front of my mother, facing my father and my other brother Ardco.

'It's not Mum's fault!' cried Nedco.

Ardco saw me standing at the door. 'Here he is. Ask him yourself!' he announced.

My mother turned to me, with a sad look in her eyes. 'Mecco, is it true you have been to the Dunes of Croll, and through the forest of Gundi?'

My family glared at me, waiting for my answer.

'Yes,' I said obstinately.

My mother's hands rose to her face in shame. She looked up and asked, 'Have you ever spoken to anyone from another creed?'

'Yes,' I replied in the same tone, and they looked at me in horror. I lowered my voice and continued, 'It's okay. They are good people.'

'I told you he would be a problem,' said my father. 'We should not have taken him in.'

My mother looked at me, then at my father. 'What was I to do?' she said. 'She was my only sister. I could not leave him to the fates.' She turned back to me and said, 'I am sorry, Mecco. I should have told you earlier.'

'Please,' I said, 'then tell me now.'

'You are the son of my only sister,' said my mother, 'who died of a broken heart at your birth.'

'Then who is my father?' I demanded.

They both looked at me. She said, 'She would never tell us. We think he was of another creed.'

As I stared at them, I knew they were lying. But with all that had happened that day, I never pursued it. Nedco started to walk over to comfort me. Ardco and the person I thought was my father stopped him then said, 'No one is to know of this, or we will have to send you away.'

I sat down. I felt lonely, so lonely, as the world and family I thought was mine was disintegrating in front of me. My only compensation was that deep inside, I knew I was different. I went to the room we three boys shared. I lay on my bed and reflected on my 14 years in this house. As I lay there, I could hear my family arguing. I knew then, I had no option. Tomorrow, I would have to leave this house, if not for my sake, then for my family's.

During the night, strange dreams filled my sleep. There were great cities, with high snow-covered mountains, enormous waterfalls cascading into wide lakes, and even dragons. I saw my friends and me sailing in a beautiful boat and riding horses.

The following morning, I woke early. How strange I felt. I knew I wanted to meet the lords and Elves at midday as they had requested, but I worried that my friends would not turn up. Gathering what I thought I would need and packing it in my knapsack, I made my way silently out of the room. I waited at the top of the stairs, listening to see if anyone was awake then sneaked down to the kitchen to eat something. Then I packed some food to take with me. Something deep inside warned me it was to be a long quest, but I was strangely full of optimism.

I left a letter for my mother, or should I say aunty, and my family, explaining that I thought it would be better for me to leave so as not put them in a compromising position. I took my last look around the house. I would miss nothing except my older brother, now cousin Nedco, who was always kind to me. I left the house without glancing back, no matter how tempted I was.

As I walked into the street, Peto was waiting for me.

'What are you doing here so early?' I asked.

'I'm not sure. But this morning, after waking and the dreams I had last night, I knew I must be here waiting for you.'

'I'm not going to school,' I said. 'I'm going to meet the lords and Elves.'

'I'm going to school,' said Peto, 'so it will not cause suspicion. But do not fret. I will meet you in the forest at midday. I will make an excuse for your absence.'

We walked together to the end of our street then went our separate ways.

6
CHAPTER

The First Day in the Forest

The morning was clear and warm. The magpies and currawongs were performing their morning warbles. As I walked to the edge of the town, I sensed a new chapter beginning in my life. At that moment, I had all intentions to embrace it with gusto and passion. My past was nothing but a lie.

It was still very early when I arrived at our meeting place, so I made myself comfortable against a tree and faced the morning sun. For an hour, I sat writing in my diary. As the morning wore on and the temperature began to rise, the birds stopped their warbling and whistling. In the quiet, I could hear someone coming. It was way before our arranged time, but as the footsteps grew closer, I sensed it was Peto.

He looked anxious as he sat next to me. Without hesitating, he asked, 'What on earth happened last night at your house? I returned home at recess to get my lunch. As I walked past your house, I heard a commotion. I went in. Your mother was crying. Your father was saying good riddance. Your brother Nedco told me you had left home.'

I relayed what had taken place the night before and added, 'I don't think I will be going back to Malla. I don't think any of us will for many a year.'

'What do you mean?' asked Peto. 'I will meet those Elves and cloaked men as I'm curious to see what they have to say. But I'm not going anywhere with them.'

'Peto.' I looked him in the eye. 'You must be aware of the force that is exerting itself upon us. I don't think we have much choice.'

'I have,' he said, 'and I will not be talked into going anywhere if I don't want to.'

'We will see,' I replied. I could tell he was in one of his defiant moods, so I didn't push the subject. We just sat there in silence, waiting for the others to arrive.

The sun had moved further overhead, and we were now sitting in the shade of the tree when we heard the laughter of Rocco and Wecco. We stood to greet them.

'I was not sure if you would turn up,' I said.

'We had these strange dreams last night, and when we woke this morning, we knew we had to at least see what they had to say.'

We had just made ourselves comfortable when Ricco came running out of the forest and dived down between us, announcing excitedly, 'This is brilliant, an adventure with Elves and wizards.'

'They are not wizards,' said Peto. 'They said they were lords.'

'Well, I think they are wizards, only pretending to be lords,' said Ricco.

'Tell them what happened to you last night,' Peto said smugly.

I relayed the story to my friends then Peto started again about not going anywhere with the lords. We sat arguing while waiting to see if Jula would turn up. She was always late but we were used to that.

The sun was now directly overhead but still no sign of Jula. My friends thought she must have decided not to come, and we were about to make our way to meet the lords and Elves. I could sense she was on her way when Wecco announced, 'I'm going to see why she has not turned up.'

So I joined him, and we walked back along the track, looking for her. On the way he asked me, 'Do you have any intentions with Jula?'

I reassured him and said, 'We are just friends.'

I loved them all and would never jeopardise our friendship. In fact, my feelings for Wecco were much stronger than I would have liked to admit. At that moment, Jula came running towards us, her face covered in tears.

'I had to sneak away without my family knowing,' she cried. 'I had to leave a note for them under my pillow so if I did not return, they'd eventually find it and know I was all right.'

With our arms around each other, we walked back, talking about the dreams we had and how different we now felt. What would happen to us if this adventure did come to pass?

When we reached the meeting place, Lord Arcon was also there. He looked impatient and announced, 'We must move quickly. We must be there by midday.'

We set off in haste, and as we entered the clearing, we saw the relief on the faces of the Elves and Lord Sebcon. They greeted us with hugs and such affection; it was as if we were long-lost friends. We sat in a semicircle, and Lord Arcon reiterated how important it was for us to be together.

'Now you and the Elves of Rew will be our chance to defeat or weaken the Evil. For the next five days, none of us can leave this clearing. And I mean none of us.'

Peto was not at all impressed at this. He carried on about having to return to the town before sunset. This was not unusual for him, as he could become quite uptight at times. We had seen these tantrums before and just ignored him.

There were many questions we needed to ask, and we hoped for some clear answers. Lord Sebcon felt our anxiety and began by telling us what and why we were chosen: 'We, the four lords of Mardascon, and the wizard Naroof have known about the prophecies of the Elves for hundreds of years. We decided to help with the quest as our ancestors always helped in the past. Lord Revcon and Lord Devcon, the younger of the lords, are staying in the south but should be here in the next five days. If not, you shall meet them along your journey, and they will help the quest seekers as much as possible.'

So now we had another title, as well as the Six of Croll, we had the quest seekers!

Then Carew, who was an expert in Elvan history, told us their story: 'The first parchment told of three things we Elves had to do. The first was to somehow create a situation to bring you six together.'

They began to laugh as they told us of the plan they had devised and how they had executed it. It was they who had made the trap in the forest. They told us how they tricked Jula into entering the woods and how they pushed her into the trap, how they got Ricco near the edge of the trap so he would hear her sobs. They laughed even more when they told us how they pushed Ricco into the trap. Ricco was not impressed that they were all having a good laugh at his expense. He walked off in a huff and joined Peto. So now we had two sitting together, both in a mood. The rest of us continued asking questions.

'Why us? And how did you know where we would be found? Why were the Elves involved?'

Drew took over the story and told us how it came about that there are four Elves on the quest. 'Although', he added, 'the prophecies said only three, one more won't go astray.' He went on, 'Your names were in the prophecies. And it was our duty to bring you together. It was lucky that you and Peto were friends. The second task was to make sure that on this day, the last day of summer in the year of Mort in the Elvan calendar, all of us are here.'

While this was going on, Peto and Ricco were making plans to leave before sunset. *A Bover and a Dation working together, what next?* I thought.

Luckily, Lord Arcon had noticed what they were up to. He had manoeuvred himself behind the tree near where they sat. Just as they were about to leap up and run away, Lord Arcon grabbed them by the scruffs of their necks and lifted them, and their feet continued running in mid-air. We began to laugh, which only made them more furious.

After the commotion had died down, Lord Arcon continued telling us about this evil power. 'He is slowly taking over the world under the pretence of being a good leader. And one of the minor wizards, called Drascar from the city of Bossak, has also defected to the Evil.' He continued, 'Many, many years ago, at a time when the world was in harmony, an evil man arrived who stirred up trouble between the creeds. The Elves, the wizards, and the lords of Con all tried to fight this evil but could not match the power he possessed. Only the Three Oracles have the clues of how to defeat him. The problem is we only know the whereabouts of one Oracle, who dwells in the caves of Mooloo. But the caves have remained hidden to this very day. All this was predicted in the ancient Elvan chronicles.

The Evil went on to create havoc among the creeds, forcing them to hate and distrust each other even more. We think that is how he gets his power, by devouring the hatred he has created.'

He hesitated for a moment. 'Remember, there may be many creeds, but they all come from only one source. The power of your innocence is what can destroy this evil. The most important thing you have learnt so far is that just because someone is from another creed, that does not make them a bad person. Also, memorising the book of your creed does not make a good person. It means only that you have a good memory. Understanding the truth and reason of your book is more important.'

He nodded his head as he stared at us. 'To show your ringlets, scarf, emblem, or your robes and beads does not a good person make, only a good follower of that creed. It's good to have pride in your ancestors, but don't let their prejudice blind you to where you should be going. Built within all of us is a need to search for the truth. Once you give up that search and accept the brainwashing of only one truth, you give up that power. The nameless, the Eternal, or whatever you wish to call him, put the seed of searching for the truth in us all as part of the whole. That seed must be given the chance to grow, or the Evil will take over. All of your creeds have their good points and try to create stable communities. But they are so scared of the other creeds gaining too much power. They think they are losing their identity. If we think we are losing something, we will lose it. We can also be good if we work at being good. When you dress to express what creed you belong to, it also becomes a straitjacket of your prejudice and shows the lack of knowledge of the Supreme. It also announces to the world your insecurities. But enough of this. Now, Carew will explain to you the history between Man and the Elves.'

Carew stepped forward and began to address us: 'Many, many years ago, as it is written in ancient Elvan, there was a distant land. The exact name has been lost in time, but we call it the Old World. This is where the Elves, Dwarfs, and Man originally come from. They travelled here across the sea thousands of years ago. After a time and for different reasons, they went their separate ways, never to be in contact again. The lords we kept in contact with every hundred years or so. Of the Dwarfs, neither the Elves nor the Lords have seen hide or hair of them. There was also another race that followed, called Goblins. They became servants of the Evil and were told by him to abduct women and breed with them to create a new form of Goblin. This is the problem now: they are much harder to identify and now live among man. We will have to teach you how to pick them out, as they are the enemy. They are called Menlins. That is all you need to know at the present. We will tell you more as needed.'

Lord Arcon stepped forward. 'I do not wish to alarm you, but we all must stay here for five days and nights.'

Peto and Ricco stood up and said, 'No way, not us. We will be leaving at sunset.'

'This I cannot permit,' said Lord Arcon.

'If we do not return by sunset,' Peto said defiantly, 'the town will send out a search party.'

Lord Arcon said in a confident tone, 'If they do, then you may return with them if you wish, but only after sunset.' Arcon knew the townsfolk would not find them and said this only to pacify them.

Meanwhile, Carew, trying to distract us, began telling us parts of the history of the Old World: how there were great wars and conflicts that were settled with the help of Elves, Men, wizards, Dwarfs, and another small race whose name has been lost in the past. No one knows what happened to them. They never followed the Elves, and there is no translation of their name from ancient Elvan. It is said they are still in their little part of the Old World.

We were mesmerised and sat listening for hours without a sound. As the day drew on, a sense of dread came over me, and it was getting stronger. I noticed Lord Arcon was a little agitated as well.

He looked at me and said, 'Yes, Mecco. Do you sense it as well? Come with me. The rest of you wait here, and we should not be gone long.'

'Aren't we supposed to stay here?' I asked.

'Stay close to me, and all will be fine,' he said.

I followed him out of the clearing and into the forest.

'You feel it as well, don't you?' he asked again.

'Yes,' I answered, 'but I'm not sure whether it is evil, except that it is strong.' We only took a few steps when we heard loud, agitated voices. I knew they were a group of Bovers by their accents. We made our way cautiously towards the voices. As we arrived at a clearing, we saw them. And I was right. It was a group of Bovers, and they were looking for Jula. They were armed. They approached us and asked what we were doing in the forbidden forest.

One of them pointed at me. 'He is the one. I read it in her diary. What is your name?' he demanded.

Lord Arcon raised his hand to my mouth to stop me answering and said, 'Who wants to know?'

The oldest of the group, who must have been their leader, stepped forward. 'We are looking for one of our children,' he said, 'who has been missing from school, and we believe a Dation has abducted her.'

'She was not abducted. She came of her own free will. You do not have to worry about her,' said Lord Arcon. They had swords and knives and started to encircle us. Lord Arcon moved me behind him saying, 'Come closer at your own peril.'

I was now becoming aware of a power within me. With great confidence, I declared, 'I am Mecco, and Jula did come of her own free will.'

The young one then said, 'See, he is the one. Get him!'

They rushed at us. Five grabbed Lord Arcon, pushing him to the ground, and three grabbed me. I began to fight them with a power that was beyond my understanding. Eventually three more joined in, and they overpowered me, pinning me to the ground. They began dragging me back to town.

Suddenly, Lord Arcon commenced spinning round slowly, getting faster and faster like a willy-willy, throwing all the Bovers to the ground. He then moved towards the ones holding me, still spinning. As he came closer, they let go and began to run out of the forest and the leader turned and said, 'We will be back, mark my word, and we will find you. Tell Jula if she does not return tonight, she will be sentenced to death by our law for defying her father.'

I lay motionless on the ground, covered in dust. Lord Arcon walked towards me, picked me up, and carried me to a log, where he sat me down. He held my hands and asked if I was all right. He looked at me with such concern, something that I had never experienced from my own father. It was to such a degree that I felt embarrassed and had to look away.

I eventually turned to face him and said, 'I don't know what they would have done to me. I owe you so much. I am in your debt.'

He kept a hold of my hands. 'No,' he said, 'my duty is to protect you so you can finish your task. There is nothing for you to worry about.'

'But I am worried, and why should you put yourself in danger?' I replied.

'If you and your friends complete your task, it will be beneficial for all and especially me. I will explain all when the time comes. Now we must get back to the others.'

That was strange. What did Lord Arcon mean by 'especially to him'? I decided to ask him when next we had a quiet moment.

'Hurry, we must be back before sunset, or we will be lost,' he said.

'Why, what is so special about being back before the sun sets?'

'You will find out in due course. Now let's go.'

We both ran towards the clearing and just made it as the sun was setting.

As we entered, we saw that the Elves were finishing painting marks on the large trees surrounding the clearing. I wondered what it was for. Peto and Ricco were still kicking up a fuss, but Lord Sebcon had them restrained. He and the Elves had also made a shelter. They had a large canvas cloth attached to pegs on the ground, which they then stretched over two arched saplings, pulling it tight and anchoring it with pegs at either end and on one side. It was about four paces long and three paces wide with a half a pace open at the front to roll under. It also had a flap that could be closed. They had also dug a deep trench all the way round, as a runoff for rainwater. The trench was so deep it looked as if they were expecting a flood.

As the last rays of sun disappeared behind the distant hills, we were ushered into the tent. Peto and Ricco were still making a commotion. Ricco said, 'The searchers from the town will come back tomorrow, and all of us will be in grave trouble.'

Drew disagreed and said quite confidently, 'They will not be back tomorrow, I can assure you, and we have only five days to teach you how to defend yourself.'

'You couldn't teach a girl how to fight,' said Peto.

'Listen, young man,' Drew said. 'You all have to learn how to defend yourselves. There will be great danger out there, and the Evil One knows of you and will have his Menlins out searching. Even worse, the Seven Pernicious, the pestilence, the most evil of his sentinels, will also be looking for you. They see, smell, and sense good. There are many things you have to learn. You must all be aware of the power you now possess, and it is our role to teach you how to best utilise it. We will start first thing in the morning. But now we must eat.'

'I have some fruit,' I said, 'but it will not last five days.'

'We will have that for lunch tomorrow,' said Drew, 'but tonight, we have something special.' Drew opened up a flat parcel and broke up the contents into thumbnail-sized pieces and handed one to each of us. Rocco sat there speechless and looked at his piece.

'Is this all we have to eat?' asked Peto.

Drew responded. He was rather annoyed. 'Eat it first, then if you want more, just ask.'

We put it in our mouths and started to chew. It felt as if my mouth was full of lamb and potato stew, my favourite meal. The others experienced the same, a mouthful of their favourite food.

Rocco was in ecstasy. 'Mine is like roast chicken, no, it's like fried fish, wait, it's like green curry.' I think he ended up going through just about every meal he'd ever eaten.

'Strawberries and cream, yummy!' was Jula's only comment. It was magic Elvan cake that we had been given. Little did we know they were to be a great help through the quest, although we used them sparingly.

7
CHAPTER

The Next Four Days in the Forest

The second day in the forest arrived abruptly. Surprisingly, we all slept well and woke at exactly the same time. *Very strange*, I thought.

'Drew,' I asked, 'it is very strange that we seem to go to sleep and wake at the same time. Why is that?'

'I don't know,' he said.

'Could it be magic?'

'Could be or maybe not.'

As we spoke, Lord Arcon stuck his head in the tent. 'There is an old saying, Mecco.' He butted in.

'If for counsel to an Elf you go,
Expect a yes and expect a no.'

It is known that Elves avoid questions as much as possible. They don't like giving advice.

'I wouldn't say that,' Drew responded.

'You make up your own mind, Mecco,' said Arcon.

Rocco couldn't wait to get out of the tent. His first words were 'What's for breakfast?' Everyone looked at him in disgust. I think this was Rocco's way of getting attention.

He would often disagree with us and was known for his loud comments. He had two older sisters and a younger brother. And this was his burden. He craved affection but he never got it. He was overweight and not a handsome child, yet his younger brother was like an angel: long blond hair, the bluest of eyes, and clear olive skin. His family doted on this brother. He was also a good-natured boy: caring, considerate, and well-mannered. Everything he did or said was praised.

Rocco wanted the same affection from his family, but whenever he did something nice or caring like his brother, it looked contrived and they would joke about it. He learnt from an early age to say and do very little. He built barriers to protect himself from the pain. He also learnt that he could get attention by disagreeing with everyone present. At least then he was noticed. At times he hated his brother but didn't blame him for his misfortune. In fact, he loved and protected him. When other boys at school made fun of his angelic looks, it was Rocco who came to his aid.

Drew, shaking his head, handed us another piece of Elvan cake. This time, we didn't rush eating it. We sat there savouring our tiny pieces for ages. And as we did, I became aware of a force emanating from the vicinity of Lord Arcon. He was still walking round the perimeter of the clearing as though looking for something. Suddenly, he sang out to Lord Sebcon and the Elves to join him.

Drew told us to stay put and added, 'Please do nothing unless we say otherwise.'

As I watched them join him, I noticed something strange. The trees seemed larger and the undergrowth thicker. There was also a large fallen tree trunk about eight paces from the tent, half in the forest and half in the clearing. The part of the tree in the clearing looked as it did last night, but the rest of it appeared to be rotting. *That's impossible*, I thought.

Also, the marks of white paint that the Elves had placed on the trees yesterday looked as if they had been painted many years ago. The lords and Elves had moved into a semicircle facing a section of the forest as if waiting for something to emerge.

We continued eating as all seemed to be fine. Then they came back, except for Lord Arcon. We were still enjoying our piece of Elvan cake when Lord Sebcon interrupted us. 'Enough with the eating, we have to start your training. Since there are six of you and six of us, we will pair up. I shall train you, Mecco, and Lord Arcon will train Wecco.'

Drew was paired with Jula, Tarew with Peto, and Carew with Ricco.

Jarew was not impressed with having to train Rocco. 'How can I train someone so fat?' he complained.

Lord Sebcon replied, 'You have the challenge, and we shall see how good you are as a trainer. But if you wish, I will take on the task of training Rocco.'

This played on Jarew's pride. 'No,' he said,' I will train him.'

They took us to different parts of the clearing to begin the training. Our first task was to learn how to handle a sword and knife. To start with, we did exercises with imaginary weapons. We all complained about it, but once we started, we found it exhilarating and rewarding. We stopped for a drink and ate the fruit I had brought along. We recommenced after forty minutes, and we started on hand-to-hand combat. We were all quite good at this as we spent many an hour wrestling on the beach—except Jula, but she tried hard, and with practice, we knew she would get better. We finished our training an hour before sunset and sat around eating and asking more questions.

Carew told us more about the history of the Elves and how he was a direct descendant of Jamatta, the first High Elf of the New World. It was something he was very proud of, and we noticed how much he enjoyed talking on the subject. As he was talking, I noticed the other Elves discreetly go around and repaint yesterday's faded white marks. Lord Arcon ordered us into the tent to rest. Sleep was instantaneous that night. We put it down to all the exercises we were mastering.

The next day was more training. The third night, we again slept well and woke simultaneously, just as the first rays of sunlight hit the mountains to the west. Once again, the forest appeared denser, the white marks on the trees had faded, and the half-rotten tree trunk was even more rotten. But I thought this could not be. *It must be my imagination.*

'Today, we start with exercising the power you have,' said Drew. First, we had to see how high we could jump from a standing position, secondly how high we could jump over an object. Peto and I had no problem jumping over things as we used to run and dive over the waves, so we used the same technique. Our friends were not as competent as us and had to do more practice.

'None of you have become aware of the power of movement you possess,' said Lord Sebcon. 'When one of you prepares to jump, the rest of you must use your power and think about helping him to achieve more height. Now, help each other when you jump.'

Lord Arcon did his usual inspection around the perimeter of the forest. He seemed extremely preoccupied with his tasks. Rocco was the next to try to jump.

'Okay, Rocco,' I said, 'this time we will help you.' As he jumped, we focused on helping him. To our surprise, he went flying about four paces high and came down with a thud. He lay there moaning and groaning. We ran over to see if he was okay.

'Thanks a lot,' he said, 'you guys did that on purpose.'

The Elves were laughing, and Drew said, 'When you lift him high, you just don't let him fall! You must let him down gently. At least until you all learn the technique.' For the rest of the day, we practised all we had been shown. It did get easier.

Lord Sebcon then explained, 'The Elvan parchments say it is possible when you are together to build an invisible barrier for protection, but it will only work when you concentrate very hard.'

We set about to work on this, but could not see any barrier occurring. We threw stones from where we stood, but no invisible barrier seemed to appear. One stone just missed Lord Sebcon. He turned abruptly and a little annoyed and said, 'What are you lot doing?'

'We can't make any barrier,' said Jula.

'Try it again,' said Lord Sebcon as he picked up a stone and threw it as hard as he could. We flinched as it hurtled towards us. But before it reached us, it bounced off an invisible force.

'It is possible,' he remarked, 'to move objects through the force field from the inside, but objects cannot enter from the outside. This skill will be one of your best defences.'

We were getting very excited about our newly acquired magical powers as they slowly came to fruition.

At midday, the Six of Croll sat down for a rest while the Elves and the lords gathered at the clearing's edge. They seemed rather occupied again with something. But we had our own worries as Peto and Ricco were devising a plan to leave the forest. We tried dissuading them.

'There is a more important deed for us to do', I said, 'than to run away from what fate has in store for us.'

'It's okay for you,' said Peto. 'Your family doesn't care what is happening to you. But mine will.'

'We are worried that sooner or later, someone from the town will find out where we are,' said Ricco. 'And the longer we stay away, the more trouble we'll be in.'

For the remainder of the afternoon, we went back to our practice as if nothing was wrong. As the day drew on, Peto and Ricco seemed more content, and the rest of us hoped they had forgotten about their escape plan. We sat eating and asking more questions about our task. Drew explained to us about the parchments, adding that not even he knew what was in store.

Just as the sun was setting, Lord Arcon ordered us into the tent as with the previous nights. We fell asleep and awoke in the morning at precisely the same time. I could not help thinking how strange this was. This was the fifth morning. Peto and Ricco were the first to leave the tent, and they immediately ran towards the forest. Lord Arcon jumped up and ran after them. As the three entered the forest, they seemed to vanish into the thick undergrowth. Lord Sebcon and the Elves stopped us from following them. They looked at the area where they had disappeared.

Lord Sebcon said to the Elves, 'I hope he reaches them in time.' The Elves led us to the centre of the clearing and told us to review the martial arts we had learned so far. Lord Sebcon walked round the perimeter of the forest as Lord Arcon had done the previous days, scouring every part of it.

The day dragged on. We stopped for some lunch, and as the four of us sat resting, I realised I had not seen an animal or bird in the clearing since our arrival. That log I had noticed on the first day intrigued me as half of it had now rotted away completely. The white paint on the trees had faded again. As the day progressed, Lord Sebcon and the Elves grew agitated. About an hour from sunset, they walked over to us.

It was Drew who spoke. 'We must talk. Please, sit down.' We made ourselves comfortable and waited for Drew to begin, and he looked extremely worried and then announced, 'We are in a dilemma as the prophecies state there must be six children for the quest or it is the end.'

Jula walked over and patted him on the shoulder, saying, 'It will be all right. Lord Arcon will find them. They could not have gone far.'

With great intensity, Drew moaned. 'Lord Arcon has only till sunset, then it will be up to us to do what we can.'

We sat watching the sun set in silence and then, with only five minutes to spare, Lord Arcon suddenly appeared with both runaways struggling under his arms.

He put them down, looked intently at the setting sun, then abruptly ordered, 'Quickly, into the tent.'

As we entered, he added, 'Sleep. We will discuss this tomorrow.'

Surprisingly, again we fell asleep and awoke simultaneously. This was really becoming quite a strange coincidence. We left the tent to have some breakfast while the lords of Con and the Elves went off to talk.

Peto and Ricco relayed to us their story: 'We rushed into the forest, and just before our feet landed, everything seemed to be moving at an incredible speed. Animals and birds were just a flash. But once our feet hit the ground, all was normal. We took one step, and then Lord Arcon appeared behind us. He grabbed us and pulled us back into the clearing and told us to get in the tent, so we did.'

'But you were gone all day,' said Jula. 'How could he have got to you so quickly?'

'No, we were only gone a few seconds,' said Ricco. 'I could not understand why we had to get straight back into the tent and, more surprisingly, how we all went to sleep so quickly.'

'I said you were gone all the day,' Jula announced angrily, 'and the Elves and Lord Sebcon were very worried.'

As they were telling us what had happened, I looked around at the forest. Again it looked different: the trees were much taller and the undergrowth so thick there would be no way out. The half a log that looked completely disintegrated yesterday now had new saplings sprouting from where it had been. And the white paint had faded again. There definitely was something strange going on here, I thought. I told the others how I had not seen an animal or bird the whole time we'd been here and how quickly the forest had grown. Eventually, the lords and the Elves returned and sat down next to us. 'We must talk,' said Arcon. 'We only have to wait till midday to go. I cannot emphasise enough how important it is that we get through this morning. Please go and finish your lessons and practise all you have learnt. Then later this morning, I will explain everything to you.'

8
CHAPTER
The Parchment Revealed

We completed the training program. I thought we had done well, and I thought Drew was also pleased. But I didn't think the lords were very impressed. It was mid-morning and we were called over to join them at the tent. We made ourselves comfortable, sitting in a semicircle around Lord Arcon.

'First, I will let Drew explain about the parchments.'

'When we left on this adventure,' Drew began, 'we were handed a roll of parchments by the high Elves of Gong. We were told instructions would be revealed to us when needed and we should follow them to the letter. As we told you before, when we entered the forest of Gundi, the parchment revealed our first task. There were three requests. The first was to bring together those that were to be known as the Six of Croll. The second was to bring the six here for five days and nights to impart our knowledge. That we have done, all except two disciplines. The first is the Elvan act of disappearing, which we cannot transfer to you. When the Elves moved to the forest of Gong from the forest of Gundi, there was no need for us to hide from Man as it was so secluded. So over the years, we lost the ability to disappear. In fact, it was very difficult at times for us when we were trying to get you together. You nearly caught us on a few occasions. The third request was to retrieve something from an old building in the city of Malla then travel to the river Condoor. It also said when we reach the lake of the black swans, we must recite the riddle of the rivers, and a boat will appear. The problem is we don't know the riddles.'

Jula rather smugly said, 'I know the riddles of the rivers. I learnt them as a child.'

Arcon sighed, saying, 'That is good news. I only hope they are the same riddles. So it is only one thing we have failed in. Let's hope it will not cause us a problem in the future.'

Tarew, who was holding the parchments, started to act strangely then stood up and said,

> *The three Elves know deep down inside*
> *How to vanish and how to hide.*
> *One of the Six has the ability as well.*
> *And when it occurs, he will be able to tell.*

We looked at Tarew in amazement. He sat back down as if nothing had happened.

'Repeat', Drew asked, 'what you just said, Tarew.'

He looked bewildered. 'I didn't say anything.'

'Look at the parchment and see if a new message has appeared,' said Drew, 'and if so, read me what it says.'

'We know what it says,' he replied. He lifted the parchment and looked, then said, 'There are only three messages on here.'

'Then look at the second page of the parchment,' said Lord Arcon.

Tarew rolled out the second page, looked down, and to his amazement, another message was appearing.

Lord Arcon, now rather annoyed, said, 'Please read it to us.'

Tarew then repeated,

> *'The three Elves know deep down inside*
> *How to vanish and how to hide.*
> *One of the Six has the ability as well.*
> *And when it occurs, he will be able to tell.'*

'So', said Lord Arcon, 'three of you do know, but which three?'

'I have never even tried,' said Drew, 'and I don't think I would know the first thing about it.'

'Well, somewhere in your subconscious, you know. And which one of the Six has the power?' asked Lord Sebcon.

'One of the five,' added Jula sarcastically, 'as the message said, he will be able to tell, so it must be one of the boys, and that would be right.'

We looked at each other, trying to fathom which one of us it could be. The Elves tried to vanish but with no luck.

Lord Arcon announced, 'Before we leave, we must work out the vanishing.'

We spent the next hour practising what we had learnt as the Elves attempted the vanishing.

Lord Arcon announced, 'We can stop for a light snack, and I will tell you how the Evil has been working on all the creeds and creating problems between them.' We made ourselves comfortable and began to eat and Lord Arcon began our history lesson:

'All the creeds have positive aspects. They teach fair and honest things and show a good way to live and die. They developed by the thoughts of great holy philosophers. But you all must be aware that evil men have taken over your creeds. They have taken every passage from each of your books and reinterpreted them to suit their own agenda. To forgive someone for a mistake or bad deed against you takes much more strength and courage than revenge. Now all your elders teach is revenge. Once you take revenge, you are dragged down to their level. Read your books of truth, but make sure you read it with an open heart and no hatred. Be careful of others' interpretations.

'The great philosophers of your books never intended their philosophy to be used for evil. There will be times when decisions will have to be made. Some of them will go against the belief of your creed. But always keep in mind, the six of you must come first, no matter how it goes against what you have been brainwashed with in the past. Remember that it is not the creed that makes a good person, but a good person that can make the creed good.

'The Anonymous gave us the seed to search for the truth. If we accept only one truth, we give up the challenge and a purpose in life to find all the truths. The Anonymous is all the truths. The Anonymous does not care what house of worship you pray to him in. Hatred, revenge, and destruction do not show him respect. A good word spoken or a good deed done—these are the things that show him respect. The challenge for all of you is to put behind the destructive beliefs that your creeds have conditioned in you. It is imperative you spend the rest of your life deconditioning those corrupt beliefs.

'That is why I tell you that the Evil can manifest itself through the thoughts of others and his struggle for power is over the bodies of good.' He hesitated for a moment then went on, 'Sometimes the Evil may triumph, but he will never conquer. Now we must rest, as soon you shall start on your journey. The other lords will arrive this afternoon, bearing news. It will depend on this whether only the Elves will escort you or whether we will also be able to accompany you on your journey.'

9
CHAPTER
The Departure

Drew handed us a piece of Elvan cake, and we munched on it for ages. The lords and the Elves had moved to the far side of the clearing and seemed preoccupied and were having a discussion without us. We all felt a little rejected, as we were the ones with the quest to undertake.

Lord Arcon looked over. Realising we were restless, he called us over and said, 'Please do not take offence. We are discussing things that are not your worry. Go over all you have been taught, and we shall leave the forest as soon as our friends arrive.'

We spent a good hour going over the exercises and felt quite pleased with ourselves. The high-flying technique was our most promising, I think because we enjoyed it the best. We stopped and joined the Elves, who were still trying to fathom how to vanish but with no luck.

Eventually Tarew said, 'Why don't I ask the parchments, as they may give us a clue?'

'Okay,' said Drew. 'What have we got to lose?' So he asked the parchments, 'How are we supposed to know how to vanish? Please give us a clue.'

For the next few seconds, nothing happened. Then Tarew stood up and said:

The vanishing trick, for you to learn,
Is to move your mind, then in turn,
Your body will follow where your mind will go,
And that is how you are to know.

Tarew sat down, looked at his feet then looked up, and asked, 'Did anything happen?'

'Yes,' said Drew, 'now read the parchment.'

'How is that a clue?' Tarew demanded.

Lord Arcon had wandered over and was listening to the proceedings. 'I think what it is saying is, you don't actually vanish but can move to another place by projecting your thoughts. And your body travels so quickly that it looks as if you disappear.'

Suddenly, Drew vanished and then reappeared in front of the tent twenty paces away.

'Yes!' he shouted, and then he was back. 'That's it. You must think of some place in your mind, and your body travels there instantly.'

Tarew and Carew tried and succeeded. Tarew was a little slow, as we could see him move. It was quick but we still saw him. He would need practice, I thought. Jarew tried but with no luck. He became quite angry.

Now they looked at us. Lord Arcon asked, 'Which one of you can do it?'

I knew I was the one but did not want to spoil it for the others. So they all had a go with no luck. Then it was my turn.

'It must be you,' said Peto, 'because you are the only one not to have attempted it.'

So I thought of inside the tent and next thing I was there. If they had looked, they would have seen the flaps of the tent swinging. I stayed in there for ages, and when I didn't return, I could hear Jula calling, 'Okay, you can come back now.'

But I stayed put until Lord Arcon became agitated and said, 'That's enough, Mecco. Come back.' I did with a smile on my face.

'That was not funny,' said Drew. 'We were beginning to worry that you might have vanished for good.'

'Remember what happened to the boy who cried, "Dragon!"' Carew added. That was Carew's first pearl of wisdom but was not to be his last on our quest.

'No, we don't,' said Peto and Rocco.

'Well, one day I shall tell you the story,' said Carew.

The three Elves and I then spent the next half hour practising the vanishing. We could only travel about twenty-five paces or so and realised we would have to spend much more time working on it. We did develop the technique with time, and it was to prove a great asset on our adventure.

'That is the one thing', said Lord Arcon, 'we lords have not mastered, although the wizard Naroof has promised us he will teach us the technique.'

It was well after midday, and Lord Arcon was becoming more anxious. He was at the perimeter again, searching for something. I started to sense a manifestation of sorts, coming from where Lord Arcon stood. I walked over to him.

'You can feel it, can't you?' he commented then asked. 'Is it negative or positive?'

'I'm not sure, but I don't think it is evil. So it must be good.'

Right at that moment, there was movement in the undergrowth, and two men appeared, one on a black horse and one on a white horse.

'Oh great, you have made it,' announced Lord Arcon.

The Elves and Lord Sebcon walked over, and the rest of us followed as the men dismounted their horses. They greeted and embraced each other as if they had not seen each other for years. The two were introduced as Lord Revcon and Lord Devcon. The six of us looked quite puzzled, as we were told that the other lords who stayed behind were much younger. But these looked the same age, or even older. We were told to do more exercises as they moved to the centre of the clearing for a meeting. It looked very intense, with hands waving and pointing in all directions.

Then somehow I overheard Lord Arcon say, 'We will have to split up. Drew, your group and the six will have to follow the instructions of the parchments. We must try to find out what is happening in the valley of Kassob and seek help from the wizard Naroof.'

There were strange things happening to me: my hearing, for instance. If I looked at someone, even if they were a long distance from me, I could hear what was being said. It was not actually a sound, but more like a thought. I also had this strange feeling whenever the Six of Croll were together; it felt as if I could harness some mysterious power.

Eventually the four lords joined us and explained that they had a task to accomplish. They would have to go to the city of Kassob to visit the wizard Naroof. They were to leave us to continue our quest with only the help of the Elves. We were to depart immediately for the river Condoor via our town of Malla.

We protested and voiced what we were thinking: 'We cannot return there, as we would be in grave danger and, in Jula's case, even face death.'

'You have nothing to fear,' said Arcon. 'The Elves will be with you and will protect you. Besides, you now have the power to protect yourselves. It is important that you return there. There are things you must do before you can continue on your quest. I think you will find a lot of changes in Malla. So be prepared!'

Lord Arcon then asked to speak to me alone. 'Mecco,' he said, 'you are the one who can focus the power of the six. It is a great burden, but you have no option. I also must tell you of the Pestilence. They are seven dragons with evil riders who can sniff out good. So be aware of them.' He laid his hands upon my shoulder, looked at me and continued, 'Now you must start the quest. You must do it with great conviction.'

This was much more than I ever wanted, but much less than I ever dreamed for my life. The Lords bid us farewell and left with a sense of urgency. We were not to know of the tragic circumstances that would befall them, nor would we see them for months.

10
CHAPTER
The Real Departure

Before leaving, the Lord Arcon handed to Drew two small bags full of silver and gold coins. 'Keep them well hidden and only use in an emergency.'

Then they made their goodbyes with an Elvan bow, and the Elves sent them on their way with the sign of travellers' luck. The Elves packed up the tent and bid farewell to the clearing with their usual bow, as if it were alive.

We moved off towards the track where we had entered six days ago, but it had completely vanished. *How could this be?* I thought.

Then Drew, as if he knew what I was thinking, said, 'Not to worry. We'll make a track.'

They moved ahead of us, hacking a clearing as we followed. How they knew which direction to take was beyond us. We six could not understand how the forest could grow so fast. We thought it must be magic.

Finally, after an hour of hacking the undergrowth, we reached where we thought the edge of the forest should be. But no, it was not the edge and still they hacked away. It seemed much larger and wider than when we first entered. We eventually found the old road and followed it back to town. It was overgrown and in need of repair. I could not remember it being this bad before.

Jula and Wecco were walking close to each other. Over the last six days, they had grown much closer and were hardly ever out of each other's sight. As we drew nearer to the town, we noticed there was no smoke rising from the chimneys. This seemed extremely strange.

'Why do we have to return to Malla?' I asked Drew.

'Is there not a library or large building called a museum in your town?' Drew asked. 'That is where we must go as it holds certain information important for the quest.'

'Yes, we used to spend long hours there reading and looking at exhibitions and things,' said Rocco and Wecco.

'Good,' said Drew. 'Show us the way.'

'I don't think they will let us all in together,' said Rocco, 'and I don't know what they will say when four Elves arrive with us.'

'I don't want to go back there,' said Jula. 'It is too dangerous for me.'

'We must stay together,' said Drew. 'That way no one can harm us.'

'Okay,' she said, with little conviction.

Arriving at the first row of houses, we six gasped, as they were run-down and dilapidated. They looked deserted. We fell silent, not knowing how this could happen in the short time we were away. We then came to the little cemetery of the Dation, which had gravestones covering the whole hill, even up to where they say the witch was buried. I could only remember it being half-covered. We became anxious, as we could not see one person in the town.

We asked the Elves what had happened. 'We cannot be sure,' they explained, 'but hopefully we shall meet someone who can tell us.'

The next corner we were to take would lead us to Jula's house. We could see how nervous she was as we drew closer. As we turned the corner, we saw that the whole front of it had been burned out. She ran over screaming, 'What has happened, and where are my mother and father?'

Wecco followed her and put his arm around her, saying, 'It will be all right. They have probably just moved.' We followed them over cautiously. What a mess! I could not fathom why it looked as if the fire had occurred ages ago, as there were trees and plants growing in which would have been the front room.

The Elves looked at each other, then at us, and Drew said, 'We must talk. There are things we must tell you. We were hoping it would not be this bad or shocking, so now the truth you will have to know.'

At that precise moment, an old man screamed from the end of the street, 'What are you doing here?'

The Elves pulled up their hoods as we approached him. There was something familiar about him, but I could not put my finger on it. His eyes were extremely sad, and it looked as if he were carrying a great load upon his soul.

As he approached, he looked at me and started to cry uncontrollably. 'Why did I let you go?' he said. 'I should have stopped you then. Now you have come back to haunt me. I'm sorry, Mecco. Forgive me.'

Who is this man, and how did he know my name? I wondered.

'Stay calm, Mecco,' said Drew, 'and I will take care of this.' He took the old man by the arm and walked away, talking with him.

'How do you know my name?' I screamed after him.

He turned around and asked, 'Is it really you, Mecco, or just a ghost?'

'Yes,' I said. 'It really is me. Who are you, and how do you know my name?'

The old man started crying again and said, 'I'm your brother, or rather, your cousin Nedco, but why do I see you as you were when you disappeared?'

We six stood bewildered as Drew walked back to us and whispered, 'Fifty years have passed in those five days in the forest. The clearing where we stayed is an old Elvan part of the forest, and it still holds magic. The parchments foretold it to us. If we did not get you to stay the five days, all would have been lost.'

I looked around me and said, 'Look, is not everything lost already?'

Jula was crying, the old man claiming to be my brother was crying, and the rest of us were dumbfounded. Was it our departure that caused this to happen? Or was it the creeds accusing each other of our abduction?

'It is nearly sunset,' said Drew. 'We should find shelter. Let us go.' We followed Drew in a daze and eventually found an old temple of the Aldation.

The old man claiming to be my cousin said, 'I can't go in there. I will be struck down.'

I went over to him and reassured him it would be fine. As I looked closely at him, I realised he really was my cousin, but fifty years older. He must have been at least sixty-eight years of age.

We moved into the house of prayer and settled down to rest. Ricco, Peto, and Rocco were sent out to find food.

Rocco was not impressed and demanded, 'Why can't we have more Elvan cake?'

'It should only be used in case of emergencies,' said Drew.

The rest of us made a fire from the old pieces of wooden beams that had fallen from the rafters. Outside, the lingering touch of winter filled the air, but the longer days were anticipating the arrival of summer. The boys arrived back with some fruit and vegetables. Jula found an old pot and made up a stew of sorts. Wecco and Jula had also found some fresh herbs to add to it, and the Elves also added some. It turned out to be a very scrumptious and filling meal.

I was still curious about what had happened by the perimeter of the forest on the second day. So as we ate, I asked Drew, 'Why did Lord Arcon spend so much time pacing the edge of the forest? And what was all that commotion on the second day, and why all the painting of the trees?'

'Questions, more questions,' he said then went on. 'That was a magical Elvan clearing, and the special paint helped its magic. To anyone walking by in the forest, it looked empty. Lord Arcon was just making sure no one would step into the clearing, for if they did, they would have seen all. On the second day, he sensed the approach of some Menlins and called us over. They were searching the forest for you six and were heading towards the clearing. They were not aware of us, but we could sense them. To them, the forest clearing looked completely empty. So hopefully there was no need for them to enter. One screamed out, "Let's have a rest in this clearing!" and had just placed one foot inside the perimeter when the captain pulled him back and said, "There is no time for rest. The Seven are waiting at the edge of the forest and would know we have stopped looking." Thankfully, they moved off as it would have thrown our quest into disarray.'

We continued eating the stew, and I wondered how it would have been had they entered the clearing. We felt refreshed, strong and ready for any challenge after eating. I think it may have had something to do with Elves' herbs. We sat around the fire in silence. The old man could not take his eyes off me. The Elves were still wearing their hoods so as not to frighten Nedco.

Drew sat up and asked of him, 'What disaster has befallen this town?'

'Fifty years ago,' said Nedco, 'when you all disappeared, each of the creeds accused each other of abduction. The Kabs attacked the Bovers. At first, the Aldation and Dation stayed out of it, then for some reason they also started to attack the Bovers. Hundreds of their homes were burned, and they started to retaliate. More homes of the other creeds were destroyed in the aftermath. This dragged on for years. None could leave their homes alone without being attacked. After maybe fifteen or twenty years of this, seven powerful lords arrived on seven of the most evil-looking fire-breathing animals with an army of the vilest-looking men. They took over the town and ordered all the people between the ages of thirty-two and thirty-four to assemble. The seven evil lords walked among them, not asking a question, just smelling and groping them. The townsfolk were so afraid they never protested, for fear of these evil creatures. All the people who lined up told us later that they could feel the evil in these lords.'

Tarew responded in a tone of anger and disgust, 'Did not you feel the evil in the rest of you?'

'It was not our fault. It was the Bovers and Kabs,' said Nedco.

Tarew stood up with such loathing, and he was about to say more, when Drew placed his hand on Tarew's shoulder and said, 'It happened many years ago, and our task has just become more important.' They both sat down, and we were reminded that Drew had this calming effect on everyone he came in contact with.

Nedco continued relaying his story, and I could sense tension from Rocco and Wecco towards Ricco. I stopped the old man then looked at the others and said, 'Our role in this quest has become much more complicated. It will take great concentration and wisdom to overcome what has happened in the past. But overcome it we must. As the lords of Con said, "Only together can we halt this evil."'

They calmed down, and I knew the power and love we all had for each other would come through. Nedco continued, 'They announced they were looking for five men and a woman of about 32 to 34 years of age and offered a reward. The Bovers, who were so disgusted with the girl who had left all those years ago, told them that five boys and a girl had disappeared into the forest twenty years past. They then sent out search parties to comb the forest. Weeks they spent looking with no luck, and for the next seven or eight years, they returned the same time every year and went through the same process. The hatred grew between the creeds—until most people had been killed or left the town. I survived, as I went looking for you in the forest and set up a camp there for years on end. I knew that there was something special about you. When I did return to the town, most people had left. Only a few old people stayed on.'

We six sat there just looking at each other, and Drew said, with extreme fear in his eyes, 'They were the Seven Pernicious, the most evil of his sentinels, and the Menlins are the army of Evil. Have they been back in the last few years?'

'Yes,' said Nedco. 'They were here three weeks ago, and before that, they had not been here for many a year.'

Carew looked at Drew and said, 'Those poor seven dragons and lords who have turned to the evil—if only they knew.'

Drew shook his head and added, 'This is more serious than we anticipated. We were hoping if we kept you hidden in the magic space, as the years passed, they would either think the legend was a lie or you would be too old to pose a threat. Hopefully they are not looking for six children and four Elves.'

Nedco looked at the four hooded children and said, 'Four Elves. Is this true?' The Elves threw their hoods back off their heads to reveal who they were. 'The armies of evil were asking about three Elves,' said Nedco. 'What is happening to the world? Elves, evil lords on dragons, armies of strange men, and so much hatred.'

'So where did most of the inhabitants of Malla go?' I asked.

'Some left for other places,' said Nedco, 'but most started a new town called Mallaville that is further down the coast. That is where most of your families now live.' This news cheered us up a little, and we talked of visiting it one day.

'We must rest tonight,' Drew announced, 'as tomorrow we start our search for a clue that should be in your museum. Then we must depart up the river Condoor to the city of Basscala, where the parchments should reveal to us the next move.'

As we lay down to rest, Jula asked Carew, 'What did you mean by those poor dragons?'

'That is a very sad story,' said Carew. 'And one day I will tell you. But for now, we must rest.'

11
CHAPTER

The Message in the Museum

We finished the leftover stew for breakfast, packed up the gear, and set out for the museum in the heart of town. It took us about an hour to walk there, and we walked in a daze, passing all the dilapidated official buildings. As soon as the museum came into view, Drew sent Carew ahead to see if it was safe. Carew used his vanishing technique and returned in no time at all to say the place was deserted and looked safe. It was a strange feeling, walking up the steps of a place I often visited—the last time was only a week ago, yet now the building was a ruin.

'What is it we are looking for?' asked Jula. The place was empty and quite eerie, and we entered with anxiety. We stood at the entrance, looking along the hall at the large marble pillars running down each side with shattered display cases tipped over or just empty. The floors were black-and-white marble covered in dust and debris. The enormous window at the end of the hall had been smashed to pieces. There were three-level galleries all with the same size marble pillars supporting each floor and then the roof. From each gallery, one could look down to the ground floor. We stood there remembering what an impressive building it was, yet it was only a week ago when we last saw it in all its splendour.

Jula asked again, rather agitated, 'What is it we are looking for?'

'There should be some large, flat silver plates with ancient Elvan design on them,' said Drew. 'They hold something that the parchments have told us to retrieve.'

We walked round the building, looking everywhere, but with no luck until late in the afternoon, Ricco screamed out from the top gallery, 'They're here in this dusty old glass case.'

We rushed up to the top floor. The Elves used some magic chant, and the case unlocked by itself. There were three dust-covered silver plates that the Elves cleaned to reveal a strange writing that even the Elves could not decipher. We stood in a semicircle while the Elves tried every magical chant they knew, with no luck. Finally, they chanted, 'Biggil, baggel, boggel boo, tell us what we need from you.'

We burst into laughter, thinking how desperate they must have been to recite that, as they turned and gave us a dirty look. The afternoon passed and the Elves continued without success and they were becoming very worried. They announced, 'We can't move on until we have deciphered the message.'

Peto was growing impatient and reached across Drew, grabbing one of the plates. As he did, he dropped it and it fell on its side, spinning slowly to a halt. As it spun, words came from it at the same speed the plate was spinning. We looked in wonder and Drew picked it up and spun it around again on its side. The words were clearer, but not in a language we understood.

Drew turned to Carew and asked, 'Can you understand any of it?'

'It is very difficult,' said Carew, 'but it is definitely ancient Elvan. The more one listens, the more one hears.'

As the adventure continued, we realised Carew had a saying for just about every situation.

'I will listen a few more times,' he added, 'and also to the others. Leave me here. The rest of you, go and see if you can gather more food for the journey.'

We went in different directions in the town. Wecco and Jula, of course, went together. Peto and Ricco also paired up, and Rocco went with Jarew. That left Drew and me to be together, and I was pleased.

We had gathered quite a large amount of supplies, and on our return, we placed them in the centre of the room. Jula and Wecco also found another large pot, so they cooked another great vegetable stew, although I wouldn't have said no to a nice leg of mutton or a chicken stew for a change. I had not had a piece of meat since I couldn't remember when, or even a piece of cheese or fish would have been fine. In fact, that would have been lovely!

While we ate, I wrote in my diary. Every time I wrote now, I seemed to be trying to catch up with events. Carew joined us, looking a little worried, and said, 'I have deciphered some of the message from the plates but not all, and I will have to continue later.' After our meal, we bedded down and left Drew and Carew to continue deciphering the Elvan plates.

Wecco lay down next to Jula—nothing unusual there. Peto lay next to me, resting his head on my outstretched arm. He put his palm on my cheek and turned my head to face him. He looked at me and said, 'I miss our days swimming and surfing.'

I knew he cared for me deeply but not the way I wanted him to.

'So do I,' I said, 'and one day, maybe it will come again.'

Deep down, I knew those days would never return, and Peto would grow too embarrassed to ever show me the innocent love he had for me. Times pass and so does life. I looked to see Peto peacefully asleep, his head resting on my shoulder. The tenderness he showed me compensated for the ache in my arm. In the morning, I woke to Peto's arm around my neck, and I lay perfectly still, feeling safe with all my friends around me.

Carew and Drew spent the whole night going over and over listening to the plates.

'I think we have deciphered the message,' Carew announced.

The company rose, freshened up, then came back and finished off last night's stew. We sat quite nervously anticipating what Carew had to relay to us.

'The first plate revealed to me that we must retrieve four silver emblems that represent all your creeds,' he announced, 'and keep them safe till the parchments reveal what we must do with them. The second disk I think said, "The first Oracle in the Mountains Blue must be visited and questions asked."'

'I don't get it,' said Rocco. 'First the parchments tell us to get a boat, now the plates tell us to climb a mountain. How confusing is that?'

Drew was quite disgusted and snapped, 'When one travels up a river, one rises, and the Mountains Blue are the source of the river of Condoor.' He then turned to Carew and asked, 'So what did you find out about the last plate?'

Carew was holding it tightly in his hand, and he answered, 'This one I'm having a problem deciphering. We will have to take it with us.'

Drew demanded that we leave for the river as soon as possible but first insisted that we find the emblems of our creeds.

'I have mine around my neck,' said Jula.

Wecco, Rocco, and Ricco nodded their heads in the affirmative. 'It's the same with us,' they said.

Only Peto and I had no emblem. Our creed did not believe in exhibiting our signs quite as blatantly as the others did. We all knew what it looked like though, so off we went on a search.

Wecco and Jula found a large box full of them. Peto and I took one each and placed them round our necks. Nedco had been tagging along with us, and I felt I had to ask him if he would like to join with us, knowing full well his answer.

We bid him goodbye and told him he must not tell a soul of our task or it could jeopardise everything. He promised to say nothing and handed us a sack full of cheese and bread that he had spent the night making at the old bakery. The Elves bowed with their customary politeness and thanked him for his kindness.

Then Carew added, 'May your shadow always cover fertile soil.'

We set off through the town to the river Condoor. It was the spookiest feeling, seeing it half in ruins, when for us we'd only left a week ago. As we walked in silence towards the river, we all thought of our family and friends who now would be dead or have left for Mallaville. The old familiar sights, now dilapidated and overgrown with vines and other plants, made us all quite depressed. The day was warming up, and I could see from the look on Peto's face that he was reminiscing about going surfing or for a swim in the ocean.

We arrived at the river's edge. We stopped and looked at the dunes and forest in the distance.

Wecco wondered aloud, 'Where will this journey take us, and will we ever return to these places of our childhood?'

Jarew looked at the dunes and forest, then at us and said, 'You have not seen a true forest yet, but you will, then you will be in awe, so look forward to your adventure.'

Drew turned to Jarew and thanked him. Hopefully the tension was being broken down between those two. *Let's hope so*, I thought.

'Which is the way to the lake of the black swans?' asked Drew.

Jula, because she knew the riddles of the river, thought she was the most important person on this trip. She stepped forward and announced, 'It is where the river widens and connects to a large lake about two kilopaces walk from here.' She then turned to us and said, 'Okay, let's go.'

We looked at each other and rolled our eyes, as though to say, 'What is she on about?' Then off we went.

Rocco was already complaining about how far it was and was demanding to know when we were going to have lunch. I threw him a piece of cheese to keep him quiet for a while. We arrived at the lake at sunset. The water was clear and still, and on the far shore, there was a flock of black swans. Upon our arrival, they started to glide over the water towards us.

'I think we should eat,' said Tarew, 'before we start to sing the riddles. I will try to finish deciphering the last plate.' By the time the swans arrived at our side of the lake, we had finished most of our meal, which consisted of fruit, cheese, and bread that had been given to us by Nedco. We threw the scraps to the swans, and they devoured them appreciatively.

When the swans finally finished, Drew turned to Jula and said, 'Okay, Jula, let's hear your singing voice before it gets too dark.'

Jula stood and moved towards the shore of the lake as if she was walking to the edge of a stage and commenced singing.

> 'The black swans dwell where the water is deep.
> The boat still lies with the rest of the fleet.
> But with these words sung in notes so true,
> The boat will rise and burden you
> Across the water and over the sea.
> Up the river it'll take you and me.
> To places far upon your quest,
> Where the trees are tall and the world's at rest.'

They all looked in anticipation, but nothing transpired. There was no sign of a boat or even a ripple on the water.

'It was probably her singing,' said Rocco. 'One of the Elves should sing it. They have better voices.' Jula was not impressed with this at all and swung around, glaring daggers at Rocco.

All of a sudden, Jarew jumped up and said, 'I have it.' He spun the plate one more time and smiled, adding, 'I know what the last plate says.' He wrote something down, handed it to Jula, and said, 'Sing it again and add this verse at the end.'

Jula sang it, adding,

> 'The boat will travel, and take you there.
> With wind in her sail, strong and fair,
> Starting where the palms are tall
> And finishing where the waters fall.
> Princess Elandra will raise her head,

And take you where the riddle says.'

Fifty paces to our right, there was a clump of palms, so we walked over and Jula sang it again. This time the swans, who had followed us, suddenly took flight, and the water around where they had been started to bubble and foam. A mast appeared slowly on an angle, and then the bow stuck its head out of the water, and indeed it was a head; in fact, the carving of a beautiful Elvan princess appeared. Then slowly the whole boat surfaced. We all looked in wonder as the boat settled and water flowed down her sides, emptying into the lake, and Jarew said, 'There are many songs in ancient Elvan about the Princess Elandra, but we never knew it was a boat as well we sang of. Now we know the context of all those songs.'

As we stood there looking, the boat started to drift over towards the shore, stopping under a branch of a large forest fig tree. We realised that was how we were to board her. One by one, we walked along the branch and dropped on to the deck. It was the most beautiful ship I had ever seen, and I have never seen one since like her. The carvings of Elvan design were all the way along the railings, and the deck was made of highly polished wood. The single mast also had painted Elvan designs on it. The sail had a large black swan on a white background, and it fluttered gently in the breeze.

Carew looked up at the sail and said, 'This is incredible. In one of our songs, it says Princess Elandra was turned into a black swan because her father forbade her to see a certain Elf. He was banished and she ran away to look for him. She could only look for her prince in the dark of night, so she painted herself black, camouflaged like a black swan, and spent the rest of her life searching for him.'

'Oh,' said Jula. 'What a beautiful story, did she ever find him?'

'We do not know. There was never an end to her story,' said Drew.

We looked over the boat and found there were four rooms. One was obviously a kitchen, and the other three, of the same configurations, were for sleeping. They consisted of a bench seat that started at the door and continued all the way round the room to the other side of the door. There was also a large oblong piece of wood lying on the floor, which we found out later could be converted into a table. The benches we could use for sleeping on as well as for sitting. Under each of the benches were weapons and beautifully woven Elvan chain-mail vests, kilts, and boots along with a sporran for storage. Jula couldn't wait to put hers on. She commented, 'They are so light but also so strong.'

Each set of clothes was neatly folded with a sword and knife placed on top. As we tried them on, we realised Jula was right, and surprisingly, the ones we chose seemed to fit us exactly. The swords were encased in elaborate Elvan-designed sheaths, with the correct balance and length for each of us. There was also magic Elvan rope as fine as a spider's web but as strong as steel. Jarew struggled with his, and it looked as if it was for someone much shorter and fatter than he was.

After we finished dressing in our new outfits, there was one left over. We thought it must be a spare one, but it wasn't. In fact, Jarew had taken one that was not meant for him—this we were to find out later on the quest.

We sat down in one of the rooms, admiring our new outfits and weapons, when Drew said, 'If you are still hungry, we can eat a little more and have a good night's rest.' This pleased Rocco greatly, and he got stuck into the food.

'When is the boat going to move?' asked Peto. 'It is still stationary.'

'We have not asked her to move, have we?' Jarew said sarcastically, annoyed that he didn't look as good in his outfit.

'Sorry, I'm not familiar with Elvan protocol,' replied Peto.

We settled down and joined Rocco to eat a little more, and Jula asked some questions about Elvan history and then requested, 'Carew, could you teach me a song about Princess Elandra?'

This really pleased the Elves, and they promised to teach her one. We five boys thought, 'She is so smart that Jula. She knows exactly what to say and when to say it.'

'I will tell you all an Elvan story,' said Carew. 'What would you like to hear?'

'We don't mind. You pick one,' said Jula.

'Then I could tell you about the dragon Silvertail.' He hesitated, then added, 'No, that would take too long, so I will talk about the early history of the colonies.' There was a groan of disappointment, and we all replied, 'No, tell us about the dragon Silvertail.'

He shook his head and added, 'I hope I'm not creating a rod for my back. I shall tell you about when the Elves first landed in the New World and how they first set up a village in the forest of Gundi.'

He began, and we were listening intently to his tale. Eventually, Drew interrupted and said, 'I think we should get some rest. Carew can continue this story some other time.'

We ended up placing the cushions on the floor and went to sleep with the sound of water lapping against the boat. I had Peto on one side and Wecco on the other and my new Elvan friends scattered around the cabin. I don't think I have ever felt so safe before or since in my life.

12
CHAPTER
The Lords of Mardascon

The lords of Con rode off in haste to the north on their white, black, and two grey horses. By lunchtime, they arrived at the village of Hawks, tethered their horses at the local inn, and entered. It must have been an awesome sight for the locals to see these tall, imposing hooded men enter the low-ceilinged inn. They made their way over to a cubicle at the darkest end of the tavern, seated themselves, and Lord Arcon perused the room.

After a few moments, he whispered to the others, 'Be careful as there are two Menlins seated over in the far corner, and I sense they may have already worked out who we are. They must not leave here, or they will relay to the Seven our whereabouts. This at all costs we cannot permit to happen. Revcon, come with me, and we will try to confuse them with words. Devcon and Sebcon, you go and find out about food, and if there is a guide or boatman to take us across the River Hawk. But be discreet!'

Lord Arcon and Revcon walked over to the two Menlins, who to most of us would have just looked like two rough-looking men with tattoos. They sat themselves on either side, and this is how the conversation went.

'Morning, gentlemen,' said Arcon, 'and how are we this beautiful sunny morning?'

You see, Menlins have a problem with good manners. They looked at him and said, 'We don't want to talk to you two, so go to *glupgar*.'

Now, *glupgar* is a very bad word, much worse than *hell*. It is so bad that there is no exact translation and nothing even close can explain it.

'Now, now, gentlemen,' said Arcon. 'That's no way to talk, and you seem such nice-looking men too.' Menlins also have a problem with being complimented; in fact, they have a lot of problems. You know the type; they go through life blaming everyone else for their troubles, and because they have a scapegoat, they continue making the same mistakes. I found out later on in our adventure that there are some Menlins who have broken their bad habits and have become good people simply by accepting responsibility for their actions. But I will tell you of that much later. This compliment made them even angrier, if that is possible.

Now, when Menlins get really angry, they lose their train of thought, and this was Lord Arcon's intention. Lord Arcon then used some of his powers of hypnosis, and said, 'This is a strange dream. You only think you see and speak to us, but it's just your imagination. You have been searching for us for so long that you have started to imagine we are here.'

The other two lords arrived back at the tavern, stood near the door, and nodded in the affirmative from across the room to let Arcon know all was organised.

Arcon went on to say, 'We are going to leave now, and when we slam the door, you will wake up and realise it was just a dream, brought to fruition by your obsession with us.'

The lords rose and moved to the door where the other lords were waiting. They quietly left the premises, but as Lord Arcon stepped outside, he pulled the door hard behind him with a loud bang. The two Menlins jumped in their seats then looked round the room, picked up their drinks, and continued as if nothing had happened.

The other lords had procured some food and a guide to take them across the River Hawk. They would have to make two trips, as the barge could only take two men and two horses at a time. Devcon and Sebcon went first and the other lords waited for the barge to return.

Back in the tavern, the Menlins were still seated, drinking and staring across the room. Then one said to the other, 'What in the *grosfuss* does *fruition* mean?' *Grosfuss* is another bad Menlin word.

'Why have you *glupgar* asked me that? I just had a dream that the lords we seek were here and were talking to us,' he replied.

'There is something *glupgar* strange about this, as I had the same dream.'

'What in the *grosfuss* are we to do?' said the other. This went on for ages, backward and forward between the two of them.

Finally, the innkeeper who was watching the proceedings got fed up with their talking. He walked over and screamed at them, 'Shut the *glupgar* up, will you?' That's how Menlins can affect you if you are not careful. The innkeeper then added, 'Yes, there were four men here, and two spoke to you.'

The Menlins suddenly jumped up and left the tavern in a rush, throwing some coins at the innkeeper. They stood outside, arguing about the situation and what to do, when one of the Menlins looked towards the wharf and saw the last two lords tying up their horses for the crossing. One of the Menlins pulled out a horn and started to blow it, making a hideous sound, as evil as one could imagine.

As the barge made its way across the river, the lords looked back and realised their plan had been foiled. But at least they had the advantage of paying the guide to stay on the far side of the river for a few hours, and they hoped that would give them a head start.

They rode north in silence, knowing that the Menlins would get a message to the Seven Pernicious sooner or later. At sunset, they decided to stop, for the horses were worn out and in need of rest and food. They dismounted and let the horses graze while they sat down to eat and discuss their circumstances.

'I think the situation calls for us to separate', said Lord Sebcon, 'and take two different roads to the valley of Kassob. That may at least improve our odds of getting to see the wizard and getting his advice.'

'I agree,' said Lord Arcon, and he continued, 'Two should take to the forest and two take the valley road. That should confuse them, as they will be looking for four tall men. The two who take to the woods will have the best chance of getting through. We will rest here tonight and leave first thing in the morning. Now how are we to decide which two for the road?'

'One grey each way', said Sebcon, 'will be best.'

Lord Arcon agreed and said, 'Throw your staff in the air, and whoever it lands closest to will go with you and the other with me.'

He flung it high, and it spun round and round, landing near and pointing to Lord Devcon, who said, 'I go with you, Lord Sebcon, and Lord Revcon will go with you, Lord Arcon. Now for the decision of who takes which route—this will be difficult, as whoever takes the road will have the harder task.'

Lord Arcon suggested a game of chess, but that would be difficult for four to play. So they decided on the Black Witch, a card game. This would make the decision, and the winner would take his partner via the forest and the losers the road. Arcon knew taking the road would be very risky, so he decided to try and lose. Black Witch is a very similar game to what is today called Hearts. The cards were dealt, and Arcon looked at his hand. Not very promising, it was a very mixed hand. After the first hand, the scores were Arcon thirteen; he was stuck with the Black Witch. Revcon, also thirteen, was caught with all the hearts. The game continued, and after the sixth hand, the scores were Arcon forty-one, Revcon eighty-six, Devcon seventy-six, and Sebcon fifty-six. The cards were dealt, and as Arcon picked his up one by one, he could not believe his hand—practically perfect to try and get them all and cost his opponents twenty-six points each. He passed three cards to the right. Lord Revcon contemplated for a while then passed his three on to Arcon. As he picked them up, he could not believe what fate had given him. Devcon led the two of clubs, which was won by Revcon with the king. He led back another small club, and Arcon had no choice but to take it with his ace. The ace of spades was the only card that could stop Arcon. He led his ace of diamonds. Revcon and Devon both followed suit. Sebcon happily tossed his ace of spades, thinking he was rid of it. That was exactly what Arcon wasn't hoping for. He had the lead and knew no matter what he did, he could not be beaten, so he laid his top four spades and his top five hearts on the table.

'Look at them and weep, gentlemen,' he announced.

Each of his opponents received twenty-six points, and both Revcon and Sebcon broke the hundred. Arcon had won.

So now the decision was made: Lord Sebcon and Lord Devcon would take the road. Lord Arcon was not too happy about this, as he knew it could be the road to suicide if they were not careful. None of the lords slept well that night.

The next morning, they packed up their gear with hardly a word. Lord Arcon handed them a map with directions to the valley of Kassob.

'Now this is an old map,' he emphasised, 'so bear in mind there may be changes. You should have at least four villages where you can get supplies, but be very wary on entering them. Try to leave it until late at night. The Menlins will be a problem, but not your main worry. If you sense or hear the Pernicious, split up and go different ways and plan to meet up further along the road, as they can smell when there is good.'

Then, bringing their left hands up in front of the left side of their chests and slapping them with their right palms, they bowed their heads while opening their arms, bidding each other goodbye with the Elvan sign of traveller's luck. Then they rode off in different directions.

13
CHAPTER
Ashes of Wood

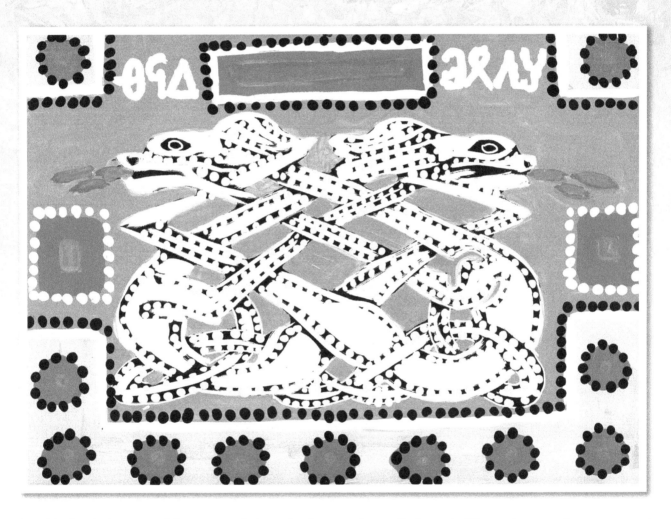

The lords Arcon and Revcon rode into the forest and travelled north. The undergrowth was not too dense in this part of the forest, so they made quite good progress on the first day. Their plan was to reach, within three days, the secluded village of Woodchisel, where the guild of woodcarvers dwelt. The inhabitants of this village had such empathy and understanding of the environment that whenever they felled a tree, five more were planted around the clearing to replace it. The woodcarvers were a group of artists who would find dead or old fallen trees and give them new life by carving out what the tree expressed. The knots, branches, and rings dictated to the artist how the carving would end up. Throughout the world, their works were renowned for their exemplary quality of craftsmanship and their ability to express the spirit of the log. Every spring, they would take their works to the villages and towns for hundreds of kilopaces around and sell them or exchange them for supplies.

The second day was a much harder ordeal, as the forest had thickened and paths had to be found or made. By the third morning, they were still ahead of schedule and anticipated arriving at Woodchisel by midday. They mounted and rode off.

After riding for about three hours, they arrived on a crest of a hill with a view which extended for hundreds of kilopaces. From way off to the north, they noticed smoke rising. It was not just smoke from a few chimneys but from a large fire. Nothing was said, but this troubled the lords. In their thoughts, they hoped it was just a bushfire, which is not uncommon in these parts.

After a few hours' ride, they arrived at Woodchisel. All except one house in the village had been burnt to the ground. The woodcarvers and their families were standing around in a daze, looking at a large fire that blazed in the centre of their village. Lord Arcon suddenly realised what was burning. It was the last year's harvest of fallen, carved trees. Now what would the artists and their families have to live on for the rest of that year? The lords entered at a slow pace, dismounted, and walked up to the group of men, women, and children standing by the smouldering fire.

'Good people of Woodchisel,' said Arcon, 'our hearts feel your woe. The grief of your loss will be felt around the country when the news of this disaster reaches the towns and villages where you sell your works.'

The leader of the guild, Lanetto, moved forward to welcome the lords to Woodchisel with a traditional greeting. What a sad greeting it was. 'Lords, welcome,' Lanetto said and added,

'Our homes are yours to dwell in,
Our food is yours to eat,
Our beds are yours to sleep in,
To rest your weary feet.'

He bowed a deep bow of respect that is rarely seen these days.
Lord Arcon responded with the traditional guild's reply.

'Thank you for your houses,
Thank you for your beds,
Thank you for your food,
And a place to rest our heads.'

He then bowed slowly with a tear in his eye and with such empathy for their losses. If any of you had been at that meeting, you would have had a tear in your eye as well.

Lanetto then went on to tell them what had happened to Woodchisel, describing how an army of brutish men and even smaller creatures led by four foul men on fire-breathing, winged dragons had destroyed their village.

'Smaller creatures,' said Arcon. 'How did they look? And were there only four foul men? And did you say on fire-breathing dragons?'

'Yes,' said Lanetto. 'There were only four and they were on fire-breathing, winged dragons. The small creatures looked short, stout, and very ugly.'

'They must be Goblins,' said Arcon. He looked at Revcon and whispered, 'Where were the other three Pernicious?'

'And Goblins too,' said Revcon. 'But I thought they died out hundreds of years ago!'

'That was one rumour, but the other was they went underground. That now sounds more feasible,' said Arcon. 'So now we have Menlins and Goblins to deal with, as well as the Seven. Our biggest worry now is that the Pernicious have developed more power and their young dragons have metamorphosed into fire-breathing dragons. Lanetto, if you could spare two horses to carry us on our trip today so we can give our steeds a rest, tomorrow morning we will send them back here. We must be in the city of Kassob in three days.'

'Yes, of course you may,' said Lanetto, 'and I will travel with you, as I have to let the wizard Naroof know what has happened here.'

Lanetto got four horses for the lords and two for him and organised as much food as he could. The lords rested under the trees near the burned-out village while their steeds grazed. Later that afternoon, the three departed for Kassob.

14
CHAPTER

On to Garlarbi

The other lords, Sebcon and Devcon, had travelled for two days without an incident or any sign of other travellers on the road. This was very unusual, for generally this was a busy thoroughfare. They arrived late on the evening of the second day at the village of Guy, which consisted of about fifteen houses and a tavern, which seemed to be closed even though it was only ten thirty in the evening.

The lords attempted to wake the innkeeper with a tap of the door and then a bashing. Finally, he arrived, not very impressed. 'Yes, gentlemen, what do you want?' he growled.

'We are looking for lodgings and a meal,' Lord Sebcon replied. 'You seemed to be closed early,' he added.

'We have no choice,' said the innkeeper. 'There is a curfew on the village. There were a hundred soldiers here yesterday, and they told us to close up by six every night or else. I thought it was them coming back. Come in quickly and shut the door.'

He turned the lamp down low and continued, 'You should be very careful out in these days with all the strange things that are happening. Only yesterday, four creatures riding fire-breathing, winged dragons landed here and seemed to be smelling around the houses, and the soldiers warned us to stay indoors, so we obeyed.'

The lords looked at each other. 'Then it is true', said Sebcon, 'that all have metamorphosed, which means the Evil is getting stronger if they can now breathe fire. The quest will be even more difficult. My main concern is where the other three evil creatures are. We must move on tonight. We cannot wait till morning. Innkeeper, can we buy some food from you, rest, and feed our horses for a few hours? Then we will be gone.'

The innkeeper looked at them and said, 'Gentlemen, please, stay here tonight. It will not be safe on the road with those creatures roaming around.'

'Thank you,' said Lord Devcon, who until now had been very quiet. 'We have no choice as we must try to be at the city of Kassob within three days.'

'Even with fresh horses, good weather, and no creatures on the road,' said the innkeeper, 'it would take at least five days, and there are also those evil men roaming around, posing as soldiers.'

'Thank you, innkeeper, but for the safety of the village, we must depart tonight,' said Devcon.

They rested for a few hours, bought some extra food from the innkeeper, then departed.

They travelled for five hours, stopping for a rest before daybreak. The sun rose quickly over the eastern sky, but thankfully by eight o'clock, there were large dark-grey clouds covering the sun, a stroke of luck for the lords as this would force the Pernicious to fly low and they would be seen from a distance.

As soon as the sun was completely covered, they started on their way again. They travelled for another day, so far so good. They rested till midnight then moved on till morning.

It was a little clearer the next day with breaks in the clouds where the sun shone through, creating patches of light across the countryside. They waited, hoping the rainclouds would return, but no luck. By ten o'clock, they decided to take a chance, as the village of Garlarbi was only twenty kilopaces away and there they would find help and fresh horses to carry them, giving their own steeds a welcome rest.

They had been travelling for two hours and they were approaching the upper reaches of the River Hawk when they heard a loud screech in the distance. The lords turned round to see a flying Pernicious far off in the distance, gliding over the mountain from where they had just come.

'Ride on, Lord Devcon, in the direction of the pine forest,' said Sebcon. 'Stay hidden and wait for sunset. I will ride the other way and hide in the ghost gum forest in the other direction. Stay low and try and cover yourself with anything you can find to hide your smell as well as camouflage yourself. Send your horse White Wind on ahead to draw them away. Wait till the sun sets, then we will meet up on the riverbank south of the bridge.'

They both patted their horses affectionately then rode off like the wind in opposite directions, reaching cover in plenty of time. Lord Devcon told White Wind to fly in the direction of the bridge, cross it, and continue on to the village of Garlarbi. He covered himself with mud from a waterhole then rolled in dry leaves and lay under a thick shrub. He could hear screeching and the flapping of wings from one of the Pernicious as it cruised above the trees of the pine forest. He lay there for a few minutes, and slowly, the screeches decreased and the flapping of its wings grew quieter as it flew off in another direction.

The Pernicious flew over and landed near the edge of the ghost forest. He and his dragon steed began sniffing and then made the most horrifying scream. All the birds and animals cowered in their hiding places. It circled around the edge of the ghost forest, sniffing and waiting. Three more Pernicious arrived on their dragon steeds, dismounted, and also started sniffing around. Lord Sebcon had sent his steed Grey Cloud on to cross the river a kilopace up from the bridge. As he entered the water, one of the Pernicious remounted, rose up, and flew in that direction. Grey Cloud was halfway across the river when the Pernicious dived down and sank the claws of his dragon steed into Grey Cloud's head and pushed him under the water. He went down, then pushed himself off the bottom of the river. Grey Cloud was only ten paces from the far shore, when the dragon dived again, grabbing his head between its claws and pushed him under a second time. The dragon hovered overhead, still holding on to Grey Cloud, forcing him to stay under.

Lord Sebcon could hear the screaming of the Pernicious and sense what was happening, but he dared not move. A few minutes passed and all went quiet, then the Pernicious arrived back to join the other three and began the sniffing. Lord Sebcon began to sense the closeness of evil creatures. He was hoping the sun would set before they got any closer. He was lying under a clump of leaves, but he hadn't had time to cover himself in mud so his goodness would be much easier to smell, and smell him they did.

They moved in slowly and quietly with the dragons following till they had surrounded the pile of dry leaves. In one pounce, the four Pernicious grabbed him, and their screams could be heard from many kilopaces away. They tied him up and dragged him out of the forest, attached him to one of the dragons, then flew off.

Lord Sebcon was taken to the evil stronghold of Malfarcus, the place where the Evil dwelled, and they tortured him for weeks on end, trying to find out the whereabouts of the Elves and the children and why Lord Sebcon was helping them.

15
CHAPTER
The City of Kassob

The two lords and Lanetto travelled for three days without further incident and by mid-afternoon, they arrived at the castle of Kassob. The gatemen took their horses to stable. The head gatekeeper showed them the way to the main hall through the labyrinth of houses, shops, and inns that surrounded the castle. The people here were a lot different from those in Malla. None of them displayed any outward sign of any creed. This made it difficult for people to develop a prejudice, and people either liked you because you were a good person or disliked you if you were not. No one was judged by what they did or didn't wear or what creed they followed.

The city was enormous, probably housing a million people at least. The city itself was situated on a terraced mountain starting at the base and finishing at the castle on top. Each terrace consisted of a row of four-storey terrace houses and a wide street with footpaths. On the high side of the street, the terrace houses were eight storeys high but only four storeys on the next street up. So as one stood in the street, it looked as if there were four-storey houses on the lower side and eight storeys on the other. The windows on the eight-storey side were very small and all barred, and the roofs were all fortified so they could be used for defensive purposes. There were rope bridges strategically placed along the houses from the top of the four-story side to the middle of the eight-storey side, connecting each level. These bridges could easily be cut in case of attack. Each entrance to the middle level was only as wide as a man could enter sideways, and had a thick metal door that slid down in slots to seal it when needed. On each level, in direct line with the main gate, was a wooden lift with weights connected that could transport a horse and cart up to the next level.

The fortification of the city was quite an ingenious invention as on each level it created an eight-storey wall and the street was completely exposed, making it easier to pick off an attacking enemy if they breached the first terrace. The main gate was also only wide enough for a cart to enter and had a solid metal door that slid down to seal it. One of the most appealing aspects of the city was that all along the outside edge of the eight storeys were large planters with vibrant green vines hanging down all around the city. From a distance, it looked like a mountain of green with a castle on top.

As the lords ascended to the first level, they were speechless. They had heard rumours about the wonder of the city of Kassob but never expected anything like this. The rest of the way, they observed the hustle and bustle of a vibrant city. As they reached the sixth and last level, they could see out over the plains of Kassob, with farmhouses scattered about and the land cultivated with different crops. There was an enormous forest surrounding the valley, extending all the way up to the snow-capped mountains in the south-west.

The two lords entered the main hall of the castle, which was vaulted in cedar with large windows set six paces from the ground that cast light all through the hall. The floor was made of cedar planks about a hand wide and polished to a high shine. Hanging from the base of the windows to the floor were large tapestries depicting different scenes that obviously had significance to the history of the castle and city. The two lords stood in awe as they waited to see the great wizard Naroof.

After a few minutes, two guards came out of an annex and escorted them to an adjoining chamber that was obviously used as a smaller meeting or dining room. The lords sensed the arrival of the wizard and looked at each other.

'Can you feel the good he projects?' asked Arcon. The door at the end of the chamber opened, and an old gentleman with long silver hair entered. He was wearing a cloak of silver with Elvan designs embroidered all over it. The two lords bowed low and said, 'Greetings from the south, my lord.'

The wizard returned the bow and said, 'Welcome, did you have a safe trip?'

'We two have arrived here in relative ease,' said Arcon, 'but what has happened to our friends we do not know. We hope they are safe and that they may arrive soon. We are here to beg your help.'

The wizard gestured to the table. 'Where are my manners?' he said. 'Please, gentlemen, take a seat. You must be weary after your travels.'

As the lords made themselves comfortable, the wizard continued, 'The tides have changed and not in our favour. I know why you are here. I have known about the Elvan parchments for two hundred years and dreaded this time, although fifty years ago when the Six never eventuated, I was hoping it was just a myth. Now that you have arrived, I know otherwise. Have the Elves accomplished their task, and are the Six safe?'

'Yes,' replied the lords, and Arcon added, 'But we have heard rumours about the wizard of Drascar and the city of Bossak. Is it true?'

The wizard nodded in the affirmative and went on to say, 'The wizard Drascar has crossed over to the Evil and taken the city of Bossak with him through force. I must add, how this came about I do not know. I can only imagine the Evil is holding some power over Drascar. We have been receiving refugees from our sister city of Bossak, and that is the only news we have. We have heard reports that if any sign of rebellion or disorder occurs, then the culprits are hanged from the city walls. We do have reports that the city of Bossak is preparing an army to attack Kassob. The army is made up of Menlins and Goblins.'

'Goblins,' said Revcon. 'So it is true! I thought they had died out and there were none left in our land.'

'I thought the same,' said Naroof, 'but my source says they are definitely Goblins. There also have been sightings of the Pernicious and their winged dragons, which means the Evil has grown stronger and the seven have metamorphosed their young innocent dragons into flying, fire-breathing dragons. The innocence of the Six of Croll is our only chance. You will have to leave tomorrow and travel to where they are. And pray tell, where is that?'

'The first Elvan parchment is the only clue to their whereabouts,' said Lord Arcon. 'It instructed them to go to the river Condoor and recite the riddles of the river, and a boat would appear for them and take them on their quest. We do not know in which direction they have gone.'

'They could only go up the river or out to sea,' said the wizard, 'and they have not gone out to sea, as I would have been informed, so up the river it is. There are only three places of importance they could go: the falls of Nebbia Circum, the city of Basscala, home of the lords Sebcon and Devcon, or perhaps the hidden caves of Mooloo, where one of the Oracles is supposed to dwell. Do you anticipate the arrival of your friends in the near future?'

'We were hoping they would be here waiting for us,' said Lord Arcon, 'as they took the road, which is quicker, and we took the forest track.'

'Had you arrived a week ago,' said Naroof, 'I would have come with you to help on the quest, but under the circumstances, I must stay with my people. They will need my leadership in this time of war, and the city will need to be prepared to defend itself against the armies of Bossak. I suggest you make your way down the River Hawks to Hawksfort and sail along the coast to the river Condoor. There I will supply you with a ship and crew. There are also three northern Elves on their way here to offer assistance. One, I hear, is a great sailor, and if we plead with him nicely, he may accompany you down the coast. If the threat from the city of Bossak continues in this direction, we will have no choice but to ask the Elvan archers from the northern forest of Woolinbar for their help.'

Naroof gave some orders to his guards, then he turned to the lords and added, 'Tonight we have a feast for the three northern Elves and the leaders of all the guilds in the city, and you are welcome to join us. My guards will show you to your quarters. Freshen yourselves, and we will see you here tonight. Now I must talk with Lanetto of the rumours circulating about Woodchisel.'

16
CHAPTER

Three More from the Year of Rew

The lords followed the guards, rested, bathed and changed into the fresh clothes that had been left on their beds, and returned to the great hall. As they entered, the last of the nine great oak tables were being placed and set. They were ushered into a large antechamber and offered drinks of cider, ale, or a pink wine in large crystal glasses, which came, I imagine, from that northern part of the world famous for its crystal.

When the room was full, everyone was ushered into the main hall and seated. The wizard Naroof was seated at the centre of a long table on the stage at the end of the room. On one side of him were seated three majestic Elves, and on his other side were three empty seats. The lords were ushered to two of them. On either side of the lords and Elves were seated the leaders of the guilds, all with black armbands which we found out represented the loss of the village of Woodchisel.

As the lords made themselves comfortable, the one vacant chair at the official table looked rather conspicuous. As the party was settling down, two solders escorted Lord Devcon to the last seat. The other two lords looked in amazement, and both said, 'You're safe, and where's Lord Sebcon?'

Devcon looked down, then back up to face them. 'He has been taken by the Pernicious,' he said. 'I will tell you all after the speeches.'

All the guilds were presented and waited in anticipation for Lanetto to tell them about the destruction of Woodchisel. He relayed how the four Pernicious had led the attack on Woodchisel and how a Menlin captain had interrogated him—how each time he answered a question with a response they did not wish to hear, they would burn one of the houses. The Menlins then piled all that year's carved wood that had been loaded on to carts for sale in the towns into a heap in the village square.

The last question was, had the lords of Mardascon travelled through this village?

'And they had not, but still they set fire to the carvings', Lanetto said, 'and left us with only one house for shelter.'

The goldsmith at the other end of the table responded with a sympathetic reply and a promise of support in food and men to help rebuild the village.

The wizard Naroof then addressed the hall. 'My honoured guests, the Elves of the northern forest of Woolinbar, the lords of Mardascon, our friend Lanetto, leaders of the guilds, ladies and gentlemen, the winds of evil are blowing in our direction, as we have heard from Lanetto about the destruction of Woodchisel and the burning of their year's labour. I have also, at this very moment, just been informed of the devastation of Garlarbi. No doubt there will be more bad news to come, which is why we have called this meeting to order.

'We must prepare for the attack from the armies of the Evil. Grocers of Kassob and farmers of the valley, now is the time to harvest as much food supplies as you can, to be stored in the city. If need be, you can use the basement of this hall. The siege may last for months or even years. Every able-bodied man must go and help the farmers with their harvest and transport the supplies as soon as possible.' The wizard went on to talk about preparing an army and asked the Elves, 'Would it be possible for your Elvan archers to teach the men of Kassob how to make and use bows and arrows?'

The Elves bowed low and agreed to ask their elders for help. 'We are sure it would be no problem.'

As the meeting came to an end and people started to leave the hall, one could already hear songs being sung about the approaching ordeal.

Pickle your pork, salt your sardines,
Conserve your cucumbers, and dry your beans.
Smoke your salmon, store your seed.
Save it in barrels till you have need.
For out of the south comes the evil beast,
And we will need stores for a year at least.
So stew your pears, apples, and plums.
And keep them stored till good times come.

Singing ho ho hody heigh-ho, pack the barrels as high as they go.
Singing de de dedy dum, preserve your apples and your plums.

Then Lord Arcon and Revcon turned to Devcon and said, 'Well, what happened?'

The three Elves and the wizard joined the lords, and introductions were made. The Elves were called El Masrew, Bayrew, and Wayrew, and they also wished to hear the tale of Devcon.

Lord Devcon looked at the awaiting company, and as he recalled the event, his face grew long and sad. He hesitated, and then went on to tell them what had transpired.

'I had hidden in the nearby forest and Sebcon had gone to the ghost gum forest on the other side of the valley. We sent our steeds on as decoys. I covered myself in mud and leaves and hid under a bush. At one stage, I could hear the beating wings of the dragon above where I lay and thought, *This is it*, but it then took off in the direction of the ghost gum forest.

'I lay there for what seemed like hours, hearing their evil cries every now and then. Just before sunset, the valley echoed with the screams of success from the Pernicious, and I knew then that they had Lord Sebcon. I stayed there for another hour, then walked cautiously towards the river and waited in hope, but in my heart, I knew they had him. As I waited, sitting on the banks of the river, the body of Grey Cloud floated by, with claw marks all over his head.'

'Grey Cloud dead and Sebcon captured—that is bad news,' said Arcon.

Devcon nodded his head then went on, 'I waited for another few hours in hope, then decided to continue on to Garlarbi. About a kilopace from the village, White Wind was waiting. I knew there was something wrong, as he would have gone straight to Garlarbi, so on we went with great anxiety, arriving about midnight to devastation. The town was completely destroyed and not a soul there. I spent the night nearby and woke to the sound of angry people returning to the village. They informed me it was an army of Menlins and Goblins who had attacked the village and they just had time to get to the caves—the mention of Goblins at the time I found hard to believe but could not dispute the evidence. They gave me an extra horse, and here I am.'

'Do you know how many were in their army?' asked Naroof.

'I don't think there were many,' replied Devcon. 'It was just a scouting party.'

'Good, they have not left Bossak as yet,' said Naroof, 'so we still have time to prepare.'

Devcon looked at the wizard, the Elves, and the lords. 'Goblins? Is this true?' he asked.

'Yes, we have not seen them ourselves, but the description definitely says Goblins,' answered Naroof.

17
CHAPTER

Princess Elandra

I t was a still, clear morning, with only the sounds of the birds and the gentle rocking of the ship *Princess Elandra*. The Elves were already on the deck, checking the rigging and all the equipment. I had no idea Elves would be good sailors.

As I thought this, Drew looked at me strangely. 'There was a lake in our forest,' he said, 'on which we all learned to sail at an early age. When our ancestors arrived from the old country, there was a prophecy instructing the Elves never to lose the art of sailing: "As you needed it once in the past, you will also require it in the future."'

How did Drew know what I was thinking? Slowly we climbed on deck, and I could see the excitement and fear in the faces of my friends. I stood and wondered what was to become of us. Carew then asked *Princess Elandra* in Elvan to depart for the city of Basscala. I assumed that was what he said, as the only word I truly understood was Basscala, although he seemed to go on for ages. I think it is a way with Elves; they seem to have a lot of pleasantries in their language. Then, without us being aware, *Elandra* moved off slowly. At first, I thought it was the fig tree moving, as I could not feel the motion.

After realising we were moving, the six of us moved to the front of the boat, three each side of the carved head of Princess Elandra. It seemed as if she was smiling, and I would swear she looked out of the corner of her eye at us. We had never been in a boat before, and it was frightening and exciting all at the same time. Although the water was running fast downstream, we were still moving at a good pace. I could tell by the speed the foreshore was passing.

'It should be an uneventful trip,' said Drew, 'as we are the only ones who know what the parchments said, and I don't think the Evil will look for us on the water.'

The day passed uneventfully until late in the afternoon when the river narrowed and the current ran much faster. The *Princess Elandra* drifted out of the main stream to the southern shore, where it was much calmer, and continued. Drew looked at the map and had noticed there was a large lake coming up around the next bend. Before entering the lake, the river narrowed even further, with steep cliffs on either side.

'Something is worrying *Princess Elandra*,' Drew announced. 'She senses danger up ahead.' As he said this, *Princess Elandra* drifted to shore before the bend. Then he added, 'I will go ashore here. Stay put in this calm section of the river, and I will check the place out and return before sunset.'

We waited for an hour, and the night was beginning to fall fast with no sign of Drew. 'Why can't we start sailing up the river', said Rocco, 'and collect Drew further upstream?'

'We must stay here till *Princess Elandra* is ready to move on,' said Carew, 'as she feels the flow of the river and senses the danger on the shore.'

I could tell Tarew was getting worried about Drew, and as the sun set, he said, 'I need to go. I think Drew is in danger and he needs my help.'

'No, Drew told us to wait here,' Carew said with authority, 'and wait here we must.'

The night dragged on with still no sign of Drew. *Princess Elandra* remained stationary. The Elves told us to go downstairs and rest. This we tried, but there was no hope of sleep, because we were listening to every sound. Then we felt a slight rock of the boat, and we knew she was moving—very slowly, but she was moving.

We came up on deck, and the night was very dark without a moon. In fact, it was so dark we could hardly see the banks of the river. The six of us stood gazing into the darkness with only the sound of lapping water piercing the silence. The Elves told us to be very still and not to say a word as sound travels over water very clearly. As our eyes adjusted to the dark, we could see the faint outline of the steep, ominous cliffs against the stars. As we approached the cliffs, we could hear the sound of people talking, loud and rough around the bend on the north side of the lake.

'Menlins,' whispered Tarew, and Carew added, 'Goblins.'

We six looked at each other, and I thought, *What have we got ourselves into? Menlins, Goblins, and the Seven Pernicious, not to mention the Evil himself.*

The Elves raised their fingers to their lips, telling us, 'Shush, be quiet.'

Princess Elandra moved slowly and quietly, passing the cliffs and hugging the southern shore. The noises that came from the Evil camp sounded very excited, and we were all thinking the same thing, 'Had they captured Drew?' although none of us were game to mention it.

After an hour of slowly sailing along the southern shore, their voices slowly faded to silence. 'Mecco,' said Peto, 'we can't leave Drew back there. We must do something.'

Jula and Wecco agreed. 'With all the new tricks, self-defence, and sword fighting we have learnt, surely we could rescue him.'

'The next time we are close to the bank,' I said, 'I will use my disappearing trick and go ashore, but don't let anyone know.'

'We should come with you,' said Peto, Jula, and Wecco.

'It won't work if we all go,' 'I said. 'The Elves would only stop us. It would be better for just one to go. Take the others below. I'll wait for the right time to get ashore.'

My chance came within minutes as *Princess Elandra* had moved towards the shore, as if she read my thoughts. When we were close enough, I projected my mind to where I thought the shore was, and then I was gone. There was a loud splash. As you may have guessed, I misjudged the bank! The Elves peered with all their might to see what had made the sound. I kept myself very still, and thanks to the moonless night, they did not see me. I was a good swimmer and thankfully was only two strokes from the shore. I dragged myself soaking wet up the bank, realising I would have to spend more time perfecting this trick.

I travelled back along the shore till I came to the cliffs where the river was at its narrowest. This time, I had to make certain I projected myself across the river without making a sound, so as not to give the enemy warning of my approach. I saw a large branch leaning out halfway over the river and thought that would be the best place to materialise, but I didn't trust my balance.

So I changed my mind and, seeing I was already wet, decided to swim across. It would be much safer, and I could then swim all the way. Halfway across, I felt the speed of the river increase. If I didn't do something soon, I would be swept past the cliffs and too far downstream.

From this distance, I could see the northern bank of the river, so I tried the disappearing trick and projected myself from the water to the far shore, thankfully without a sound. I moved cautiously around the shore till I saw the lights from their fire. I kept myself hidden behind trees until I had a clear view of how many there were, and if Drew was their prisoner.

There, at the edge of the camp, was a wooden cage hanging from a tree. And sure enough, Drew was in it, with his arms tied behind his back. They must be aware of his vanishing ability, and that was why they had him in a cage: it is impossible to project yourself through material things. There were only five of them, two Goblins and three Menlins.

The leader was the ugliest Menlin one could imagine, and they addressed him as Captain Yobtowoy. He was a very evil Menlin. You could tell as the others were quite scared of him. I sat there for ages, trying to devise a plan to rescue Drew, and then it came to me. I would project myself into the tree above where he was hanging, and at the first opportunity, I would hang down and let him out. He could then project himself into the forest. As I waited, I had a strange eerie feeling like something was trying to warn me not to attempt it.

The night was still dark, and I told myself it should be fine as long as I was quiet. I hesitated for a moment, then thought, *Nothing ventured, nothing gained.*

In a split second, I was in the tree. I materialised on the branch above Drew and thought how lucky I was it was a wide branch. But was I in for a big surprise? A net came up around me, and a bell started to ring as I struggled to get free. There was also a Goblin sitting in the tree, and he immediately started to spin the net round and round, tightening the trap.

If I had known then what I found out later, that Menlins and Goblins always went in even numbers, I would have been more careful. I could see Drew looking up at me and shaking his head in disbelief. Captain Yobtowoy marched over, looked up, and laughed arrogantly, saying, 'The Seven will be very pleased with us. We now have one of the Elves and one of the children.' They unlocked the cage and threw me in with Drew.

'Didn't you receive my projected message?' asked Drew, shaking his head.

'That's what that strange feeling was. I didn't realise it was from you. I'm sorry,' I said.

'We can't cry over squashed mushrooms,' said Drew.

'How did they catch you?' I asked.

'There was a large branch protruding over a part of the river,' answered Drew, 'and I projected myself onto it and there waiting was a trap. They somehow are aware of our vanishing abilities. How they know is beyond me as we have only just become aware ourselves.'

'What are we to do now?' I said.

'We do nothing,' said Drew. 'We can only hope the lords arrived in Kassob and have got the wizard Naroof to join our quest, and that he will rescue us.'

While all this was happening, the Elves were questioning my five friends about my whereabouts. Jula and Wecco, after much persuading, finally told them what I had done. Jarew was so angry with them he ranted and raved for ages. Over the duration of the quest, we learned that Carew had a saying for just about every occasion. And on this one, he said, 'Misfortune always enters through a window left open,' then he said exactly what Drew had said to me, 'It's no good crying over squashed mushrooms. We now must devise a plan. We cannot leave them both there.'

Jarew argued against trying to rescue us, saying, 'It would jeopardise the quest.'

'The quest cannot proceed without Mecco and Drew,' Tarew said. Jula told me later that she thought Jarew had an obsession with power and was trying to take over the leadership of the quest, so if Drew was not there, he had no opposition.

The *Princess Elandra* made the decision for them. She turned around and started sailing across the lake to where the Evil soldiers were camped. She landed them about a half a kilopace up from where their camp was situated. On the way they devised a plan. The first priority was for Tarew to use his new powers to go and find out how many there were. They changed into the Elvan chain mail, attached their swords and knives, and waited for Tarew's return. He was not gone very long and, on his return, was really impressed with them in their Elvan regalia, all standing in a line along the side of *Princess Elandra*.

When he came back on board, Tarew said, 'I think we have an army here.' He continued, 'There are only six of them, and with Carew and my ability to vanish, we have a fighting chance.'

The plans were for the two Elves to project themselves into the centre of the camp and make a disturbance, then return straight out again. The rest were to stand at different sections around the camp and make a lot of noise at the same time. When they started to attack one of them, the others were to back them up. While this was going on, whoever was in the best position was to get Drew and me out of the cage.

When this finally happened, even Drew and I were shocked by the noise, but the element of surprise worked, as Carew and Tarew had us out in no time and we could then use our vanishing trick. Yobtowoy had Peto by the neck and was cursing and shaking him like mad. Ricco was hanging around Yobtowoy's shoulders with one arm and trying to cut him with his knife with the other. In retrospect, it looked very funny, as he was flying everywhere. Later, when I heard Ricco's version, he insisted they would have overpowered Yobtowoy without anyone's help. Two of the Goblins and one of the Menlins had run off. We had no problem overpowering the last Goblin and Menlin, but Yobtowoy was another story. Ricco had sliced his arm in three places and this made him angrier, and he would not let go of Peto.

Drew and Tarew came to their rescue saying, 'Let them go, or this Elvan sword will pierce your side.'

Yobtowoy looked at them with such hatred but let go of Peto.

Ricco jumped off Yobtowoy's shoulders and said, 'We had him under control. We didn't need your help.'

Red-faced and choking Peto turned to Ricco and said, 'I did.'

Yobtowoy looked at the two children and said, 'I will not forget this', as he looked down at his bleeding arm. Yobtowoy then turned to face the other Menlin and Goblin and said, 'Those three *grosfuss* who ran off will be the sorriest *glupgars* when I get hold of them.'

'You won't be getting hold of anyone,' said Ricco.

We marched our prisoners back to the *Princess Elandra*, feeling very proud of ourselves. We had no idea what to do with them but knew we could not let them go. As we drew close to the *Princess Elandra*, she moved away from the shore. She was letting us know she would not take any evil things on board. What were we to do?

Drew had a plan and said, 'We should spend the night here, tie the prisoners to a tree, and I will make an Elvan sleeping draught that will put them to sleep for at least a week.'

Drew put it in some water and left it by the prisoners. Tarew and Drew stayed guard to make sure they drank some during the night. They did. In fact, they fought over it. As we ate our evening meal, we asked Carew to tell us the story of Silvertail.

'First, I must finish what I was telling you last night,' Carew said. As we ate, he continued his story of how the Elves first lived in harmony with Man. But as the years passed, Man developed bad traits and became coarse and rude. The Elves had no option but to completely disappear from the lives of Man. He told us of the first High Elf, Jamatta, who had tried every type of diplomacy with Man, to try to help them, but to no avail.

Drew said, 'I think that's enough for tonight. You must get rest, so now go off to sleep.'

In the morning, when we went out to see the prisoners, they were fast asleep and nothing could budge them, so we hid them under some bushes, covered them with leaves, and continued with our journey.

18
CHAPTER
What a Secret to Be Told

The *Princess Elandra* knew exactly where she was going and headed straight across Lake Condoor to where it converged back into the river. By midday, we were more than halfway across the lake. The shore was many kilopaces away, and as this was our first experience in a boat, we six were a little worried. The Elves seemed a little occupied with something and kept looking off to the south.

Eventually, Drew came over and addressed us: 'From tomorrow, my friends, we will have to be on our guard. I predict it will take about a day till those Menlins and Goblins get a report back to their superiors. We only have till tonight to travel safely, which is the reason the *Princess* is travelling in such haste, to get back into the river before night falls. If we travel all night, we should make it to the city of Basscala by morning. It is the home of the lords Sebcon and Devcon, so we will find refuge there.' It was close on sunset, and there seemed to be a flock of black birds travelling down from the southern mountains and in our direction.

'Go down to the galley,' said Drew, 'and get on your Elvan chain mail in preparation for battle, but stay there until we call you.'

'These are the black crows of Malfarcus,' said Carew, 'messengers of the Evil. They were once the great crows of the forest living in harmony with all other creatures, but somehow the Evil holds power over them.'

The Elves then spoke something in Elvan. I think it was about the *Princess Elandra* camouflaging herself. We went downstairs and waited. We could hear the cries of the crows of Malfarcus, but it sounded as if they were travelling on past the boat. I must get myself out of the habit of saying 'boat' as I don't think the *Princess Elandra* likes it somehow. I speak aloud when I write my diary, and every time I said 'boat' (see, there she went again), she seemed to shudder. From now on, I would say *Princess* or *Elandra*.

Anyway, what happened was the Princess's mast, which was situated forward, settled back to cover most of her. She changed the colour of her sail to a blue similar to the lake and let her sail flap in unison with the movement of the water, so from high above the crows could not spot her. After ten or fifteen minutes, the crows had passed by, and all was clear, so *Elandra* hoisted her sail and set off.

We arrived at the entrance of the river just as the sun set over the western hills. The Elves joined us in the galley, and we ate some fish stew that Jula had prepared that morning with all the leftover vegetables, loads of wild coriander, and two large fish that Rocco had caught. Jarew thought the fish were bitter, but the rest of us ate all we could. Besides, I think Jarew was jealous of Rocco catching all the fish, as he never managed to catch one.

Princess Elandra continued sailing the whole night, and we rested peacefully. We woke early and ate the leftover stew. Carew then went on to the deck to teach Jula a song about Princess Elandra. Rocco and Jarew were still arguing about the fish, and I was pondering what fate had in store for us. Drew was in deep thought, sitting by himself at the stern of the boat—sorry, at the stern of the *Princess*.

These powers that I was developing felt rather strange, and at times, I could sense my friends' and the Elves' thoughts. I found myself tuning into Drew's thoughts, but there were so many conflicting arguments going on in his mind that I could not decipher exactly what they were, though it was obvious they were stressing him out.

As we turned around the last bend, the city of Basscala appeared on the horizon, shimmering in the morning sun. We were all anticipating the wonder of a great city but never expected this. We were still about five kilopaces from landing, and we stood at the bow, mesmerised by the splendid sight we saw. Drew walked over and put his arm around me and asked to see me alone. I followed him to the stern of the boat (another shudder from the *Princess*).

He looked deep into my eyes, grabbed my hand gently, and pulled it towards him. He then placed a leather and silver armband covered in Elvan runes into my palm, closing my fist tightly. He then placed a fine silver chain with a tooth attached around my neck.

'These are magic and were given to me by my mother,' said Drew. 'I think they will do more good with you. The runes on the armband will change and warn you of imminent danger. The tooth is a dragon tooth from Silvertail and will also help you. I must add I'm not sure how.'

'But I don't read Elvan,' I said. 'How will I know what it is saying?'

I was gazing at the armband, and he lifted my head to face him. He looked at me with great concern and said, 'I think now is the time.'

I looked back at him, thinking, *What on Central Earth is he talking about?*

'I sense you are beginning to understand Elvan, and your magical powers will develop at great speed from now on.' He placed his hand over my heart.

'Somewhere deep within you, there is the knowledge.' He took both my hands in his and held them. He looked at me, hesitated, then stressed, 'You are part Elvan.'

We stood there for ages not speaking, just looking back down the river. Drew then put his arm around my shoulders and said, 'You are my cousin, but do not mention this to the others, not even the other Elves, as they are not aware of your bloodline.'

He walked back to the others. I just stayed there looking downriver, thinking, *So that's where the powers were coming from. What other surprises are in store for me?*

It was hard to believe it had been just over a week since I was told that my mother and father were not who I thought they were, informed of the quest, met lords and elves, found out my brother (who was now sixty-eight) was my cousin, sailed on a magic ship, been captured by Goblins and Menlins, and now told that Drew was my cousin and I had Elvan blood. What next? I turned to Drew and said, 'I don't want this. I didn't ask for it, and it's all too much for me. I want to go back to the life I had.'

Drew looked at me, shaking his head, and said, 'You don't have any say in it, Mecco. The die has been cast, and what is to be will be.' I was not happy about what he said, and he sensed it.

'You're an Elf and have lived with magic all your life. I have not, and in fact, I don't like it. I am starting to feel everyone's problems and thoughts. And when they are sad, so am I. The burden is too great for me.'

'Mecco,' he whispered, 'I'm here with you all the way and will do my best to take some of the load off your shoulders.'

19
CHAPTER

The City of Basscala, Mountain of Stars

I stood looking back over the river in a complete daze. All of a sudden, I became aware of a commotion at the bow of the boat, and turned around to see the city of Basscala in all its glory. It was situated halfway up the mountain, and from the river to the entrance of the city, there was the longest avenue of steps. There were rows of (I think they are called) Liquid Ambers on either side, creating an avenue of trees that shaded the steps.

On one side of the steps, there was an inclinator attached to weights and pulleys in a large tower at the base of the steps. This took stores and visitors up to the main part of the city. On the other side of the steps, there was another mechanical contraption that continually carried water in buckets from the river up to the city.

On either side of these contraptions were rows and rows of terraces, each one rising vertically about five paces and fifty paces wide, cultivated with every crop and fruit tree you could imagine. Scattered on some of the terraces, where the trees were tall, were sheep grazing. These terraces were designed for defence as well as for farming.

The water that was carried up to the city was stored in large stone dams on the mountaintop and used for cleaning, the sewerage system, and watering the terraces. It was an ingenious use of water, as the city was hosed down completely late every evening, with the water winding its way down the gutters, cleansing the city and eventually arriving to be evenly dispersed to irrigate the terraces.

There were also large underground stone compost and sewerage pits that were emptied regularly when the contents had decomposed. These were used for fertilising the terraces. Nothing was wasted; all organic material was recycled. It was the cleanest and most efficient city that one could imagine.

I also found out later that there were no burials and all who died were crushed into blood and bone and returned to their loved ones as fertiliser and planted under trees or shrubs that relatives could name and maintain. The city itself was also terraced and went all the way to the top of the mountain. Along the top and down the sides was a great stone wall with towers dispersed evenly along it. Defensively, the city was designed a little like the city of Kassob, but without a castle at the top.

We docked and were welcomed by an official in a splendid outfit. Something about *Princess Elandra* made all the locals excited. They were talking loudly and pointing at her sail. We were ushered to the inclinator, which slowly transported us up the slope, and as we arrived at the gates, the company turned to admire the breathtaking view. We stood there in wonder, looking over the river and the plains of Basscala stretching as far as the eye could see.

Then an official interrupted us and escorted the company to the most elaborate quarters and invited us to join them for their midday meal. Drew accepted and the Elves bowed low in their customary fashion, and we followed suit. On one of the top terraces, a feast had been set up. The tables had been laid out under the grapevines which covered angled trellises. The cool of the rock terraces, the shade of the grapevines, and the view. I ask you, where better could one dine?

We obviously were honoured guests, as we were ushered to the most elaborate table with the best views. As we sat, a tall, elegantly dressed woman with the most beautiful ebony skin walked towards us. She stopped at our table and introduced herself. 'Welcome to Basscala. I am Vice Lord Chefskicon. And do you have any news of Lord Sebcon and Lord Devcon?'

'We left them a few weeks ago, and they were going to see the wizard Naroof. We have not heard from the since then,' said Drew.

As they talked, Rocco whispered to Jula, 'She is a woman. How can she be a lord?'

'I have no idea but if she has the same abilities, then that's fine with me,' responded Jula then she asked the lord, 'What was all the commotion about down on the wharf?'

The vice lord smiled at us then said, 'There is an old song, sung about the arrival of a magic ship with a large black swan on its sail, which would herald the arrival of a company of Elves and special children. Later we will get someone to sing it for you. I hope the song has some truth to it.'

Rocco sat impatiently listening to all this while tapping the table with his fingers, waiting impatiently for the meal to arrive. Jula, disgusted with Rocco, was doing her utmost to kick him under the table to shut him up.

Carew patted Jula's hand and said, 'Give him enough rope, and he shall hang himself.'

I looked across at Tarew, who was in some type of trance. He was reciting something to Drew. I could hear or sense everything he was saying. These powers that were developing in me, at times, were scary. From where I sat, I could hear Drew say to Tarew, 'The parchments have revealed something. You were just in a trance. We must have a meeting after this meal. Pass the information along.'

As the news made its way around the table, Peto turned to me and was about to speak, but before he had time to open his mouth, I said, 'I know, as soon as we finish eating, there is a meeting.'

He shot me a surprised look but said nothing. After some speeches of welcome, we asked to be excused. We thanked the lord and the Basscalati for their hospitality, then returned to our room and waited for Tarew to unroll the parchment. He unrolled it with such deftness and laid it on the floor. We waited in anticipation, and then slowly the Elvan runes appeared. Drew asked Tarew to read it aloud. From where I sat, I could see it and read it as well, but I kept my silence.

When you reach the place where the rainbow shines,
Go behind the curtain and start to climb
Forty steps up and ten across
And there will be revealed all that was lost:
The magical weapons of Elvan past,
Waiting to be claimed by the eleven at last.
After you have done this, step forward, please,
The one who is mixed, of many a seed.
Waiting here is a question to be asked
But only from one who has already passed
The trials of Elf and the trials of Man
And only is he the one who will understand.
So step forward, please, and listen hard with your ears
For the Oracle only answers every fifty years.

'So, what does it all mean?' asked Wecco. 'And where does the rainbow shine?'

'If you recall the song about the river,' said Drew, 'it said, if I remember accurately and Jula will correct me if I'm wrong, "starting where the trees are tall and finishing where the water falls".'

'Waterfalls have rainbows,' said Jula, 'and the curtains are the falls.'

'But what about the sentence where it says the weapons are to be claimed by the eleven at last?' asked Jula. 'There are only ten of us.'

'Maybe there is a spare one like what was left in the *Princess*,' said Jarew.

'Well, let's worry about that when we get there,' said Drew. 'For now, we must continue up the river and with haste as the Evil must be aware by now, we are here at Basscala.'

We were hoping that the lords and the wizard Naroof would be here, but deep down inside, we knew it would be at least seven or eight days before they would arrive, if at all.

Drew met with Chefskicon and explained to her what had transpired. We added that she should prepare the city's defences for war as the Evil was assembling his troops in the south. Chefskicon argued that she had no orders from Lord Devcon and that Lord Sebcon had not been seen for fifty years, so why should she create panic in the city? Drew continued, explaining all that had happened and that Lord Sebcon was still alive with Lord Devcon, and they had left to beg help from the wizard Naroof.

Drew then asked, 'Did not Lord Devcon explain anything before he left?'

'He was too preoccupied with other things', replied Chefskicon, 'and left a few weeks ago. He did say there may be trouble, but he did not elaborate.'

'Well, I'm elaborating now,' said Drew. 'At least organise a section of your men so if need be, they can organise the rest of the city at short notice.'

She agreed to this and set out a plan in case the Evil attacked.

I knew what Drew was thinking—that there was no doubt the Evil would attack the city eventually. Drew went on, 'Tomorrow night, the ten must depart. We leave for the Falls of Nebbia Circum.'

'Then tomorrow night, we will have a farewell feast for your departure,' said Chefskicon. 'Tonight and tomorrow, we will store provisions on the *Princess* for your quest. I also suggest you take four horses, as the river gets narrow and will be hard for the *Princess Elandra* to navigate. Further up the reaches, there is a track on the shore where it would be possible for the horses to tow you upstream. Even with good weather and the horses, it will take at least ten days to reach the falls of Nebbia Circum.'

That night, we all slept in the same room. I was glad as it made me feel safe. I think the others felt the same way, as we all slept well. The city faced west, and the sunrise was spectacular as it hit the mountain to the west.

I sat out on the top terrace and looked over the river winding its way through the long wide valley, with a distant view of the lake. This would be a difficult city for an enemy to capture as the lookout towers had at least a 270-degree outlook and everything could be seen for hundreds of kilopaces around.

Drew came out and sat by me, placed his arm round my shoulder without saying a word, and I felt safe. We both sat there admiring the sunrise for ages.

The others started to awaken, and we could hear Rocco asking his usual question, 'Where does one get breakfast around here?'

Carew retorted, 'Most things one craves can be good for you in moderation but taken to excess will devour you. You shall become a slave to it and lose all perspective.'

'I don't care. I'm hungry,' he shot back.

The door behind us opened and Peto joined us, and sitting down next to me, he placed his arm around me as well. Wecco and Jula were the next to arrive. Eventually, all of the company except Rocco sat watching the sunrise with our arms around each other. These friends that I trusted and had grown to love, I hoped would be with me for my whole life. I knew there would be danger and even death in store for some of us. But if giving up the quest and danger meant not meeting these friends, then lead me on to danger.

The Elves spent the rest of the morning discussing the city's fortification with Chefskicon while we went swimming and diving off *Princess Elandra*. I could sense it made her happy that children were having fun.

The evening arrived, and the feast was magnificent with every type of fish, poultry, meat, cheese, fruit, and vegetable one could imagine. The wine, ale, and cider flowed all evening, but we never touched it as we had seen what evil too much drinking had done to people in our village. Although the Elves did partake, they did so sparingly. Peto had to try it and had stolen a few glasses, but the next day, he paid for it.

Drew lectured him about drinking too much and said, 'You are too young. There will be plenty of time to experience these things.'

Then Carew came out with one of his pearls of wisdom and said, 'Remember, Peto, a mistake admitted to is a victory.'

Then Drew added, 'The one warning I give you is "Do not drink." If you have strength of character and moderation, that is the magic answer to a good life.' As he was saying this, he also looked at Rocco, who in just ten days had become much fatter.

As the sun set behind the city towers, we walked down the long flight of steps to the wharf, reboarded Elandra, and the Vice Lord Chefskicon bade us farewell:

> *'On the Condoor River, may the tides be fair.*
> *And where you wish, may they take you there*
> *With the wind in your sails and the sun in your face,*
> *To arrive safely at your chosen place.'*

The Elves had given the world such beauty and had influenced the good in people. The courtesies, manners, and greetings all come from Elvan influence. I am aware of the decline of good manners, so by the time you read this book, Elves would have not been seen for many a year, and I bet good manners and courtesy have left with them. Drew stood up and responded to the Vice Lord Chefskicon:

> *'May the winds blow from the snowy mountains high,*
> *In the long summer days, when it's hot and dry.*
> *And in the winter, when the nights they freeze*
> *May the warmth come from an equatorial breeze.'*

The Elves all bowed low, thanked the Basscalati for their help and the gift of four most beautiful horses. Their names were Seafair, Treefair, Skyfair, and Greenfair. We followed suit and bowed in gratitude; the Basscalati returned our bows and bade us farewell. See what I mean about Elvan influence and manners? If one sets a good example, society will follow.

The provisions had been stored in one of the empty rooms, and we had been given enough to feed an army. I thought to myself, *We must put a lock on the door. Otherwise, Rocco will end up like the side of a barn.* The horses had been stabled at the stern of *Princess Elandra.* I wondered, *Should I say* stern, *or would that offend her as well? I must ask Drew at the first chance.*

With *Princess Elandra,* there was no need to cast off, as she was not tied up and had just stayed waiting for us. She sensed the direction we needed to go and slowly moved away from the wharf as we waved at all the Basscalati bidding us farewell. We still didn't get to hear their song about Princess Elandra.

As we moved up the river, the light was slowly fading, as night was about to fall. We sat with the horses at the stern of *Princess Elandra* and watched as the Basscalati lit candles. What a lovely sight to see! The night grew dark, and the city lit up like a mountain of stars. There is a tradition among the Basscalati that when a friend departs on a long journey, a candle is lit and kept aflame until they think their friend cannot see it any more. It is then extinguished and saved till they return then relit.

20
CHAPTER
The Arrival of Friends

After the grand feast, the speeches and farewells, we were rather weary, and we retired for a good sleep. The Elves had taken it in turns to keep watch without incident, and *Princess Elandra* had travelled steadily but calmly. We had offered our services to keep watch, but the Elves insisted we sleep. At sunrise, we met on the deck to admire the beautiful morning. And for the rest of the day, we just sat around and went for an occasional swim when we got too hot. Lately, I had noticed how my friends' muscles had developed as their bodies reached manhood. As I stood on the edge of the railing, I glanced down into the water at my reflection, and to my surprise, my body too was developing muscles. As I stood there, I flexed them, feeling very proud.

'What are you doing,' screamed Peto, 'you big whoos!'

I just dived into the water, knowing whenever Peto made a derogatory comment, it was usually jealousy.

'Why do you always pick on Mecco?' said Wecco.

'He thinks he is so amazing sometimes with his magic powers, and now look at him thinking he is a great warrior,' said Peto.

'Just ignore him,' I said. 'It's only jealousy.' He then swam off in a huff.

Thankfully, so far we had seen neither nose nor nail of the Evil.

The day went quickly, and the sun passed overhead on its way to set behind the mountains way off in the distance. I was sensing things from *Princess Elandra* that were quite disturbing and realised she was worried about something.

Drew and Tarew came over. 'Something is bothering *Princess Elandra*,' said Drew. 'We must be on the lookout. Tell the others.'

I relayed the messages, then we positioned ourselves at strategic intervals around the railings and kept a lookout for anything strange. The one thing I noticed was that there were no laughing birds, magpies, or the famous white screeches to be seen or heard.

'Can any of you sense the crows of Malfarcus?' Drew asked.

Strangely, the dragon tooth felt heavy and the armband had begun to glow, but as it was daytime, I didn't notice it. The Elves all focused and so did I discreetly. Suddenly, *Princess Elandra* turned into a small bay with overhanging trees. Slowly, she manoeuvred in as close as she could. It was just in time as the sky turned black with thousands of crows.

'We must be as quiet as possible,' Drew said and added, 'It is strange they are travelling in such a large group. Never have I seen anything like it before, and it looks as if they are on their way to Malfarcus.'

We stayed hidden till night had fallen. It was quiet, and everyone was down below eating, except Drew and me. He asked how I was.

'Fine,' I said, 'but I'm not sure what this quest is all about or what the Six of Croll have to do with it and how we can help. I feel like my life is like a jigsaw that has been tossed into the air, and I have no idea where to start.'

'I am not sure either,' said Drew. 'I don't know exactly what we Elves have to do. I only know that we were chosen, and that is such an honour for an Elf. You should look on it the same way. If some greater power chose you, take the honour.'

'But how do I know it is not the Evil that has chosen me and is leading me down the wrong path?'

Drew leant across over the rail right next to me and said, 'Mecco, you know the difference between good and evil. You know it is wrong to kill, to steal, to hate, and to enslave people who do not have the power or ability to fight back. You know it is wrong to manipulate, abuse, or exploit. For the world to be a better place, we must have an empathy and understanding for all. This must be at least the one thing you have learnt from your five friends. You are all of different creeds who were brainwashed into believing that yours was the only truth. Yet look, are they not good people? Strangely, those who believe the most end up suffering the most. Your creeds breed hatred and mistrust of each other. I ask you, if one of the creeds is the truth, then why is it that they all suffer the same? The sad thing is we Elves know that it is the same anonymous power that gave rules to those four great philosophers to help their people through bad times. But the Evil has manipulated weak men to focus on hatred, exploitation, and blaming all the other creeds for their problems, and to never accept any responsibility. Do you not know it is the children of the world who have the power? You six are the example.'

I looked at Drew as he was talking, and thought, *He is such a good person—I mean, Elf.* He put his arm around me.

'Thank you, Mecco, I know you are the same.' And we stood there peering into the dark till Jula's voice pierced the blackness. 'If you two don't come down to eat soon, Rocco will devour it all.'

I smiled and sensed Drew was smiling as well as we both made our way down to the galley. I felt a lot better after our talk. I must write that in my diary straight away so I could remember to tell the others.

We had just finished eating when *Princess Elandra* started moving. The night was very dark and the sky full of clouds, a blessing for us. Hopefully, we would travel all night without an incident. This time, we insisted we take turns at keeping watch: Drew and I, Ricco and Jarew, Tarew and Peto, and Carew and Jula all took turns. Rocco was not asked and was happy just to sleep.

While Drew and I did our watch, I thanked him for his wisdom and advice. I looked at him and wondered how old he was in Elvan years. He looked 16 or 17 in our years, but if stories were true, he could be 50. Should I ask him? Maybe not, he might take offence. Maybe one day.

The night passed without incident and the morning arrived to the songs of the magpies, currawongs, and the white screechers, so we knew we were in for a safe day of travelling. The summer had arrived with a vengeance, and the clouds had cleared to reveal a bright sunny morning. In fact, it was such a hot day we spent most of it swimming around the *Princess Elandra*. Pushing each other into the water, diving and bombing from the mast filled our day. I could feel how this made the *Princess* happy to see children and Elves laughing and having fun. By the end of the day, we were all so exhausted and were glowing from a touch too much sun. We ate our dinner then straight off to sleep, except Peto and me, as we took the first watch.

We started our watch, but within minutes, we both fell into a deep sleep and we were only woken by the sudden stop of *Princess Elandra*. We both fell on to the deck with a thud then struggled to regain our footing. Looking to the shore, we saw standing in the dark two Goblins who were ready to board *Princess Elandra*.

I screamed out to the others, 'Goblins attacking!'

Peto and I drew our swords and confronted them. 'Take one step on this boat, and you will die.'

The leader stood his ground, saying, 'I have taught a lesson for less of an insult. How dare you!'

By this stage, the others had come up on to the deck, half-dressed in their armour and struggling to get into the rest. The head Goblin stepped forward and said something in a language I only half understood.

'Put down your weapons,' said Drew.

Peto and I puffed out our chests with pride. 'Yes, put down your weapons,' Peto said to the Goblins.

Drew turned to us sharply and said, 'No, your weapons, you fools. These are Dwarfs from the Far West. I hope they forgive you for your insult.'

Drew welcomed them aboard and added, 'Please forgive our ignorant friends. It is my fault. I never prepared them for Dwarfs. We were not expecting you so early on the quest, if at all. Please come aboard.'

The two stepped on to *Princess Elandra*, placed their axes on the deck, and bowed low to the Elves. The Elves returned the courtesy.

The head Dwarf looked at us perceptively. 'So these are the six?' he asked. 'I only hope they have better luck knowing the Evil when they meet him.'

I bowed low, then grabbing Peto, I pulled him reluctantly down to the same position and asked, 'Please forgive two young, ignorant boys for their stupid mistake.'

He looked at us, and shaking his head, he said, 'Thankfully, it did not cost you your lives, but beware, next time you may not be so lucky. It may be the Evil in disguise. You should be perfecting the skills of your sixth sense. If you had, you would have known we were not evil.'

I should have known they weren't evil. Neither my armband nor dragon tooth reacted. It was still very early morning, and the Dwarfs introduced themselves. The leader was called Dolark and introduced his companion as Soltain, whom we ended up calling Sol. By this time, *Princess Elandra* had drifted back out into the middle of the river, and Drew invited them to rest. We all went inside, except Jarew and Rocco as they were to keep watch. We spent the rest of the early morning trying to catch up on our sleep.

21
CHAPTER

The Splitting of the Company

We woke to another beautiful morning, then climbed on deck and had a hearty breakfast as we sat admiring the day. My friends and I thought this was more like a holiday then a quest. The Elves and the Dwarfs sat talking at the stern of *Princess Elandra*.

'Why do they do that?' asked Ricco. 'I thought we were supposed to be the most important part of the quest.'

'I agree. I shall talk to them,' I said and walked up to where they sat. 'Excuse me,' I announced. 'There is alarm among the Six as to why we are left out of certain conversations. I thought we were the main reason for the quest.'

Drew looked at me with pity in his eyes and said, 'I am so sorry. We are just catching up with the history of the Dwarfs. We did not think it would interest you.'

'Maybe we are not interested,' I said, 'but it would have been nice to be asked.'

Then Wecco piped up from behind me, 'I'm interested.'

Then Jula placed her hands on her hips and, looking at Wecco, asked, 'Don't you think I would be interested as well?'

'I can't read your mind,' said Wecco. 'If you're interested, you don't need me to ask for you.'

'So is that how it's going to be?' Jula turned on her heel and stormed down into the cabin, with Wecco following to make amends.

'We're interested,' said the rest of us, so Drew apologised with much sincerity and asked Dolark, 'Would it be okay if the Six joined the conversation?'

'Not a problem, please join us,' said Dolark. 'It would give us great pleasure to tell you our history.'

By now the rest of my friends were standing behind me, waiting to hear the Dwarf's story. The tension between Jula and Wecco was, I think, frustration, for we knew how much they really cared for each other. I went down and told Jula and Wecco that it was fine to come up and listen to Dolark give us a Dwarf history lesson.

'I'm quite happy here, thank you,' she said.

'Thank you,' said Wecco sarcastically. 'I would love to join you and hear their history.'

Wecco and I returned to our friends, leaving Jula to sulk.

Dolark, who was also the holder of Dwarf history, went on with his story: 'Thousands of years ago, when the great migration occurred, the Dwarfs of the great mountains had mined them of all their wealth, and the war of wars had just finished. Our elders had decided to leave our ancestral mountains and travel to a new beginning. The ancient Elves of Central Earth had kept from us this place of great beauty with mountains of immense wealth.' As he made this last statement, Dolark turned and looked down his nose at the Elves.

'There was a reason for that,' said Carew. 'Our ancestors were trying to keep from Man its whereabouts. We never know who let the secret out, but once known, it spread like wildfire over the Old World. We only hoped the Evil would never venture so far, but as we know now, he did.'

At this point, while we were all engrossed in the story Jula sneaked up quietly and sat unnoticed at the rear as Dolark continued, 'We packed up what goods we could carry and departed for the New World. When our ancestors arrived, there were already a lot of Men on this part of the continent, and for many years, we worked in harmony with and for them, mining the mountains. Over time, Man grew greedy, and we knew it was time for us to move on. So our ancestors travelled west, over the Mountains Blue and much farther west than anyone had travelled before.

'They arrived at this mighty mountain range which held great mineral wealth, which we mined for centuries. But during our lives in that part of the great continent, we became mindful of other things besides mining for wealth. We had mined for so many years that we had emptied mountains of their riches, and what did we have to show for it except a greed for material wealth?

'Then suddenly one day, a great philosopher arrived in our midst. He showed us an appreciation and awareness of the beauty of the mountains, sky, and countryside that outshone any diamond or mineral we could ever mine. From then on, our focus was on moderation to mine only what we had need of, and we worked hard to repair the mountains we had ravaged.

'Over time, we became aware that mining is not all there is to life. That was about three hundred years ago, and since then, things have changed. Our mines are either used for our homes or left for nature to reclaim them, with our help. The great philosopher was the Dwarf Sidlark. We have never been approached by the Evil, and I don't even think he is aware we survived our journey to the west.

'Our histories tell us of all the ancient wars and the Evil that once tried to take Central Earth and how we had a hand in stopping the outcome in his favour. The ancient Elvan prophecies were given to us as well. Two Dwarfs were sent to the east, looking for the Six and the Elves fifty years ago. Lord Revcon informed them that the nine had been hidden and would not reappear for another fifty years. So the two Dwarfs returned west. We have been chosen to take their place, so here we are.'

We all sat in awe, listening to their tale and wondering what help they would give us. Drew asked Dolark, 'If we needed the help of a Dwarf army, could it be arranged?'

'Yes,' he said, 'but time would be needed, as we are so far west it would take at least two months by foot, or twenty days by boat, if that could be arranged.'

'At the moment, it is not necessary,' said Drew, 'but we must not rule it out.' Drew then asked, 'Do you have a way of getting news back to your elders?'

'Yes,' said Soltain, 'some of the white screechers could carry the news back for us.'

'How could they do that?' Rocco butted in.

'That is how we found your company,' said Dolark. 'Since our change of heart towards the environment, we have developed great rapport with the white screechers. They are our messengers, and they keep us informed of what is happening in the east.'

By this stage, the Dwarfs wished to hear our side of the story and more of the history of the east and why there were four Elves instead of three. I started by relaying how the Six of Croll had come about. Then Drew carried on telling them how it developed that there were four Elves and continued with the rest of the tale up till the present. By this time, it was midday, and Rocco, to the surprise of none, was the one who reminded us that it was time to eat.

Tarew and Carew offered to go down to the galley to prepare an Elvan feast. Rocco was getting excited, anticipating Elvan cakes, but that was not the case.

'The Elvan cakes are only for emergencies,' said Drew. But Rocco was not to be disappointed; the meal was a feast. As we ate, I noticed Carew looking rather sad and sensed he was a little jealous of the Dwarfs telling their story. Later, I would ask him to continue with the Elvan history.

Princess Elandra had travelled for five days without a stop, but by mid-afternoon on the sixth, she started to slow down, and we could see why. The river was getting narrow, and she could not harness the wind so well any more. We looked on the northern shore for the horse track that Chefskicon had told us about, and there it was: clear and right next to the river without a tree or obstacle blocking the track. We unloaded the horses and harnessed them together, then attached a rope from the horses to *Princess Elandra* and off we went again. We were making such good time that we thought we should be at the falls of Nebbia Circum in perhaps ten days or even less.

Drew was by himself leading the horses, so the next time *Princess Elandra* drew close to the edge, I jumped ashore. And draw close she did, within seconds of me thinking about it. She seemed to sense everything I felt. Drew did not see me, and I walked up behind him. Before I could say anything, he turned and said, 'Hi, Mecco, have you come to help me?'

'Yes,' I said. 'All the others are resting. I saw you here by yourself and thought that perhaps you might like company.'

'Thank you, I would,' he replied.

We talked of everything from his plans for his future, when all this would be over, to how I was going to pursue my art. He told me of his plans of visiting the northern Elves of Woolinbar forest and that he would like to do more travelling, but his parents had said, 'Elves never travel far from their forest, except on a quest of importance.'

As we talked, I realised he had a lot of issues in his life he needed to tackle, and I hoped he found what he was looking for, because if anyone I knew deserved happiness, it was him. I was growing very close to Drew. What was wrong with me? Why did I need the affection and attention of another male?

The afternoon flew by, and the next thing we knew was Jula crying out, 'Dinner is ready.'

Jarew and Rocco had already eaten, so they changed places with us guiding the horses, and we went in to eat and rest. We turned in early that night after leaving the horses to graze by the river, and I lay there awake for ages, thinking about my life. What did it have in store for me, and how would this all end?

It was early morning when suddenly *Princess Elandra* rocked abruptly. Those of us sleeping at the back of the room fell off our bunks with a thud. The first thought was that *Princess Elandra* had hit something, but I remembered we were moored.

'I think that's our wake-up call,' said Tarew. We stumbled out of our bunks and made our way on deck and did some exercise while Wecco and Jula cooked some breakfast. Within no time, we had harnessed the horses and set off to the sounds of the morning.

It was another beautiful day as the sun filtered through the trees and we led the horses along the track. We travelled till early afternoon when *Princess Elandra* got snagged on something, and even with the horses and us pulling on the rope, we could not dislodge her. So Drew and I dived in the river to check out the problem, but there seemed to be none.

'I don't think she wants to travel any further upstream,' said Tarew. 'She may sense something.'

So while Drew and I treaded water, the other Elves went to the bow of the *Princess* and used their magic to try and fathom what the problem was. I could sense their powers emanating from where they were, and I knew what the trouble was. She sensed Menlins and Goblins up ahead.

At the same moment, the runes on the armband Drew had given me started to glow and change and the dragon tooth seemed heavy. I looked, and surprisingly, I could read what it said. The Elves stared down at me, but I thought it best to say nothing of what I was sensing. However, I swam across to Drew and whispered to him about being able to read the armband and what it said about the enemy being close by. Drew asked me to say nothing. He told the company he had sensed the Menlins and Goblins up ahead.

It was now early evening, and as the *Princess* would not move, we had no choice but to stay put, so we rested the horses then ate and three of us kept watch, one at the front, back, and centre of *Princess Elandra* while the rest of us rested.

The morning came with decisions to make: what was the best route around the Evil? I knew we would have to travel by foot but sensed it best to stay quiet.

'We have no option,' said Drew. 'We must take to the shore.'

'What should we do with *Princess Elandra*,' Dolark asked, 'and does anyone have a map?'

'Since we have four horses,' I suggested, 'eight of us should take them and try to get to the Falls of Nebbia Circum. The rest should stay here and wait to see if the Evil army moves on.'

We ate breakfast while discussing the issue. The argument went back and forth about whether to split up the assorted company, which now numbered twelve.

'Something must be done,' said Drew. 'We can't sit here forever, and besides, the Evil army will be looking for us. We just can't wait for them to find us. We must separate today and move on as soon as possible.'

As the four horses were young and strong, a decision was made that eight of us would continue to the Falls of Nebbia Circum. The eight were the Elves Drew and Tarew, both dwarfs Dolark and Soltain, and four from the Six of Croll: Peto, Rocco, Ricco, and me. The other four would wait until it was safe, then sail the *Princess* back down the river, find a hiding place for her, and wait for us.

We had finished eating and spent the rest of the morning in a sombre mood. Rocco and Ricco packed up some provisions, the Dwarfs prepared the horses, and off we went. Drew had two maps: one Elvan, which was very old, and the other acquired from Chefskicon, which was more up to date. On it, there were two possible routes: the river road that hugged the south bank, or the other, which started on the north bank then branched off into the north forest. We chose the road on the northern shore, as it looked more direct and without many hills, and there was a village on the way. The decision was made to leave straight after the midday meal.

We bid our goodbyes and then mounted the horses. The band of eight went in single file with Drew and me on Skyfair, Tarew and Peto on Treefair, Soltain and Rocco on Seafair, and Dolark and Ricco bringing up the rear on Greenfair. Wecco and Jula were not very happy at being left behind to look after *Princess Elandra*, but there was no other option.

The first three days were uneventful. The road was an easy ride with nice weather, and the Elves taught us some Elvan songs, very quietly, I should add. We had turns of riding on ahead to check if all was clear. The village of Gamba was only a half-day ride, so hopefully we would arrive before sunset. And we hoped to find out news of what had been happening in this part of the world. We agreed that Drew and I should ride ahead, enter the village, and discover what we could, while the rest were to spend the night in the forest nearby, so as not to create suspicion. We organised to meet the others early next morning.

It was quite a large village with over a hundred houses and four taverns. Drew pulled up his hood to cover his face. 'We must be very careful,' he said. 'I think you should go in first, stand tall, and act more like an adult. Book a room for us and try to find out if any Menlins or Goblins have been around, then come out, let me know, and we will take it from there. I will stay with Skyfair. They must not know I am an Elf.'

The village was very quiet for this time of day, unusually quiet. I entered the inn, standing tall. Considering how deserted the village was, the inn seemed rather busy and loud. As soon as I walked in, the room became quiet, and nearly everyone looked at me. I held my head high and walked up to the innkeeper and asked, 'Do you have a room for the night?'

He looked me over and said, 'You're a little young to be out by yourself, laddie.'

'I'll have you know I'm 18,' I said. 'I just look young, and I'm here with my grandfather, who is waiting outside with our horse.'

As I said grandfather, I thought how Drew would have reacted to this and smiled.

The innkeeper apologised. 'Yes, we have a room.' He added, 'And would you like your horse stabled for the night as well?'

I lifted my head high and said, 'Yes, my man, that would be much appreciated. I will now go and help my grandfather. He is not too well. Could I also order some food to be sent up?'

He nodded in agreement, and I thanked him with a deep bow. As I walked out, I could sense them all looking at me. I told Drew what had taken place and he was not very impressed about having to play my grandfather, but he did a good performance. Truthfully, I think he overacted. His hood was completely covering his head, and I held his arm to help him.

Halfway up the stairs, he turned to me and said sarcastically, 'Thank you, my grandchild,' then added, smiling, 'You will have to pay for this.'

We arrived at the room, and he asked, 'What else did you find out?'

'Nothing,' I said. 'I didn't have the chance to talk to the innkeeper. He was too busy, but I will go down later and find out what is going on. I must admit they all seemed a little on edge. I have ordered some food, and it should arrive soon.'

When the food arrived, we ate and sat there in silence. After a few hours, we could hear the inn growing quiet, so I made a move down to the bar. There were only six customers left sitting around a table in the corner and they were in deep conversation. I approached the innkeeper and sat myself on a stool by the bar.

'How are things in Gamba?' I asked, which has today become quite a common way of asking what's happening in one's life.

The innkeeper looked across at the group of men seated together, then leaned over the bar and said, 'Do not bow like you did earlier around here. It shows you are acquainted with Elves, and there are evil men and Goblins looking for Elves and children, so be careful.' After scanning the tavern, he went on to say, 'Things have not been good here for many a year, what with the Goblins, evil men, and those seven depraved things on winged dragons.' He added, 'The times, they are changing.'

I turned and was about to leave the bar when one of the six men sitting at the table came over to me and said, 'I overheard your conversation. We are a band of travelling actors going from city to town, and from town to village. Please, will you join us? And we will tell you all that is happening in these strange times.'

He introduced himself as Waiden then introduced the others to me, but I cannot remember their names, except Allimrac, his assistant. He was much older than I was, about 24, I would say, although he seemed sad and quite insecure. My newly acquired Elvan instincts and armband were not giving me any negative warnings.

'Thank you, I will,' I said.

He told me about the plays he had been in and that at the moment, the band was doing a performance of *Poppy*, about an overpowering mother who makes her daughter into a famous dancer.

He then went on to tell me about the destruction of towns and villages by an evil army of Goblins, strange Men, and these seven destructive creatures. The seven creatures were the most evil things they had ever seen. He described how they would sniff around all the children in the towns and villages in search of something or someone.

I looked at the band of actors and announced, 'The name given to those creatures are the Seven Pernicious.'

They handed me a glass of ale, and I had to act as if I was drinking it. This was a very difficult task to do when all six were watching me, so I had to take a drink as if it was an everyday occurrence. I lifted it to my lips and took a big swig. It was the most hideous thing I'd ever tasted, but I swallowed it in one gulp, placed the mug back on the table with a thud. 'I needed that,' I said.

I then asked them where they were going.

'To the village of Bassmont at the bottom of the Mountains Blue to do three performances of *Poppy*,' Waiden replied.

As they talked, I tried to think of a way to get rid of the ale, but at all times, there was at least one of them looking at me, so I had to drink it. They continued to tell me ghastly stories about the Evil and how he had destroyed many a village that did not comply with his demands. Each time the Evil left a village, they added, he would say, 'I must thank a section of the town for giving me the information and the support. You know who you are.'

He did this with the express purpose of creating hatred among the creeds, and it worked: the suspicions fell upon them all.

By the end of the ale, I was feeling quite dizzy and said, no, mumbled, 'I must retire now and see how my grandfather is.' I stood up and then sat down again quickly. I was drunk and I had no idea how I was going to get to the stairs without falling over.

'We are going to our rooms as well,' said the band of actors.

'I think I may stay for a while longer,' I said, 'to think over some problems I have.'

'I hope we meet again,' Allimrac said. 'It has been a pleasure.'

I began to panic as I thought Waiden was going to stay behind as the others made their way to their rooms, but he said, 'Good night and good dreams,' and left with the others. They left the bar, and the innkeeper came over. 'Do you need anything?' he asked.

'No, thank you. I will be going to my room in a few moments,' I said.

He walked out into his kitchen, and I thought, *This is my chance.* I staggered over to the stairs, grabbed the banister, and hauled myself up the stairs to our room.

Drew was walking up and down the room in a state of apprehension, and snarled at me, 'Where have you been?' Then looked at me and added, 'You're drunk.'

'Maybe,' I said, 'but at least I have found out what is going on in this part of the world.' I then related to Drew what had happened.

Drew looked at me in disgust then smiled and said, 'You'll be sorry for this tomorrow.'

We went to bed, and everything was going round in circles. I felt dreadful and swore never to drink again.

Drew woke me early and looked at me with a smirk on his face. I felt and looked vile. We had breakfast although I didn't eat much. We then left to meet the others at our arranged meeting place.

They all said, 'Oh my, Mecco, you look dreadful. What on Central Earth happened to you?'

I told them what had transpired at the inn, and they all had a good laugh. We set off on the road again, bypassing the village. We were making good progress, so we stopped to eat our midday meal and devised a plan in case we encountered the Evil's army. We made plans A and B. Depending on how many there might be in the army, plan A was, if there were only a few, we would stand and fight. Plan B was, if there were many, we would ride off in different directions.

Up and onwards we travelled. Then just before sunset, I sensed something, and the runes on my armband started to change. Drew sensed it as well. He discreetly came over and asked, 'What does the armband say?'

I showed him and it said,

'Be careful where the cliffs are tall,
For rocks and stones will begin to fall.
For high above, the Evil army lies in wait,
With the seven evils in debate,
Take the next narrow path upon your left.
It may take longer, but it will be best.'

It was true. High above the cliffs of Gamba, the Seven Pernicious and an army of Goblins and Menlins were lying in wait and arguing which was the best way to catch us. Captain Yobtowoy was in charge of the forces, but the Pernicious were overseeing the ambush and Yobtowoy was not happy about this. He was telling the Seven how it should be done: 'Five of you should fly off and scour the countryside as far back as the lake, and try and find where the glupgars are. I will send half of my crew down to wait about a half a kilopace before the cliffs. When the grosfuss arrive, we can start a rockfall, and my crew can come up behind and trap them.'

This argument went back and forth for ages, till finally the Seven agreed. Five of them flew off towards the river and lake, while the other two began a search back along the road to Gamba.

22
CHAPTER

Our First Encounter with the Pernicious

We had just found the path off to the left as described by the runes on my armband and decided to take it. Before we had the chance to get off the main road, a band of horsemen was riding frantically from the cliffs towards us. The company rushed into the woods, but it was too late. They had seen us.

'Quick, get your weapons, 'said Drew, 'and be prepared for a fight. It's plan A.'

Luckily, all except Drew and I were in their Elvan chain mail, and there were only six horsemen. They were riding towards us at great speed, leaving a trail of dust in their wake. We moved back into the woods, hoping they would pass by, but as they grew closer, they slowed down to a canter. It looked as if they were prepared to fight. They were all tall, so we assumed they were Menlins. Their swords were drawn as they approached where we were hiding. They moved cautiously, as if waiting for us to attack them. The riders were by now right in line with where we were.

'We know you are there,' one of them said. 'Either let us past or fight.'

That voice sounds familiar, I thought, and then it dawned on me who they were. Not Menlins but the band of actors, and the voice was Waiden's.

I whispered this to Drew, and he said, 'Then you go out and find out what is going on.'

I walked out with my hands outstretched to show I had no weapons. They rode over and surrounded me.

'Only you,' said Waiden, 'but who are your friends that are hiding in there?'

'There is no reason to be scared of them,' I said. 'We are only travellers and when we saw you riding towards us with such speed, we thought you may be part of the Evil's army. Why were you riding so fast?'

'As we grew close to the cliffs of Gamba,' said Waiden, 'we saw a group of evil Men and Goblins standing on the top of the cliffs. We were not going to take the risk of riding past, so we turned around and were heading back to the town.'

As we spoke, I could sense something terrible deep in the pit of my stomach and noticed my armband lighting up and changing and the dragon tooth becoming heavy again.

'What is that on your arm?' asked Waiden. 'It seems to be glowing and flashing.'

At that moment, Drew sang out, 'Quick, get in the woods!'

Just as I did, two of the Seven flew overhead, uttering the most evil screech one could imagine. They circled the band of actors then descended to land about fifty paces away from them.

While this was happening, Drew had covered everyone in mud and leaves and told them to hide in any possible place they could find. He sent Dolark and Rocco ahead with the horses, thinking they might not sense a Dwarf. The Pernicious dismounted their flying dragon steeds and walked over to the band of actors.

'Who is your leader?' asked one, in the most depraved voice, as if every word was breathed out of some deep horrid pit. It sounded like 'Ha-who ha-is ha-your ha-leader.'

'It is I,' said Waiden. 'How can I help you?'

'Ha-why ha-you ha-running ha-way ha-from ha-the ha-cliff?'

'We were just out from the town of Gamba for our morning race,' said Waiden. 'We take our horses every day for a ride.'

The Pernicious started to sniff around the ground and made the most horrid sounds. From where I was hiding, I had a good view of one of them. He was tall, thin, drawn, and had the most bloodshot eyes, as if all life had been drained from him. He looked in my direction and I could feel his evil, and it made my skin crawl. He looked at where we entered the woods and saw that the horses had trampled it. The dragon steeds then made a loud scream and stamped the ground.

The Pernicious turned to the band of actors and said, 'Ha-be ha-careful ha-what ha-friends ha-you ha-choose.' Then they mounted their steeds, and flew off.

We waited a few minutes, and as we did, Wecco and Tarew looked very strange.

'I don't know what happened then,' said Wecco, 'but I could hear the thoughts of the dragons, if that is possible.'

'So could I,' added Tarew.

'I never felt a thing,' said Drew. 'I can't explain it. Can you sense anything now?'

They both shook their heads in the negative. Drew then sent me out to talk to the actors and thank them for not telling the Pernicious where we were and to ask if they could please tell no one they saw us.

'Where are you off to?' asked Waiden.

I could sense Drew telling me to say nothing, but it was too late, and I said, 'We are going to the Mountains Blue.'

'Then don't take the road,' said Waiden. 'The Evil is everywhere, and you don't want to bump into them on your travels.' He went on to say, 'Do you know that this is a magic Elvan path? Known only by a few non-Elves?'

'How come you know it was Elvan?' I asked.

'Many years ago,' he said, 'when my father was young, he told me of this hidden path that had been told to him by northern Elves. That was the reason we were riding back here, to take it to the village of Bassmont.' He added, 'I know you have Elvan friends by the way you thanked the innkeeper last night. I must admit I have never seen one, but my father spoke of Elves often. Where are the rest of your friends? Are they still hiding?'

'Yes,' I said. 'We will wait here till we think it is safe. You and your friends may go ahead of us. We have two comrades with our horses further along the track. Could you send them back for us, please?'

'Certainly,' he said, 'and we bid you farewell and may your journey be free of the Evil.'

I waited for them to move off, then beckoned my friends to emerge from their hiding places, and we regathered on the track. We looked a dishevelled bunch standing there with mud and leaves all over us. Drew insisted we wait till Waiden and his friends were out of sight before we continued our journey. We rode in silence as the evil residue that had radiated from the two Pernicious permeated our thoughts.

While this was happening to us, Dolark and Rocco had grabbed the horses and rode on along the track about two kilopaces ahead, then tied them up and waited. Dolark sat under a tree and Rocco had seen a bush full of ripe berries, and we all know Rocco. Food he could not resist, so he walked back to the bush, sat next to it, and picked the berries one by one and ate them. He made a complete pig of himself and could not stop till there was not one berry left. His face and hands were completely covered in red stain, and his stomach was so full he just went to sleep.

Dolark was still sitting under the tree and noticed how there was not a sound of a bird or animal anywhere in the forest. He sat there quietly, wondering how the rest of the company was coping with the riders. As he lay there, he could hear a slow beating sound come up the path. The instant he looked up, a hideous scream filled the silence, and there above him were two Pernicious hovering.

He jumped up and ran along the track as fast as he could in the opposite direction from where Rocco lay sleeping. One of the Pernicious swooped down and grabbed his shoulders, lifting him from the ground, about three paces high, then dropped him. He fell hard on to the ground and rolled to a stop. He staggered to his feet, felt his body to see if nothing had been broken, then off he ran again.

The other evil creature had flown ahead and landed further along the track. He dismounted from his dragon steed and waited for the dwarf. Dolark was running as fast as his tiny legs could take him. Looking up, he saw the other Pernicious straight ahead waiting for him and turned to run into the woods. But it was too late: the first Pernicious dived again, grabbing him in his talons and carrying him straight towards the second. He was struggling with all his might, but this time, he was taken about eight paces high and dropped. He landed with a loud thud, rolled a few times then came to a stop, where he lay motionless.

The first Pernicious dismounted his dragon, and they both crept over to look at what they had captured. With each word spoken, they made a ghastly sound, expelling air from deep down in their evil selves. One said, 'Ha-look, ha-dwarf. Ha-the ha-master ha-will ha-be ha-pleased.' They picked up Dolark and tied him on to one of the dragons. Then one of them began to sniffing the air around where they stood and said, 'Ha-smell ha-something ha-else.'

They nodded at each other and said, 'Ha-return', and they then took to the sky with their prize for their master.

23
CHAPTER

A Dwarf Goes Missing

The band of actors had travelled for about ten minutes when they heard the sound of the Pernicious somewhere ahead of them. They slowed down to a walk then stopped completely and waited for another few minutes till the screeching had ceased. They continued till they came across a chubby child asleep under a bush, covered in red stains. Waiden dismounted his steed and shook the child.

'What have we here?' he said.

Rocco jumped with fright and splattered half-chewed berries all over Waiden while saying, 'I'm Rocco, and who are you?' Looking around for his friend, he added, 'And what have you done with my companion Dolark and our horses?'

Waiden looked down at Rocco then to his fellow actors. 'Have any of you seen horses or another child?' They all shook their heads to say no.

'He is not a child. He is a dwarf from the far western hills,' cried Rocco in a voice of authority. 'And if he heard you call him a child, he would not like it.'

'There has never been a dwarf in this part of the world,' said Waiden. 'You must be dreaming.'

'Dreaming?' said Rocco in a state of agitation. 'I'm on a quest with five other children, four Elves, and two Dwarfs, and I can assure you I'm not dreaming.'

Waiden's assistant Allimrac added, 'Elves and Dwarfs, please! They're purely a figment of one's imagination. Maybe the berries you ate are hallucinatory and had an effect on you.'

Rocco was getting annoyed by now. 'Where's my friend and where are the horses?'

Allimrac pointed further along the track and sang out, 'Look, there are four horses tied up to a tree over there.' She smiled and added, 'Maybe that's where your Dwarf friend is, asleep under a tree like you.'

They walked over to the horses and looked around. 'Sorry, there is no Dwarf here,' said Allimrac. 'You must have imagined him.'

Rocco put his hands to his mouth and screamed out as loud as he could. 'Dolark!'

'Be quiet. There were just two Evil creatures back on the main road,' said Waiden, 'and we don't want them to know of this path.'

At that moment, the rest of the company turned the bend. Drew saw the band of actors talking to Rocco and asked, 'Could three of you children go on and see what the problem is? We will wait here. They must not know we are Elves and Dwarfs.'

Three of us walked on while the others hid in the undergrowth. I greeted Waiden with a deep bow and asked, 'What is the problem?'

'Is this red-stained young man a friend of yours?'

'Yes,' I said, looking at Rocco, who by now had a guilty expression all over his face. 'And has he caused you good people any embarrassment?'

Rocco then piped up, 'I have not caused anyone any problems. But they have hidden Dolark.'

'I think your friend ate too many berries and it made him dream,' Waiden interjected. 'He has been insisting he has lost a Dwarf.'

Allimrac had walked further along and was looking at the path and sang out, 'Look here. There are tracks that suddenly stop, and over there, they start again. But take a good look because it seems as if someone fell, or was dropped then rolled to a stop.'

She continued walking while scrutinising the track. 'Look, it happens again here, only this time whoever fell never got up to continue.' She jumped back and said in a trembling voice, 'There are dragon footprints all around this spot. I think the Evil has taken whoever it was that lay here.'

Rocco sank back to the ground. 'I didn't see or hear a thing,' he pleaded.

I shook my head in disgust and thought, *What will the others say?* Dolark was captured by the Pernicious. *What will be his fate now?*

'Call your friends over,' begged Waiden. 'I know there are Elves among them.'

I called over the rest of the leaf-covered, motley crew, but Drew was hesitant.

'They know who you are,' I said, 'and I think they are trustworthy.' I introduced the band of actors to the members of the quest, which took forever. I then had to tell my friends that Dolark had been captured.

Drew grew quite pale and worried about the Evil finding the path. 'We must make haste,' he said, 'and be as far along as possible by tonight.'

We mounted our horses, but before we left, the band of actors offered to accompany us as far as Bassmont. We thanked them. Drew had sensed they were good people, and could be trusted. He then explained to them the reason for this bizarre blending of such a bunch of characters. Soltain kept glaring at Rocco as if he was to blame, and maybe he was. Had he been awake, he might have been able to help fight them off.

Drew sensed the tension and made Rocco feel better by saying, 'Thankfully you were asleep. You could have been quite possibly captured as well.'

The band of actors then mounted their steeds, and we went on our way. There were no stops for elaborate meals on this section of the trip. Drew urged us to make haste and Waiden agreed, so we rode all day and night, with only a few half-hour breaks to graze and rest the horses. These were our only chances to eat, and it consisted of only raw vegetables or fruit. I'm sure you can imagine the look on Rocco's face. The last break just before sunrise was to be a rather strange one for me.

Waiden sat next to me and asked many questions on many subjects. He then looked right into my eyes. 'You are a handsome young man,' he said, 'and I hope when you are older, we meet again, as I would like to talk to you about a certain subject.'

I felt as if he was reading my thoughts, and I felt rather uncomfortable. But I also felt as if he could be trusted, and that he somehow knew, deep down, who I really was.

24
CHAPTER
The Town of Bassmont

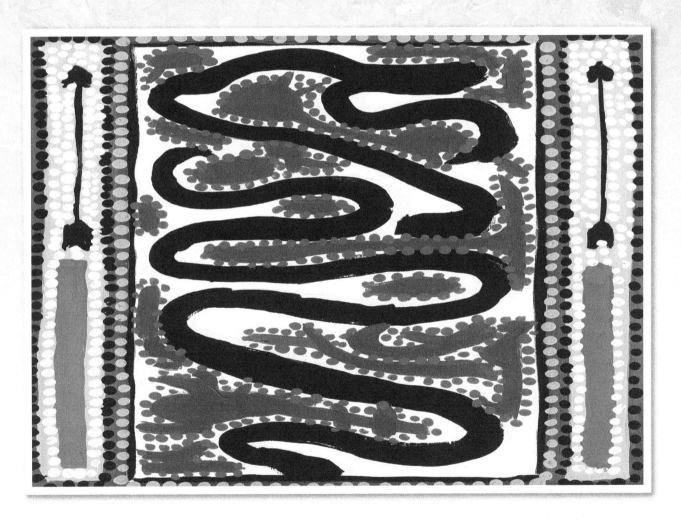

We continued riding till the sun was high on the horizon. It was then that we saw the village of Bassmont off in the distance. The whole morning, not a word was spoken between Waiden and me. Occasionally, I caught him staring at me. I would return his glances, and I could feel myself blushing with embarrassment at what I felt. I just wanted to jump from my horse on to his and hold him close.

As we drew nearer to the village, Drew turned to me and announced, 'I sense there is no danger from the Evil.'

I nodded my head in agreement and added, 'Yes, I sense no evil vibes in this district.'

Rocco expressed a deep sigh of relief. Immediately, he asked, 'Could we have breakfast first?'

The villagers of Bassmont were obviously scared when they saw ten horses with riders all converging on their village. They were preparing to repel the invaders when they saw it was Waiden and his band of actors, whom they knew and admired.

The village was a strange configuration. It was a miniature version of the city of Basscala, complete with terraces and crops. The village was situated halfway up the mountain. The villagers welcomed us, stabled and fed our horses, then ushered us up the steps towards their town hall to meet their elders. The Elves and Soltain had their hoods pulled over their faces so as not to scare the inhabitants.

'We should rest here a few hours', Drew whispered, 'and get some supplies.'

'I don't agree,' I said. 'I think we are wasting time and should continue on to the falls of Nebbia Circum.'

'Good manners never cost anything,' said Drew, 'and we may need their help in the future. Besides, the falls are only seven or eight hours' ride from here, if the map is correct.' He then asked Waiden, 'How trustworthy are these villagers?'

'The elders here have had contact with Elves,' he replied, 'although it was many years ago. But they can be trusted.'

The split second before we entered the hall, the Elves looked at me, and I sensed the Evil was close. Then my armband started to change and said,

'*High above, and to the south*
The Evil has sent out his scouts.
So move fast and hide yourself
Before his scouts they send for help.'

At that exact moment, from high above, the screeching sound of two Pernicious echoed from the skies. They circled the village and then flew off in haste towards the south.

'We have been spotted,' said Drew. 'We will have to leave now. I will explain to the elders.'

Drew explained all, except where we were headed, then added, 'We hope we have not brought bad fortune to your village.'

The head elder, Longstep, replied, 'We know of the evil which is seeping into the land. Somewhere, the line must be drawn. If it is here, then here it must be. This may be a small village, but we have good fortifications and good men who will defend our town.'

'We must leave before they return with an army,' said Drew. 'If we are not here when they come searching, they should leave you alone.'

Just as Drew said this, there was a trumpet sound off in the distance.

Longstep turned to face us. 'Too late, they're on their way. We must prepare to defend the town.'

'But if we are not here,' said Drew, 'all will be fine.'

'It is too late,' said Longstep. 'Look at the distant hill.'

There, all along the ridge was an army of the Evil with three Pernicious hovering above. Even from this distance, I could tell Yobtowoy led it.

Drew said to Longstep the elder, 'The company must be on its way as we have urgent business to attend to.'

'We should come with you for support,' Waiden said.

'No,' said Drew, 'we must do this alone.'

Longstep then said, 'We have a song about Elves, children, and Dwarfs that was given to our ancestors many, many years ago. It predicts your arrival and said we should help if possible.' He fell silent as if in thought then added, 'I have a plan. We have a secret tunnel leading down to the river Underhill, which then flows into the river Condoor. The tunnel is large enough to take your horses with you, and that will give you a few hours' start. We will let the Evil forces in to look for you, and by the time they realise you are not here, you will be well on your way.'

'Are you sure it will not create a problem for your village?' asked Drew.

'No,' replied Longstep. 'I have a plan to distract them. Leave now and do not worry yourselves.'

Drew bowed low and thanked him for his help. We followed suit. Drew then said,

'May Elvan luck be upon your town.
When the rains are needed, let it come down.
When the time for harvesting is due,
May the sky be always crystal blue.
Whatever luck you wish yourself
We wish ten times more, plus good health.'

The elders bowed in return and thanked them for Elvan luck. Then Longstep added, 'It is good to eventually meet Elves. Now we hope the Evil will finally be expelled from this land.'

'We must depart as well', said Waiden, 'and ride on to our next engagement.' The band of actors bowed and thanked us for our company on the road, then mounted their horses.

Have you readers taken notice of the influence the Elves have had on this world? Their manners have influenced even the actors.

I looked at Waiden. He looked at me. There was no way of saying what I wanted to say. I walked over to him, reached up, and shook his hand. Looking deep into his eyes, I said, 'Thank you for all your help. I hope we meet again someday soon, when all the evil is gone from the world. Thank you again, Waiden, and goodbye.'

Longstep had sent for the horses and then led us through a secret door and down a wide tunnel. The craftsmanship was much admired by Soltain, and he insisted that it had been built by Dwarfs many years ago.

'It may be so,' added Longstep, 'as our history says that it was always here, and we never knew who built it.'

Halfway down, we came to what looked like a four-arched intersection, but two exits had been blocked up. Soltain stopped, looked at the writing over the arches, and said, 'See, there over each arch, the old Dwarf words for *up*, *out*, *deep*, and *deeper*, and the mark of the great tunnel-digger Bidlark.'

'Those two tunnels were bricked up many years ago,' said Longstep, 'as they just went deep into the mountain and there was no end to them. They say that many a man was lost in them over the years and no one could find their way out.'

'There would have been an ancient Dwarf sign over each intersection,' said Soltain, 'and had they made the effort to get it translated, they would have had no problems finding their way out.'

We continued with Longstep leading the way with the light from his blazing torch flickering off the walls and ceiling. The horses were not very comfortable in the tunnels with their heads just missing the roof and the torch smoke flying in their faces. Longstep assured us we would be there in about fifteen minutes. The company was now whittled down to seven: four children, two Elves, and one

Dwarf. We were still in our Elvan kilts, vests, and boots, and we carried our weapons. To this day, I still marvel at the strength and lightness of them and still have mine packed away in a special box with all my other souvenirs of our adventure.

As we walked, my mind was going over many things but especially that strange experience with Waiden. How it was playing on my mind! I also wondered what was so important about going to the falls. What could it reveal to us that we didn't already know? We were aware of the hatred between the creeds and the evil creeping into the world. More to the point, what were we supposed to do about it?

Drew stopped and waited for me to catch up. He said, 'I asked myself the same questions when we were waiting in the forest of Gundi. But after meeting you all, I realised it is your innocence and the trust you have in each other that will defeat the Evil.' He smiled and added, 'Of course, with the help of us Elves.'

I had to wonder whether Drew could sense everything I felt.

We arrived at the exit of the tunnel, which had a large stone door on metal wheels that covered the whole entrance. There was a set of pulleys that moved the stone door across. Longstep asked Soltain if he could understand the writing on the top of the arched exit. Soltain walked back inside and peered up. 'Hold the torch closer, please.'

After a few moments, he said, 'Yes, it is an old Dwarf incantation. If one needs to open the door from the outside, all one has to do is recite it.'

He went on to read it three or four times to memorise it. Old Dwarf sounds very strange but is very similar to our language, but with a strong accent.

Drew turned to Longstep and said, 'You must return quickly and cover our tracks with old garbage or anything that has a strong odour, as the Seven Pernicious can smell where we have been. If they realise you have helped us, they will cause great trouble for your people.'

We bid our last farewells then mounted our steeds. With Dolark captured, Rocco was riding solo and was a little unsure. But thanks to Seafair, we knew he would be safe.

25
CHAPTER

Ride Along the River Underhill

We rode off in haste along the river Underhill towards the river Condoor. There was a well-worn track on one side that paralleled the meandering of the river. Had it been another time, I would have spent many an hour appreciating the beauty of the river that bubbled and flowed over rocks into large, deep crystal-clear pools.

As we rode, I had glimpses in my mind of the fun we all would have had diving and swinging on ropes from the branches that hung over the pools.

Drew's hand patted my knee, and he said, 'Don't worry, my friend, good times will come again.'

Now I was really worried. *I think he does know everything I'm thinking.*

Within twenty minutes, we reached the fork where the two rivers joined, and we turned left to travel up the Condoor. Here the track started to climb steeply, and it was not quite as well trod as the first section. The rock pools were larger, and the bubbling over the rocks turned into a roar over boulders, with the occasional small waterfall. The further we rode, the steeper the incline and the harder it was on the horses.

While we were riding on towards the falls of Nebbia Circum, the forces of evil had descended and surrounded Bassmont. Three of the Pernicious and Captain Yobtowoy had demanded to speak to Longstep, threatening to turn the town upside down if they did not hand us over to them. Longstep was a good speaker and told the Pernicious and Yobtowoy that we had been there but they had turned us away from the town for fear of punishment from the great wizard Drascar.

The Pernicious sniffed for a very long time around the entrance to the town hall but they were rather confused. Longstep had covered our escape route by spilling a large pot of soup over the exit we took after we left the town hall. He then told the Evil that there had been a banquet the night before, which was the reason for the strong smell of food. The Pernicious continued sniffing around for a while longer then followed the trail back to the gates.

They spent ages smelling around the gates where we entered the town but could not find our trail, and they were very upset. At Yobtowoy's insistence, they took two hostages.

'I shall find out the truth from these glupgars,' he said, 'you mark my word. If you have hidden the Elves and children, your town will be in big trouble.'

26
CHAPTER

The Falls of Nebbia Circum

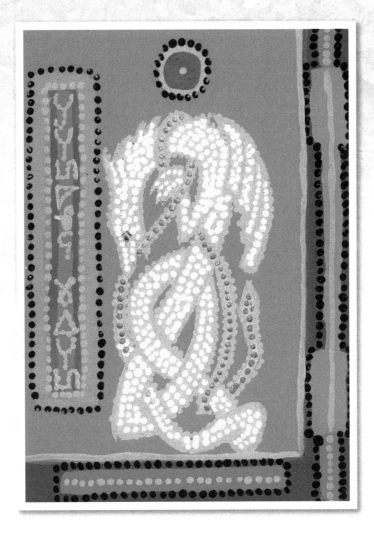

Judging by the map, we should have been about two and a half hours from the falls when Drew suggested a break to rest the horses for ten minutes as the going was quite tough for them. Of course, Rocco was the first to ask what there was to eat.

Drew looked at Rocco and, shaking his head, said, 'I know exactly what Carew would say now. You would eat someone out of house and home!'

The Bassmontians had given us enough supplies to last at least another week. Drew was not so worried about how much we ate, so while the horses grazed, we ate to our hearts' content. After a while, the company remounted, and we set off. The Elves were singing quietly now, and that made us feel a little better about our quest.

'Why are you always singing?' asked Rocco.

'Forests are magical living things, and you must sing to them,' said Drew. 'Why do you think birds sing so much? It's because it makes the forest happy, and it in turn makes those who are singing happy.'

Soltain was not too happy though, saying, 'How can you sing when one of the company has been captured by the Evil?'

The Elves apologised and stopped singing, and this made an unenjoyable journey more miserable. It also made me aware that I was still worried about *Princess Elandra* and the rest of our friends. Little did I know they were safer than we were and, at that very moment, were travelling up the river Condoor.

It was now starting to get quite dark, and with the rainforest canopy shutting out most of the sun's rays, we knew we had to make haste to be at the falls by sunset. We were having difficulty finding the track, and in some places, it was much too steep for the horses and we had to lead them. Fifteen minutes passed, and it was now too dark to continue. So we decided to camp for the night.

I know now why they are called rainforests, as the humidity was so heavy drops of water fell continuously from the leaves of the trees. We were all rather wet, though it was not raining and the sky was clear above the forest canopy. Luckily, Drew had one of the Elvan tent covers, and he set it up over a low-hanging branch. We huddled under it for protection, and we spent the night trying to get some rest.

I lay there listening to the drops of moisture landing on the tent and the sound of the river rushing down the slope and over the boulders. This was the first chance I had to think about Waiden, and I wondered if I would ever see him again. I thought about how I loved my friends and how they loved me, but knew they could never give me what I sensed Waiden could. Their love was platonic, whereas mine had a much deeper need. The thought of my friends knowing my secret also worried me. I tried to think instead of how we were to rescue Dolark from the Evil.

Drew, who was next to me, put his arm round my shoulder. 'Mecco, all your friends love you,' he said. 'This I know, and they would support any choice you made in your life. The question of Dolark's rescue is also on my mind.'

I felt safe with Drew and I think he loved me too, in his way, though I can't help thinking he has issues himself to deal with. And there was that question again: could he sense all my thoughts?

We spent a rather sleepless night, then about five thirty, when we finally had dozed off, we were wakened abruptly by a loud screech. We knew exactly what it was. Luckily, we were well hidden under the rainforest canopy so the Pernicious had no way of flying down and spotting us. Soltain then responded with a loud screech, and we all jumped in fright.

'What are you doing?' asked Drew.

'It's not a Pernicious. Don't you think I know the difference by now?' announced Soltain. 'It was the call of the messengers of Master Baylib, the head of the Dwarfs.'

There was no replay, so we decided to move on straight away in case he was wrong and the Evil had dispatched a force along the river. After ten minutes, we realised that the terrain was too difficult for the horses as they were slipping and sliding everywhere.

A difficult choice was called for. Rocco was to stay with the horses while the rest of us continued on. At first, he was not very impressed and asked, 'Why do I get left to look after the horses all the time?'

'Rocco,' replied Drew, 'the last part of this journey requires a lot of climbing which will be quite difficult, and besides, someone must look after the food and provisions.'

A smart tack by Drew, I thought. This line of argument convinced Rocco in a split second.

Soltain by this time had had enough and, in an emotional state, asked, 'Why do none of you care what has happened to Dolark? I know I'm only a guest on the quest, but we offered our services to help against the Evil. One of our company has been captured, and none of you are saying what we are going to do about it.'

Drew walked over to Soltain, bowed deeply, and said, 'Soltain, please accept our apologies. We have been considering the subject of Dolark's rescue. I'm hoping when we get to the Falls of Nebbia Circum, where we may find magic weapons that have been predicted to be there. That will give us more power and hopefully the Oracle will reveal a plan of attack to defeat the Evil. We have not forgotten Dolark's plight, but our first priority is to get to the falls. Then, and only then, will we be able to organise a plan to rescue him, and that we will do, I assure you.'

Soltain looked relieved and apologised for his outburst then said, 'Well, let us depart for these falls immediately.'

Off we set while Rocco made himself comfortable under an Elvan tent and bade us goodbye. I knew exactly what he was going to do as soon as we were out of sight. He would look through all the provisions to see what was there and maybe have a taste, just to see what it was like. Who knows what will be left when we return? I wasn't sure it was a good idea to leave Rocco alone with the provisions.

The track by now had completely disappeared and had become steeper and more slippery. Tarew and Peto had become very good companions and were helping each other up the steeper parts; in fact, it was so steep in places we all had to help each other up. The river by now had become a continuous chain of small waterholes and waterfalls. The sun was just rising and we were upon the steepest part of the climb, when another loud screech silenced the roar of the water, and we shuddered and looked up, except Soltain, who turned and made a screech of his own.

Tarew screamed, 'What are you doing? If it is the Pernicious, they will hear you.'

Soltain turned to us and said exasperatedly, 'It is not the Pernicious, I assure you. Please believe me, it was a white screecher, a messenger of the Dwarfs.'

He screeched again, but it was too late. The bird had flown off. As we continued our climb, we became aware of a faint distant roar above the sound of the rushing water. And as we continued, the roar grew louder and louder. And we realised we were approaching the Falls of Nebbia Circum. Ten minutes later, we dragged ourselves up and over the last incline. There before us lay a large semicircular lake, with falls cascading from a hundred-paces-high cliff into the water below. This created a mist of spray that covered half the lake, and with the morning sun shining, the most vibrant rainbow hung over it.

We were at the falls of Nebbia Circum, the source of the river Condoor. As we surveyed the lake, we noticed there were three rivers cascading down the mountain from different parts of the lake, and we realised they all joined the Condoor further down the mountain. We had just followed one of the tributaries up the southern side of the mountain. We stood there in wonder; even Drew who lived on a lake with a waterfall was in awe of the sight. We looked across the lake to the northern side, where a forest of large cedars and forest figs grew on a gentle incline up to the top of the mountain.

How are we to get behind that fall of water?' I thought. We will all be crushed before we get within twenty paces of it. I realised Drew was thinking the same thing. Could I read his mind as well, or was I imagining it?

After absorbing the beauty of the area and regaining our breath, we pushed on towards the falls. It was a shame we never climbed up the northern side, as the walk to the falls there was along a sandy beach, but our side just large boulders and slippery rocks. If the old saying 'No pain no gain' rings true, then we were to gain everything we had come for. We slipped and skidded our way around to the edge of the lake. We arrived at the falls and spent hours looking for a possible way to penetrate them, but without any luck. What were we to do now?

27
CHAPTER
The Five Go On

While all this was happening on the road to Bassmont, our friends back at the boat had their own problems, not with the Evil, but with *Princess Elandra*. They tried every way of getting her to turn around and sail back to Basscala, but she would not budge. Carew tried every ancient Elvan riddle and chant without any success. After a whole day of this, he suggested that they all sit and try to sense what was wrong with *Princess Elandra*. This they did, and in no time at all, they found out the problem. In fact, there was no problem. She would not sail back to the city because the Evil army had moved on. Now she was ready to continue up the river Condoor.

The four debated this but in the end realised it would make no difference what decision they came to. *Princess Elandra* wanted to continue, although Jarew was not too keen on the idea. Eventually, Carew and Jarew scouted along the river for a few kilopaces then returned and said there was no sign of the Evil, so they launched *Princess Elandra* out into the middle of the river and set off. It turned out to be a very slow trip as there were no horses now and they had to take it in turns to tow the *Princess* along the river. She helped as much as she could, but with the narrowness of the river and the height of the forest, hardly a breeze reached her.

Around midday, just as they stopped for lunch, there were loud screeches, and the company went into defence mode, thinking it was the Pernicious. *Princess Elandra* made no attempt to hide herself, and this worried our friends, who were running around in a frenzy. Suddenly, five large white birds with yellow crests came diving through the trees then glided down and perched on the railing and one began speaking Elvan to Carew. Jula and Wecco could not believe it; they had seen these birds all around the forest of Gundi all their lives but had never seen one talk as clearly as these. After five minutes' conversation with Carew, two flew off in one direction, while the other three flew off in a different direction.

Carew turned to the rest of the crew and announced, 'They are messengers of the High Master of the Dwarfs, Master Baylib.' He then relayed the message.

'Master Baylib wishes to know if the Dwarf army was needed. And how are things progressing with the quest? I ordered two messengers to inform Master Baylib of our progress and one to inform the lords. The other two I sent to search for our eight companions and to let us know what is happening in these times of dread, in this part of the world.'

After the commotion had died down, they cast off and continued towing the *Princess* along the narrow river. At the next bend, they could see the Mountains Blue rising to a great height in the distance. They estimated a day and half travel and they would be at Nebbia Circum. They continued till the sun nearly set and then fell shattered on the deck, drowsy with exhaustion. They ate the meal Jula had prepared with hardly a word, and then collapsed on the bunks and were asleep in no time at all. They rose early to a clear beautiful morning, had their breakfast, and set off.

There was a slight breeze in their favour. This took the pressure off pulling *Princess Elandra*, but as the day drew on, the breeze abated, and by the end of it, they were towing her again. By nightfall, they had entered a part of the river where the forest had been cleared on one side and the fields extended all the way down to the river's edge. They decided to continue for a few hours to pass this section then turn in.

That night, there was a little drama as Jarew and Carew argued about who was the best to take command.

'As I was one of the three mentioned in the parchments,' announced Jarew, 'the task should be mine.'

Carew argued that he was the eldest and had more experience in travel, and he should be leader. With two such healthy egos, the fighting went on for ages.

Jula and Wecco started to laugh. Jula then said, 'Whoever wins this argument will only be ordering the other around, as we will not take any notice of whoever wins. We have got this far by discussing any problems democratically, and we don't intend changing now.'

Carew began to laugh as well, but Jarew was not impressed. He ate alone and sulked the rest of the evening. After the commotion had abated, they decided to turn in early and get a good night's rest as they were so worn out from towing *Elandra* most of the day. During the night, Jula woke to the sound of talking on deck and perused the room to see who was missing and realised Jarew was the only one not in his bunk. Up the steps she slowly sneaked. Peering along the deck, she saw only one figure but she had no doubt there were two different voices talking. Suddenly, the figure turned just as she ducked her head below the cabin door, and it began walking towards her. She tiptoed her way back to her bunk and acted as if she was asleep while Jarew stood at the door, checking out his friends before finally hopping in his bunk.

The morning arrived with the sun rising over the distant plains, and the motley crew were very pleased to find there was a stronger breeze blowing in their favour, allowing them to make good progress without the task of towing *Princess Elandra*. The Mountains Blue were towering over them by now, and they knew they must be close to the falls. As they turned the next bend, there in front of them was a small lake with three small waterfalls cascading into it.

Jula said, 'That's not so impressive. I was expecting a large lake and towering falls.'

'That's not the Falls of Nebbia Circum,' Carew said. 'By the map, these are called Basslake and Forkfalls. Nebbia Circum is at least another two- or three-hour climb up the mountain.'

The lake was wide enough for the *Princess* to use her sail to advantage, and they crossed it in no time, stopping near the eastern falls, where there was a small beach that backed on to a gently sloping pine forest. They had a conference and decided to wait there for a day, as the rest of the company might not have arrived. I was jealous when they told me what fun they had: how they went swimming and diving from the falls, lying on the beach and having a good time while we were trudging up the opposite creek.

The following morning, they left the *Princess* and walked up the slope by the eastern falls. It was a lovely day, and the walk was quite easy. It was only the last hour where it became quite steep. The forest began to thin out, and a slight roar could be heard in the distance. They continued, and the closer they came to the top of the hill, the louder the roar. When they finally reached the crest of the hill, they stood in wonder at the view, a beautiful lake and, on the far side, the falls of Nebbia Circum.

'Whoa, now that's impressive,' said Jula. 'I have never seen a rainbow so vibrant.'

They walked along the small beach towards the falls. As they approached them, the spray grew stronger, and everything was covered in moisture. The trees close to the falls were covered in elk, stag, and bird's-nest ferns collecting the moisture, and every rock was covered in rock orchids of every description. Poor Rocco—being into gardening, he would have loved this, and I knew the others would tell him how beautiful it was. I can just see him now complaining about being left with the horses. They looked around the vicinity to see if we had arrived. When they saw no sign of us and as the five-hour hike had exhausted them, they decided to sit in the late morning sun and wait a few hours, hoping for our arrival. They were very worried about us, although they would not let on to each other.

Suddenly off in the distance, Jula saw a white speck appear on the horizon. She pointed and said, 'Look.'

Carew jumped with joy. 'It is a white messenger. Hopefully, he has some good news.'

The bird landed on the grass next to them, walked over to Carew, and began to speak in the common tongue.

'The Evil's army has destroyed Bassmont and preparing to march on the city of Basscala. The Dwarf army has been summoned to help and is on its way. I also heard the call of a Dwarf from under the forest canopy on the western side of the creek that leads from the lower lake early this morning. Shall I go and take another look?'

'Yes, go,' said Carew, 'and see if it is the Dwarfs and our companions. Let them know of our position and if they have found a way past the falls.'

The white screecher flew off in the direction of the southern shore, making deafening screeches.

28
CHAPTER
The Company Rejoined

The morning was half over. We gave up all hope of finding a way past the impenetrable wall of water. We were sitting on the rocks about a hundred paces from the falls, when out of the blue came loud screeches from across the lake. We looked up, and in the distance was a white messenger flying towards us. As it drew closer, Soltain made a replying screech, and the bird veered in our direction, gliding peacefully without a sound. We stood under the canopy of the forest, and Soltain voiced our thoughts. 'He may have news from the others, or at least news from Master Baylib.'

The messenger was no more than a hundred paces from where we stood when three shadows passed over the lake and an evil screech of a Pernicious pervaded the day. In horror, we looked up as the talons of one of the dragons grabbed the messenger, ripping one wing clean off, leaving it to fall into the lake below. As we watched this, we became aware that the rest of our friends were watching the same drama unfolding from the other side of the falls, and they became aware of us.

Within seconds, it was all over, and with one last horrifying scream, the dragon and the Pernicious flew off with its prey clutched tightly in its talons. We stood motionless with only the sound of the falls breaking the silence. As they became specks in the distance, they made this loud horrendous cry, as if they were in great agony. We were to find out much later what the reason was for their agonising screech.

It was only a few seconds, though it seemed like ages when Drew broke the silence. 'Speed is now of the essence, as the Evil knows we are here. How do you feel about swimming across the lake?'

We all answered fine except Soltain. A plan had to be devised as we could not leave him here alone as the Evil without a doubt would send more of the Pernicious back when he learned of our whereabouts.

Soltain suggested, 'I could retrace our steps to where we left the horses with Rocco, inform him of the events, and we could travel back to the start of the river Condoor.'

Drew was worried about him going back alone and insisted he come with us.

We set about making a raft by tying some fallen logs together with vines. We stripped off our heavy clothes and chain mail down to just our shorts, then tied them to a makeshift raft with Soltain lying on top. We set out across the lake, pushing with all our might. The water along the edge was quite warm, but as we moved into the centre of the lake, it turned extremely cold. Hopefully the amount of kicking we were doing would keep us warm till we reached our companions on the other side.

Poor Soltain was soaked by now from the spray from the falls. As we approached halfway, the wind changed, and the mist from the falls now completely covered us. We could not see where we were going.

Peto started to panic. 'Why did I ever come along in the first place?' he complained. 'This is a waste of time. There will always be evil in the world. We should have just made the best of it.'

'Shut up, you silly boy,' said Drew. 'You may be right about evil being always in our midst, but you have no idea what you are taking about. When the opportunity arises, I will explain some things to you. For now, just keep kicking.'

'Great,' replied Peto, 'just keep kicking. Do you know what direction we are going? We could be heading straight for the falls.'

Drew started to get angry now and slapped the water with his hand. 'Are you deaf? The roar of the falls is on our left, so if we continue to keep the sound to our left, sooner or later, we'll arrive on the eastern shore.'

Within ten minutes, I could feel the water getting warmer and realised that we must be approaching the shore. Without warning, we emerged from the mist of the falls, only about a hundred paces from the beach. The rest of the company were now wading or swimming out to meet us. Wecco, Carew, and Jarew arrived and started to laugh and to splash us with water, but when they saw the look on Soltain's face, they stopped. They told us to swim ashore and they would take over pushing the raft.

Jula had four Elvan blankets and wrapped them around us. We had to share them, so Drew and I huddled together, as did Tarew and Peto, who were laughing and slapping each other in fun. Drew and I were facing each other and the warmth of our bodies and the blankets was expelling the cold. I found myself looking straight into Drew's eyes. I don't know whether he sensed my thoughts or I sensed his, but we both became embarrassed and moved away at the same time. The rest of the company had laid our things out in the sun to dry and were hugging us like long-lost brothers. We were all pleased to see each other. It allowed me to forget what had just happened with Drew.

'Where are Dolark and Rocco?' asked Jarew.

'Let them have a rest,' said Jula, 'and some food and they can tell us while they eat.'

Drew faced our friends, looking very serious, and asked, 'Have you found a way behind the falls?'

'We have not looked as yet,' Carew replied, 'but we'll go now and see what we can find while you eat and get your strength back.'

'We will eat on the way', said Drew, 'and tell you about our journey thus far. We should make haste and be gone from this place, as the Pernicious will return with reinforcements. Also, how is *Princess Elandra*, and is she safe?'

'We left her at Basslake,' said Jula, 'and she is well hidden under a large forest fig tree.'

We packed up our gear and dressed, then headed along the beach in the direction of the falls, explaining as we walked what had happened to Dolark and Rocco. We continued along the beach until we reached the edge of the falls. By now, the roar was deafening, and we had to yell to be heard. The water was falling here with more power than on the western side. There seemed no way of piercing the curtain from this side either.

'Remember, the riddle said forty steps up and ten across,' said Carew, 'so we must find a path of sorts and climb the cliff.' I was about to take the first step when suddenly that feeling came over me again. I looked at Drew and could see he sensed it as well. I looked at my wrist, and sure enough, there appearing was an Elvan message. So I read the Elvan runes aloud.

'When you enter this place, there is something you need.
Ask the parchment, then you can read.
When you enter this cave, what you must take.
And heed it well, for your own sake.'

Drew was shaking his head as I finished, and the other three Elves looked at me with curiosity and suspicion, as did the rest of the company. I was aware instantly of my error. I should have let Drew read it. Now questions would be asked. Sure enough, the three Elves turned to Drew and asked, 'What is going on here, how come a mortal can read Elvan?'

Drew looked at me then at the rest of the company. 'I was instructed by the elders to teach one of the six the Elvan language,' said Drew, 'and that's what I have been doing. That was why I gave Mecco the magic wristband so he could practice. We must not waste time. It is important that we get to the Oracle as soon as possible.'

I don't think he convinced them, as they still looked at me with suspicion.

Drew turned to Carew and asked, 'Do you have the parchments with you?'

'Yes,' answered Carew as he rolled out the parchment then asked it, 'What do we need for this part of our quest?' Then the Elvan runes began to appear on the parchment, and Carew read it aloud.

'A sentry guards where the Oracle lives.
So take with you some food to give,
To distract the sentry from his chore.

Then knock three times upon the door.
But also be careful of this beast.
For his eyes are open when he sleeps.
But he watches well when his eyes are shut.
So be very careful of that mutt.'

'Have you any spare food?' asked Drew. 'Our provisions were left with Rocco and the horses.'

'Not much,' said Wecco, 'but I will return and get what we have left.'

'What does it mean', I asked Drew, 'by "his eyes are open when he sleeps"?'

'Stories tell of a great hound that would keep watch over the Oracle with his eyes shut', Drew said, 'and sleep with his eyes open.'

Carew rolled up the parchments, and we waited for Wecco's return. Then we attempted to climb at different parts of the cliff face. Some of us were having great trouble as the rocks were so slippery.

Eventually, Tarew sang out, 'Look there.' He was about three paces up the cliff face and pointed to his left.

We looked at where he was pointing but could not see anything. I climbed to where he was and became aware of steps cut into the rock. I beckoned the others up, and they followed. The steps were well camouflaged, and it was not until we reached a certain height they could be seen. The sight of the steps cheered us up and we continued with the climb, and we counted another thirty-seven paces. Still, there was no way across, so we continued. Just a few more steps and we became aware of a ledge that traversed across and behind the falls, so off we went. Ten steps, and there behind the wall of water was a small entrance. This must be the start of the caves of Mooloo!

We were hidden behind the wall of water and just in time as the evil screech of the Pernicious could be heard over the deafening roar of the falls.

Drew asked, 'Can anyone see how many there are?'

Jula was at the end. She looked out and said, 'It looks like there are only two.'

We stood there for ages, not moving, then I said, 'Okay, let's proceed into the cave. That's why we are here.'

We climbed in, and it opened into a large cavern with an enormous domed ceiling. There was a large light well, allowing in shafts of sunlight that hit the western wall. A rocky island situated twenty paces back from the edge of the falls achieved this, and in the centre of it, there was the light shaft. There were also unlit torches around the walls. But there was no sign of the Oracle.

29
CHAPTER
The Task Revealed

By now all of us were in the cave, and we moved over to the western wall to dry off in the sun coming through the shaft. Curiosity got the better of Jula and Wecco, who were not as wet as us, and they went searching for any signs of the Oracle.

As we were drying off, Sol commented, 'It looks as if the cave was of ancient Dwarf workmanship, but I could not be certain as Dolark was the expert on Dwarf history.' It just looked like a big cavern to me with a hole in the roof.

Jula and Wecco arrived back with news that at the end of the cave there were three tunnels going in different directions, with writing over each one but still no sign of the Oracle.

The sun was so warm coming through the opening in the cavern. Without the cold wind, we dried off in no time at all. We moved off towards the three tunnels at the end of the cavern. I was becoming a little anxious. I wondered if there really was an Oracle and if so, I had no idea what it was I had to ask them. We stopped at the entrance of the tunnels.

Carew looked at the writing and said, 'Part is in ancient Elvan, but the rest I can't understand. Over the right cave, the Elvan part says "under". On the left it says "through the", and the centre says "to the". The other writing is some other tongue. I have no idea from where.'

Sol looked up, pointed, and said, 'These were built by dwarfs. There is the mark of Bidlark the master digger and the writing is ancient Dwarf, but I am not sure exactly what it means.' He contemplated the words for a few minutes, then said, 'Over the right, I think it says "water or lake", over the left, "descent or fall", over the centre, it is definitely "word".'

'If we combine the Elvan and Dwarf words,' said Carew, 'they say, "under water" or "lake". I think it's "under lake". The second is "through the descent or fall". I think it's "through the falls". The last is definitely "to the word". That's where we will find the Oracle.'

So the choice was made. We lit a few torches, and off we went along the tunnel.

As we walked, I said to Sol, 'These tunnels are so smooth and perfectly round, Bidlark must have been a great builder.'

His pride showed as he lifted his head and answered with great authority, 'Yes, this is definitely Bidlark's workmanship.'

As the adventure went on, I came to realise that the Dwarfs were quite an insecure lot, although very proud. We walked on for approximately ten minutes, arriving at another large cavern with another light well that was much smaller. The light seemed to fall straight down to one place on the floor, and in and around it was discarded scraps of food and bones. The question on all our minds was who left all this rubbish and where were they now? Was it the sentry who was guarding the Oracle? And would we be the next victims for him to devour? We gazed deeply around the dark cavern but saw no sign of any vicious animal or the Oracle. What was our next move?

Carew froze on the spot, pointed, and said, 'Look over there in that corner.'

We turned and peered into the dark. All we could see were two shining red eyes, and as our eyes adjusted to the dark, there, sitting so still, was a large black dog or wolf. Drew pulled out his sword. He was the only one with a weapon, as we had hidden ours near the beach with our Elvan chain mail.

'The food is the distraction,' said Tarew, 'and I think we should place it over near the light so the animal can see it. That's where all the scraps have been left.'

'That is a good idea,' I said, 'and if he stays long in the light, it will be more difficult for his eyes to adjust and see where we are.'

'I think it should be fine,' Drew said. 'Remember what the parchment said, he sleeps with his eyes open. But we should not take any unnecessary risks.' Then he asked Tarew, 'Please take the last of the provisions and place them in the light, then come right back.'

As Tarew walked to the area of light, the animal's eyes closed half-shut and followed him. He placed the last of the food in a pile right in the centre of the light and turned to walk back. He was not quick enough. He took just one step, and the large hound jumped out to block his way. Tarew stopped in his tracks, but the hound moved towards him slowly with a snarl and his fangs showing. Tarew started to move back step by step as the hound crawled closer and closer.

'Get him close to the food!' Drew screamed. 'And then try the vanishing trick.'

We all shuddered a little, for we knew Tarew was having trouble with the vanishing, but if he could get back here, we could use the invisible force field to protect us. Tarew was terrified, really terrified, and it showed on his face. He would not be able to control the vanishing, and something must be done.

Drew knew precisely what I was thinking, and in an instant, we both had projected ourselves to Tarew's side. This startled the hound, and he stopped in his tracks. This was all the time we needed, so we grabbed one arm each and said, 'Now.'

Within a split second, we were all together again. The hound turned and focused on us. He started to move slowly and confidently in our direction.

'Now is the time to use our invisible force field,' said Drew. He only had to mention it, and in seconds, it materialised.

In this dark cave, the barrier was quite obvious, but the hound still moved towards us. He moved up to the barrier and sniffed around. He then tried to enter, but the force field threw him back. He growled at it, made a second attempt with the same outcome. He gave a few growls then walked back to the food we had left.

Now was our chance. With the force field around us, we moved over to the door that he had been guarding. I knocked three times, then with a creak, the door opened to reveal a statue standing with burning candles surrounding her. To our horror, the statue had gaping holes where her eyes should have been. Tentatively, we all moved into the candlelit room. Suddenly, the door slammed behind us, and the statue started to speak. To our surprise, it was a soft and gentle voice that asked,

'Who are you all who come this way
To ask and hear what I have to say?
I need you all to speak loud and clear
To reach each crack and crevasse so I can hear.
So go ahead and say your piece
So I can get back to my deep sleep.'

I looked at Drew, who returned my glance. 'Well, ask her something,' he said as I stood there thinking what to ask.

'Where should we go?' I asked. She replied,

'No, you all must tell me who you are
and where you're from.
So you can be sure the answer
will not be wrong.'

I spoke first, then each of us in turn said our names and where we were from. We had finished and all was silent for a few moments then the Oracle said,

'There is something wrong, with the Elvan three.
There is one extra, who should not be.'

Drew told her why there were four Elves rather than three, and she turned her head in the direction of the four Elves.

'Please, Elves, repeat what you said,'

she asked and so they did. After what seemed like ages, she added,

'What is it you wish to know?'

'We don't know what we are supposed to ask you,' I said. 'We were instructed to come to see you because of an ancient prophecy.'

She then looked in our direction with her gaping holes for eyes and said,

'In the caves of Nebbia Circum, I the Oracle wait.
And here behind me is a chest for you to take.
Read the inscription, but take heed.
And there you will find the magic weapons you need.'

We moved around behind the Oracle, and sure enough, there was an old Elvan chest with ancient runes inscribed on the lid. We looked at Carew, waiting for him to decipher them. It seemed like ages although it was only seconds when he said,

'The one of mixed blood and the Elvan three,
Place your hands on the lid and sense the key.
The lid will open, upon this day
To reveal the weapons for the Evil armies to slay.'

I spoke up before anyone had a chance to say a word and said, 'I am the one of mixed blood.'

Peto looked at me and said, 'You told me you didn't know who your father was.'

'I don't,' I replied. 'But I know he is from the south, so I must be the one.'

I could feel Drew's relief, as the secret of my Elvan bloodline remained ours. The next question now was which of the three Elves were to place their hands on the chest. I knew what Drew was thinking: that Jarew should not be one of the three, as the warning said, 'Take heed.'

Before Drew had said a word, Jarew turned on his heel and said, 'I was one of the three chosen from the year of Rew, so I should be one of the three to open the chest.'

Drew turned to Jarew. 'There is something you must know. On the night we were chosen, there was one more who answered the riddle correctly, although he was not with the twelve.' Drew went on to tell the company about how Tarew knew it and answered correctly, and that Jarew had made mistakes. We then took a vote on what to do. It went in favour of Tarew. The look on Jarew's face was one of hate and resentment and was to have consequences later on with our quest.

The three Elves and I placed our hands on the lid with the rest of the company looking on and Jarew standing back in a huff. I could sense that he wanted us to fail. The four of us concentrated on the key to unlock the lid, and then in the silence, we heard a click. We hesitated for a moment then lifted the lid, and there inside were nine bows with an assortment of arrows of different lengths, with a variety of feathered flights and nine old Elvan daggers.

Jula and Wecco said, 'We don't know how to use a bow and arrow.'

'Not to worry,' said Drew, 'we have one of the best Elvan archers with us. He may be not too good at vanishing, but at using a bow, there is none better. He is our mate Tarew.' He added, 'There must be some reason why they were left for us, so at the first chance, Tarew can teach you how to use them. Now we must ask the Oracle why and what we are to do.'

We each picked up a bow and some arrows, and it was strange how each one was the correct height for each of us. Jarew grabbed one also, but we knew it was not for him but for Rocco, and kept silent. We all felt a little strange, as there were none for Soltain.

He sensed our discomfort and said, 'Bows are not for me. I have a Dwarf axe and a sword.'

We moved around to face the Oracle again. They looked at me, waiting for me to ask the question. I looked into the deep holes where her eyes would have been and asked, 'Great Oracle in the caves of Mooloo, please tell us, what are we are to do?'

Turning her head, she looked down to face me and said,

'The Evil in this world, you can never defeat,
But you can suppress it and make it weak,
And this is the task which was given to you,
To disarm this evil, you and your crew.
With the magic weapons now in your hands,
It is the time to make your plans.
The band you wear will help you more,
But feel it deep, within your core.
Man has the ability to reach new highs,
To use his soul and then take flight.
He commands the world to obey his needs
Without thinking of consequential deeds.
The angels of light may come your way,
But there are deeds and challenges, which you must pay.
The ancient city that is underground
Was lost for years but now is found.
Have clues for you on the walls to see.
But be careful of faulty personalities.
Mankind's influence equals mankind's fate.
If you leave it too long, it will be too late.
For one day soon, when the Elves depart this time,
The Dwarfs and angels follow, with the lords behind.
When all have gone, what will you do
By yourselves, just struggle through?
Let us hope the seeds will germinate,
And the search for the truth will bring a new fate.
In fifty years, if you are back to plead,
Then I will know you did not succeed.
So do your best to balance the score,
Then I can sleep forevermore.
There is one more thing I say to you.
These are not the caves of Mooloo.
The caves you seek are from here far
And your guide will be a shining star.

We looked at each other, not knowing what to make of the riddle, except that we had to defeat the Evil, but that we knew. The only new thing was the mention of angels and the reference to a shining star. I asked Drew what he made of it.

'They are warnings for mankind,' he said. 'I think she is saying that all the greed of mankind will have to be paid for one day. There is a mention that we Elves, Dwarfs, and the lords may be departing this world someday.'

'But what about the mention of angels?' I asked.

Drew looked at me in a strange way as if he were hiding something. 'Even among Elves, angels are only a superstition,' he said, 'but there have been times when some Elves have sworn to have seen them. And there was the mention of an ancient city, and that these are not the caves of Mooloo. For now, we must get back to Rocco.'

'If you don't believe in angels, you will never see one,' said Carew. 'Only those who believe see them.'

There was silence. Then I said, 'We must be very cautious leaving the chamber as the wild hound may have polished off our offering.'

We opened the door slowly, and to our surprise, the hound was standing on a plinth completely still with his back to us, guarding the door. We stood there wondering how we were to get past the beast.

Ricco said, 'Throw a stone over in that direction and see if he chases it.'

This we did, but he didn't move.

Drew asked Wecco to pass him the torch and he held it out towards the animal, and to our surprise, we found it had turned into a statue. We moved off very slowly back to the tunnel we had come down, hoping he would not come back to life.

As we reached the entrance, we started to walk faster and faster up the tunnel, and just as we arrived at the large cave, my Elvan band started to glow. But this time, I sang out to Drew and asked him to read it. I said it was too hard for me, but I knew what it said.

'Beware ahead, the Evil waits,
So take another exit before it's too late.'

We had to choose which tunnel to take, left or right.

'The left says under the lake,' said Carew, 'and the right through the falls. I think right would be the best choice.'

Thus the right it was, and off we went hurrying along the tunnel. Just in time. The moment we entered the tunnel, a group of Goblins and Menlins entered the main cavern and were lighting torches and beginning to search for us. The tunnel went down and down for ages. When we reached the bottom, we found two more tunnels, one going to the left, and the other to the right. Soltain made a quick decision and off to the right we ran. We could hear the Evil's army getting closer and closer. Then all of a sudden, the tunnel changed direction and began to climb. It became steeper, and every fifty steps or so, there was a carved-out section in the wall—we found out the purpose of them later. The Evil creatures were gaining, and we could now hear their footsteps and knew they were close behind.

Soltain suddenly stopped, looked up, and said, 'There is a message in ancient Dwarf over the carved-out section which says,

'To clear the tunnel, step inside.
Then pull the lever and wait a time.'

'I know what it means,' said Soltain. 'Keep running. When we see the enemy close behind, and we come across the next carved-out section, then we all jump inside. Trust me on this. I know what I'm doing.'

We kept running up and up, and slowly we were running out of breath. Gaining on us and in clear sight were the Menlins and Goblins.

'Now in here,' Soltain screamed. We all jumped in and there was just enough room for us to squeeze in.

'One of you help me with this lever,' Soltain said. Ricco grabbed and pulled on it, but it didn't budge.

'This is when we need Rocco,' Sol said then looked around at Drew and me and yelled, 'You two, quick, help us.'

We grabbed the end of the lever, jumped, and down it came. Then without warning, from way up the cave, we could hear a roaring sound getting louder and louder. Of course, Peto had to stick his head out to look back at the Evil. As he did, he saw the look of fright on their faces as they all turned and ran. He then looked up the tunnel and pulled his head back just in time, as a perfectly round boulder flew past us and continued rolling down the tunnel.

'Now is our chance,' said Sol. And off we went again. We continued and came upon a fork. Which one to take?

'The left, it says through the falls,' said Sol. 'On the right, I don't know, but if we take the left, at least we will end up at the falls.' So off we went again.

We ran for about ten minutes. Then the cave stopped, and there was only a small tunnel, just wide enough for one person to slide down. We all hesitated.

'If Bidlark built it,' said Soltain, 'it will be safe.'

We agreed it was our only hope, although Sol looked a little worried, thinking he might end up in the lake.

'We will go first,' I said, 'and wait for you just in case we do end up in the lake.'

Sol looked at us puffed out his chest and said, 'I will go first', and off he went. We followed, holding on tight to our bows and arrows. One by one, we went sliding down this perfect, smooth tunnel, eventually flying out at the side of the falls, through the curtain of water, and landing in the lake only a few paces from the sandy beach where we first began to climb the falls. Luckily, we were not far from the shore, and the water was not so deep. We helped support Sol as we swam to shore. I thought, *One day I must ask Sol, why is it Dwarfs never learnt to swim?*

'Quick,' said Drew, 'we must get the gear and the raft and be across the lake before sunset.' Sol still looked a little terrified.

'Don't worry,' said Drew. 'You can get on the raft again and we can push it across the lake, but we must be quick.'

Peto arrived back with all the gear, piled it on the raft with Sol, and we set out across the lake. We headed straight for the mist of the falls, just in case the Pernicious were around and the Evil's army would come out of the caves. So far, so good. We got about halfway across when we heard the screech of a Pernicious, but we kept going. Poor Sol was shaking with fear and clinging to the raft for dear life. We could feel the water getting warmer and knew we were close to shore, so we had to take it very slowly. I swam ahead to see if it was safe. It looked fine, so I swam back to get the rest of the company. One by one, we ran up to hide in the forest canopy with our clothes and new weapons. The sun was just about to set, so Drew and I went back, dismantled the raft while our friends dried themselves and we then rejoined them.

30
CHAPTER

The Departure of the Second Company

The lords, Elves, and the wizard continued to discuss the situation for many hours, when an assistant interrupted and whispered into the wizard's ear. The wizard excused himself and left the hall. The rest of the party continued the discussion. A few minutes passed, then the wizard returned with another two guests. The party fell silent and gazed at the two strangers, and before anyone could say a word, the wizard introduced them as Mordlark and Benlib, Dwarfs from the western mountains.

The party stood and bowed. Then El Mazrew said, 'Many ages have passed without word from the Dwarfs, and we never knew what had happened to your people. Now, out of the blue, in a time of dread when the Evil grows strong and his armies advance all over the world, you return, hopefully with good tidings.'

The two Dwarfs bowed their heads, and Mordlark said, 'We of the west have known about the Elvan prophecies for a thousand years. Fifty years ago, we sent two Dwarfs to the forest of Gundi, but they could not find the company of children and Elves, so they returned. But recently, we had news from the white screechers of the east that the company had been sighted, so two other Dwarfs were dispatched to help them. The screechers also explained that the Evil was growing strong. Master Baylib knew our services would be needed. We have been preparing our armies and are ready at your request.'

'Your timing is perfect,' said Lord Arcon, 'as we have just received news that the Evil is gathering on the southern borders with the intention to attack the cities of peace. We know of three cities that already have fallen into the Evil's clutches: Bossak, Blarak, and Howsark. They have played right into the Evil's hands and are making it difficult for the good to succeed in weakening the Evil. We have also heard news that if Basscala does not surrender to the Evil, then an attack is imminent.'

Lord Arcon then asked, 'Could you send word to your armies of our plight? And if they could help us defeat or weaken the Evil, we would be forever in your debt.'

'That can be done by white messengers,' said Mordlark, 'but they will take a few days to arrive. And it would take about five or six weeks for the armies to march from the western mountains.'

The wizard Naroof interrupted and said, 'We have an armada of ships at Hawksfort, at the entrance of the River Hawk. They can travel at great speed and could meet your armies at the beginning of the Great Bay at the south-western edge of the continent in less than a week. Then they could transport them back to Basscala or, if it has fallen, then back here to Kassob. Could you dispatch your messenger immediately, and if it is possible, could your white screechers find out any news of the whereabouts and progress of the company of children and Elves?'

'Your company is doing fine,' replied Mordlark. 'Master Baylib sent two Dwarfs to assist them, and the last we heard, they have arrived at the Falls of Nebbia Circum. Unfortunately, one of the Dwarfs has been captured by the Evil.'

He turned his gaze to the lords and said, 'The other bad news we have from the messengers is the Evil is gathering his forces to march on the city of Basscala as we speak. We will go immediately and send a message to Master Baylib to start the armies on the march to the beginning of the Great Bay to meet the armada.'

The Dwarfs bowed and left the hall, and the party continued their discussion about how to defeat the Evil, now with much more hope.

The wizard Naroof lifted his hand to silence the lords and the Elves then asked, 'Could two of you take charge of the armada and escort the Dwarf army to Basscala?'

Lord Arcon turned to face El Mazrew and said, 'Your skills as a sailor are famous, so we should take charge of the fleet.'

El Mazrew agreed and added, 'Wayrew can stay here a few days and teach the inhabitants how to make and use bows and arrows. Bayrew should sail up the coast and take news to the elder Tarvin of the northern Elves, then return back down the coast, picking up Wayrew. Then he will meet us at the entrance of the river Condoor.'

The Dwarfs returned to the hall. 'The messengers have been sent to Master Baylib,' they said, 'and five dispatched to find the quest seekers.'

'I have changed my mind,' said the wizard. 'Now we have the men of Kassob being shown by the Elves the art of making and using bows. I think my presence with the armada would be beneficial. It is better to stop the Evil at Basscala than wait for them to arrive here.'

The night grew late, and a second company was formed consisting of the wizard Naroof, the lords Revcon, Devcon, and Arcon, the Dwarfs Mordlark and Benlib, and the Elves Bayrew and El Mazrew. They would leave early the next morning and travel together to Hawksfort.

31
CHAPTER

When the Pernicious Hit the Dust

Morning came with the hint of rain, and Naroof's company departed early on their journey to Hawksfort. The eight had a horse each, loaded with plenty of supplies, and headed for the River Hawk.

'The morning brings us luck,' said Naroof. 'With this overcast sky, the Pernicious will be forced to fly low, and we will be aware if they sight us.'

Thankfully the morning passed without incident and the rain held off, and they made good time. By nightfall, they had arrived at the upper reaches of the River Hawk and set up camp.

'Two of us must stay on watch,' said the wizard Naroof. 'We must not slacken for a moment.'

The night passed without an incident, except for something that happened during the watch of El Mazrew and Mordlark. They were sitting staring into the distance when six or seven glowing shapes appeared on the horizon. They moved overhead and seemed to be hovering at a distance, then suddenly disappeared. They mentioned it to the others and concluded they must have been white screechers, although the Dwarfs were not convinced they were messengers.

Morning arrived with the trees by the river covered in a light dew and the sounds of birds welcoming the day. They hoped this was a good omen. There were breaks in the clouds, and the rays of the sun coming over the eastern horizon were hitting the tops of the trees, making the dew sparkle like diamonds. With so much beauty, it was hard to believe there was such Evil in the world.

After a light breakfast, they saddled up and departed. As the day lengthened, the clouds dispersed, and the sun hit the damp ground. The humidity was oppressive. Luckily, the shade of the river gums protected them from the hot sun and kept them out of sight from the Pernicious. But this was not to last.

As they travelled down the river, they came to a section where the meadows extended right down to the river's edge, and there were no trees for at least two kilopaces. By now it was midday, with the sun shining brightly overhead.

'We should not expose ourselves to this danger,' Naroof warned. 'We can either wait till nightfall or enter the river and drift down with the flow.'

They decided on the latter, as they could not risk wasting more time. They entered the water two at a time at intervals of five minutes. Lord Arcon and Devcon went first, Revcon and Mordlark next, then Benlib and El Mazrew, and Wizard Naroof and Bayrew to follow. The first four arrived without incident, drying themselves as they waited on the banks under the gums.

Benlib and El Mazrew were about halfway and drifting slowly, when from the south a loud screech penetrated their journey. Two Pernicious dived down towards them with the talons of their dragon steeds outstretched. The four waiting on the bank looked on, unable to assist their friends, but the wizard Naroof had sensed the Evil and had entered the river and told Bayrew to wait. He was only a hundred paces from them and moving quickly downstream.

El Mazrew and Benlib had moved into the shallows. Benlib had his compact axe in hand while El Mazrew had his bow loaded, ready for the Pernicious as they dived. El Mazrew fired his first shot. The arrow bounced off the wing of the leading dragon. He was trying to reload when the dragons swooped across the water and went straight for them. El Mazrew was knocked to the ground by the first, and the second took hold of Benlib, scooping him up with one talon. But not for long, as Benlib was swinging from side to side while hacking away at the dragon's other leg with his axe every chance he could. The screeches coming from the creatures were bloodcurdling. Within seconds, he was released and fell into the shallows, uninjured except for his pride.

El Mazrew had regained his footing and was reloading when the wizard sang out, 'Aim for under their neck. It is where they are most vulnerable.'

The two Pernicious circled and prepared to dive a second time. They headed straight for them, flying low on the same trajectory across the river, giving El Mazrew no chance of taking aim. The horses had run off, and the two were completely exposed. The creatures were only fifteen paces away, and there was no hope of placing the arrow under their necks.

Then out of the blue, a sudden bright flashing light came from the direction of the wizard and hit the two Pernicious, knocking them off course. They were forced to climb, and this gave El Mazrew his opportunity to fire. The arrow left the bow, entering one of the dragons' necks with such force that the arrowhead was protruding out the other side. The Pernicious screamed with pain as its dragon dived headfirst into the riverbank. The Pernicious jumped off his steed and was about to pull out the arrow when the wizard sang out to El Mazrew to fire again at the same spot. He had already reloaded his bow, aimed it, and fired.

The Pernicious turned and looked at him with such hate and started to move towards him. El Mazrew looked at the Pernicious moving in his direction. Not having the time to reload, he was now vulnerable to attack. As the Pernicious drew closer, it started to stagger and El Mazrew noticed that although he had only shot the dragon, there was also blood flowing from the neck of the Dragon's rider.

The other Pernicious hovering above gave a mighty scream in unison with the dying dragon, and at the same time, the Pernicious fell dead to the ground at El Mazrew's feet just as the wizard arrived. The remaining Pernicious circled overhead then flew off south.

Now that it was over, the two heroes started to shake with fright and sat down as the rest of the company arrived on their horses, dismounted, and ran to their companion's aid. The wizard went straight to the Pernicious to make sure it was dead, and then joined the company.

'You have done a great service for the good, El Mazrew and Benlib,' said Naroof.

'There will be songs written about this deed, and this will go down in the history of man and Dwarf as well as Elf. I already see the chapter: "When the Pernicious Hits the Dust".'

From this experience, we learned that if the Pernicious were killed, then their dragons would die, and vice versa. There were tears in El Mazrew's eyes as he walked over to the dead dragon, patted his head and said,

> *'Fare ye well, to you I command*
> *And on this last journey, I give you my hand*
> *For the agony and pain to take away*
> *And a safe trip for you, I pray.*
> *May the sky be blue and the water warm.*
> *May the rain be gentle without a storm.*
> *May the grass grow thick on the mountainside.*
> *May a warm breeze caress your silver hide.'*

El Masrew's hands moved slowly over the dragon's head as he spoke the final comforting words.

> *'So fare ye well, my noble friend.*
> *Now your pain and agony is at an end.*
> *On a peaceful sleep, drift away*
> *To reawaken on a new day.'*

32
CHAPTER
The Battle of Hawksfort

The wizard's company pulled themselves together and rode on with great speed, for now the Pernicious knew their whereabouts and would return with the Evil armies. They rode on till close to midnight when the salt spray from the ocean saturated the air and they knew they were close to Hawksfort.

Hawksfort had been preparing for days to repel any forces of the Evil. Scouts from the fort had become aware of the eight riders, and word had been sent ahead to open the gates. As the riders turned the last bend, the harbour came into sight, and they saw the sails of the fleet gently waving in the breeze. The lights of the fort shone brightly, and the welcoming embrace of the open gates and soldiers warmed the hearts of the company.

As they entered, the men of Hawksfort watched as this strange company of Dwarfs, Elves, and wizards dismounted their steeds. The captain of the fort greeted the company with much respect. The captain introduced the company and escorted them among the men. The wizard asked how they were and thanked them for their courage; the rest of the company did likewise.

The men of Hawksfort were aware of the advancing armies, and they had felt abandoned. But with the sight of Naroof and this strange company walking among them, their hearts rose and hope was in their thoughts. The wizard explained all that had happened and told them about a great Dwarf army coming from the west.

The men of Hawksfort spoke among themselves of the old tales of great lords, Elves, and Dwarf armies and they began to sing old songs telling of such things.

Naroof then explained that an attack on Hawksfort from the armies of Menlins and Goblins was inevitable. So be prepared, he told them.

'Are the ships in readiness for sailing,' he asked,' as we must leave on the earliest possible tide?'

'They are all shipshape and ready to go,' responded the captain, 'but the tide is against us at the moment. It will turn at six this coming morning. That gives us time to show you to your quarters and get you settled on board.'

'We need the smallest ship of the fleet,' said the wizard, 'to sail up north with the Elf Bayrew to get news to the northern Elves of our plight.'

The captain pointed to the ship anchored at the far end of the fleet. 'That is her, the *Hawkalinna*,' he said, 'small but very yaw.'

The fort's captain introduced the wizard and company to the ship's captains, then ushered them on to the head boat of the armada, the *Silver Sky*.

They made themselves comfortable, and by three o'clock that morning, they were ready to depart.

Suddenly from upriver could be heard a muffled sound of trumpets and drums in the distance. As the night drew on, the sound grew louder, a warning of the approaching armies of evil. The scouts had all returned to the fort, the gates were locked, and the fleet was pulling up anchor. There was still an hour to wait for the tide to be in the second company's favour, and the armies of Evil were approaching fast. The sun was still a way off from rising, although the early morning light was illuminating the clouds in the east.

In the distance, the matching armies with large red banners and three Pernicious hovering overhead could be seen advancing on Hawksfort. With this sight, the hearts of the men of Hawksfort grew dark, so Naroof asked to be rowed ashore and marched among the men, encouraging them as much as he could.

The fortifications of Hawksfort were another ingenious construction, with a high cliff facing the ocean. With the fort facing inland, it was ingenious how they used the fast-running Hawks River as a large moat. There was only one drawbridge crossing the river. In front of the forty-foot wall of stone, there was a large empty paddock that stretched all the way to the banks of the river. At intervals along the wall, turrets were strategically placed.

The company began to worry about the safety of the soldiers and whether they would be trapped with no way of escape if the Evil took the fort.

The captain reassured the company. 'There would be no problem,' he said, 'as there are tunnels all through the mountain that lead to different escape routes. And we have a contingency plan in case of the Evil breaching the fort. There is also a secret cave that leads to a ship prepared for an escape if need be.

'The tunnels were built by Bidlark, the master Dwarf builder,' he added, 'and I had the signs translated from ancient Dwarf so the soldiers are aware of all the booby traps. That will help them escape if need be. So please do not worry, the soldiers will be fine.'

Mordlark and Benlib's chins rose high with pride when Bidlark's name was mentioned. There was still half an hour to go before they could set sail, and they could now see the Evil army's weapons of war: giant catapults and gigantic bows with arrows ten feet long, with large balls of material for lighting. There were red wooden forts on wheels, with extendable ladders protruding from the top, being pulled by strange animals, a cross between an elephant and a dragon, *dragophants*.

There was also a long flat red wooden machine on wheels, also being pushed by the same type of animals. On first glance, the group was not aware of its function, and the enemy were still too far away from the fort to use their artillery.

The tide was about to change, and this would be their only chance. The problem was, they could only leave the harbour one at a time and in single file, which left them vulnerable. Slowly they moved out into the main stream. The wind was coming from the north-west and in their favour. Naroof was on his way back to his ship when the first rock from the Evil's catapults landed about a hundred paces from the last ship. Another rock landed, this time only twenty paces from the small boat returning Naroof to *Silver Sky*. The sailors rowing lifted their pace, and with a bash, the small boat crashed into *Silver Sky* and Naroof scurried up the side.

'I think we will make it out to sea,' said Naroof as he set foot on board, but just as he said that, a lighted arrow came flying overhead and just missed the sail of the second last ship.

'Maybe I've spoken too soon,' he added. The fort, which also had catapults stationed much higher, had started to launch their attack. There were clouds on the eastern horizon, blanketing the sunrise, which made the battle look quite spectacular, what with the flaming arrows coming at the ships, and the flaming balls of fire from the fort landing all around the enemy.

As the company watched the battle take place, they realised the purpose of the long flat wooden machine on wheels. As it approached the river, the contraption extended itself and moved over the water to reach the far side and anchor on the bank. It was hollow inside, about two paces high and twenty-five paces wide so the enemy could run along inside without fear of arrows.

As it landed, it extended and dropped another section at each end that was to be used by the wooden forts as a bridge to traverse the river. As the company watched the contraption ford the river, a flaming arrow passed overhead and landed on the stern of the second ship, spontaneously bursting into flames. Within seconds, her crew had buckets of water dousing the flames and, in minutes, had it under control.

More flaming arrows passed overhead, and one went straight through the sail of the last ship, the *Hawkalinna*, but luckily it did not catch fire and she could still sail. The next flaming arrow hit its mark fair in the centre-deck of the fifth ship and burst into flames spreading up the mast and mainsail with incredible speed, finally engulfing the deck and wheel.

The confusion that ensued created another problem: the ship was out of control and heading straight towards the fleet, specifically towards *Silver Sky*. Most of her crew had jumped overboard and were being picked up by the following ships or swimming ashore. Now their problem was how to manoeuvre out of the way of the burning ship heading straight for the Silver Sky. The first four ships had sailed out to the safety of the open sea. The next two, having had to slow down to pick up survivors, would be out of range within minutes. Only *Hawkalinna* and *Silver Sky* were left to somehow get past the flaming ship heading towards them.

Without warning, the *Hawkalinna* swung out of the line and headed slowly alongside *Silver Sky*. We could see what Bayrew and the captain were endeavouring to do: placing *Hawkalinna* in the course of the burning ship would save *Silver Sky*. The whole crew of *Silver Sky* stood looking towards Hawkalinna, anticipating the disaster to come.

There were only a few paces separating the two ships, and Bayrew was at the wheel, steering a steady course between *Silver Sky* and the burning ship. The other two ships had now reached open water and were safe. Then suddenly, for no apparent reason, the burning ship changed course and passed by the stern off *Silver Sky* and *Hawkalinna* by centapaces and headed straight towards the breakwater.

The crew of both ships sighed with relief then noticed the wizard in some kind of daze and aiming his staff at the burning ship. So it was not luck, but Naroof who forced the burning ship into the breakwater. They slowed down to pick up the last few stragglers from the burning ship as she crashed and exploded on the breakwater and then they headed out to join the rest of the fleet.

33
CHAPTER

The First Company Rejoined

We sat huddled together under a large forest fig, with the Elvan blankets around us for warmth. The canopy of the forest was our cover from the Pernicious, and at times, we could hear their screams above the roar of the falls. We decided to wait a few hours before making a move back down to Rocco and the horses. Eventually, we set off but it ended up a bit of a disaster as there was no moon and we slipped and fell our way down the slope in the dark. We had no choice but to continue. We would look a sorry sight when we arrived as we were covered in bumps and bruises. But we did make reasonable time and knew when we were getting close, as the earthy smell of the horses filled the air.

The night was very dark under the canopy of the rainforest, and it must have been about one o'clock when we finally arrived, to the relief of Rocco. To our surprise, there were plenty of provisions left, and we squeezed into the tent and sat with the Elvan blankets wrapped around us and ate. We relayed our story to Rocco, while he sat in complete silence.

'Where is my bow and arrows then?' he finally asked.

I knew this was going to be a problem as Jarew had taken the last bow even though it was not the right size for him, and we all knew it was for Rocco.

An argument then followed with Rocco saying, 'If nine bows were left for the quest seekers, then one would have to be mine.'

Of course, he was right, but how were we to get it from Jarew without drama?

Soltain then said, 'If all the bows matched up to the height of each of the Chosen, then it should not be a problem.'

We looked at each other with relief as Soltain made this statement, knowing it would get the rest of us of the hook.

Jarew had no intention of letting go of the bow, and he held it tightly in his hands. 'I was there when they were found,' he said, 'so I am keeping it.'

Rocco was about to say something else, but before he had the chance, I handed him my bow. Drew tried to stop me, but I felt it was best for the company. Both Rocco and Jarew blushed with embarrassment, but Rocco still took the bow, though it was way too tall for him.

Carew interjected with one of his pearls of wisdom, 'It is sad that the bow is plucked more than the harp these days.'

When things settled down, we finished eating then continued to rest for a few hours. Drew hadn't said much the whole time and I could sense something was bothering him, so I concentrated and sensed what it was. I moved to his side.

'Don't worry, Drew,' I said. 'With all of us back together, we will have the power to get back to *Princess Elandra* without incident.'

'I know,' Drew said, 'but there is another worry.' And as he was saying it, I sensed what it was: *something terrible was happening at the village of Bassmont.*

I sat with Drew but I sensed he wished to be alone, so I rejoined the others, who had already fallen asleep. I lay down and tried to rest. The company slept very well, as we were so exhausted, except Drew, who was worrying about the next part of our quest. It preyed on me and stopped me from having a good night's sleep as well.

The morning arrived with the threat of rain upon the sky. We packed up and moved off down the western creek.

'The other side of the lake was much easier than this side,' said Peto.

'We had no choice. We had to collect Rocco and the horses.' I added, 'Besides, the Evil would be thinking we would take the easy way and would search there first rather than this way, which is more secluded.' We had turns at riding the horses, and in no time at all, we arrived at the fork, where one track went on to Basslake and the other up to the entrance of the tunnel to Bassmont. Drew had been quiet the whole morning, and I knew what he was thinking.

'You are not going to Bassmont by yourself,' I said. 'I think half of us should go down to the *Princess*, and the rest go on to Bassmont and find out what has happened.'

As Drew was still feeling guilty about picking Tarew in place of Jarew to open the chest, he said, 'Jarew should come to Bassmont with Soltain, Rocco, Peto, and you, Mecco. The others should take the horses and go back to see if all is fine with *Princess Elandra*.'

There were the usual complaints from the company. They were not too pleased about having to take the horses and travel back to the *Princess* as they wanted to come with us, but we convinced them it was best. We bid our Elvan farewells, which were now becoming a habit, and departed our different ways.

We arrived back at the entrance of the tunnel, and Soltain recited the ancient Dwarf riddle. The door slowly opened, and off we went along the tunnel. We passed the intersection where the two tunnels had been bricked up. We continued until we reached the secret door where Longstep had shown us through only a week ago. We listened intently for any sound at all but we could not hear a thing, so Drew opened the door very slowly and peered out. Within seconds of the door being opened, the smell of smoke entered the tunnel. One by one, we walked out to the deserted hall that was half-burnt down and still smouldering.

We walked over to one of the windows and looked down upon the village, or what was left of it. We found out later that the Evil had taken two villages as hostages. One of them had succumbed to the torture and told them about us arriving and leaving through a hidden passage.

Longstep would not tell them where the secret door was, so they killed him by hanging him over one of the terraces, then burnt the village down, scattering all the inhabitants. The deep guilt that Drew carried from then on was a heavy burden for him. In my way, I tried to relieve some of it by projecting happy thoughts to him, but by doing this, I received some of his guilt.

We stood for ages looking over the half-destroyed village, when we noticed that there were still evil forces sifting through the burnt ruins. We ducked down, but it was too late. We had been spotted. We ran back to the door, but by now they had seen where it was, and even closed, they would break it down eventually and get in. We ran off down the tunnel, arriving at the bricked-up intersection.

'I have my axe with me,' said Soltain. 'I could break a small hole for us to enter, and we could lead them along the tunnel, get them lost, then return and escape. But if we continue running along this one, they will eventually catch up with us, and that will lead them to *Princess Elandra*. As Bidlark built them, there are sure to be some booby traps along the way that could help us.'

So Soltain bashed away with the back of his axe and made a small hole for us to get through, but not large enough for the Menlins to enter. They would have to spend more time making a larger hole. Although the Goblins would be able to enter straight away, we knew they wouldn't follow us without the Menlins. We climbed in with only two torches.

The caves were full of cobwebs and smelt damp, as if they had been filled with water. They didn't feel like a nice place to be.

'This cave will suit the Goblins no end,' said Drew. 'It is like one of their homes.'

I was apprehensive taking this route as the sign in old Dwarf said, *'Deeper.'*

Soltain reassured us that there would be other signs along the way to guide us and added, 'There must be another exit somewhere.'

So off we went trudging along this foul tunnel, which after years of neglect and closure looked nothing like a Dwarf tunnel. We walked quickly for approximately fifteen minutes, before arriving at our first intersection.

Here there were six tunnels. Soltain held up the torch to read the signs. Three said *'Deeper'*, one said *'Up'*, and two said *'Cliff face.'*

Soltain announced, 'I have a plan. Drew and Mecco, take one of the torches and run up one of the tunnels for about five minutes or until you come to another intersection then return. Jarew and Rocco, take the other torch and do the same thing in one of the other tunnels. When the enemy arrives here, they will sniff around and will be confused and not know which tunnel to take. If what they say about Goblins and Merlins is true, then they will argue for ages. I don't need a torch, but I will do the same in one of the other tunnels. We will meet back here in ten minutes and take one of the tunnels to the cliff face. Now go.'

We did as we were told and arrived back as arranged. Jarew and Rocco arrived back at the same time, and we waited for about three minutes then started to worry about Soltain. Another minute passed.

'I will go up the tunnel to look for him,' I said. 'The rest of you take the tunnel on the left to the cliff face, and we will catch up.'

'You are not going alone,' Drew said. 'I will come with you, and the rest of you wait here for five minutes, then take the left tunnel to the cliff face. If you hear the Evil approaching, just go, and we will catch up somehow.'

They were not too happy and argued to the contrary but did as we asked. Drew and I took one of the torches and started to run up the tunnel Soltain had taken.

Poor Soltain! What had happened to him was that he was walking along in the dark when the tunnel suddenly started to decline. He kept on walking but the decline grew steeper to a point that he started to slip. He fell on his behind and slipped all the way to the bottom of the trap, landing with a crunching sound that he could not make out.

We began calling his name, and after a few minutes, just as we approached the corner where the tunnel began to decline, he responded. He told us to be very careful, that it was one of Bidlark's traps and that the floor gets so steep that one slips right to the bottom.

As we turned the corner and as the light from our torch hit him, there he was, lying at the end of the decline against a wall, and among a pile of old skeletons. We laugh about it now, but at the time it was not so funny. We could not go any further as we would end up sliding into the trap. We noticed that every few paces on the left side of the tunnel, there were bricks protruding from the wall. And two paces above them were handgrips to hold onto. We realised these were for walking along to avoid the trap. Luckily, Drew had his Elvan rope, and we threw it to Soltain. It was not quite long enough, so Soltain had to rearrange the old bones to make a sort of ladder so he could reach the rope.

Within a few minutes, we had him out and were running back to the intersection, arriving just in time to enter the left tunnel to the cliff face as we heard the Evil forces arriving. The others had left only minutes before. We finally caught up with them just as their torch was going out.

Now we only had one torch, so Soltain went ahead with it to light the way. Then he hesitated and said, 'The floor is starting to decline. We must be careful turning this corner.'

Sure enough, it was another of Bidlark's traps, but this time we were prepared for it. One by one we walked along the bricks protruding from the wall while holding on to the handgrips. It was rather scary—one slip and down we could go! Rocco, being the last, was finding it very difficult, what with his weight and being unfit. He was only two bricks away from safety when he slipped. As he fell, he grabbed the last brick and was screaming out for help just as the Evil's forces turned the corner.

Drew tied a noose from the Elvan rope and threw it to him. 'Now grab it,' said Drew, 'and put it over your shoulders.'

Rocco screamed, 'I can't do it. If I let go, I will fall.'

'You have no choice,' said Drew, 'If you don't, the Menlins and Goblins will get you, so hang on with one hand and do it.'

So Rocco let go with his left hand and slipped the rope over his shoulder just as his right hand slipped and he went crashing into the wall. Luckily, we all had hold of the rope, although he very nearly dragged us all in with him. Eventually, we pulled with all our might and slowly hauled him to safety.

Soltain glanced up and announced, 'Look, there is a message in old Dwarf saying if we remove the last brick, then water will flow.' He hit it with the back of his axe to loosen it, and as it came free, a gush of water came flowing out behind it. Then about five paces further up the tunnel, we heard another pop, then another, and bricks started to pop out of the wall, with gushes of water escaping from the gaping holes where the bricks had been.

We had to move fast, or we would have been washed into the trap too. We got past just in time, as it became a raging torrent. As the forces of Evil flew round the last corner and onto the decline, the leaders tried to stop but the ones following were not aware of what was ahead and pushed them into the trap.

Off we went again, sopping wet, running along with Soltain carefully leading the way. Now the tunnel became a steep incline, and as we ran, we could hear the sound of the enemy screaming as they flew into the watery trap. We continued for another ten minutes and passed another Bidlark trap hanging from the ceiling, consisting of rows and rows of razor-sharp stakes protruding only an inch from the ceiling.

Soltain said, 'There will be a lever somewhere to set it off but we can't look for it now.'

We ran for another ten minutes, arriving at a small opening that led us out to a cliff face. As we emerged onto a narrow ledge, we realised we were at Basslake and there diagonally across to the left, sitting calmly under a large clump of trees was *Princess Elandra*. But how were we to reach her from this height?

34
CHAPTER

The Return Trip Down the Condoor

We looked for ways to climb down the cliff face, but there was no ladder or steps and where we stood was at least a hundred paces from the water. Jarew searched along the narrow ledge and eventually found a small waterfall with a slide cut into the rock face that zigzagged half the way down then spilled into the lake. Now we knew how we could get down, although it was still about forty paces' drop to the water. And there was still the problem of Soltain and his inability to swim.

We stripped off to our shorts and tied all our gear together wrapped in an Elvan blanket so it would float and sent it down ahead of us. Drew and Jarew went first, laughing all the way.

'See, it's not that hard,' I said to Soltain. It was a smart move of Drew's to pick Jarew to come to Bassmont as I think sliding down that water slide was the first time I heard him laugh.

Drew waved back to us. 'It's easy. Come on!' he screamed.

We convinced Soltain that it would be fine, and Peto and I would be on either side of him. The three of us linked arms and sat on the edge of the slide. We shouldn't have laughed, but the look on his face was too much. And off we went, Soltain with a look of dread, and us trying not to laugh. We landed with a gigantic splash, and straight away, Soltain began to struggle. Then to make matters worse, Rocco came flying through the air and landed right on top of us. Poor Soltain didn't know what hit him.

By this stage, *Princess Elandra* had become aware of us and sailed over to where we were floundering in the water. Peto and I were having a hard time convincing Soltain to relax. We tried explaining to him that if he stayed calm, we could support him. Boy, were we pleased when the *Princess* arrived and Wecco and Ricco jumped in and helped us with Soltain as we thought we were going to drown.

The horses were all on board, and as soon as we placed our feet on the deck, the *Princess* knew exactly what to do: she headed straight for the river Condoor. It was the safest we had felt for days. Jula and Wecco prepared a meal for us, as the smell of food hit our senses and we realised how hungry we were. Halfway through eating, I could sense Drew's thoughts pulling him down. I then realised that somehow, we all were sensing them as the whole company had long faces. Then suddenly we seemed to cheer up and I could sense the power of *Princess Elandra*. Being aware of Drew's guilt, she projected how glad she was to have the company all together again, and this seemed to relieve the tension a little.

By now, it was late afternoon, and we knew that if we could avoid the Evil till sunset, we would be able to travel all night and perhaps be back safely at Basscala by tomorrow afternoon. We stood leaning on the rails, watching the sunset.

Then out of the blue, a white messenger glided in and collapsed on the deck of *Elandra*. It looked as if she was on her last legs. She had feathers missing and peck marks all over her body. Soltain moved to pick her up and laid her gently on an Elvan blanket. She looked up and spoke to the Dwarf. Sadly, they were her last words. Soltain stroked her and spoke soothing words that we could not understand, but we felt their comforting effect. She lay there with her head in Soltain's palm as her eyes slowly closed and the last ounce of life left her body. The Dwarf gently wrapped her body in a piece of Elvan blanket while reciting a Dwarf eulogy, then placed her carefully on the moving current of the river and bid a last farewell which went like this:

'The crest of yellow upon your sole
Will lead you to your final goal.
Your feathered wings on your final night
Will carry you on your very last flight.
So do not fear this trip you're on,
For part of the New World you will become.'

We stood there watching as the white messenger drifted off slowly down past the bow of *Princess Elandra*. The four Elves then stood up and placed their open right palm over their left chest and slapped the back of their hand with their left palm bowing as they opened their arms, and Drew said,

'May you travel east on this gentle stream.
As if it were naught but a wondrous dream.'

It never ceases to amaze me how much influence the manners of the Elves have had on this world. If they leave, as the Oracle predicts, what will become of man? A few minutes passed, and Soltain turned to us. 'The news from the messenger is not good,' he said. 'She said the port of Hawksfort has been destroyed and the Evil is mustering his forces to march on the city of Basscala. The lords have sent a message to Baylib for the Dwarf army to help. She also mentioned something about an armada of ships that had travelled to meet the army and was transporting them up the river Condoor as we speak. She also added that Dolark has been transferred from Malfarcus to the city of Howsak. It was the crows of Malfarcus who attacked the messenger.'

Our cooks had prepared another great meal, but after the news, we were not that hungry, except Rocco. We rested while *Princess Elandra* travelled all night and into the first few hours of morning. She then manoeuvred herself into a small creek covered by large trees and moored there. Did she sense something evil up ahead?

35
CHAPTER
The Trip to Lake Eople

By seven in the morning, they were beyond range of the flaming arrows. *Hawkalinna* had turned left and headed north while the rest of the armada travelled south. The wind was still in the company's favour, and they were making good progress. The crews of the ships were hanging over the railings of the starboard side, watching and feeling helpless as the attack continued on Hawksfort. The clouds that had covered the eastern horizon were moving across to the west, and a storm was in the air. But to the south, the weather still looked fair. Hopefully they could stay in front of the storm, though Bayrew in *Hawkalinna* was heading right into it. Let's hope he doesn't get seasick.

Once the rain started, it pounded the enemy for two days, making life difficult for them, but when it stopped, they continued their attack. The battle of Hawksfort raged for another eight days. On the last, the enemy had manoeuvred their mobile wooden castles contraption with ladders across their drawbridge and had mounted an assault.

The contingency plan was put into effect. Two thirds of the castle's company had retreated to the ship in the secret cave and put out to sea. The last third had taken horses and escaped along the Dwarf tunnels that led to a beach twenty kilopaces long on the northern side of Hawksfort. There they would be safe from the Evil's forces, as the first fifteen kilopaces of the beach had sheer cliffs that the Evil could not descend. By the time the Evil had breached the fort, it was deserted except for Bidlark's booby traps that were set, waiting for unsuspecting victims of which there were many.

The escape ship travelled north then sailed up the River Kuta to the triple lakes of Bulla. There, they rejoined the rest of the soldiers, who had escaped on horseback along the beach and travelled overland to Kassob, bringing with them the bad news of the fall of Hawksfort. For the Elf Bayrew, it was a difficult trip as the storm raged for two days. When the weather finally cleared, he realised he was a day behind schedule.

The captain and Bayrew took turns at the wheel and arrived at the entrance of the River Bacca, only six hours behind their estimated time of arrival. They sailed upriver till they came to the lake of the northern Elves, Lake Eople, where they received a splendid welcome. The news of the advance of the Evil and the need of help from the Elvan archers was relayed to the elder Tarvin. Within minutes, the call had travelled through the forest, and the Elves were all gathering under their sacred tree to hear the news and prepare for the march to support the city of Basscala. I was told the speech given by Tarvin was one of the most inspiring in the history of Elves, and I wish someone had written it down.

While this was going on, Bayrew was wondering how he was to pick up Wayrew now that Hawksfort was controlled by the Evil. After Tarvin's speech, the Elves cheered and went off to their respective parts of the forest to prepare for the march to Kassob. Bayrew approached Tarvin and explained his predicament.

'That is easy,' said Tarvin. 'We have a message from Wayrew saying he is safe in Kassob. I have sent a messenger to let him know that you are here and he can return immediately. He should be here within two days. You can then sail back down the coast and rejoin the rest of your company at the river Condoor.'

36

CHAPTER

The Trip Back to Lake Condoor

The wind had swung around to the north-east and was still in favour of the fleet. The armada's cruise down the coast went smoothly. By the morning of the third day, they had passed the entrance to the river Condoor. If they continued at this pace, they would be at the Great Bay well ahead of schedule.

It only took the fleet six days, and they arrived well ahead of the Dwarf army. The fleet lay anchored in a quiet bay surrounded by large cliffs of sandstone, well out of the wind and weather.

'We should be safe here,' said the wizard, 'as the environment on this part of the continent is not congenial to Goblins. But to be on the safe side, I will send out scouts to make sure, and to find out how many days' march the Dwarf armies are from us.'

Little did the second company know that the Dwarf army was only a half day's march away, and at the head was Master Baylib himself, their supreme commander. It is rather unusual for a master of the Dwarfs to lead his armies, but this was an exceptional course.

The scouts returned with the good news that the Evil troops were nowhere to be sighted and that the Dwarfs would be arriving later that afternoon. The captains prepared their ships for their arrival and arranged a feast so the armies could eat and settle in, before the fleet left on the late evening tide.

The army arrived and were evenly dispersed on board each of the eight ships, offered food, and told to rest. The army was much larger than expected, and a third had to sleep on deck under Elvan tents. Mordlark and Benlib left to meet and escort Master Baylib to *Silver Sky*, where the wizard and the rest of the company were waiting to greet him. As Baylib set foot on the deck of *Silver Sky*, the wizard, lords, and Elves bowed low, and El Mazrew welcomed him with an appropriate Elvan welcoming that went,

'We welcome you aboard this boat.
You and your company bring us hope.
We hope to repay to you sometime,
When the Evil is gone and there is no more crime.
Until that time, may you rest in peace,
Eat well, sleep well, and rest your feet.'

Master Baylib turned to the company and said, 'The ancient books of Dwarf history tell of the etiquette and manners of the Elves, and I see they did not lie. It is good to see that some things don't change. Now, who is going to bring me up to date with the affairs in the east?'

The wizard offered his hand and led him down to the main cabin, and the rest of the company followed. Food was brought in, and they sat to eat, bringing Master Baylib up to date while planning what to do next.

'I have had some news from the white screechers, my messengers,' said Master Baylib, 'and only yesterday sent six more to try and find the company of children, Elves, and Dwarfs for an update of their state of affairs. The white messengers have relayed to us the news that the Evil has retreated from Hawksfort and are marching back to meet up with their armies coming from the south. They are setting their sights on Basscala.'

'Would it be possible, 'asked the wizard, 'for you to get a message to Kassob and the northern Elves tomorrow? I would like you to inform them to send the Elvan archers and all the able-bodied men to march to the northern hills overlooking the valley of Basscala. It must not fall to the Evil. If the Elves and the men of Kassob come from the north and we and the Dwarf armies come from the east, we may be able to cut them off.'

The meeting continued till close to midnight, when the bells were sounded to bring up the anchor and the fleet to set sail. The company went on deck to a clear starlit night to watch the proceedings. The breeze had swung around to the west and had lost a lot of its power, but at least there was a breeze. Once the fleet had left the port and had turned north to travel up the coast, the company retired to

MALCOLM POOLE

their allotted cabins to rest. Because of the lack of space, each cabin was full, and the decks were also covered in sleeping Dwarfs.

The company woke to the smell of vegetables, fish, and herbs frying and met in the main galley for a hearty breakfast. Some of the sailors had stayed up all night trailing lines to catch fish. The breeze had picked up, and they were now making good progress. The company continued discussing their plan of attack.

It was to go something like this: They planned to arrive at the river Condoor late in the afternoon and sail all night, hopefully under cover of darkness, and finally anchor in Lake Condoor, where they would be able to find a hiding place for the ships and drop of the Dwarf army. There would be one problem: a full moon was forecast the very night they were to arrive at the river Condoor. They spent the rest of the trip hoping the weather would be overcast.

Back at Lake Bulla, two white screechers had delivered the message from Naroof to the High Elf Tarvin. Within hours, the Elvan archers were beginning to prepare to depart on their march to help defend the city of Basscala. Tarvin had sent a messenger ahead to Kassob to inform Wayrew that there had been a change of plan. He was to report back to Lake Bulla at the earliest possible time. This he did and was back at the lake before the archers departed on their march. As he entered the secret meeting place, he saw Bayrew standing by the side of Tarvin, waiting impatiently for him to arrive. He walked up to them and bowed respectfully.

'Well, are you ready to go, Bayrew?' asked Wayrew.

'We were only waiting for you,' Bayrew replied, 'and now you are here, we can set sail.'

They bade farewell to Tarvin and the Elvan archers while wishing them success. Then the *Hawkalinna* set sail across Lake Bulla and down the River Kuta back to the ocean, then continued down the coast to the river Condoor. The trip was very pleasant compared to the sail up the coast. In fact, they arrived two days before the fleet and were hiding under a large forest fig tree on the far side of Swan Lake, waiting for the arrival of their friends.

144

37
CHAPTER

Up the Condoor

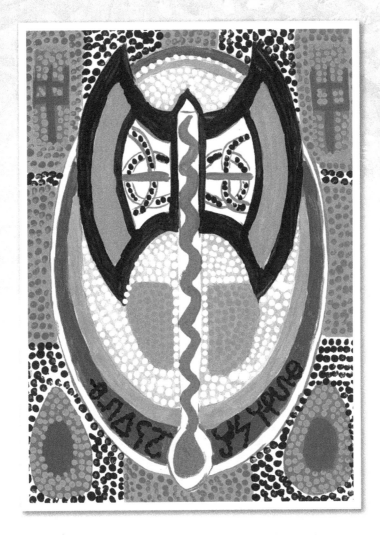

For the fleet, the trip up the coast went like clockwork, and they arrived at seven on the evening of their fourth night at sea. The sun was well set and the full moon had not yet risen, so the fleet headed straight into the entrance of the river Condoor. They made their way slowly up the river, arriving at Swan Lake at nine thirty, just as the moon was showing herself over the north-eastern sky. As the moonbeams hit the south-western shore, they could see the outline of the *Hawkalinna* anchored by the upper mouth of the river Condoor.

The fleet sailed towards her, and on arrival, they anchored one after the other in a line with *Silver Sky* next to *Hawkalinna*. Bayrew and Wayrew transferred aboard *Silver Sky* even before the anchor was dropped, and the second company was reunited again. They were welcomed aboard with great respect, enthusiasm, and lots of bowing.

After all the pleasantries, they were filled in on all that had happened and introduced to Master Baylib. The wizard then sent eight men out to round up or buy at least eighteen horses to tow the ships up the river, in case the winds were not in their favour. They sat around, discussing their plan of attack as the fleet set sail up the river Condoor. Their plan was to travel as far as possible up the river to Lake Condoor before letting off the Dwarf army to continue on foot to the city of Basscala.

The night passed with only one incident. At four in the morning, about an hour from the entrance of Lake Condoor, a lookout called the alarm that there were five or six flying Pernicious hovering above. When they got on deck, they were nowhere to be seen. The lookout swore he saw them fly directly across the face of the full moon, although he did say there was a strange glow about them. There was no reason to disbelieve him, so the army and crew of the ships were put on alert.

The morning was very cold and the river was now covered in a faint mist, and hopefully that would be in their favour and hide them from the Pernicious and any other Evil scouts. It was an uneventful day; in fact, it was pleasant sailing up the river. The breeze was still quite strong and thankfully in their favour, and they entered Lake Condoor just as the night was falling. This was to have been the most difficult part, as the fleet would be fully exposed as they sailed across the lake. But luck was in their favour, as clouds had gathered high in the eastern sky and would hide the moon. The wizard made the decision to forge ahead and head straight across to the upper Condoor.

The breeze had grown stronger, and surprisingly, they sailed across the lake without any mishap or even a sighting of the Evil and arrived at the upper reaches by first light. One by one, the fleet entered the river, and with the help of the strong breeze, they made good time. They continued travelling as far as possible, but as the river grew narrower, they had no choice but to use the horses they had acquired earlier. Although there were only two horses per ship, their help was invaluable. The plan was to disembark the troops as far up the river as possible to conserve their energy for the battle ahead.

It was mid-morning, and the weather continued turning colder. From the railing of the ships, one could see the breath of the horses as they dragged the fleet upstream. Winter was on its way, and the further they travelled, the colder it became. The wizard and the company were on deck, looking at the weather and hoping the wind would not turn and come from the mountains of snow. This would make things difficult, as we found out the Dwarfs had a real problem with the cold. The wizard had sent out scouting parties to investigate further up the river, and all but one had returned. The three that had returned had news that all was clear, at least for the next ten kilopaces. By midday, the last scouting party had returned with news of an encounter with Evil's forces. And it was bad news as two of their companions were killed in the skirmish.

They reported to the wizard, and the leader said, 'We had travelled about fifteen kilopaces upstream and had stumbled on an evil party of Menlins and Goblins, six of each, and a fight occurred. We were outnumbered and had no way of defeating the Evil forces. We lost two men in the process. But we put up a good fight, and in the end, they ran off. We followed them for a few kilopaces, eventually losing them, and then returned here.'

'They would have reported back to their leaders our whereabouts by now, so we must make haste,' the wizard said in a worried state.

Just as he finished talking, six white messengers glided in and landed on the railing and screeched. Master Baylib, Benlib, and Mordlark came running on deck and approached the messengers. A few minutes passed, then two of the birds stretched their wings and launched themselves from the railings, flying in unison back down the river.

Master Baylib turned to the rest of the company, who had now gathered on deck. 'Bad news,' he said. 'The Evil army has made camp on the hills to the south-west of Basscala, but at least they have not attacked yet. One white messenger had perused the city and said it is well fortified, and could withstand many an onslaught from the enemy for months. I have also sent two messengers to see what progress the Six and their company are making.'

'Can the white screechers get a message to Basscala?' the wizard asked. Baylib nodded in the affirmative then asked, 'What is the message?'

'I estimate if we travel today and tonight', said the wizard, 'and march the rest of the way tomorrow, we should be at Basscala tomorrow evening or thereabouts. The fleet can also travel up as far as it can without endangering itself in case it is needed for support. If your messengers could inform the city of Basscala along with the Elvan archers and the men of Kassob that we will be arriving late tomorrow or first thing the following morning. We will attack the enemy on their south-eastern flank. If they could attack the enemy from the north-eastern flank, it will take pressure off Basscala, who then can attack the enemy from the east.'

'It would be difficult,' said Baylib, 'as these messengers only speak Dwarf, but we could fasten a message to their legs and they can deliver it.'

'Will it be safe?' the wizard asked anxiously.

'If they travel back along the river, then inland they will be fine,' answered Baylib. 'It may take a little longer, but they will arrive well before tomorrow night.'

'Good,' said the wizard. 'Then please send it.'

Baylib spoke to the birds as the wizard wrote out two messages. He handed them to Baylib, who attached it to the birds' legs as he scratched under their necks. The four birds gave a squawk and then flew off back down the river.

The wizard still looked a little worried, so Baylib added, 'Do not fret if the white messengers get captured. They know to eat the message.'

38
CHAPTER

Leaving the Princess Again

The morning arrived with a mist covering the river, a prelude to the arrival of winter, and we were hoping this would be in our favour. But *Princess Elandra* would still not move. We were no more than a day from Basscala, but we had to trust her—she had not let us down so far. One by one, we awoke, and we sat huddled in the cabin with Elvan blankets wrapped around us. Then out of the blue, Tarew stood up straight. His blanket dropped to the floor and he said,

'Avoid the city, and travel high,
To where the white hats touch the sky.

On the road towards the mountain blue,
There is a message waiting for you.'

He sat down and looked at us, then said, 'It happened again, didn't it?'

We nodded in the affirmative as he pulled his blanket off the floor and wrapped it around his shoulders, and then opened the parchment and read the message again. This happened often to Tarew whenever the parchments needed to get an urgent message to us. We sat discussing the gist of the message while Wecco began cooking breakfast.

'Why are you doing that without me?' demanded Jula.

'No reason,' he answered.

'Well, don't start without me next time,' she said with an air of authority. Although they were fond of each other, at times there was a power struggle going on between them.

We laughed and Rocco said, 'Well, I don't care who cooks but hurry up.'

As we ate, we discussed the message and came to the conclusion that the white hats were the snow-capped peaks that rise on the far side of the Mountains Blue. Drew laid out the old map and we searched for any mention of more caves.

'Should we not first go to Basscala?' I asked.

'If the parchment says to avoid it,' said Carew, 'then we should.'

Drew then unfolded the second map, and we studied both. 'There is no mention of caves on either map,' said Drew, 'but there is a reference to an underground city that disappeared thousands of years ago. It was supposedly inhabited by an ancient race, but there is very little knowledge of where they went or whatever happened to them. There is also a mention of a door halfway up Mount Gatta. I shall read to you what it says on the map:

'Take the door of silver and gold,
And it will keep you from the cold
Through the mountains blue it winds,
And to your destiny in half the time.'

'With winter coming on,' Drew added, 'I doubt we shall make it before the heavy snows arrive.' He then continued studying the map for ages while we finished eating.

'All the roads over the mountains eventually join up', said Drew, 'and pass within a few kilopaces of Malfarcus. There is an alternative. There is a creek that is only a kilometre or so downstream from here, which branches off the Condoor and climbs up the mountain, crisscrossing a few roads. It then joins a road that travels south to the pass of Malfarcus.'

At the mention off Malfarcus, we all stared at Drew, knowing this was the stronghold of the Evil. Drew reassured us that the old map said the pass was kilopaces from the Evil's fort, and to get to it, we would pass close by the city of Howsak, where Dolark had been taken. He showed us on the map and the Dwarf Soltain took great notice of where this was.

'Would it not be easier to rescue Dolark', Soltain asked, 'now he is away from Malfarcus?'

'Let's wait', said Drew, 'and see what eventuates.'

'I bet if it was an Elf or one of the six, you would be devising a plan by now,' Soltain said sarcastically.

'Soltain, my friend,' said Drew reassuringly, 'as we speak, I'm mulling over a plan, so please be patient.'

Jula broke the silence that followed by wishing to know more about the ancient race who dwelt in the underground city. Carew offered to tell us all the Elves knew at a later date.

'We're all in this predicament because of the greed of man,' Soltain announced annoyingly while staring at the Six.

'Well,' said Peto, 'listening to the history of the Dwarfs, it sounds like you were a greedy lot once, destroying mountains and countryside for a few trinkets.'

Drew took the floor and said, 'Man has missed the point, and placed all his trust solely on the laws he himself implemented. What he should have been striving to search for was his inner conscience. Your conscience when asked a question will always answer what is best for you, without any thought of how it would affect others.'

'What do you mean?' asked Jula.

'We all have another us,' he continued. 'I think you call it the subconscious. Man has pushed it down and will not acknowledge it. That is why Man has become base and greedy. But you must learn to use your inner ears and listen to your subconscious, as it knows intrinsically right from wrong. And if you ask truthfully, "Is this really good for me?" your subconscious will take everything into account: how it will affect the people, the town and environment and answer you truthfully, although at times it may seem contrary to what your conscience demands.'

At this, some of us nodded in the affirmative while others were not sure they comprehended what he said.

'Man is not aware that his subconscious is immortal and connected to the whole and, when asked a question, will answer for the whole. Your conscience will disagree often with it, because it has been brainwashed by greed, a thirst for power, and your creed. But when you learn to hear with your inner ear, though at times it may sound alien, it is your connection to the Supreme.'

His last words on the subject were that the division created by the creeds had done more to hide the Supreme from man than all the blasphemy ever spoken.

While we spent this time listening and arguing, *Princess Elandra* had begun moving slowly and finally coasted into the creek that Drew had shown us on the map. She travelled up as far as she could go, stopping with a thump before we finally realised what had happened. She had anchored next to a large rock ledge that protruded out into the creek at exactly the height of *Princess Elandra*.

'The decision has been made for us,' said Drew. 'We must prepare to depart first thing tomorrow morning.'

39
CHAPTER

A Most Pleasant Dream

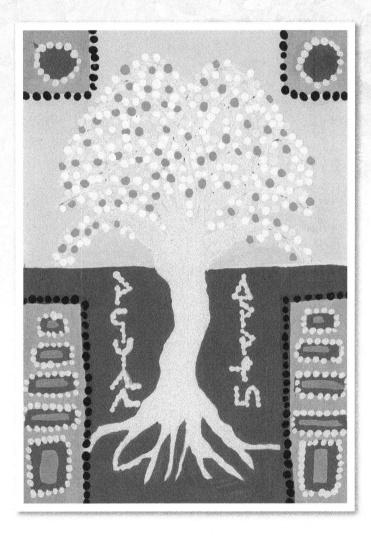

We woke to another misty morning without a breath of wind. The mist hovered low over the creek as the birds began their morning ritual of song. We ate our breakfast silently, watching the wild animals making their way down to the creek for their morning drink. As the sun rose higher in the sky, we packed our provisions and stepped on to the rock ledge.

'Let the horses go to graze,' said Drew. 'If *Princess Elandra* decides to leave, the horses will follow her.'

We did as Drew suggested, then bid *Princess Elandra* farewell.

Drew knew what I was thinking and turned to me. 'Don't worry,' he said. '*Princess Elandra* will be fine. She will sense whether she should stay here or travel back downstream. Remember, she is a magic Elvan ship.'

I felt I should bid the *Princess* farewell again as I was worried about leaving her alone, but as I did, a sense of calm came over me. I realised it was her letting me know she would be fine. I threw my pack over my back, and the eleven of us trudged off, loaded to the hilt with supplies.

We had only travelled for five or ten minutes when Rocco started complaining, 'Is it far? How long will it take? When are we stopping for lunch?'

Finally, Soltain had had enough, turned, and said, 'Please, will you stop with the whining?'

Rocco, for the rest of the day, never said a word and sulked at the back of the group. This never really worried us.

The first few hours of the day were easy going as the track was mostly level and pleasantly peaceful without Rocco's complaining. But as the day drew on, the path along the creek started to rise, and this slowed us down. It was now late afternoon and the air was getting cold, so we stopped to eat and make camp. This finally cheered Rocco up, although sometimes I thought it was better when he was sulking.

Drew and I took the first watch. We sat next to each other and talked quietly so as not to disturb the others. I could sense his worries and his guilt about Bassmont, and I was wondering whether he could sense my thoughts.

He looked at me and smiled. 'Don't worry,' he said. 'Your secret is safe with me.'

What did he mean? Was he aware of that strange experience between Waiden and me, or could Drew also sense that I cared for him deeply? Now I was becoming more paranoid, but he put his arm around my shoulder, not saying a word, and just held me. We had been sitting silently there for what seemed like hours when high above, I saw specks of light fly across the night sky.

'Did you see that?' I asked Drew.

'What?' he replied.

'I just saw seven lights flying across the sky.'

'Maybe shooting stars,' he said.

I sensed he was hiding something from me, but I did not let on and said nothing. Peto and Rocco came out to relieve us. Drew went straight into the tent. I sat with Peto and Rocco for a few moments and talked, waiting for Drew to fall asleep before I entered the tent. When I entered, he was fast asleep, but his blanket had fallen off so I picked it up, covered him, and tucked in the sides, then lay down next to him and went to sleep.

We woke to the smell of diced vegetables and mushrooms frying in butter. What a treat on a cold morning! Wecco and Jula had risen early and found some wild mushrooms and herbs and used some of the vegetables we had in our provisions. After such a hearty breakfast, packing up and setting on our way seemed easy. We travelled for five hours before stopping for a rest and lunch. We then walked another hour and came to where the creek crossed a well-maintained road.

'Why can't we take the road?' I asked Drew.

'West would take us straight to Malfarcus,' he said, 'and if you're asking me, I think there would be too many Evil Goblins and Menlins travelling up and down that road.'

There was no more argument from us when he mentioned Goblins and Menlins. So we kept to the creek.

'What is in the other direction?' asked Soltain.

Drew hesitated. 'Howsak,' he said eventually, then added, 'I'm thinking about a plan to rescue Dolark, but for now, I think we should continue.'

So on we went, although I could sense Drew's dilemma about how to rescue Dolark. We continued till the last rays of the sun set behind the mountain to our west. We then stopped and made camp, ate, then rested.

Drew and I went on first watch again. I was a little uncomfortable, knowing Drew could sense my thoughts, so I focused on other matters.

Drew then turned to me, held my shoulders with both his hands, looked right into my eyes, and said, 'Do not be troubled, Mecco. I love you too, although I can't take it as far as you would wish, for I would lose all my powers.'

He was still looking into my eyes. I knew how he felt for me, and it was deep. I sat there for a few moments, pondering what he had just said. He was still looking at me, and I turned with embarrassment and stared into the forest.

A few more moments passed. *Did I just imagine that*?

We never said another word till we were relieved from our watch, and then it was just goodnight. I felt uncomfortable, and when I went back into the tent and saw there was a space between Rocco and Peto, I lay down there. Drew had to lie down at the far end of the tent by himself. I lay awake for ages, pondering over what had just happened. Did I just imagine what he said as it was what I would have liked him to say? And if he did say that, what did he mean by losing all his powers, and how come I now had all these powers?

Tomorrow, I would find a discreet way to ask him if it did happen. I lay there for ages and could not sleep, so I walked out into the fresh air. Fresh? It was more like freezing. Winter was definitely on its way.

Ricco and Carew were on watch and were sitting with their backs against a large tree. I walked and sat down out of sight of them. With the Elvan blanket around my shoulders, I sat there thinking about all that had happened to me this last year when I suddenly saw, directly in front of me, three softly glowing shapes standing together no more than fifty paces away. Strangely, I was not scared. I looked at them and waved. I don't know why I did that. Then they waved back at me. As quick as they materialised, they disappeared.

Next thing I knew, I was sitting by a beautiful crystal-clear lake, with a waterfall cascading gently into it. Drew was coming out of the water and smiling at me.

He walked over to me, grabbing my hands he pulled me up and said, 'Come for a swim.'

I stood and looked at him. He seemed so happy without a worry in the world.

'Come on,' he said. 'I'll race you. Last one in is a toadstool!' He ran off over the pure white sand with me in pursuit. We both arrived at the water's edge at the same time and dived. We surfaced simultaneously, and he was laughing as he emerged. He then splashed me with water, and I began to laugh as well.

He was such a nice, kind Elf, no wonder I liked him. We swam into deeper water and dived down. There were schools of brightly coloured fish swimming out of our way as we both touched the sand on the bottom and pushed ourselves up again to the surface. As he surfaced, he screamed, 'Last one to the falls is a drongo,' and off we swam, stroke for stroke, arriving at the same time at either side of the falls.

He then dragged himself up on to a rock ledge at the edge of the waterfall and was standing with the water cascading over him and yelled out, 'Come on over here, my friend.'

I swam over to him and he put out his hand to help me up. So I reached out and grabbed it and pulled him back into the water. He landed directly on top of me. When we both resurfaced, we were laughing hysterically. Eventually we climbed up onto the rock ledge. We stood there looking back towards the beach through the fine curtain of water. I could not believe how happy I felt, and I could feel Drew's happiness as well.

'Come on,' he said, as he pointed to a rope ladder that hung down at the far end of the rock ledge. He ascended it with ease, with me following as fast as I could. We arrived at the top of the falls, and the view over the rainforest and lake was unbelievable. He placed an arm around my waist, and I rested mine over his shoulder and we stood staring over the view. I could not find a word to describe how I felt. It was every positive adjective I have ever heard rolled into one. He removed his arm and grabbed my hand, smiled at me, and said, 'Okay, let's jump.' And we did.

Next thing, I looked up and there was Drew kneeling in front of me with water running down his face. He was holding my hand and saying, 'Quick, you'll get soaked sitting out here. It's pouring.'

He pulled me up by the hand put his arm around me and walked me to the tent and said, 'Dry yourself and get some sleep. We have a big day tomorrow.'

He slapped my arm and said, 'Goodnight, see you in the morning, my friend.' The way he said 'my friend' was exactly how he said it in the dream, if that's what it was. He walked to the far end of the tent and lay down. I just lay there in a daze, my mind confused, trying to decipher what was fact and what was fantasy.

40
CHAPTER

A Decision Made

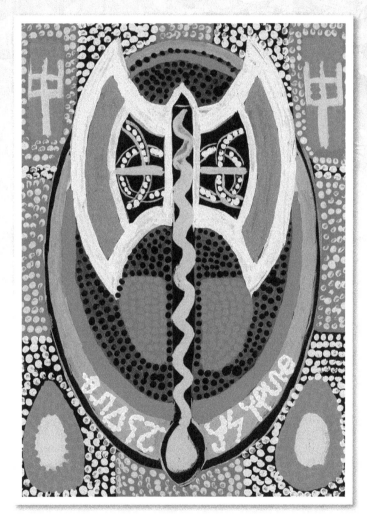

The morning arrived and it looked promising as the rain had stopped, but there were still plenty of clouds hovering in the south. The temperature was much colder, and at this altitude, there was the possibility of snow. Jula and Wecco made breakfast again and in fact seemed to like preparing it. Besides, if they did breakfast, they realised they didn't have to have a turn of taking watch.

Rocco was the first out of the tent and headed straight for the food. *What's new?* I thought.

After finishing, his response was, 'Is that all there is?'

'Those who complain most', said Carew, 'are the most complained of.'

I don't think it had any effect on him as he still continued to complain about everything. The company seemed rather despondent this morning, or was it our overwhelming sense of guilt about not trying to rescue Dolark? As we ate breakfast, I sensed Drew was preoccupied with the same issue. I would have liked to think about what happened last night, but the Dolark problem was too heavy on all our minds.

Suddenly, Jula stood and said in a matter-of-fact manner, 'Why can't we disguise ourselves and enter the city of Howsak, discover where Dolark is being held, and rescue him? Don't forget, we now have these new abilities and our magic Elvan chain mail and weapons.'

Jula, I think, was just verbalising what we were thinking. We agreed that something had to be done. For the next few hours, we talked about a plan and decided that some of us would wear the emblems and dress of two of the creeds, go into the city, and find out all we could about where Dolark was.

There was another problem now. Which two creeds would it be? Finally, a decision was made. Because there were two Kabs and two Dations among us, the choice was made for us. Jula was uncomfortable dressing as a Dation and Ricco unhappy dressing as a Kab, but with the Elves and Dwarfs having to dress up as well, they were finally convinced it was the only way not to be noticed in a big city like Howsak.

Carew came up with one of his pearls of wisdom and said, 'How the sapling is trained is how the tree will lean.'

We were not sure of what he actually meant, but I think he was referring to how our creeds had brainwashed us. On that note, we packed our gear up and started our trek to Howsak. We made our way back, and we stopped about twenty paces from the road and walked parallel to it under the cover of the forest. It was more difficult than the road, but it turned out to be the best decision as during our hike, there were three groups of the enemy that passed by us and all were travelling to Howsak, so we thought. As the day drew on, we came across a fork in the road, the right one to Howsak and the left to Basscala. The enemy was taking the left fork, we guessed, and it simultaneously dawned on us why.

They were reinforcements for the battle of Basscala, which we were unaware was to take place within the next few days. We continued for the rest of the day on the road to Howsak. We passed many more armies of men: first a group of Kabs, then Aldations, finally Dations who had been recruited from Howsak by the Evil and were marching to assist in the destruction of Basscala. As we watched, we noticed there were no Bovers in the armies and wondered why.

By nightfall, we could see the towering walls of the city. Towering was an understatement. I don't think ever in the history of Man there has been a city with such incredibly high walls. We stopped within sight of the city where the forest was still dense and made camp.

The decision was made that only four should enter Howsak so as not to create suspicion. Peto and I changed into our Dation disguise, while Rocco and Wecco changed into their Kab outfits. The four of us left to enter the city with the intention of getting more clothes to disguise the rest of our company. This was not a big problem. We would find clothes that teenagers could wear which would fit our friends' fine. Rocco and Wecco did the same and we met back at our camp by midnight and handed out the outfits we procured.

Then we rested till morning. As most of the leaves had fallen from the deciduous trees, we had to move deeper into the forest and hide under the evergreens for cover. We had a cold breakfast of the last of the fruit and raw vegetables then changed into our disguises. We laughed when Carew and Jarew had to have ringlets pulled over their pointed ears but at least they were covered. Drew and Tarew had to have their hair combed in a strange way to cover their ears, and they sure looked funny. It was the best we could do. But even with a funny hairstyle, Drew still looked handsome.

We set off and entered the city at different times. Our first stop was the markets, knowing this to be the best place for gossip. As we walked around, we could feel hatred emanating from the Kabs and Aldations towards us. Rocco and Wecco sensed the hatred towards them from the Dations and the Aldations. We bought provisions, and in the process, we who were dressed as Dation asked questions of the Dations about what was happening. The others did the same with the Kabs. Where was the prison situated? Why were there no Bovers in the city?

By nightfall, we had all returned with our stories of the hatred we had experienced coming from the creeds, and the reason there were no Bovers. The Evil had devised a plan to get control of Howsak by turning all the creeds against the Bovers to create hatred and take control of the city. He then kept control by turning the remaining three creeds against each other. This was what the Evil had been doing over hundreds of years, yet none of the creeds were aware of it. We also found out where they were holding Dolark, in the prison of Howyard.

That night, Drew, Tarew and I went back into the city disguised as Dations, found the prison, then examined its weaknesses. Drew told us to wait for him, and he would use the vanishing and enter the prison when next the gates were opened. We waited for only a few minutes, and he was gone. We waited in the shadows of the prison wall, and it seemed like forever before he returned. When he did, he looked dreadful.

He looked at us, and the only words he spoke were 'Let's get out of here!' And off we went. On the return journey to our camp, we asked if he had seen Dolark.

'Wait till we get back to the camp,' he said.

We both looked at him and wondered what was wrong. We walked back as fast as we could without making ourselves conspicuous, and I could sense the problem was major. When we arrived, they were all waiting with bated breath, especially Soltain, to hear what the best way was to rescue Dolark.

'Right,' Drew said. 'All sit down, please.'

We looked at each other and knew this was going to be serious.

He began, 'I saw Dolark, but he was unconscious and chained to a wall. I assume he has been tortured. On the way back, I have been devising a way to get him out but have not made up my mind as yet. The one thing I do know is it will not be easy. We will talk about it tomorrow. I will sleep on it tonight.'

He was not the only one sleeping on it. We all had a restless night, thinking about poor Dolark.

During the night, the temperature had dropped quite drastically, and there had been a slight dusting of snow. As we ate breakfast, we discussed the rescue plans.

'Dolark is being held in the southern tower,' said Drew. 'Do any of you have any suggestions?'

'Why don't we use the vanishing', said Tarew, 'to rescue him?'

'Thank you, Tarew,' said Drew, 'that's exactly what I've been thinking. Mecco and I are the best with the vanishing. We will practice today with you, Soltain, using you as a substitute for Dolark, to see if we can get it to work.'

He looked at the confused Dwarf and continued, 'With Mecco and me on either side of you, arm in arm, we will see if and how far we can transport you. If it does work, that is how we will have to rescue Dolark. He will be too weak to walk by himself.'

So for the next four hours, we tried over and over again. It worked but we could only travel about ten paces, and we knew that would not be enough.

'Why don't we attempt it with three of us?' Tarew asked. 'I have been practising at every opportunity, which is the reason over the last few days I was always at the rear of the trek.'

Jarew laughed and said, 'Please, if I can't do it, I don't see how you can. They should just practise with two.'

Tarew was very disappointed. Seeing it was his idea, he thought he should have been given the opportunity to try it, and I was inclined to agree. We worked for another hour but had only extended it to twenty paces. It was better but still not good enough.

Tarew then pleaded, 'Please, let me have a go.'

I saw the look on Tarew's face. 'Let him try it,' I said. 'It was his idea, and we couldn't do any worse.'

So we tried it again, this time with Tarew. I stood behind Soltain with my arms around his chest and an Elf under each of his arms. We decided to go all the way from our camp to the road, but we did not tell the others. Strangely, I knew this time it was going to work as I could sense Tarew focusing. We concentrated with all our strength. Then on the count of three, we disappeared and materialised on the road fifty paces away. The company had no idea where we had gone. Tarew was so pleased and screamed out, 'We did it!'

41
CHAPTER

The Prelude to the Battle of Basscala

The Evil armies had been gathering for days on the south-western slopes of the hills that surrounded the valley of Basscala. Even though there had been snowfalls, more men were still arriving every day from the fallen cites of Bossak, Blarak, and Howyard. The Evil was building to a formidable force. Over the next three days, the enemy had grown to encompass the whole south-western side of the valley, which was now covered in the red tents of the Evil that stood out against the snow-covered hills.

There were also black dots scattered over the red tents and on the snow. These were the black crows of Malfarcus. Inside the largest red tent ever seen were the traitor wizard Drascar, the six remaining Pernicious, and the Goblin and Menlin captains in a meeting discussing the battle of Basscala.

Captain Yobtowoy had the floor and was demanding to attack Basscala later that afternoon. 'The sun would be setting,' he said, 'which would shine straight on the city. The inhabitants would have to look straight into the setting sun. This would make it hard for them to see our army advancing. The longer we wait, the more chance the enemy will have to get reinforcements.'

The wizard Drascar stood waving his staff for silence then addressed the company of evil leaders. 'I do not discuss tactics with captains,' he said. 'What I say we do, and I say we wait two more days.'

Yobtowoy and his followers grudgingly sat down with growls and grunts, but the wizard Drascar bashed the floor with his staff.

This soon stopped the disgruntled complaints. 'Tonight the high wizard of the South', he announced, 'will be here, and he will tell us what to do, so you all must return here by six to show your respect.'

That night when all the Evil's captains and leaders had re-congregated in the large red tent, the black crows of Malfarcus began their crowing to signify the Evil's arrival. Suddenly, the Evil appeared; from where, no one saw. He materialised in a second to stand between the wizard Drascar and the Six Pernicious. The power of this evil thing was way beyond anything the world had experienced.

The strange thing about him was everyone saw him as one of their own: the Menlins saw a Menlin, the Goblins saw a Goblin, and the men of whatever creed they were saw a man of that same creed. The only things that stayed the same were his staff, cloak, amulet, and the armband he wore. The large red tent grew silent as they became aware of his presence. He perused his audience slowly. His presence demanded the attention of all.

They waited with bated breath for him to begin. 'Today is our day,' he said, 'and we will defeat our enemy. Their so-called liberal ideas that are forced upon us will be shoved down their righteous throats. We have our beliefs and they will not be destroyed. Their so-called understanding and tolerance will be their downfall. This is only the beginning of our quest for power. The fall of Basscala will lead the way. Tomorrow we attack.'

Yobtowoy glanced across at the wizard Drascar with contempt and satisfaction as these words were spoken.

The Evil then raised his hands over his spellbound audience and continued, 'You who are here today may not be here tomorrow night, but those of you who do not return will be in paradise.'

The spellbound group rose and cheered, and with this support, the Evil's power grew stronger.

He held up his hands again for silence then continued. 'Tomorrow morning I will address the troops, but for now, depart, rest, and remember the enemy must be destroyed.'

The captains and leaders of the Evil armies walked out of the red tent with such pride, each thinking their leader was one of their own. They were repeating to each other, 'Paradise will be at the end of tomorrow, and may you reach it with little pain.'

Across the valley in Basscala, the city was prepared for the worst. They had stored all their provisions and summoned all the farmhands working in the fields to retreat to the safety of the city. As the workers made their way back, they herded with them cows, sheep, and goats and wagons of straw, placing a certain number on each terrace, except for the first, which had been cleared of all the trees and was now completely exposed, so there was no cover for the Evil.

As all this was happening, the armies of Elvan archers and the men of Kassob, who now were also fairly good archers, had marched south and were hiding in the woods on the northern hills of the valley of Basscala, waiting for some sort of sign. Just before sunset, two large white birds being chased by a flock of black crows landed and were screeching in some strange tongue. Some of the men of Kassob were trying to chase them away.

'Stop,' screamed out an old Elf. 'These are legendary messengers from the Dwarfs of the west. It is the black crows that are the Evil's helpers.'

Five of the crows dived down and were heading straight for the white messengers with their claws outstretched. Suddenly a whoosh of arrows passed by the white messengers and found their targets, and the five crows fell dead to the ground.

The old Elf approached the white messengers slowly with his hands open and faced up. One jumped on to his hand, moved his head down to his leg, and with his beak, handed the Elf a rolled-up message.

The Elf called out to the High Elf Tarvin. 'Lord, here is a message,' he said, 'from the western Dwarfs,' and handed it to him.

Tarvin unrolled it and read it, then turned to his companions. 'Tomorrow will be our day,' he said. 'The lords and the Dwarf armies are in the forest on the hills to the south-east and will wait for the Evil to make their assault on Basscala. Once the Evil reaches the first terrace, they will attack them from the south-east. We must wait for a signal, and it will be a large rocket fired from the south-eastern hills, and then we join the battle. If no rocket is fired, then we must wait till we see the Dwarf armies attacking the Evil at their camp and charge down to support the Dwarf armies.'

At the same time, two other white screechers had landed on the top terrace of Basscala, with a message for Vice Lord Chefskicon explaining the plan. All that night, the city prepared its men along its first walled terrace. And on the top terrace, the slingshots and large crossbows were mounted and ready to repel the enemy.

The lords, wizard, Elves, and the Dwarf armies had landed and begun their march north along the riverbank. The scouts had been arriving back with the news that the Evil had a large army camped on the hills to the south-west and so the decision was made to make camp on the south-eastern hills of the valley. The forest was quite dense there, giving them more protection from the snows. The company arrived late that evening and set up camp though no fires were permitted, in case the enemy had not been informed of their arrival.

A meeting was called in the wizard Naroof's tent. In attendance were the Dwarfs Mordlark, Benlib, and the master Dwarf Baylib, the lords Arcon, Devcon, and Revcon, the northern Elves Bayrew, Wayrew, and El Masrew, and five of the fiercest Dwarf captains. The only light they had was from the wizard's staff that glowed strong on the faces of the co-conspirators as they ate and talked of the day ahead.

The strategy was planned. They were to wait till sunrise, hoping the enemy would attack Basscala. As soon as they reached the first terrace, the signal was to be fired to let the archers and the city know the battle was to begin. If the Evil did not attack the city, then the Dwarf armies would attack the Evil. This would give the signal for the Elvan and Men archers to attack from the north-east.

The meeting finished with the plan to give a speech to the company and army an hour before sunrise. They all left with the customary Elvan farewells and retired to their respective tents. Wayrew went straight to his to write down all that had happened on his part of the quest against the Evil. The hour arrived, and all the confederates had eaten and armed themselves and were quietly waiting for the wizard Naroof to arrive. The three Dwarfs, the three Elves, and the three lords were now mounted on their steeds, with the Dwarf armies in formation ready for battle, when the wizard appeared on his pitch-black horse with his silver cloak shining in the light of his staff.

He called the company to gather close to listen to what he had to say. I'm glad Wayrew took notes of his speech as this is how it went:

'People of this world, the time has come to stand against this evil source which threatens our world. We must show all the creeds that if they wish to follow their creed's beliefs, they may, but there must be no criticism or blaming the other for problems that may occur. All the creeds must accept responsibility for this disaster. This enemy wishes to destroy all free thinkers. They even punish and murder their own kind who disagrees with them. As you know, there are followers of the creeds in Basscala and Kassob, but they don't wear their beliefs on their sleeves. A scarf may be burnt, a ringlet cut off, or an emblem destroyed, but if it is in your heart, it is safe.

'The city of Basscala has always been a city that has contributed great thinkers and askers of questions, who are not brainwashed to accept one train of thought. They read the books of all the creeds and even earlier philosophers, in a search for knowledge. We who are free thinkers must defend this city from the evil brainwashers who play the ignorant against each other to gain power. But remember, do not blame the ignorant as they know no better. And do not try to force them to look for the whole truth, as the force you exert will only reaffirm their prejudices. They must come to the truth of their own accord.

'The city of Basscala has always been a city of example, never forcing their view on others, but showing the way only by their model of tolerance and compassion. We must keep this in mind. If the time comes and we must take prisoners, then show them some compassion and forgive their ignorance as only from this will the good prevail.

'The Elves have always understood the search for the truth. It is the truth itself. For only when we accept one truth do we leave ourselves open to justifying the wrong we do. We must not play the same game as the Evil, but show forgiveness and help in a positive manner.'

As this speech was taking place, way off in the forest, seven gleaming lights were listening to it. And the High Elf Tarvin on the hills of the north-east and Lord Chefskicon in the city were giving similar speeches to their respective armies.

42
CHAPTER
The Battle Begins

The morning arrived, and on the snow-covered hills of the south-west, the Evil armies had gathered, waving, shouting, and waiting to hear the speech of the Evil.

The wizard Drascar held out a hand for silence then bashed the floor with his staff. 'Listen,' he said, 'and listen well to what our master says.'

He then stepped back, and from out of thin air, the Evil appeared and his forces broke into spontaneous applause. The Evil waited till the crescendo of cheers ceased.

'Let me speak to all of you here', he said, 'about the situation that has occurred. Our coalition forces, from the cities of Bossak, Blarak, Howyard and my forces have encountered opposition from three groups: the wizard Naroof with the lords of Con, the Dwarfs of the west, and the Elves. They are against the creeds. They are not like us, who will allow the creeds to stay as they are, with no intermarriage or intermingling. That is what we fight for. Do we want the so-called coalition of good to tell us what we should think? Our commitment to destroy the enemy is consistent with the ideals of the creeds. We don't need to be told that our creeds are wrong. You who are here today are helping your fellow citizens to a free future. The peoples of the cities of independents are behind you. When we take this city and liberate it from the enemy, the occupation will not be indefinite. Our goal is to seek an independent and free Basscala. We need to make the New World great again.'

The armies of the Evil stood proud and cheered. And the sound could be heard for tens of kilopaces around. But for the inhabitants of the city and the allied armies, it sent a chilling sensation up their spines.

The Evil held up his hands for silence and continued, 'The people of our cities are united behind all of you. For this historic mission to succeed and triumph, all that is necessary will be done. We serve the cause of freedom that everywhere and always is a reason to fight. And those who return will celebrate the victory tonight, and those who do not will be in paradise.'

The roar his followers sent up was even louder this time, and they chanted, 'Hail Master, Hail Master.'

The power of this evil wizard was growing stronger each day, draining the evil from all his forces. Remember, each of the creeds along with the Goblins and Menlins all thought he was one of them. So they cheered on and on, 'Hail Master, Hail Master,' thinking that when they won, it would mean they would be in control of the city. The roar of the Evil armies echoed through the hills and sent all the birds and animals fleeing from the valley.

The Evil held up his hand again for silence. 'Now is the hour for the coalition to take its prize. The army's generals know the plans. Heed them well, and may the reward of victory or paradise be waiting at the end of your day.'

The final roar went up, and the drums of the enemy began to pound. The Evil armies started their march down the snow-covered hills and across the valley of Basscala to the city.

Escorting the Evil army were large wooden forts on wheels with ladders, being pulled by those strange elephant/dragon-like animals. Being pushed by the animals were the large, flat, wooden retractable drawbridges for crossing the river that hundreds of the Evil had entered. Their artillery consisted of catapults and large crossbows that were being dragged into place. From the city, the view looked terrifying: the red tents on the hills and the red machines waving large red and black flags of the Evil. Also among them were the flags of the wizard of Drascar and banners of all the cities. Following all this was the Evil armies dressed in red and black.

The wizard Naroof was telling his compatriots to hold their ground and wait till the enemy had reached the first terrace. The Dwarf army stood waving their white banners with their emblem of a gold sun setting behind a dark mountain with a golden pick, a shovel, and an axe all crossing each other. The three Elves sat proudly on their small horses next to the wizard and the lords. Across on the northern hills waited Tarvin and the Elvan archers, carrying their banners of blue with a silver tree on it. The men from Kassob were also holding high their red and brown flags on which were depicted the abstract wings of a dragon.

The Evil armies by now had positioned their artillery, and were beginning to fire large flaming balls and arrows at Basscala. The long red wooden machines had reached the river and were extending their retractable drawbridges across to let the Evil armies land on the shore. The flaming arrows and balls were not doing much damage, as the city was made of stone and covered in greenery so most of the balls were bouncing off and the arrows breaking.

The first mistake the Evil made was to attack at dawn. Just as they had positioned themselves, the sun was rising behind the city, so it was shining directly into their faces. This was the advantage the allies needed. This gave them time to herd all the livestock grazing on the terrace into the safety of the city.

Meanwhile, the first group of the Evil forces were spewing out from the contraptions fording the river and were now only a hundred paces from the first terrace. The wizard Naroof fired the rocket and sounded the horns of attack. Off charged the wizard's forces out of the forest, with the Dwarfs following behind, with their swords waving, axes by their sides, and carrying their special shields.

The Dwarf shields were an ingenious invention, three feet across by four feet high with a half circle at the bottom and a half circle cut out at the top. When needed, they could be turned on their side, with alternating Dwarfs holding one in the left hand and down low, and the next Dwarf holding the other in the right hand and above, linking to form a solid wall for protection.

Across on the hills north of the city, the allied archers had fired their first volley. At that precise moment, Basscala's artillery rose above the third terrace and began to rain down balls of fire upon the red wooden machines of the Evil.

One of the first flaming balls hit one of the retractable drawbridges. It burst into flames and, within minutes, started to disintegrate and float down the river with the Goblins, Menlins, and Men all fighting each other for debris to keep them afloat. The archers had now left the safety of the forest, but they also had ingenious shields. Each was five feet high and three feet wide with a four-inch-wide cross cut into the centre, enabling them to aim through and fire their bows. The bows were attached to and were also the handles of the shields, but could be dislodged in seconds and used freely.

As the wizard Naroof and the lords charged down the hill, they looked across and could see the blue shields with the silver tree making their way down the slope towards the enemy. At this point, more of the enemy had traversed the river through its drawbridges, and the Evil army was arriving at the terraces. The large red wooden forts with ladders had also moved over the drawbridges and had positioned themselves at the base of the first terrace. There was one group of the enemy at the great gates. They were ramming and bashing it, with more of the Evil's troops gathering behind them.

It was now time for the city to send down even larger balls of flames that would explode after fifteen or twenty seconds, sending pieces of flaming debris over the enemy. Ten of the balls were ready on the top of the third terrace. As they started to roll, they were lit, and as they rolled down, the wind fanned them. By the time they reached the enemy, they were glowing and they exploded, causing havoc.

The Elvan and Kassobian archers were now taking it in turns to fire. And there was a continuous rain of arrows landing around the Evil's army. Many were felled. The Evil, on his dragon steed, was overlooking the proceedings from the snow-covered hill with an anxious look on his face.

The company from the southern hill was now only three hundred paces from the south-eastern flank of the enemy, just by the river, and in minutes would be engaging them. The enemy's archers had turned, and they were now firing at the company charging down the hill. The riders and horses thankfully wore Elvan chain mail that was protecting them. Now, the Dwarfs had turned, joining their shields together for protection, and they were advancing rapidly in lines.

The inhabitants of Basscala, to this day, still talk of what an incredible sight the lines of Dwarfs marching towards the Evil were. The wizard, lords, and Elves were riding through and breaking up the Evil's line of attack, forcing the enemy to run in all directions. Those who ran up the hill came face to face with the Dwarfs, who surrounded them, forcing them to drop their weapons.

The battle continued all morning. The Evil continued sending waves of his troops but made no progress, what with the balls of fire from the city raining down on them and the arrows from the allied archers also taking their toll. The Dwarfs from the south had also completely surprised and thrown the enemy off balance.

The enemy was now starting to panic and run in all directions. The Evil had underestimated the forces of good. He turned to the wizard Drascar, ordering him to sound the retreat as the Six Pernicious took to the air, screeching the order to his armies. Within minutes, the enemy had turned their artillery around and traversed the river and were heading back up the snow-covered hills, which had now turned to mud with the archers still firing after them and the Dwarfs in hot pursuit. By mid-afternoon, the valley was free of the enemy, who were now packing up their tents and marching off to the loud cheers from the grateful Basscalati. Scouts were sent out to make sure the enemy had left completely. Then the wizard, lords, Dwarfs, Elves, and Men from Kassob met at the steps that led to the gates of Basscala.

43
CHAPTER
Basscala Rejoices

The great gates were opened, and Vice Lord Chefskicon walked briskly down to greet her fellow lords and allies. She glanced around at the odd-looking fraternity, welcomed them, and asked, 'Where is Lord Sebcon?'

The lords and wizard dismounted, turned towards Chefskicon, and hesitated.

'We are sorry but we have bad news: he has been captured,' Naroof stated, 'and we have no idea where he is. We fear the worst. But tell us, please, have you seen or heard of the fellowship of twelve?'

'Yes,' said Chefskicon. 'They passed this way a month or so back, but we have not seen or heard of them since. Please, where is my hospitality? Come, and bring your friends with you.'

They were welcomed into the city and a feast prepared for them under a large white canopy hanging from the same terrace where the twelve had eaten the month before. As they walked towards the terrace, Master Baylib summoned three white messengers, gave them the good news about the outcome of the battle, and sent them out to find and relay the news to the quest-seekers and to bring back news of them. The fraternity of defenders of Basscala stood and watched as the screechers flew off towards the mountains. Vice Lord Chefskicon then ushered them to the seats closest to the large fireplaces carved out of the stone terrace walls.

'Listen,' she said, 'the Basscalati are already singing about the victory.'

As the allied company took their seats, they listened intently and could hear a song being sung in the distance. It went like this:

> 'The battle began on an early winter morn.
> There was snow all around and the sound of a horn.
> The Evil charged down and across the river.
> With their artillery of flaming arrows and balls, they delivered.
> The Elvan archers came from out of the north,
> With the men of Kassob showing their worth,
> Raining arrows down upon the enemy as they charged,
> Slowing them down as the great door they barged.
> And from out of the south, as the sun did rise,
> The Dwarfs charged down, with axes by their sides
> Waving their swords and holding their shields,
> Waiting for the enemy to begin to yield.
> And we of Basscala, we did the same,
> Sending down balls of fire and arrows aflame,
> With the help of the allies, the enemy drew back
> Along the valley, up the hills, for their tents to pack.
> By the end of the day, the enemy had departed.
> Leaving us to clean up and our lives restarted.'

The lords and the wizard were now comfortably seated in the large white marquee on the terrace. Tarvin entered with two other Elves and a man. The three Elves bowed respectfully; the Man did likewise but not with the same sincerity. The lords and the wizard rose and bowed in return.

Naroof asked Tarvin, 'How are your archers and men?'

'We have two Elves and a man dead and six injured,' Tarvin said. 'And did you have any casualties?'

Naroof looked mortified and said, 'No, we were very lucky. The fireballs of Basscala rained down and scattered the enemy into disarray, and it made our task much easier.'

Tarvin then added regretfully, 'Six Elves and I must leave tonight to escort our departed companions back, so they may cross the lake of Eople and be planted in the great forest of Barrington.'

'Will you not stay for the feast?' asked Chefskicon.

Tarvin bowed his head slightly in sorrow, then added, 'The victory is good. The Evil has been sent on his way. But the families of our companions will need to take them on their last trip across the lake and into the great forest, where they will be buried under young saplings. As the trees grow, they will henceforth be called by the names of the fallen Elves. All must be returned from whence they came.

Farewells to all of you brave people. My archers will stay with you till the Evil one has been captured, then send them home to the great forest.'

Tarvin and his six companions bowed again, and the wizard and company returned the gesture, and brought their right hand up to their heart, slapping it with their left hand, to signify travellers' luck. The seven Elves departed, and the company sat back down.

The feast arrived, but for a victory, it was a very sombre celebration. As the meal was coming to a close, the wizard turned to the company. 'This is not the end,' he said. 'We must pursue the enemy back to his castle before he has time to regroup. Only then will we have the chance to free the cities of Bossak, Howyard, and Blarak.'

The company retired to their rooms, with the armies being billeted in the great hall and other parts of the city. The morning arrived with another light flurry of snow, much to the disappointment of the Dwarf army, who by now had added another layer of clothes. I never understood how they could continue marching wearing so much. They joined the Elvan archers and the men from Kassob, had their breakfast, and began to move out of the city. What a sight to see, the flags and banners waving as they marched down the great steps between the avenue of trees, clothed in their late autumn colours! A contingent of barges had been assembled across the river, and the combined forces marched across them and up the valley, led by the wizard, the three lords, the three Elves, and the three Dwarfs all on horseback.

44
CHAPTER
The Rescue of Draylib

We practised the disappearing for another hour; with each attempt, we became more proficient. Later that afternoon, the three of us dressed in Dation attire and set out for the city, with the wishes of all for success—although I knew Jarew's was not sincere. I could sense he would have liked us to fail.

We arrived at the city late in the afternoon and decided to have a meal at a small tavern with the sign of the Dation on the door and wait till the evening was fully upon us. We sat, ate, and listened to the conversations that were taking place in the tavern.

One old Dation was arguing with a faction of young Dations. 'Why are we all blaming the Bovers for the problems at the moment?' he asked. 'If you ask me, it's not the Bovers who are causing all these troubles, it's that wizard Drascar. He is being manipulated by some greater evil. Why does he want to destroy the city of Basscala?'

The young faction turned on him. One said, 'You silly old man, don't you know anything? The Bovers have control of Basscala, and we must destroy them.'

I sat and listened to the conversation taking place and realised how stupid we once were to have been hoodwinked into thinking that our creed was the only truth, and how sad these people were blocking their intelligence with prejudice. Two of the men walked over to us and asked our opinion. I was about to say something when Drew squeezed my hand and looked at me intently. I knew what he was thinking, so I bowed my head, with my finger over my lips, to signify we were not to speak as we were in mourning. In the end, the old man was shouted down.

He left the tavern, shaking his head and saying, 'The hatred you have for the Bovers and the other creeds will be repaid tenfold to you.'

This was something we six slowly became aware of over the years of this adventure. When one does a good deed, it comes back double, but evil is always repaid tenfold.

It was now mid-evening and time to make a move to the prison of Howyard. The three of us rose and I was about to bow, but Drew stopped me just in time, as they would have found it strange. It has been so incredible how the manners and the goodness of the Elves have permeated my thinking and behaviour, and how sad it is that one must hide one's manners. We walked slowly towards the prison so as not to create suspicion and to search for dark corners that we could use as stopping points on our way out of the city.

We arrived at the prison and waited in the dark for the door to be opened. Drew went over the plan and schooled us on the best way to get to where Draylib was being held. The plan sounded very dangerous to me. We didn't have to wait long till the gates were opened to let in three soldiers.

Drew grabbed our hands. 'Now,' he said, and in an instant, we were inside, standing together in a dark corner.

As we passed, the evil soldiers one turned and said to the others, 'Did you feel that gust of wind?' The other two looked at him.

'What wind?' asked one of the other soldiers. 'There is no wind tonight, and if there is, who cares?' And then they moved off. We waited a few moments till the soldiers had gone and the guards had relocked the gate.

'Keep hold of my hands', said Drew, 'and use your power with mine, and I will guide us to the balcony.' Drew was looking not at the first balcony but further up, and I could sense where he was intending to project us. 'Now,' he said, and within a split second, we materialised under the arches on the balcony of the third floor. Tarew stood completely frozen and looked a little pale.

'From here,' Drew said, 'we will climb up the centre tower which is unmanned. When we reach the top, we will have to use all our power to travel across to the southern tower.'

On hearing this, poor Tarew turned grey. Upon reaching the top, we walked out on to the battlement, looked down then across at the southern tower.

Tarew and I looked at each other. 'Will this be possible?' I asked Drew. 'It looks a long way.'

'Do not be afraid,' he said. 'The distance is less than what we were practising yesterday. We can see the other battlement on the southern tower, and on the count of three, focus with all your skill.'

Again in a split second, Drew and I materialised on the balcony, but Tarew was standing on the very edge of the parapet looking down, frozen. Drew yanked him down before he had time to think.

'Don't worry. You will get better,' he said. 'Now it gets difficult.'

We walked around the battlement to a window on the far side, and there we could see Dolark hanging in chains from a wall. Luckily, there was only one guard by the door.

'We must distract him somehow,' said Drew, 'so we can get in and overpower him before he raises the alarm.'

The plan was that I was to make a noise at the window to distract the guard, then Drew and Tarew would enter the chamber and use the vanishing to get close before he realised what had hit him, and then hopefully disarm him.

I waited till they were at the door then made a sound like squawking. It worked; the guard came over to the window. In an instant, Drew and Tarew materialised just behind him while he was looking out the window. Tarew knelt behind him, and as he stepped back, Drew pushed him over, jumped on him, and covered his mouth. He was so startled that he didn't have time to say or do anything. Tarew then jumped up and grabbed his arms, and they tied him up.

Dolark was a sight; his body was battered, bruised, and limp. Drew grabbed the keys from the guard, and we walked over to our poor friend, unlocked the chains, and gently lowered him to the floor. He made a few groans and looked up. Tears entered his eyes. He could not speak, but his eyes thanked us. We told him to hang on and that we would be safe in no time. We asked whether he could stand. It was a silly question; we should have known the answer by just looking at him. We carried him outside, then Tarew began walking towards the steps.

'No,' said Drew. 'We must go back the way we came.'

Tarew really went pale, and I didn't feel too well either, but Drew reassured us that we had travelled much further with Soltain this morning and he was heavier than Dolark. I placed Dolark's arms over the Elves' shoulders, which they held in place. I stood in front, facing forward with one of his legs under each of my arms.

Drew then looked at Tarew and said, 'This may not have been the way we practised, but we can do this.'

We stood looking across at the centre tower for what seemed like ages.

'Concentrate,' said Drew, 'and on the count of three, we go. One, two . . . Stop,' said Drew abruptly. 'I can sense the doubt in both of you. You must have faith in our friendship and power. Only then can we do this. We had no problem this morning. We did it countless times. We are travelling less distance than this morning, so please trust me.'

'I am sorry,' said Tarew. 'It's not you I don't trust, it's me.'

Drew looked at us both again and smiled. 'I trust you,' he said, 'so please trust yourself.'

'I trust you,' I said. 'Let's go!'

'Yes, let's go,' said Tarew as he puffed out his chest.

'Okay,' said Drew. 'On the count of three: one, two, three—'

Suddenly, there we were on the battlement of the other tower, all in one piece.

I sensed a sigh of relief from Drew as we materialised. We carried Dolark as gently as possible back down to the first-story balcony and waited till the courtyard was clear. We got in position and down we went. This time there were no doubts in any of our minds. We were now hiding in the dark corner, waiting for the gate to be opened, and at this time of night, how could we be sure it would be opened until tomorrow? We were standing holding Dolark, when two solders left their guards' room and walked within four paces of where we stood. Their smell was putrid, and as they passed us, Dolark let out a groan.

One of the guards asked, 'Did you hear that?'

The other replied, 'No, your hearing is playing tricks on you.'

Then they continued on their way. We stood there for what seemed like over half an hour, but it was only a few minutes before the gate was opened. It was fortuitous for us that more soldiers were arriving.

'This is our chance,' said Drew. 'As soon as they enter and are about to close the gate, we make our move.'

We waited while two of the soldiers began talking to the gatekeeper. The three were standing blocking our escape.

'This may be our only chance till morning,' Drew said. 'We must vanish over the top of them.'

At this statement, we both frowned with doubt.

'You can do it,' said Drew.

Tarew looked at me for support, and I knew that if I showed doubt, he would sense it.

'Yes, we know,' I said, 'whenever you are ready.'

Drew held up his thumb to signify one, then his next finger for two, then his middle finger for three and we were suddenly outside under cover by the shadow of the wall. As we passed by the three Evil soldiers, there was a gust of wind, and they looked around to see where it had come from. We waited for a few moments in the dark till the gates were closed. Now, we relaxed a little and slowly moved from one dark corner to another, moving ever closer to the western gate of the city. When we were in sight of the gate, we became aware of some commotion happening back in the centre of the city and knew that they must now be aware that Dolark had been rescued. We now had to move fast to exit the city before they closed the gate. Otherwise, there would be no way of escape.

Before we realised what was happening, a trumpet sounded. The gate came crashing down before we had time to use the vanishing. There was no hope of us getting over the famous walls of Howyard. Now we were in big trouble.

'We must go back to the tavern,' said Drew, 'and somehow get a room for the night and smuggle Dolark in.'

We started to move back toward the tavern when from up the hill came a bunch of soldiers looking in every corner and lane. We stood there waiting, not knowing what to do.

'Quick, in here,' someone sang out and ushered us into their house then closed the door and turned their lamp down. We stood silently in the dark as the soldiers moved on past the house. After a few moments, the man turned up his lamp, the light lit his face, and it was then that we saw who he was. It was the old man who had argued with the young Dations in the tavern.

'Thank you,' we said. 'They are after our friend whom we have rescued from the prison.'

'I knew there was something odd about you three when I saw you in the tavern,' he said as he stared at us, 'so I waited outside, and when you left, I followed you to the prison Howyard. Then when you disappeared, I knew you must have magic powers, and quite possibly be from Basscala. I lived there for five years many years ago, and they were good and powerful people. They never had the problems or the hatred that we have here, and all the creeds lived in harmony.'

He then eyed off Dolark. 'He is not a man,' he said. 'What is he?'

Drew pushed me forward to speak. 'Please understand,' I said. 'These are strange times, and the Good needs help from all. This is our friend Dolark the Dwarf from the western mountains.'

He gazed at him and then turned to Tarew and Drew. 'Are you two Dwarfs as well?' he asked.

'These are my friends also,' I said and asked, 'Have you ever heard about Elves?'

Tarew and Drew threw back their hoods.

He sat down and stared at the two Elves. 'Yes, when I lived in Basscala,' he said, 'I heard songs about Elves but never thought they were real.' He sat there for a long time staring at the two handsome creatures.

'Well, they are real,' I added, 'and here are two, Drew and Tarew, Elves from the forest of Gong, and your name, sir?'

He continued staring at the two Elves and stammered as he pronounced his name. 'I am Ruary the Wanderer,' he said. 'And why are the soldiers after you?'

'We are on a mission', I answered, 'to destroy or at least weaken the Evil that has taken over our world. The Evil had our friend in your prison.' I looked at him and knew he was good and added, 'We must get out of the city as soon as possible. We have companions waiting in the forest outside your city. Can we trust you?'

'Yes,' he said defiantly, 'if you are trying to destroy the Evil that has pervaded our lives, I will help you. Stay here this night, and first thing in the morning, when the gates are opened to let in the farmers and traders, I will scrutinise the situation for you. For now, make yourselves comfortable and rest. Your friend can sleep in my bed, and I have food on the stove.'

He made up makeshift beds for us then dished out large helpings of a chicken, olive, and vegetable stew that was simmering on the stove. When we had finished eating, he made up a pot of fresh mint, fresh rosemary, green tea, and Drew sprinkled some herb on top. We sat there quite content while Tarew fed Dolark spoonfuls of stew, which restored him to the point where he wanted to know all that had happened so far. We spent an hour or so bringing him up to the present, with Ruary listening to every word we said. It was starting to get late, so I suggested we all rest, as getting out of this city would be a task and a half.

We made Dolark as comfortable as possible and then turned in ourselves. We all had the best sleep we had had for ages: I think it must have been the special herb Drew had sprinkled on top.

45
CHAPTER
The Rescue Continues

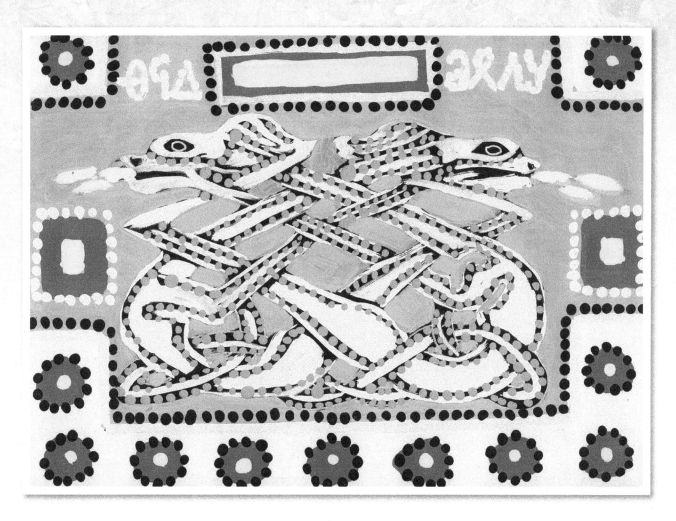

The following morning was bleak, overcast, cold, and another dusting of snow covered the streets. Ruary had just arrived back from checking out the situation at the main gate.

'It does not look too promising,' he said as he walked in the doorway, shaking the snow from his jacket.

'Thankfully,' said Drew, 'the weather is in our favour.' Then he turned to Ruary and asked, 'Have they opened the gates yet?'

Ruary looked worried. 'Yes,' he said, 'but they are searching all those who are leaving the city, and there is a wait of about an hour, causing a crowd to gather.'

'That could quite possibly be in our favour,' said Drew. 'With all the people milling around, we can mingle with them, then use the vanishing when the time is right.'

He turned to Ruary and said, 'Can we rely on your help?'

'Yes,' he roared with great gusto, 'and what would you have me do?'

'I am not sure of a plan as yet,' said Drew, 'but we will think of something when we consider the circumstances.'

Within five minutes, we were on our way. The rest and the food had restored us and had even given Dolark some much-needed energy. He could now speak and walk a little by himself. Ruary gave him a walking stick to use, which came in very handy on the walk back to the gate. So Ruary gave Dolark some old clothes a hat and dressed him as an old man. Drew and I went ahead to suss out the best way of approaching the gate, while Tarew and Ruary helped Dolark walk down to our meeting place.

As we stood scrutinising the situation, we realised this was not going to be easy. Vanishing from this side of the gate would be fine, but where could we materialise? It was daytime, and there was no place to hide us outside the gate. As we waited, a covered wagon came rolling past on its way to the gate, and the old man driving it greeted Ruary.

As soon as the wagon passed, I asked Ruary, 'Is he a friend? And would he be willing to let us materialise in the back of his wagon when he gets through the gate?'

'I doubt it,' answered Ruary. 'He has worked for me over many years. He is a mangy old codger and only does what he must. But what I could do is tell him I need a lift, and when we pass the gate, I will distract him while you do your trick.'

We agreed it was probably our only chance, so off went Ruary to ask the old man for a lift. We mingled with the crowd, then positioned ourselves behind an empty dray and waited for the wagon to pass through the gate. Then, just as he had promised, there was a commotion, and everyone was pointing and looking up at the sky. Now was our chance. Drew counted to three and off we went, landing in the back of the wagon with a bang, and the only clue was the canvas flaps waving about. But we were in, and the wagon master had no idea as he was still distracted by Ruary's ploy.

As soon as we landed, the smell of rotting apples pierced our noses. The wagon was travelling back along the road from which we had come, so we stayed hidden, waiting for the right moment to use the vanishing to get into the forest.

But Ruary looked back into the wagon at us in a strange way. He was trying to tell us something, but we could not understand him, so we motioned to him that we were getting ready to depart. But just before we were going to vanish, the wagon stopped. Then the wagon master stepped down, and Ruary took the reins and waved goodbye.

'I will return the wagon tonight,' he said, 'loaded with the apples, and don't worry, you will still get your wages.'

Then off we went again. He then turned around quickly and said, 'Do not leave the wagon yet. I didn't create that commotion. It was three flying creatures who were obviously searching for you and your friends, and they are still flying around.

We looked at each other, and our first thought was for our friends in the forest.

'All of you should stay here with Ruary,' said Drew, 'and I will vanish up to our hideout and see if all is well.'

Drew departed, and Ruary drove on slowly. It was no more than a few minutes when he returned. We could see by the look on his face that all was well. He told us our friends had seen the three

Pernicious flying in the distance and that gave them time to cover themselves with mud and leaves and hide.

'They are travelling under cover of the forest and will meet us further along the road,' said Drew, then asked Ruary how far he was going.

'All the way to the apple orchards in the valley of Prill,' he answered.

'Would it be too much of an inconvenience if we accompanied you at least to the beginning of the valley of Prill?' Drew asked.

Before he could answer, we turned a corner, and there waiting a couple of hundred paces ahead were two Pernicious.

'Get out of here quick!' cautioned Ruary, and the three of us grabbed Dolark and used the vanishing to project us into the forest.

We made our way to our friends and laid Dolark under a tree and covered him with mud and dried leaves. Then we did the same and watched what was taking place at the wagon. As Ruary drew close to the creatures, he pulled up, and one of the riders hopped off his evil steed and marched around peering into the wagon.

He then jumped in and began sniffing and snorting. Eventually they flew off, back to the main gates of the city, and Ruary continued on his way. Once the evil creatures were out of sight, he slowed down and waited for us to join him. Drew and I made our way out of the forest, leaving Dolark to rest under a tree then projected us back into the wagon.

'Is it okay that we join you?' asked Drew. 'It will not put you in danger.'

'It is fine,' said Ruary.

'I promise we will leave just before you descend into the valley,' said Drew then hesitantly added, 'Would more travellers be welcome?'

'If they are fighting the Evil,' he answered, 'fill the wagon.' He then burst into a song:

> *'Empty the wagon of apples and fill it with your friends.*
> *Take them on their journey over hills and 'round bends.*
> *Help them on their quest against the Evil force,*
> *Then maybe all the creeds will take another course.*
> *I feel so good today, now I think that I can cope.*
> *With this company in this wagon, I feel that there is hope.*
> *So I'll crush the apples for cider and make a toast to the quest*
> *And hope they defeat the Evil, I know they will do their best.'*

When Ruary had finished singing, Drew tapped him on the shoulder and asked, 'Could we stop on the crest of the hill and wait for our friends?'

'I think it would be too exposed,' Ruary replied. 'There is a large grove of evergreens just over the hill. We could hide under them and wait for your friends there.'

'We will return and meet them', Drew said, 'and then fetch them to the grove.'

46
CHAPTER
The Company Reunited Again

By now, most of the snow had melted, and the wagon was approaching the grove of trees. It slowed down and eventually came to a stop and waited under the canopy. Poor Dolark, who had fallen straight to sleep under the tree, was now to be woken and moved again. We used the vanishing to move him to the edge of the forest near the grove of trees. Cleaned of the mud and old leaves, he was then bundled into the wagon, and we waited for the rest of the company to arrive.

We didn't have to wait long: out of the forest they arrived, and in no time at all, they were introduced to Ruary. Now they could show their enthusiasm, and there were hugs all around as excitement erupted at seeing Dolark and his rescuers—even though they had to be careful hugging poor Dolark as he was so bruised.

Ruary turned around and said, 'Make yourselves comfortable.' Then he lifted the reins and said, 'Come on, fellow, off we go.' The horse roused, and we were on our way again.

We then had to relay every detail of the rescue to our companions as they sat there in wonder. As we did this, we become conscious of why the Pernicious never smelt us it was the smell of rotten apples that permeated the wagon that concealed we had been there. Jula and Wecco had brought the last of the food with them, and we sat and devoured the lot.

As we ate, Dolark told us of his ordeal, saying, 'The Pernicious took me to Malfarcus, where I was chained to a wall in a cell and left hanging without food for days on end. I was interrogated and beaten. Then they moved me to another space, where I had a view into the adjoining cell. I assumed the man being tortured there was Lord Sebcon. The Menlin in charge was Yobtowoy, and he made me watch and threatened that I would be next. Then one day, the most evil, vile presence appeared in Sebcon's cell. My blood ran cold as he stood standing in front of Lord Sebcon, not saying a word. He never raised a hand to him, but whatever he did, the pain must have been excruciating, as Sebcon screamed in agony. After an hour of this, Sebcon fell unconscious. Before the Evil left, he told Yobtowoy to take me to Howyard, for what reason I knew not. They tied me in a bag and threw me over a horse. When they finally got me to the prison of Howyard, they started more torture till I eventually fell unconscious. The next thing I remember was you rescuing me.'

The day drew on. We were nearly at the entrance to the valley, and we had to plan how to get more supplies and start back on our trip to the caves of Mount Gatta. Ruary suggested that the rest of the company wait at the entrance to the valley of Prill while he and I travelled on and bought food and supplies for our trip over the Mountains Blue.

By mid-afternoon, we had arrived, and the company left the wagon and retreated into the forest while Ruary and I went on to collect the harvest of apples from the farmers of Prill. This took the rest of the day, and in the process, I bought more food, fresh bread, preserved peaches, cheese, fresh vegetables, smoked beef, legs of lamb, and of course, apples. Hopefully, this would keep us going for weeks. With winter on its way, I also bought some wool-lined jackets and boots called Ugg that the valley of Prill was famous for. It was too late to travel back that night, so we stayed with friends of Ruary. He told them I was his offsider so that we never had to tell them anything.

We departed early the next morning and were just about back at our meeting place when we heard some screeches. My first thought was that it was the Pernicious, but as we drew closer, I could see three white screechers flying down to where our company was in hiding.

'I must not stop for long,' Ruary said. 'If the evil creatures are still in the immediate vicinity, they will think it strange, so be prepared to get all your provisions out as quick as possible.'

As we drew close to our planned meeting place, I beckoned the company over to help me unload the supplies as soon as we pulled up under the canopy of trees. They arrived to help, and quickly, we had the supplies relayed from one to the other and into the forest.

Ruary bid us farewell and wished us good luck in defeating the Evil. As he did, the Elves bowed and returned his thanks with the Elvan sign of traveller's luck, and we all followed suit.

As he drove off, he turned around and added, 'I hope to see you all one day when the world is a better place.'

The wagon turned the sharp bend, and he was gone. The company then retreated into the forest, and the decision was made to continue immediately to the caves of Mount Gatta.

I turned to the dwarfs and asked, 'Before we set off, what was the news from your messengers?'

'The news is good and bad,' said Soltain. 'The lords, the wizard, and the Dwarf army are at this moment attacking the Evil army from the southern hills surrounding Basscala. The Elvan archers from the northern forest and the Kassobian Men are attacking from the northern hills and are winning the battle for Basscala. The bad news is that the Evil will probably be retreating in this direction. We have also sent back news of our progress and whereabouts with the messengers.'

We packed up our belongings and moved off in single file, each carrying some supplies, except Dolark, who was still hobbling along with the walking stick Ruary had given him.

Tarew handed Dolark a silver handle with Elvan runes and said, 'Please use this walking stick. It has magic and will help you.'

Dolark looked at it. 'It's only a handle,' he said.

Tarew held it out beside him, and it extended to the ground. 'It will adjust itself to fit your height,' he said.

Dolark took the handle and held it out. Sure enough, it extended to the exact length for his height, and he thanked Tarew generously.

Rocco then asked Dolark if he could use the other walking stick and Dolark handed it to him. He will do anything to make life easier for him!

We made our way back to where the roads split to Basscala and Malfarcus. We took the one to Malfarcus for half a day then stopped, made lunch, and rested.

Drew unfolded the map, and we planned our route over the Mountains Blue. Dolark was not looking too well, so we rested much longer than we should have. Soltain suggested we go ahead. They would follow at a slower pace to take the pressure off Dolark. Rocco seconded this and offered to stay with the Dwarfs, but we all knew why: he was finding the going tough with the extra weight he was carrying, and I don't mean supplies.

But Drew had a much better idea. He, Tarew, and Carew made up what they called an old Elf travel seat made of two long poles with another joining them in the centre. It looked like a stretched H with an extra cross bar and a seat fashioned like a swing made of Elvan rope for support, which was attached to all three poles.

'What are you making?' asked Dolark.

'It's a special Elvan chair to make it easier for you to travel,' said Drew.

'Please, you don't have to do that. I'm feeling much better.'

'Five strong young men here will have no problem taking the extra weight,' said Drew as Rocco stepped back so as not to be chosen as one of the Elvan chair bearers.

Drew added, 'We will help as well.'

With one of us at each end of a pole and taking it in turns, we made much better time, and we gave most of the food supplies to Rocco, who wasn't very happy. Dolark was not happy about this and insisted he was capable of walking himself, but he eventually gave in and sat on the Elvan seat.

We travelled till late afternoon then made camp. We never lit a fire, just sat in our Elvan tent, wearing our new sheepskin jackets and boots, and eating the bread, smoked beef, and cheese. I must add that the sheepskin jackets and boots were a hit. The wool was on the inside with the sheep leather on the outside, and the boots had a special sole that gripped any type of surface. The jackets were bulky, but the Elves insisted on wearing their hoods as did Jula her Bover scarf.

We rose early, and as we opened the tent flaps, we saw that more snow had fallen during the night. After a quick breakfast of Prill apples and dried apricots, we set off again. We made excellent time, stopping for a quick lunch, and then continued. As the afternoon drew on, the terrain slowly began to rise. In the last hour, it became even steeper, and we were finding the going a little tough. The higher we went, the deeper the snow became, and with Dolark in the Elvan seat, it slowed us down. We made camp, ate a hearty meal, and then spent the night huddled in our warm lamb jackets in the shelter of our Elvan tent. The morning arrived with even colder temperatures with the hint of more snow in the air. We packed up our provisions and set off.

Dolark insisted on walking by himself, saying, 'I feel much better now, and with this magic Elvan walking stick, I should be fine.'

This section was very difficult and we were rather weary, but we were cheered up by Drew when at lunch he looked at the map and announced, 'There is a path about two kilopaces ahead that leads to a pass over the Mountains Blue. It looks a much easier climb.'

We made our way to the track that Drew had pointed out on the map, but all the way there, he seemed preoccupied with other thoughts. I tried sensing them, but he was hiding them so well that all I could make out was something about Lord Sebcon. We made camp that night, twenty paces from the track for safety. I could still feel the tension in the air, but no one was game to say anything. We ate what Jula and Wecco had prepared then just sat and stared at each other.

I could not stand it any longer. 'Okay,' I said. 'What's the problem, Drew? We all know you're worried about something, but none of us know what it is.'

As soon as I said this, his barriers came down, and I became aware of what it was.

He turned to face us all and said, 'The Evil has mustered a great force of Goblins, Menlins, and Men from the city of Bossak who are now retreating from Basscala. I sense they are leaving a trail of disaster in their wake. I wish we could have somehow lent a hand.'

Soltain said with great pride in a matter-of-fact sort of way, 'With the Dwarf armies now chasing the Evil, all should be fine. We should continue with the quest.'

Dolark, who had been extremely quiet, turned to face his friends. 'Do not underestimate the Evil,' he said. 'I saw first-hand what he and his forces are capable of. I heard the Evil's messages, promising great rewards in paradise. All the men of that city were letting themselves become hoodwinked by this promise. I was in the city when all the Bovers were either imprisoned or expelled because they did not agree with the wizard Drascar to follow the Evil. So I can understand Drew's anxiety.'

Jarew snapped back at Dolark, 'Well, what could you do in your condition?'

'Not much maybe,' he replied, 'but the rest of you could.'

We spent hours arguing the merits of whether to go back to Basscala or continue the quest. In the end, we decided to sleep on it and make a decision in the morning. The night was very dark, and ominous clouds were gathering on the southern horizon, so we made ourselves comfortable in the Elvan tent and rested.

The morning arrived, and as we opened the flaps of the tent, the cold air rushed in, and the ground around our tent was now covered in a deep snowdrift. Thank the high Elves for this tent, it must have been magic as it was so peaceful and warm and so spacious, although from the outside, it looked quite small.

Our faithful cooks Wecco and Jula made another great feast for us: soup from the smoked beef, with wild herbs, mushrooms, and vegetables they had been gathering on our hike along the path. As we ate, the discussion continued. I had kept quiet through all the talking when suddenly they all turned to me.

'Well, what do you think?' they asked.

I hesitated for a moment. 'I'm not sure,' I answered. 'I know the Evil has mustered a great force, but they were repelled from Basscala. Deep inside me, I feel we should continue to the caves of Mooloo at Mount Gatta. That was our last message from the parchment. Remember, Basscala is a very well-fortified city and the wizard, lords, and the armies of Dwarfs and Elves attacked the Evil forces from three sides and defeated them. The Evil is now in retreat. Personally, I think the Evil will not have time to wreak much havoc, as I'm sure the coalition will be hard on their tail. I think we should finish our task.'

Jarew, who had during the whole discussion wanted to continue, now changed his mind and said, 'We should travel back to Basscala and lend support in defeating the Evil and not continue with the quest.'

I couldn't fathom Jarew sometimes. I knew for sure he had a problem with Drew, and I didn't think he liked me for some reason, whatever that might be, as he always opposed what I suggested.

The company looked at each other, and I was not surprised when they all agreed with me. And I knew why—because Jarew had changed his mind and wanted to go to Basscala. Jarew looked at the company with such hatred when they all agreed to continue to Mount Gatta.

We packed up our gear in silence, moved back to the path, and continued up the Mountains Blue. The air was cold and still. The deep covering of snow was not as bad to walk on as we thought, and the boots were a great help.

The morning moved on quickly, and it was a peaceful walk except for Rocco asking his usual questions: 'When are we going to stop for lunch?' and 'How much further is it?'

After four hours, we stopped to eat our lunch. As we were packing up, we heard the screech and turned to see how the Dwarfs responded. Both Soltain and Dolark returned a screech and three white messengers landed on a log.

Dolark announced, 'This must be important. The white messengers hate the cold even more than we do.' The Dwarfs spoke to them for a few minutes and gave them some bread, which they ate, then squawked and flew off.

The Dwarfs turned to us and said, 'We have good and bad news. First the bad: the Evil Goblins, Menlins, and the Pernicious are on their way back up the mountain to Malfarcus. We must move fast now and make the pass of Malfarcus before the enemy. If not, we will not get through and will be trapped on the mountain for the winter. The good news is, the army of Good is coming to our support, but we do not know when they will be arriving, as they are chasing the Evil. The white messengers are heading back to the wizard Naroof with our plan to continue on our quest.'

47
CHAPTER

On the Tracks of the Evil

The allied forces were now on their long march up the snow-covered valley, following in the tracks of the Evil. They marched till sunset, made camp, and rested the night. Scouts were sent out to make sure the enemy had not stopped and were setting up an ambush. The morning came with more snow but it was not strong enough to cover the enemy's tracks, so the armies of Good packed up and continued with their march. As they set off, they met the scouts returning with the news that all was clear.

Another day passed without any sign of the Evil. The further up the mountains they travelled, the deeper the snow became, and if it continued snowing, the tracks would become much harder to follow.

As the day was drawing to a close, three white messengers arrived with the news from the fellowship of twelve. They flew down and landed on the horse of Master Baylib and relayed their message. The birds were not looking so good. In fact, they looked terrible. If you remember, they were not used to the cold, and it was having a profound effect on them. El Masrew noticed the condition of the birds, and while they were talking to Master Baylib, he pulled out an Elvan blanket and cut it up into small pieces, fashioning a jacket to cover the backs and breasts of the screechers, then cutting holes for the wings and feet to fit through. As the white screechers were finishing their message, El Masrew rode over to Master Baylib.

'Please,' he said, 'these will help protect your white messengers from the cold.' He handed him three small jackets made of fine Elvan cloth.

Master Baylib bowed and thanked El Masrew deeply. 'Will it hamper their flying?' Baylib asked El Masrew.

'No,' he said. 'This is magic Elvan cloth, and it will hug the birds like their own feathers.'

Master Baylib then turned to the birds and spoke to them. They lifted up their wings while he placed the jackets over them. They fitted perfectly. They took off and flew away to the north-west without any hindrance from their new protection.

Master Baylib turned to El Masrew and said, 'The birds will remember you always.' Then he continued, 'There is good news. Dolark has been rescued, and the company are continuing the quest and traveling over the Mountains Blue.'

'Did they mention their destination?' the wizard asked.

'No,' said Baylib, 'only that they were continuing with the quest.'

The company of Good set up camp, and the lords, wizard, Elves, and Dwarfs sat around a fire, ready to discuss their plans. They sat there waiting for the wizard to begin, but he seemed preoccupied.

Master Baylib stood up and said, 'The Mountains Blue are very large. Do we have an idea what pass they will be taking?'

'From the last reports,' Arcon said, 'I would say the company of twelve is heading for the pass of Malfarcus.'

'Would that not', El Masrew asked, 'be playing right into the hands of the Evil?'

'No, I don't think so,' said Lord Arcon. 'The Evil would not be expecting them to travel right past the great steel doors of Malfarcus, and I'm sure if they must pass that way, they will keep themselves well hidden.'

'If we have to attack Malfarcus,' asked Master Baylib, 'what are their strengths and weaknesses?'

The whole party turned to face Lord Arcon, but it was Revcon who spoke: 'Sorry, there are no weaknesses.'

The wizard was still preoccupied in thought and now had a strained look upon his face. Revcon continued describing the fort of Malfarcus. 'Imagine', he said, 'a wide road that leads up the mountain with the granite cliffs of the Mountains Blue on one side and the gorge of Malfarcus on the other. At the very top, there is a granite bridge that fords a gorge. As you cross this bridge, you will have your first glimpse of Malfarcus. Set back off the road and further up the mountain and built into the Granite Mountain itself, the fort looms up into the sky. There in front sit the infamous steel doors that they say once entered, one is never seen again.' This last statement made the whole company shudder with dread at the thought.

El Masrew asked Lord Revcon, 'Is it true that behind the steel doors there is a large valley with an evil city full of Menlins, Goblins, and even stranger creatures?'

'Even the black eagles of Jasper', said Revcon, shaking his head, 'did not return. At the request of Naroof, he had sent three young eagles to fly over Malfarcus to gather surveillance, but sadly, none have ever returned. So it is our guess that it must be the most evil place in the world. That is all we know of Malfarcus, but they are just rumours. It may even be worse.'

Mordlark then popped up and said, 'Well, I can't see why the quest seekers would even think of going past such an evil place.'

'They must have received directions from the parchments,' Lord Arcon said, 'and with the Evil and his forces away from the fort, it would not be such a problem to get past. I'm sure they are traveling as discreetly as possible.'

Suddenly, the wizard Naroof's face twisted up. 'No,' he moaned aloud then lamented, 'The quest seekers are in grave trouble right at this very moment, I can sense it.'

He stood in deep thought for what seemed an eternity then added, 'We must all rest tonight and make a move early tomorrow. We must catch up as soon as possible with the Evil forces and distract them from their march back to Malfarcus.'

48
CHAPTER

A Disaster Befalls the Quest Seekers

The higher we walked, the thicker the snow became, and it was now slowing us down. Dolark was feeling much better now and had less trouble walking. The Elvan walking stick had a six-inch plate extended from the base of the stick, which stopped it from slipping into the snow. The day wore on and we dragged ourselves through the snow until we stopped for half an hour for some lunch, then continued till the sun was on the verge of setting. We made camp, and Jula and Wecco were about to light a fire to cook some food.

'Not tonight,' said Drew. 'We are too close to Malfarcus. A fire would be too risky, and so tonight we shall have Elvan cake.'

Just looking at the excited face on Rocco cheered us all up. Carew and Tarew quickly finished assembling the Elvan tent, and we huddled inside and munched with delight our small piece of magic Elvan cake. We had all finished savouring it, except Rocco, who chewed on it for ages to the irritation of us all. Dolark and Soltain wished to know more about the Elves, and how the Evil had acquired so much power.

Drew turned to Carew and said, 'Maybe you should fill them in with some history of the Elvan prophecies.'

'Please,' the rest of us echoed, 'we wish to know more as well.'

So Carew started to relate to us the Elvan history and their relationship with Man:

'Many, many years ago, when Man and Elves first came to these shores, we lived in harmony, side by side. The first Elvan king of the New World was Samatta of Gundi. He was famous for his wisdom in dealing with the Men who had left the Old World in the wake of the Elves. There is also talk of a great Man, Lord Malla, who led his people into a time of great prosperity with his wisdom.'

'That must be where our town of Malla gets its name,' Jula interrupted, 'but we have never heard of him in our history.'

Carew continued, 'You are correct, Jula, but your people, with the help of the Evil, erased from your history what good he did. It was his preaching of tolerance, acceptance, forgiveness, and empathy for the environment and all living things that was contrary to the Evil's quest for power.

'Once there was a famous statue of Lord Malla in your town, but it was buried after an earthquake and may lie somewhere under one of your parks. Before the rise of the Evil, Man was kind and thoughtful to his neighbour, and the world was not just about oneself, but for all. Not like the present, where you see wealthy people living in great mansions with views over your river and harbour and their properties extending all the way down to the water's edge. This only allows other inhabitants a glimpse from a distance and where there are only some allotted places possible to walk along the foreshores and appreciate the beauty of nature.

'Eventually, Man demanded of the Elves answers to complicated questions, but our answers were not good enough for them.'

'What were the questions?' asked Jula then Wecco added, 'And what were your answers?'

Carew glanced over his audience with a sad look. 'Our answers were too simple,' he said. 'They had need of a more complicated explanation. They wanted to know where they came from and why they were here. We told them there is a great powerful force that has control of the universe and everything in it. It sometimes moves in mysterious ways, and this power is all encompassing. The trees grow and die, the water is circulated around the world like blood in a vein. When we die, we are returned to the earth to create new growth. Our earth stays pretty much the same weight. The only way Man can populate more of the world is to chop down rainforests or eliminate other species. This is what Man has been doing for the last thousand years, with no real understanding or empathy with the universe. We tried so hard to explain the simple understanding of the Supreme, but they needed more. They could not understand an abstract supreme God. They needed to make him in their own image. Your creeds are the outcome of these manifestations. He is the same Supreme, only Man has made him different for his own purpose, and the Evil has taken advantage of this by playing you against each other.'

Carew then began to get a little emotional. 'All the creeds', he said, 'are so hateful and think only theirs is the true faith. How stupid you all are.'

Drew placed his hand on Carew's shoulder. 'Be calm, my friend,' he said. 'We are not here to judge, but to help. As we can see with our friends, there is hope for mankind.'

Carew calmed down and cleared his throat. 'The High Elf Samatta had been given the parchments and a magic crystal by the Elves from the Old World.'

As Carew said this, Drew's voice raised in alarm: 'Carew, what are you doing? We were to keep that a secret from our friends so it would not place them in danger if they were captured by the Evil. This may now place the quest in jeopardy.'

Carew went red with embarrassment. 'What have I done?' he asked. 'I'm sorry. I just got carried away.'

Their audience sat there looking at the Elves, waiting for an explanation.

'Okay,' said Peto, 'we wish to know the rest.'

'It's too late now,' added Wecco. 'You will have to tell us.'

Drew shook his head and said, 'The damage has been done, so go on, Carew, with the story.'

Poor Carew looked so despondent and apologised again to his fellow Elves. 'I'm sorry.'

Drew patted him on the back and said, 'It may be better that they know. Continue with the story.'

Carew continued but without the same enthusiasm. 'This crystal,' he exclaimed, 'it is said, gives its owner great powers, and this was another thing that corrupted Man, the thirst for absolute power and the crystal.'

Drew then interrupted. 'We think the quest will lead us to the crystal,' he added. 'That is why we must not let the Evil know where we are going.'

Carew was still rather upset, and he didn't want to continue. 'May I continue the history later?' he asked. 'I have lost the momentum.'

The two Dwarfs sat staring in silence at the Elves. 'And when were you going to tell us?' demanded Soltain eventually. 'We have known about the Elvan prophecies, but there was no mention of a magic crystal.'

Drew gazed at the Dwarfs then slowly turned to face us. 'We are sorry,' he said, 'but the high elves stressed the less the Six of Croll know, the better and safer it will be for all concerned. I think we have talked too long. We have a hard day tomorrow so we should get some sleep.'

Drew was trying to distract us from our disappointment that something as important as the crystal was not disclosed to us. Dolark was already asleep, and the rest of us settled down without a word. The disappointed silence was deafening.

We woke to a delicious bowl of preserved peaches and sliced apples that Jula and Wecco had chopped up and sprinkled with some sweet and bitter herbs they had collected. The company was still giving the Elves the silent treatment over the news of the crystal, but I thought they were being a bit hard on them so I carried on as if all was fine and this slowly wore them down. By the time we had finished breakfast, all was back to normal. There had been more snow during the night, and this would slow us down even more.

Drew had been looking over the map, and he announced, 'It should take us less than a day and a half if the old map is correct, and we should arrive at the old Elvan northern road to Malfarcus, which is not on any of the current maps.'

He looked at Dolark and added, 'We should have told the white messengers we would be arriving by the old northern road, and the forces of Good could have met us at the Granite Bridge of Malfarcus.' We packed up our gear and set off on our journey. We had our usual stop for lunch then continued.

As the day drew on, Jula commented, 'I have not seen an animal or bird all afternoon!'

This observation put us on edge. In fact, making this comment made every other sound seem louder. The feeling we had was of anticipating danger, and it turned out to be just that.

Just before we were to make camp, Dolark, who was feeling the strain of the difficult walk, was lagging some distance behind, so I stopped to wait for him. Just as he took my arm, I felt a tingle on my armband, I did not look at it, as my jacket was covering the band, and it was the arm Dolark was resting on. But I wish I had.

The others had not noticed us lagging so far behind and continued at the same pace. With the depth of the snow and with what was to happen next, the company had no way of preventing the outcome.

Dolark and I were dragging ourselves through the snow when he said, 'Can you hear that slight whooshing sound?'

I stopped and listened. I could hear a faint whistling. As we stood there in silence, the whistle seemed to be coming closer and getting louder.

'Yes,' I said, 'what is it?'

Just as I spoke, we both looked to see three Pernicious diving straight towards us.

'Quick, run!' I yelled. But Dolark's condition and the depth of snow gave us no hope of reaching the rest of the company.

Our friends still had no idea what was happening behind them, as the Pernicious had not made a sound. I screamed out, thinking it was the company the evil things were after. As it turned out, they had nothing to worry about, as the Pernicious were after me. Peto had turned around to see us running in their direction with me dragging Dolark behind. The Pernicious were only about fifty paces from us when their screams pierced the quiet.

At the same time, Peto screamed to our friends, 'Quick, we must help Dolark and Mecco!'

The company by now had turned around to see the drama unfold. The Pernicious were now nearly upon us, with their claws outstretched and only a few paces away. This time, fate was looking after Dolark, for just as the Pernicious reached us, he tripped and fell into the snow. The middle creature's claws grabbed my wool jacket and started to lift me. By now, the Elves had their bows and arrows out and loaded. They were firing at the other two Pernicious, who were about to descend again on Dolark.

I was jabbing at the third one with my Elvan dagger, but he still held tight as I swung all over the place. I swung myself as hard as I could and finally had the chance to stick the blade of the dagger into his thigh. He screamed and let go, and as he did, I thought maybe that was not a good idea, as I was so high that the fall would probably kill me.

As I fell and the white-covered mountainside drew closer, I could see all my friends surrounding Dolark to protect him from the Pernicious, with their bows loaded and ready to fire. I then became aware that the company was looking at me falling. And I sensed they were using their power that we had practised in the magic clearing all those months ago, to try and soften my fall. I suddenly felt all would be fine, but as I watched my friends, a look of helplessness came over their faces. Then within a second, I knew why. One of the other Pernicious grabbed me this time by the feet. I had no way of swinging up to jab him with my dagger. As I dangled there helplessly, my sword fell out of its sheath, landing in the snow near my friends. I also took of my arm band and tossed it towards Drew. I watched as my friends diminished to small dots in the snow. The three Pernicious were screeching back and forth to each other as they carried me across the snow-covered mountains, obviously very pleased with their prize. Within minutes, I could see the dreaded fort of Malfarcus looming up on the horizon. I dangled from the claws of the Pernicious, wondering what was now in store for me.

49
CHAPTER

The Valley of the Dead Fig Trees

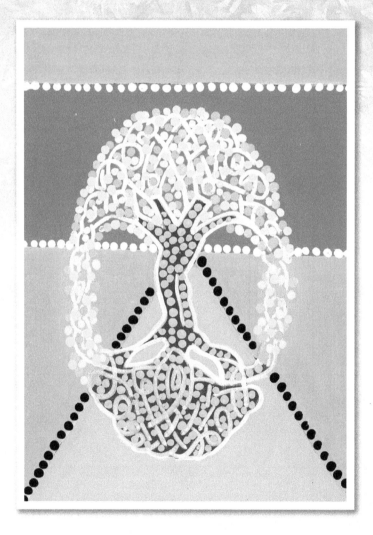

The second company woke to another dusting of snow. They ate, packed, and were ready to march off in no time at all. At that same moment, only ten kilopaces ahead, the Evil were doing the same, only at a slower pace. If we could see through the eyes of a flying white messenger, we could have seen both forces packing at once. The red banners of the Evil contrasted against the white snow and the mixed banners of the good fluttering in the slight breeze.

The day wore on, and the armies of Good were marching at a much faster pace than the Evil and making ground on them. At this pace, the allies would hopefully be at their heels before they would arrive at the start of the road which runs alongside the gorge of Malfarcus.

The men from the cities of Basscala and Kassob were marching behind the four Elves, the three Dwarfs, the lords, and the wizard, who were all on horseback. Then came the Elvan archers, who, being light-footed, had no problem with the deep snow. Last but not least was the army of Dwarfs. Because of all the other allies marching ahead, the snow was packed down and made firm; this made the march easier for the Dwarfs. The three white messengers with their new Elvan jackets now seemed to be handling the cold and had returned and relayed where the enemy was.

The wizard, who had hardly said a word, asked Master Baylib, 'Could you please send the white screechers to go and find out news of the quest seekers? I feel they have had a grave misfortune.'

The white messengers took off in a northerly direction and were only about a hundred feet in the air, when out of nowhere came two Pernicious diving down at them. Baylib screamed something, and the birds suddenly dived down in three different directions and then headed straight back in the direction of the allies. The Pernicious were following two of the birds and were only a few hundred paces behind them. The evil creatures then sent a burst of flames towards the birds. Thankfully they were too far from them to do much harm and only singed their Elvan jackets. Just as the birds approached the Elvan archers, Baylib screamed again and the messengers swung up into a vertical climb, and the Pernicious followed. At that very moment, the Evil creatures had exposed their underbellies, and a volley of at least a hundred arrows left the Elvan bows to head straight for the Pernicious.

The Evil creatures realised in a split second that they were vulnerable and turned themselves around so their armoured backs would fend off the arrows. Most of the arrows just bounced off their thick scales but a few found weak spots and the screams were vile.

Although they did not kill any of the Pernicious, they at least wounded them and forced them to retreat to their evil master. This gave the white messengers their chance to take off again and continue their task.

'The Pernicious will report our whereabouts,' said the wizard Naroof, 'so now we must make haste. We must stop them before they arrive at their fort near the entrance of the gorge. If they make it there before us, they will have the upper hand and, with only a token force, could delay us for days.'

The allied army increased their speed, and the wizard sent some scouts out to find out more about the terrain and what the enemy was up to. Naroof called his friends over for a conference and told the rest of the allies to continue the march, hoping they would catch up soon.

He turned to his friends. 'The Evil has grown in confidence,' he said. 'I can feel it in my bones. Can any of you sense the disaster that has befallen the quest seekers?'

'Yes,' said Lord Arcon, 'it is Mecco who is in grave danger. I can feel his stress right at this very moment.

'I have not met Mecco', said El Masrew, 'but feel some strange connection. If I didn't know he was a boy, I would think he was an Elf, as the vibes that I sense are very strong.'

None of the second company knew of Mecco's bloodline, except the elder Tarvin—and he was not going to reveal the secret as he thought the less they knew, the better it would be for Mecco. The one thing they all agreed on was that he was in great danger. And somehow, they knew it had something to do with stopping the Evil reaching Malfarcus. The company remounted and galloped off in pursuit of the Evil army, arriving just as they were entering the Valley of Dead Fig Trees. They knew if the Evil got back to his fort, there would be no stopping him or knowing what he would do next.

50
CHAPTER

A Change in Direction

The quest seekers stood silent and helpless as the Pernicious flew off with their friend Mecco dangling by one leg. For ten minutes they watched, speechless, till their companion was naught but a speck on the horizon.

Dolark was the first to speak and said, 'I am to blame. I was too slow and he came back to help me.'

'It was no one's fault,' said Drew. 'If anyone is to blame, it must be me. We should not have walked off so far ahead. Had we stayed together, we could have supported each other.'

'That's right. You wanted to be the leader,' barked Jarew. 'It's all your fault.'

'We are all to blame,' said Wecco. 'We never looked back to see how Dolark was. Mecco was the only one who worried about him.'

'Well, we must do something,' said Carew. 'They have obviously taken him to Malfarcus. If the Evil has not arrived back at his fort, then maybe we have a chance to rescue him.'

They all agreed and Rocco added, 'Well, the night is upon us, so we should make camp.'

'It's as plain as the nose on your face why you want to make camp, Rocco,' said Carew, and we all knew as well.

'Okay,' said Drew, 'we will rest tonight and move off very early in the morning.'

The company could see by the look on Rocco's face what he was thinking: *What does he mean by that, very early?*

'Excuse me,' said Jula. 'Are we just going to rest and do nothing about rescuing Mecco?'

'What do you suggest?' asked Jarew sarcastically.

'I don't know,' said Jula. 'You Elves are supposed to be the experts.'

'It's getting dark and colder,' said Drew. 'Let's discuss the situation over a meal in the tent.'

'Okay,' said Jula reluctantly, and Rocco added, 'I think that's a good idea.'

Carew and Tarew assembled the Elvan tent while Jula and Wecco started to prepare food. Drew felt guilty about my capture and allowed them to make a fire to cook a decent meal.

'I think it best if we split up tomorrow', Drew said, 'and you all travel to meet our allies on the bridge of Malfarcus. I will go alone to see about Mecco's rescue.' He turned to the dwarfs and asked, 'Is there any way of calling a white messenger? We must get news to the second company of our plight.'

'I will try tomorrow,' replied Soltain, 'but I don't think there will be any white screechers, as it is too cold for them at this altitude.'

Carew and Tarew turned to Drew and said, 'If you intend to try to rescue Mecco, you can forget it. We shall not let you go alone. We shall come too.'

Then Ricco and Peto added, 'We're coming too. You are not going without us.'

Then there were echoes from the rest of the company: 'We're not being left behind either.'

Only Rocco and Jarew were silent. Drew sat there and argued with his friends the best he could, but none of them would have a bar of it. In the end, the company made a declaration, although Rocco and Jarew were a little reluctant: *'If one goes, then we all go.'*

The company bedded down and spent a restless night wondering what was happening to me.

The morning welcomed the company with more snow, which had settled gently on the trees. It looked so beautiful and peaceful that it was hard to imagine there was such evil in the world. The group packed up and was standing, waiting for Drew.

'I have thought over your suggestion last night, and maybe you are correct. We should stay together to rescue Mecco,' explained Drew. 'I have been looking for a less conspicuous approach to the bridge of Malfarcus. There is an old disused road marked on this ancient map that travels along a cliff face, eventually joining up three quarters of the way along the gorge of Malfarcus. From there, we should be able to see the bridge. If our allies have succeeded in defeating or at least distracting the Evil, hopefully they will be waiting there for us.'

'So are we not going to rescue Mecco?' asked Ricco.

'Of course,' replied Drew, 'but we shall have a much better chance if we have the help of the second company. The only way to Malfarcus from here is via the northern road up the gorge. But I think it will be safer on the old mountain road I mentioned earlier. Still, we must be alert as we approach the gorge of Malfarcus, and if the second company is not waiting for us at the granite bridge, we shall rescue Mecco ourselves.'

The company moved off, trudging through the snow, but this time they stayed together.

'Please,' Drew asked Dolark, 'see if any of your white messengers are around.' But before he finished, Dolark made an almighty screech that echoed throughout the mountains. As the last echo faded, there was another screech. But this one was not an echo but a white messenger.

Dolark could not believe his ears. 'This is very strange,' he said. 'I have never known a white screecher to travel so high this time of year, but a white screecher it is.'

Dolark made another screech, and this time, the returning echoes were accompanied by a louder screech of a white messenger. Far on the horizon, three specks appeared and flew straight for the company. Within minutes, they had glided down and landed on an arm of the Dwarf.

Carew noticed immediately and said, 'These birds are wearing magic Elvan clothing that changes to suit their colouring. That is why they can cope with the cold.'

The dwarfs marvelled at the little jackets and said, 'We could do with an under-jacket like that to keep us warm. We appreciate the jacket Mecco got us, but we still feel the cold.'

'One day when time permits', said Drew, 'and we have some Elvan cloth, I will get our Elvan tailors to make you Dwarfs a magic jacket each.'

Then Jula piped up, asking, 'And what about me?' Then the rest of the company echoed her sentiments.

Drew put his hands to his ears to block out their demands. 'Okay,' he said, 'when we return.'

The Dwarfs were now talking to the messengers and relaying their news. Dolark explained that the allies were only a few kilopaces behind the Evil and were hoping to engage them before they got to the gorge. They were also greatly concerned about us, sensing there had been a catastrophe.

'Then we must let them know to what degree,' Drew said, 'and that three Pernicious have captured Mecco. We must also let them know of our plan to travel to the bridge of Malfarcus to join up with them, and if they are not there, we will attempt a rescue of Mecco ourselves.'

Dolark relayed the message to the white screechers and off they flew. The group felt a little safer, knowing their friends were only twenty or so kilopaces over the mountains. The white messengers should have no problems returning to the allies, as their white feathers against the snow would camouflage them.

But as they slowly disappeared into the distance, black dots began filling the sky. It was a murder of black crows descending upon them from the hills above. The company stood wondering if the white messengers would get the news of their whereabouts back to the second company.

Drew analysed the situation then faced the company. 'We must not stand here waiting in the open,' he said. 'It is too exposed.' So off they trudged in the direction of the old road, and after an hour, they arrived at it—although when Drew said *old*, I don't think he realised it would be this overgrown. The company came to a halt, glaring at the so-called road.

'We don't have to walk along that, do we?' asked Rocco.

'This is a very old map,' answered Drew, 'so when it says old, then it must be very old. But that will be perfect as the Evil will not expect us to take this way.' This argument convinced the company, so off they went, climbing over boulders and under overgrown bushes. Rocco did his usual moaning till it was time to make camp.

51
CHAPTER

Five Frightened Dwarfs

The two Pernicious returned to their master and relayed their news that the enemy was no more than five kilopaces away and making up ground. The Evil screamed a depraved sound, which put dread into all of his forces. He then turned to wizard Drascar and told him to assemble all his captains for a meeting. Within minutes, all of them had arrived on horseback, and were marching in a line on either side of the Evil on his Dragon steed with the wizard Drascar on his right.

The Evil than spoke very quietly, but surprisingly, all his captains could hear him. 'Our enemy,' he said, 'is gaining on us, and we must make the pass before them. When we arrive at the fort, we can deploy a small force to hold the pass, and the rest of the army can march back to the safety of Malfarcus. I have just been informed of good news by one of my six: we now have one of the Children of Croll.'

The Evil's captains cheered, then rode back to their respective forces and relayed the commands and news of the new prisoner, then the army of Evil picked up pace and continued their march.

The enemy was now halfway along the Valley of Dead Fig Trees and would be at the start of the road to Malfarcus by late afternoon. Using the river-crossing machine, they could traverse the frozen River Malfarcus that came down from the gorge, without breaking the ice. They were now only an hour's march away from their fort and the road that led up alongside the gorge.

At the same time, the allies were gaining ground and had now entered the valley. The snow here was much lighter, and the Elvan archers had moved up to the front of the army. But the wizard Naroof was still in a mood and was silent all the way. Ten minutes after entering the valley, he threw his hands up and halted his horse. 'We must stop,' he said.

'Why?' asked Lord Arcon. 'We will be on their tail in less than an hour.'

'There is the wide River Malfarcus', said the wizard, 'that crosses this dead valley, and we must take care as the Evil may have camouflaged it. We should not take the risk till we find out exactly where the river is. You all should freshen up, eat, and wait till I return from my surveillance or give the go-ahead for you to join me.'

He rode off straight towards the enemy, and within minutes, he had found where the Evil had crossed. The river was completely frozen over and covered with snow, so it was very difficult to recognise. He waved to his comrades to join him, and they rode down to where he waited with the army following. As they arrived to join their friends, the Pestilence of Pernicious and the Evil himself on his giant dragon steed landed on the opposite bank. As they landed, the Evil's power permeated the air, and fear struck the forces of good.

'Beware of the power of the Evil,' said Naroof. 'He will project different images to each of you, and you may think he is an Elf, a Dwarf, or a Man. Do not be fooled and remember he cannot change his cloak, staff, armband, or amulet. To have at least some of his power, he must be wearing at least one of those articles I have described, so have a good look at them.'

The second company stared at the Evil. But they were having great trouble concentrating on what Naroof had said. Remember, the Evil had the ability to project a similar image back to whatever person is looking at him. The Elves saw a great Elf, the Dwarfs a great Dwarf, and the Men a great Man. The cloak he wore was of the finest black silk with strange red embossed designs. His staff was at least two paces tall with red rings circling it, and his armband was of black leather with silver studs that went from his wrist to his elbow on his right arm. His amulet was made of gold and precious jewels and was displayed prominently around his neck. At the time, none of us knew how the Evil had acquired his powers, and it would be many months till we eventually found out, although we had our suspicions.

The company stood transfixed in a daze.

'Snap out of it, you lot,' Naroof finally said, 'and concentrate on what I just told you.'

They shook themselves then looked back at the Evil. He might now have looked like one of them, but they could also see he was Evil. They all concentrated and focused on his cloak, staff, armband, and amulet.

'Why must he wear at least one of those articles to have his power?' asked El Masrew.

'We are not sure,' said the wizard Naroof, 'but it is said that each of his trinkets is made of magic crystal.'

When this was mentioned, the elder Tarvin shuddered and said, 'Naroof, we must talk in private later.'

At this point, the rest of the army had arrived, and the Elvan archers had loaded up their bows and were standing along the river's edge. Naroof told the archers to wait while the rest of the army marched across the river and if the Evil things moved at all, then they should fire. El Masrew had to distract the archers from the mesmerising effect of the Evil by relaying what Naroof had said to him, and Naroof did the same to the rest of the allies. The Men and the Dwarfs started to cross the ice, but still the Evil and his Six stood there.

A third of the troops were halfway across when the wizard Naroof thought to himself, *What is he up to?*

At that precise moment, the Six Pernicious rose and flew downstream a short way then landed as hard as they could, close together at the same spot on the ice. The Elvan archers had fired their first volley of arrows, and they went whooshing through the sky towards the Evil Six. They reloaded, and waited for their next move.

The rest of the company stood watching as the cracking of the ice could be heard for many kilopaces; they felt helpless as they watched as the cracks begin moving along towards the army of Good. The wizard Naroof had called the troops back, and they were running and slipping as the cracks came closer.

The Six had risen again, and the Elves let go of their second round. Some of the arrows found their mark, but still, it did not stop the Six. This time, they landed harder with a louder thud. Suddenly the ice on their side of the river cracked and began to break up and flow away. Some of the Elves had run across to help the army as they were light-footed and could handle the ice. The others were helping their friends up the riverbank.

By now, most of the Men had made it back, but the Dwarfs were finding the going tough, although they were still keeping a good distance in front of the cracks. Those watching started to relax with the thought that they would make it. Then one of the smaller Dwarfs fell, and four of his friends ran back to help him. The company stood there in silence as the ice cracked and separated from the main ice shelf and slowly started to drift away with the five Dwarfs struggling to steady themselves.

Sitting on their horses, the second company watched helplessly as the drama unfolded. The wizard Naroof turned to Tarvin the elder and said, 'I will use my powers with that of the lords to distract the Evil. Couldn't you four Elves assist us?'

Tarvin turned to the wizard and the lords and said, 'I have not informed the three of their powers yet.'

'I think now', said Lord Arcon, 'would be a good time.'

'The lords and I', said Naroof, 'will use our power and project it to the Elves of Rew, and that will help them.'

The three Elves sat there wondering what this conversation was about, but El Masrew knew deep inside that he and his two friends were different. Tarvin the elder turned to the three Elves and told them they had special magic power and to use it to help the five Dwarfs.

Bayrew and Wayrew asked, 'What magic power and what would you have us do?'

El Masrew turned to face his friends. 'I can feel the magic,' he said, 'but why us?'

'We shall tell you why later,' said Naroof. 'For now, let us use our powers to draw the ice drift to our side of the river. Then you three go down and help them to get across to the firm ice. Do not be afraid.'

Tarvin added, 'Yes, the power of the wizard, lords and thousands of ancient Elves go with you.'

The second company stood and concentrated their power at the ice flow, and it started to steady and move towards the eastern shore. Then, from out of the blue came the six Evil creatures diving down towards the five frightened Dwarfs, who, as we know, hate the cold at the best of times and never learned to swim, so you can imagine their fear. The Elvan archers had reloaded their bows and were firing at will.

The wizard Naroof then sent a blinding flash of powerful magic towards the Six Pernicious. This distracted them from their evil task. El Masrew charged ahead and was now only a few paces away from where the Dwarfs lay on the ice shelf. Bayrew and Wayrew had moved to either side of El Masrew and were concentrating on holding the ice steady with their newfound magic power. El Masrew stepped across on to the ice shelf and held out his hand to help the frightened Dwarfs on to the firm ice.

The Six had regrouped and were ready to make another dive when the wizard Naroof sent another lightning bolt towards them. The Evil was watching and fired a powerful bolt of blue at Naroof to distract him from helping the Elves. Naroof was knocked flying off his horse and landed, dazed on his back in the snow. But by this time, the five Dwarfs and three Elves were now making a run to safety.

The Six were about to descend when the Evil made a loud, hideous cry, and the six turned and headed straight back to join their master. The Evil took off on his dragon steed with the Six in pursuit, and they faded into the distance. The good thing was that two of the Six were flying erratically. Some of the arrows must have done some damage. The three Elves helped the frightened Dwarfs back to the safety of riverbank with a sigh of relief from the company.

52
CHAPTER

On to the Fort of Malfarcus

As the scared, shivering Dwarfs and the second company stood staring back across the River Malfarcus, they knew too well that the Evil would not make the road up the side of the gorge without a fight.

'I think it best we travel upstream', said Naroof, 'to where the river is narrow and still frozen.'

The order was given, and the allies moved off, marching along the bank of the river for about three kilopaces. The Elves were the first to cross, and they were to check and make sure that the ice was firm and safe and give the signal if all was clear. The Dwarfs went next, which meant there would be help on either side if there was to be more trouble. The men of Basscala and Kassob followed, and last came the wizard and company leading their horses. The allies then headed towards the gorge of Malfarcus.

As they rode, the three northern Elves of Rew asked the High Elf Tarvin and Naroof, 'How did we come to have this magic power, and why were we not informed about it earlier?'

'Do you not remember fifty years ago,' asked Tarvin, 'when the first twelve born in the year of Rew had to answer the riddles posed by the elders and you three were the only ones to pass the test?'

'Yes,' said Wayrew. 'I remember it well. Often I have wondered what the purpose of it was and how nothing eventuated from it.'

Tarvin went on to say, 'At the same time in the forest of Gong, three southern Elves passed the same test and were set a task, which they succeeded in achieving with the help of another Elf and the lords. It was to bring together the Six of Croll. That was around the time when the Evil had come to prominence, and two of the lords, the four Elves, and the Six of Croll had to hide in a magic clearing in the forest of Gundi for fifty years. The six of Croll, the four Elves, and two Dwarfs who joined them are the quest seekers, and you three are part of that quest.'

The three Elves looked at each other, and Wayrew said, 'But, Tarvin, originally you said three Elves. How come there was an extra Elf?'

Tarvin then went on to tell the story of how Tarew joined the quest as the traveller's aid and how the Dwarfs also joined the group.

As the afternoon drew on, they could now see the cutting in the mountain that was the gorge of Malfarcus. The wizard estimated it was about three hours' march, so a decision was made to make camp, have a good meal, and get a good night's rest, then attack at first light.

The morning arrived bright and clear; the sun was low on the horizon but quite strong for this time of year, and the company packed up and set off on their march. As they approached the gorge, they could see the fortifications above and knew they had a challenge ahead of them.

The evil fort had walls two hundred paces high and was situated at the end of the gorge. From their battlements, they could see all the way up the gorge and in the other direction, over the valley of dead figs all the way to the River Malfarcus. The road passed around the edge of the fort, and a token force could hold off any attempt to pass it.

They stopped just out of range of the Evil's artillery that was strategically placed along the clifftop. Then they waited. As the day dragged on, the main company were discussing their strategy when three white messengers came flying down, landed by the Dwarf tent, and screeched. The company exited the main tent and stood anticipating the news as the three birds flew over from the Dwarfs' tent and landed on the arms of the Dwarfs. Their message was relayed to the company of the capture of Mecco and that the rest of the quest seekers were heading for the bridge of Malfarcus to meet up with the allied forces. The white screechers also added it would be very difficult to return, as the mountains were full of the black crows of Malfarcus.

'We have been attacked on two occasions,' they told them. 'But thankfully the Elvan jackets, as well as keeping us warm, have protected us from the beaks and claws of the black crows.'

'Please thank these three,' said Naroof. 'They have been a great help. Let them rest and feed them well. They deserve it.'

He then turned to his friends. 'I knew there had been a disaster with the quest seekers,' he said, 'but never thought it was this bad. Things are not looking good for us now.'

'I don't think we should underestimate the quest seekers,' replied Tarvin. 'If they work together, their power is tenfold.'

'But without Mecco,' queried Lord Arcon, 'how will they focus their power, as he was the connection between the Elves and children?'

'Please,' Tarvin said. 'There are four Elves there that know they have a duty to fulfil, and I'm sure they will do their best.'

'Maybe so,' said Arcon. 'But it was Mecco who had the power to focus them. Without his abilities, it may prove more difficult.'

'This talk is not helping,' Devcon interrupted. 'We must think of some way to help the rest of the quest seekers and to rescue Mecco.'

'The first task is to get past the gorge of Malfarcus,' added Naroof.

El Masrew was listening intently to the conversation. When it was over, he asked to speak to Tarvin alone. As they left the tent and walked over to the river's edge, they began to talk.

'Who is this Mecco,' asked El Masrew, 'and why would he hold such power, more than the four Elves?'

'At the moment,' replied Tarvin, 'I cannot tell you as I don't know, except that it was foretold in the parchments that came from the land over the sea thousands of years ago. The parchments said there would be a child by the name of Mecco who, with his five friends, would help defeat the Evil. Through his example, he would show Man a new way of understanding. When we meet up with the quest seekers and hopefully rescue Mecco, then maybe more can be revealed. In the meantime, we must concentrate on getting past the gorge of Malfarcus.'

53
CHAPTER
Another Story Unfolds

The Elves erected the tent, and the children made a small fire from wood gathered by the Dwarfs. Then Jula and Wecco made another great stew of the last smoked leg of lamb cooked with vegetables and wild herbs they had gathered earlier on the march. The company sat huddled in the tent, silently eating; all they could think of was Mecco.

'Okay,' said Drew. 'We must get a good night's rest, as the old road looks a much harder task than I first thought.'

'Really,' said Rocco sarcastically as they all bedded down.

The following morning was much colder although there had been no snow during the night. The company packed up and, finishing the last of the preserved pears, were ready to move off. Drew was pleased, as he was anxious to make an early start. Little did he realise he was projecting his anxiety to the rest of the company, and they had no alternative but to comply for their own peace of mind.

As they walked along the old road, the cliff on the left got higher and higher, the mountain on their right got steeper and steeper, and the road ahead got narrower and narrower. The wind grew stronger, and Drew took another look at the map. He realised this was another ravine branching off the gorge of Malfarcus.

The day had drawn on and was coming to a close when around a bend, they saw a gorge cutting into the mountain and, beyond that, a deserted stone village half overgrown with vines. There was a gigantic granite arch that would have to be passed to continue along the road but as they drew closer, they realised on the far side of the arch, the road had fallen away into the gorge. One by one, the company arrived at the arch and then stopped, staring down to the bottom of the ravine.

It was if they were all thinking exactly the same thing as they stood shivering silently on the edge of the gorge until their collective frustration took form in Jula screaming out, 'Well, what now?'

Then with only the whistle of the wind coming up from the ravine, a voice called back from behind the arch, 'Well, what now?'

The company jumped in fright, and Dolark and Soltain pulled out their axes.

'Show yourself', Soltain yelled, 'if you're game, but don't if you're smart.' He was obviously feeling frustrated as well.

Then the voice said, 'Show yourself if you are game.'

This time Drew asked, 'Please, could we see whom we are talking to?'

'So you want to talk?' said the voice. 'That might be fun. I have not had a conversation in decades. You know, no one has been along this road for many a year.'

'Well, could we see you?' asked Drew.

'Well, could we see you?' the voice repeated.

Jula, who was fed up with this game, screamed out, 'Well, can we see you?'

'Oh, that's it,' said the voice. 'Could we see you, or can we see you? Yes, I think this will be fun.'

Then Sol said something to Dolark in Dwarf, and there was a screech from behind the arch and the voice said, 'Silly old thing, ah. I can remember way off in my past, my parents speaking that language.' Then suddenly there was a large black bird with a red tail sitting on top of the arch, staring down at them.

'What a motley, morbid, miscellaneous mob we have here,' he said then added, 'Yes, this is going to be fun.'

'What is your name?' asked Jula.

'Oh, the hard questions first,' said the bird. 'Now, what is my name? Now, let's see—is it Chrissie wants a cracker, or is it Brucey wants a bottlebrush? Or is it Cobber wants a cuppa? I think it's one of those, or maybe it's not.'

Drew turned to his friends and said, 'We can't waste time playing these games. We must find a way around the rockfall.'

'We could use the vanishing,' suggested Carew, 'and take an Elvan rope over and attach it to that large rock then swing the rest of our party over.'

'Oh, going to ignore me now, are we?' said the bird. 'What manners! And I'm the only one who can get you through the arch and across to the other side of the rockfall.'

'And how could you do that?' asked Rocco.

'Well,' replied the bird, 'first I could tell you to read the writing at the base of the right side of the pillar, but it's too dark now, so you will have to wait till . . .' He hesitated and then said, 'Morning, yes, that's it, morning.'

'Yes,' said Drew, 'it is getting late. We should make camp now. It looks like more snow again tonight.'

'Snow,' said the bird. 'Yes, that's what it's called. I remember now.' Then the bird added, 'Please, you can stay in one of my homes. I have ninety-nine, you know, for you to choose from. This is getting better and better.'

'Fine,' said Drew. 'We will use one of your old houses tonight.'

So off they went, walking up the narrow cobbled street.

'No, no, no, you are going too far,' the bird screeched. 'Use the first house.'

'Didn't you say use any house?' asked Drew.

'Yes,' said the bird, 'but if you move too far from the gate, I will not be able to stay long and talk to you.'

'Great,' said Rocco, 'let's take the one at the end of the street.'

'That's not very nice,' said the bird.

'Yes,' Drew said in reply. 'He is giving us shelter for the night, so we must show some manners.'

So the company turned around and walked back to the house next to the granite arch. There were two empty spaces: one where a door would have been, the other a window. The interior was quite spacious with two other openings that would have been doors to their sleeping quarters. As they entered the room and started to unpack some supplies to make dinner, the bird flew onto the windowsill.

'I hope you are all aware,' he said, 'I'm the keeper of the gate.'

Rocco and Peto, who had started to make a fire, turned to their companions and said, 'That thing will not be talking all night, will it?'

'So now I'm a thing, am I?' said the bird. 'You better be nice to me, or you will never get through the gate.'

The Dwarfs had been talking among themselves while admiring the workmanship and the carving of the rooms. In fact, Dolark was thinking it was the most precise carving he had ever seen. Soltain turned to the bird.

'I have a question,' he said. 'How come you understood Dwarf?'

'Dwarf,' the bird said. 'My, I have not heard that word for many a year. That was the main language that was spoken here. It was the Dwarfs who built this village.'

'I don't believe you,' said Soltain. 'Our history never mentioned a village in this part of the east, and besides, all the Dwarfs travelled west.'

'That's where you are wrong,' said the bird. 'The village was built by Bidlook, son of Bidlark.'

If you remember, Dolark was the holder of Dwarf history. His eyes lit up at the mention of these two names.

He said to his friends, 'There is a vague mention of Bidlark disowning his son and forbidding his name to ever be mentioned.'

The bird then got really excited and jumped up and down. 'I know the whole story,' he said. 'I can tell you, I can tell you.'

'Then while we eat,' said Drew, 'why don't you tell us the history of Bidlook and this village?'

The bird became very excited. 'Yes, I can tell you, I will tell you. Will I start now?'

'Yes,' Drew said, 'why not?'

'I think we're in for a long night,' said Jula.

Carew and Tarew hung the Elvan tents over the holes where the door and window were and the company huddled around the fire. The bird had flown over to a rock shelf protruding from the wall, fluffed up his feathers, and then made himself comfortable.

He was about to begin when Jula asked, 'What is your name? We still don't know.'

The bird looked at the company and said, 'It's been so long I have forgotten.'

'Your feathers are so shiny,' said Dolark, 'I think we should call you Black Silver.'

The bird made a squawk of approval then added, 'Yes, I like that. It sounds strangely familiar. You may call me Black Silver.'

He began to tell his story. 'Many, many years ago when the world was at peace and Bidlark and his Dwarf diggers—can I say that again?'

The company nodded their heads, and the bird continued, 'Dwarf diggers, I like that, so the Dwarf diggers were building the mines, and Bidlook was his son and apprentice. They had travelled the countryside for years, building mines and tunnels for the menfolk.'

Soltain piped up and said, 'Yes, and they are still here and are famous.'

'Yes,' said the bird. 'But Bidlark became obsessive, and his gang of diggers had to work seven days a week and at least ten hours a day. This made for unrest within his crew. So the Dwarfs got a petition up and asked Bidlook to take it to his father, which he did. His father was so offended that he made them work even harder. Bidlook knew this was bad and tried to reason with him, to no avail.

The tension grew and grew. One night in the tunnels of Hawk, there was an argument between Bidlark and Bidlook over the style of the entrance. Three quarters of the dwarfs walked and stood behind Bidlook. Well, if you know the temper of an old Dwarf.' He looked at the dwarfs sitting and listening and said, 'You two would know.'

They smiled and shook their heads. Black Silver then continued, 'So at that moment, Bidlark banished Bidlook and his supporters and refused to even discuss it. Bidlook and his supporters then walked out of the tunnels of Hawk and went to the females' caves. Off they marched with their wives and children till they found this place and decided to stay here. Bidlook called it Dissident, and they began building the houses cut out of the rock.'

'So where are the Dwarfs now?' asked Soltain.

'I'm getting to that,' said Black Silver. 'The village of Dissident was a prosperous and happy place for hundreds of years till it must be about a thousand years ago, when the Evil built his fortress of Malfarcus, only a few days' march from here.' Black Silver paused with a dreamy look in his eyes. 'I'm really enjoying this,' he squawked. 'It's been so long since I've had such a conversation.'

Jula piped up, 'Excuse me! This is not conversation as you're doing all the talking.'

'Well,' Black Silver replied. 'Do you want to hear the end or not?'

'Yes, please,' said the company. 'Go on with your story.'

He continued, 'Now, to build his fort, the Evil started to quarry granite from a mountain very near here at the time of the Dwarf leader Bellark.'

Dolark interrupted. 'That's a female name,' he said. 'Why would he call himself that? And what happened to Bidlook?'

'You funny little Dwarf,' said Black Silver, 'even Dwarfs don't live forever. He died a happy old Dwarf. And Bellark was a female and one of the great forward thinkers of the day.'

This was strange for the western Dwarfs as they had never had a female leader. 'So where is she now?' asked Soltain.

Black Silver was now getting quite angry because of all the interruptions. 'If you don't be quiet,' he said, 'I will not go on with the story.'

Drew then turned to his friends. 'Okay, let's all be quiet so our little black friend can finish his story, as we must get rest some time tonight.'

'Thank you,' said the bird and continued. 'So the Evil was mining and transporting the stone away, and this was against the Dwarfs' philosophy, what a lovely word is *philosophy*. Anyway, the Dwarfs would not allow the Evil to transport the stone past Dissident, so they collapsed the road to stop the Evil. This really upset him, and for the next twenty years, he did everything in his power to destroy Dissident. First, he poisoned the crops on the upper terraces and stationed evil creatures at either end of the road to stop all travellers coming or going. Bellark decided to tunnel through the mountain and move on somewhere else, and start a new village. My family and I were left here to guard the gate.'

'How could a bunch of birds guard a gate?' asked Soltain.

'It's not a bunch of birds,' replied Black Silver. 'It's a flock of birds, and to be more precise, I'm a parrot. And we were the only ones who could stay here safely without hindrance from the Evil. Also, we could relay the magic words to bring out the shelf to repair the road so travellers could make their trip.'

He went on, 'My family have all moved on to the great perch on the horizon, and I'm the only one left. When I go, the road will never be used again.' He was beginning to get rather sad now, thinking of his departed family.

'This has been a great story,' said Drew, sensing the bird's sorrow, 'and you have told it well. When others hear it, I'm sure someone will write a song. It is deserving of one. I think we should rest now and you can finish your story while we eat our breakfast in the morning.'

The fire had turned to glowing embers.

Black Silver asked, 'Could I sleep on the ledge tonight?'

'Yes,' said Drew. 'Of course, you may, and sleep well, my fine feathered friend.'

The company settled down and was asleep in no time at all, though thoughts of Mecco still played in their dreams.

54
CHAPTER

The Taking of the Gorge of Malfarcus

The second company's army slept well, and the following morning while eating a healthy breakfast, the leaders were in the main tent, discussing their strategy for the attack on the fort at the Gorge of Malfarcus.

'I can sense that Mecco has made contact with Sebcon,' said Naroof, 'and if I sense it, then perhaps so has the Evil. We must attack the enemy as soon as possible.'

'But they are so well protected,' said Arcon. 'We will have many losses.'

Naroof for some reason looked a lot older today. I don't think he slept well, and the reason was that he had spent the night thinking about exactly what Lord Arcon had just mentioned. Naroof shook his head slightly.

'I know, Lord Arcon,' he said, 'but we do not have any other choice.' He then turned to the Elves. 'Do any of you have the ability to disappear from one place and appear in another?'

'I cannot,' said Tarvin, 'but the three northern Elves of Rew should have this ability.'

'We have only just been informed of our powers', said El Masrew, 'and have never attempted the vanishing. How are we supposed to know what to do?'

Naroof stepped forward and faced the Elves. 'If you have the powers, it will come easy for you.'

Lord Arcon added, 'I was there when the three southern Elves of Rew received their instructions, and I can explain all I know.'

Naroof faced the two lords and announced, 'I think one day I shall have to teach you the vanishing as well.'

'Is it possible for us to learn?' asked Arcon.

'Yes,' Naroof answered, 'but not at the moment.' He turned to face the Elves. 'When we finish this meeting, go with Lord Arcon. Let him tell you what he knows and try to master the vanishing. I have a plan.' He explained it to his companions and then Tarvin and the lords went off to relay it to the rest of the army.

The three Elves with the help of Arcon spent all of the day working on perfecting the vanishing, while the rest of the army prepared for the battle. As the day drew to a close, the three Elves born in the year of Rew had mastered the vanishing. They then set of to execute Naroof's plan, moving from tree to boulder and boulder to tree, using their newly acquired powers. Their purpose was to get as close as possible to the enemy to analyse their position and strength and report back to the company.

The three Elves arrived at the base of the gorge. They synchronised their time and set off in different directions. It only took them four and half hours, and they were back at their camp. The rest of the company was seated in the main tent when the three Elves pushed open the flaps and walked in.

They bowed respectfully. 'The Evil has only left a token force,' said El Masrew. 'From what we can see, they will not be able to use all their artillery. I think we three and perhaps another nine or ten Elvan archers could get above and rain down arrows upon them, and that should distract them. And this should make it easy to attack from the gorge road.'

'That is exactly what we need,' announced Naroof, 'a distraction. I was hoping he would underestimate us, and he has, but what I would also like you to do is to position some of the Elvan archers where they have a good view of the road to Malfarcus and make sure none of his army escapes and gets a message to him. This will be your business: to distract the enemy and to stop any messages from getting through. Early tomorrow morning, before the sun rises, you three of Rew must take your archers and try to get in position. Then as soon as the sun hits the fort, rain down your arrows, and we will attack from the road.'

Later when the company spoke of this battle, everyone agreed that the night before had seemed to drag on and last forever. An hour before the sun rose, the Elves left, and the rest of the army marched quietly to take up their posts. It was a crisp, clear, and cloudless morning. The sun's rays slowly made their way down the snow-covered mountains to the grey granite garrison that stood out in contrast against the white of the snow.

As the first rays of the morning sun hit the fort, the archers sent their first hail of arrows down on the enemy from above. At the same time, the other archers sent another flurry of arrows from the road. The Men and Dwarfs had connected their shields and were advancing towards the fort's walls. The Menlins and Goblins were running around like crazy trying to take up their positions when the second rain of arrows hailed down. The enemy had only one catapult manned and had so far fired only one flaming ball. They were trying to load another when the third hail of arrows whooshed down to send them running for cover.

This was the break the allies needed, and the men from Basscala and Kassob were firing up grapple hooks over the walls. Attached to the hooks were ropes with large knots in them spaced a few feet apart. The men were using these to begin to climb the walls.

After twenty minutes, the fort suddenly went quiet, and not a Menlin or Goblin could be seen. The ten Elvan archers and the three northern Elves of Rew stood waving to the rest of the army that all was clear. The wizard, lords, and Dwarfs stood looking up as the Men scaled the wall then opened the gate. When they entered, there was still no enemy to be seen.

Then, just as the company was about to ride into the fort, a hideous screech stabbed the silence, and suddenly diving down towards the Elves on the snow-covered mountain were three Pernicious with their talons outstretched. The Elvan archers had not reloaded, and the company stood helpless as the Evil things headed straight for the Elf standing on the highest point, grabbing him from behind as they flew off in the direction of Malfarcus.

The Evil things had learned from experience that grabbing the Elves from the back, they had no way of defending themselves. As the three Pernicious flew off, it became obvious who it was they had captured. And though the second company and the army had taken the fort and should have been pleased with only one casualty, they weren't for it was El Masrew whom the Evil had captured.

The army searched high and low for the enemy, but they had seemed to disappear without a trace. Then one of the Dwarfs informed the company that he had found an old Dwarf door that had been locked from the inside. 'That is how the enemy made their escape,' he told them.

'Be prepared to continue the march up the gorge of Malfarcus within half an hour,' announced Naroof to the army. He also sent six Dwarfs to see if they could get the old Dwarf door open. If not, could they somehow lock or seal it from this side so that the enemy could not come back through the same way?

The half hour had elapsed, and the army was prepared to continue its march on Malfarcus when one of the Dwarfs returned and announced, 'We had no luck with opening the door, so decided to brick it up. We should be finished shortly and then we will catch up with the rest of the army.'

The army then began their march and what a splendid sight it was.

The company led on horseback, with El Masrew's horse being led by Wayrew, then the Elvan archers all in white, followed by the Dwarfs and the Men of Basscala and Kassob. It must have been a spectacular sight from the far hills as the army stood out against the gloomy grey granite garrison.

Naroof looked even more worried and called out to his friends to come closer. He spoke in a low voice, but they all could hear what he was saying. 'The Evil now has a lord, an Elf of Rew, and a child of Croll, and this will make him much more powerful.'

'But how?' asked Bayrew. 'I'm sure they will not help him. I know El Masrew will not.'

'It's not that our friends will help him in any way,' said Naroof, 'but his Evil forces will grow more confident with our friends captured and this is what will give him the power. We must somehow create an environment of mistrust among his forces, and this will lessen his strength. But how to do this—that is the problem.'

The company marched all day then set up camp along the road just as the night began to fall and a heavy fog descended from the east. The following morning, the fog was still hanging in the air, and this would be to their advantage. The army set off, arriving at the Rope Bridge of Malfarcus by midday. By this time, the fog had lifted, and Naroof decided to set up camp.

55
CHAPTER
Three Prisoners Unite

As I hung from the claws of the Pernicious, I could now see clearly the walls of the Malfarcus. What a sight it was, built between two great mountains a few thousand paces back from the bridge and, behind it, a great bustling city. The wall joining each mountain was a hundred paces tall, and in the middle was a great steel gate that looked as if it could never by penetrated. The evil creatures carried me over the city, screeching and showing off their prize. At the end of the valley, past the city, was a large palace of black granite with a prison attached on its left. As we descended closer to the tower on the western side, I could see a group of Menlins and Goblins screaming and jumping up and down.

The Pernicious circled and dropped me into the middle of the waiting horde. Within seconds, they had me bound and gagged, shouting, 'We have a child for the Master.' I was whisked off into a cell with large open windows overlooking the city. I lay there for a few minutes composing myself on the frozen floor. I could sense another power nearby and realised it must have been Lord Sebcon. As I lay there, I knew that he was also sensing me, but what could we do? I looked around and saw another door with bars on it. I rolled over to it and peered in, and there hanging from the wall half-naked was Lord Sebcon. He looked as if he was dead but I could sense he was still alive.

He then projected some form of image of himself, which spoke to me. 'Is it truly you, Mecco?' he asked.

'Yes,' I answered, and his hanging body groaned.

'This will be the end,' his image said.

'Don't worry, Lord Sebcon,' I continued. 'The Evil was defeated at Basscala and is in retreat.' Yet I could still sense some anxiety coming from him.

'Mecco,' he explained, 'I still have some magic left in me, and somehow we must use it to get you out of this evil place before the Evil arrives back.'

'But how?' I asked.

'I will think of something,' Sebcon said, 'but we must do it before he arrives back, as he will be able to pick up our thoughts.'

'How come your body looks quite lifeless hanging there?'

'My only escape from the torture and cold', he replied, 'was to go into a type of hibernation and close off all my physical senses.'

'Have you been practising the vanishing?' he asked. So I explained to him all that had happened so far on the quest and about rescuing Draylib.

'Try and get yourself free of your restraints,' he said.

So I spent the night trying to work myself free, but to no avail. The morning arrived, and the sill of the large window looking over the city was covered in snow. I was lucky I still had my sheepskin jacket on, but I could sense the cold of Lord Sebcon and this was making me shiver. Then as the light grew stronger, a Goblin and a Menlin came with food and pushed it under the bars. Well, not really food, just slop, and there was no way I was going to eat it.

Lord Sebcon asked again, 'Have you freed yourself, Mecco?'

My answer was still no, but I added, 'I will keep trying.'

It was nearly midday when I could hear the screeches of the evil Pernicious flying overhead again, and I wondered what was to happen now. The next thing, I could hear the Menlins and Goblins making their hideous yapping and coming closer and closer, then to my surprise, they threw in an unconscious Elf. He lay there and I did my best to make him comfortable, but it was difficult with my tight restraints. Sebcon asked me what was happening and I told him an Elf had been captured and he made a groan of despair even louder than before.

'Who is it?' Sebcon asked nervously.

'I do not know, Lord Sebcon,' I said. 'I have never seen him before, but he looks older than the four Elves of Rew.'

I sat thinking what this meant, when he started to come round. He lay there looking up at me with the largest brown eyes I have ever seen.

'Are you Mecco?' he asked.

'Yes, but how do you know my name?'

'Mecco,' he said, 'you are famous. I hear that you can do great things and somehow can harness the innocence of children and the magic of Elves to produce great power.'

I thought about what Drew had told me all those weeks ago—that I had Elvan blood and one day it would develop into a strong force for good by harnessing the righteousness in the world.

'Yes, there have been strange things happening to me,' I said, 'but I'm not sure I understand, though I do feel it is for the good of the world.

The Elf then introduced himself as El Masrew from the northern forest of Barrington, one of the three Elves of Rew chosen to help with the quest.

'I don't understand,' I said. 'The quest has four Elves of Rew from the rainforest of Gong.'

'Yes, I know,' he responded, 'but we from the forest of Barrington also were acquainted with the prophecies and knew we had to send three Elves to help and that we have done. I shall tell you all later, for now we must somehow find a way to escape from this evil place. The army of good has, I hope, taken over the fort of the gorge of Malfarcus and, at this very moment, should be marching up the road to attack the Evil.' He suddenly looked round and asked, 'I sense another power of good here somewhere.'

'Yes,' I said, 'it is Lord Sebcon of Basscala. He is in the adjacent cell, but he is in a state of hibernation, though he has communicated to me.'

'It is true, then,' El Masrew said. 'You do have great powers. I can sense him but cannot receive any connection with him. Is he aware that I am here?'

'Yes, but for some reason, it has made him more anxious, although he seems calmer now. I will ask him why.'

I then spoke to Lord Sebcon and asked why he felt the way he did. His transparent image materialised.

'My first thought was bad news,' he said, 'as the Evil will be harnessing more power from the propaganda of having a lord, a child, and an Elf as his prisoners, but now I think it could be a blessing in disguise. With the power of your innocence, the magic of the Elf, and what little magic I have left, we may be able to get you two out of here before the Evil returns, although I sense he is close, so we will have to work fast.'

'And how are we to do that?'

'Use your powers,' he said, 'to let the Elf see me and hear our conversation.'

As he was saying this, I could sense El Masrew's thoughts and he sensed mine, and suddenly, he could also see and hear Lord Sebcon.

El Masrew looked at me in wonder. 'You are not an ordinary child.' He said, 'This is very peculiar. You do possess Elvan magic.'

'There is not time to discuss who has what,' said Lord Sebcon. 'We must work fast.' His first question was for El Masrew.

'Do you have the ability to vanish?' he asked.

'Yes,' said the Elf.

'Good,' said Sebcon. 'Then first you two must use your magic to untie the rope that restrains you. If you start to sense the Evil, clear your minds and project that you are still tied up.'

For the next hour, we manoeuvred ourselves into a position near the door that led to the cell where Lord Sebcon hung. We continued for the rest of the afternoon using our powers to loosen the ropes, and on three occasions, we had to cease as we could feel the dreadful overpowering presence of the Evil. It was a strange sensation, and for some strange reason, I was the only one who could see him.

He walked around and looked at Lord Sebcon and us. We all lay there quite still as if we could not move. When he left, I told the other two that I could see him and that it looked as if he was thinking we were still restrained.

While we were working to untie the ropes, El Masrew told me all about his part in the quest, the fall of Hawksfort, the sail up the coast to the river Condoor, and the victory at Basscala, and I told him about our part of the adventure.

Then just as the sun was setting and the ropes fell from our hands, we could hear the growling and moaning of Menlins and Goblins coming towards our cell. We both rolled back to where they had left us, twisted the rope around our hands, and El Masrew acted as if he was still unconscious. The wooden door to the cell swung open, and there standing looking down at us with a repulsive smile was none other than Captain Yobtowoy and his offsiders.

He looked down at us lying flat on the frozen floor and said, 'Look what we have here, a little glupgar and an ugly grosfuss.

56
CHAPTER

The Second Gate

W ecco rose early and was preparing the breakfast as the rest of the company awoke to the smell of fried vegetables and leftover smoked lamb in butter. Jula never said a word, but the company knew she was annoyed with Wecco for starting breakfast without her. Rocco was seated first in line to have his share, but there was no sign of Black Silver, as he had flown out much earlier. While they ate, all they could talk about was Mecco and how they were to rescue him.

As the discussion continued, the parrot flew back and landed on the shelf. 'Talking, talking, are we?' he asked. 'I thought I was to finish my story this morning.'

'Okay,' said Drew. 'While we finish our breakfast, you may continue your story.'

'First, I must warn you,' said the bird. 'There are a lot of crows of Malfarcus hanging around the mountain at the moment. When you leave, you must be very careful, as they will get a message back to the Evil in no time.'

He ruffled his feathers and cleared his throat and then began his story again. 'The Dwarfs had made a secret tunnel through the mountain and sent out four explorers to search for another mountain where they could build a new village. After nearly a year, they returned with news of a great mountain many miles to the north.'

The company sat listening to the story, but none were more enthralled than the two Dwarfs. Dolark, who was sitting by the window at the demand of the rest of the company because of his annoying pipe-smoking, asked, 'So where are they now?'

The parrot replied, 'When the Dwarfs left here hundreds of years ago, my ancestors were given the task to only let good travellers past the gate and told that they would send for us when they were settled in their new home. My family and I waited for hundreds of years without a sign of a Dwarf. In fact, you two are the first I have ever seen. The rest of my family moved further up and over the mountains, and I was left here to guard the gate and to wait in case any dwarfs returned one day.'

'This is very interesting,' Dolark said, 'more Dwarfs somewhere on this continent that we knew nothing of.'

'Well, maybe,' Black Silver said, 'but why did they not send for us?' He added, 'Maybe the Evil was waiting at the end of the tunnel and captured them, putting them all to work in his mines. It did seem as if he finished his fort of Malfarcus very fast, so the story goes, and it was just after the Dwarfs all left.'

'That is terrible,' Dolark said, 'if the Evil had them all working as slaves to build his evil fort.'

'I don't know if they were captured,' Black Silver said, 'but from what my family told me, the fort was suddenly finished, and it was only about two years after the Dwarf exodus. I am now eighty and my family waited two hundred years before they left, and at the time, I was only ten.'

Drew then interrupted the story and said, 'We must think about making a move if we are to meet the army of good on the bridge of Malfarcus.'

Draylib then turned to Black Silver. 'Have you ever come across white parrots?' he asked.

The bird made a laughing sound. 'They would not come this far up the mountain,' he said, 'at least not in winter. But now and then when the weather is warm, some do venture to this altitude.'

'But the last time we saw white messengers,' Dolark explained, 'they were wearing magic Elvan cloth for warmth. So maybe we will see some when we get on the road again.'

'I don't think so,' said Black Silver, 'not with a murder of Malfarcian crows hanging around and I must reiterate—that's a nice word too, isn't it, *reiterate*,' he repeated himself. 'Reiterate—now where was I? Yes, be wary of the crows.'

Jula, Wecco, Tarew, and Carew had already packed up the gear and were waiting impatiently at the door. The Dwarfs, however, were a little reluctant to make a move as they wished to hear more about Dissident.

'You're not going now, are you?' asked Black Silver. 'Do you not want to hear more stories? I have many from all the different travellers who have passed this way. There were wizards, lords, Elves, Men, and a lovely lady with magic powers called Lillipilli. She used to travel this way often but has not been this way for many a year. You must stay a day more so I can tell you. There are so many marvellous stories.'

'We thank you very much for your hospitality', Drew said, 'and the story, but we must be on our way. We have a quest to finish.'

'Tell me about it,' said the bird. 'I could add it to my other stories.'

Dolark then stood and said, 'When this quest is over, I will bring back some other Dwarfs to search the village and tunnels for clues and find out where the Dwarfs went or what happened to them.'

Black Silver started to get quite excited. 'That would be wonderful,' he said, 'and maybe they could rebuild the village and move in to live here.'

'Maybe,' said Dolark, 'but for now we must say goodbye. We do have a pressing engagement.'

The company walked through the door and assembled at the granite arch.

Drew said to Dolark, 'I think you should read the message at the foot of the pillar. I assume it is in Dwarf.'

Dolark knelt down and began to read, but it was not in Dwarf at all but the common tongue.

> *So you wish to travel along this road*
> *To sell your wares and lighten your load.*
> *Or is it to take in the scene*
> *From this mountain high into the ravine?*
> *No matter what the reason be,*
> *When you say these words, I will see*
> *That in your heart if you carry hate,*
> *Then you shall never pass this gate.*
> *But if it is good that is in your heart,*
> *Then the road will appear and you can start*
> *To travel uphill and around the bend*
> *To take you to your journey's end.*

The company circled the gate and stood waiting in the shimmering, silent sunrise. Minutes passed but nothing happened.

'Well, I told you,' said Black Silver. 'No one can pass until I recite the poem.'

'So recite it,' said Rocco.

'A please would not go astray,' Black Silver said.

'Would you mind reading the poem for us?' asked Drew politely.

'Certainly,' answered the bird, and then he recited it loud and clear.

Suddenly there was a cracking sound, and straight ahead where the road had fallen into the ravine, a shelf slid out from the cliff face and a bridge materialised over the collapsed chasm as the company looked on in wonder.

Rocco piped up, 'It doesn't look safe to me.'

'I think you should go first,' said Peto, 'and if it holds you, the rest of us will have no problem at all.'

Jula turned to Peto and said, 'Stop being a smarty. We shall all go together.'

Drew also looked a little insecure about them crossing at once.

'I think we should go one at a time,' he suggested.

But before he had a chance to say anymore, the Dwarfs stepped on to the ledge and walked across.

'If it was built by the son of Bidlark,' said Dolark, 'it will be safe.'

Black Silver sat upon the gate, laughing at the rest of them. 'You should go now,' he said. 'It only stays there for a few moments.'

Jula and Wecco then ran across, with the rest of them in hot pursuit except one. The company was now on the other side except poor Rocco, who stood hesitating.

'Come on, Rocco,' Peto and Ricco sang out. 'You don't want to be left behind as we have the last of the provisions.'

That was all the persuading Rocco needed, and off he ran. He was halfway across when the bridge started to retract, and poor Rocco went white with fear. He made his last step on to solid ground just as it completely disappeared back into the cliff. Black Silver squawked and said,

> *'When the wind is cold, may the sun be on your face.*
> *When the snows they fall, may you find a warm place.*
> *May your shoes hold firm when the ground is damp.*
> *May a safe clearing be waiting when it's time to make camp.*
> *So be on your way with good luck.*
> *And maybe one day you'll return to us.'*

The bird added, 'Well, it's just me now, as the rest have gone.'

The company waved farewell to the bird and thanked him for his kind hospitality and his stories, then moved off in single file along the ledge. The ledge was only two paces at the widest point. The air was still very chilly but that was not the company's main worry. The next section of the walk was very exposed and not just to the weather.

They continued the walk and the day drew on. They stopped to eat their lunch but only for a few minutes, then continued the walk, much to Rocco's displeasure. The afternoon was getting colder, and the mountain cast its long shadow over the company. They continued to walk as the day drew to a close, but they had still not found a safe place to camp.

Rocco was bringing up the rear and said, 'When is that good-luck clearing going to appear that the know-it-all bird talked about?'

Just as he was speaking, Dolark, who was in the lead, turned a bend, and there on his right was a small gate leading into a small cave.

'Stop your whinging,' he scolded Rocco. 'Here is a cave to spend the night in.'

The company filed in, and they were very happy with what they found. There was another space off the main cave, so they could use one for sleeping and one for cooking. The night was now fully upon them, and the cave was a welcome find. They made themselves comfortable and settled down to rest.

'Tonight, we shall have Elvan cakes', said Drew, 'and save the last of the provisions for our breakfast.' This announcement was received with great enthusiasm, especially by Wecco and not to mention Rocco, although Jula was still annoyed with Wecco for starting breakfast without her.

'Well, I insist on cooking tomorrow morning,' she said, glaring at Wecco.

The company happily munched on their Elvan cakes for a long time. Eventually they finished, except for Rocco who was munching away, to the aggravation of all. Drew was looking over the old map when suddenly Carew stood up and said,

> *'Tomorrow in this cave, you must stay,*
> *Then wait till dark to make your way.*

The evil things, they are close by,
So wait till there are stars in the sky.
Then you may set out upon your climb
And in the morn, a rope bridge you will find.
This will take you across the canyons,
And there on the other side will be your companions.
But be very careful when you cross that bridge,
As the Evil has scouts upon the ridge.'

Carew sat down again, looked around in surprise. 'What happened?' he asked.

'Open the parchments and read it,' Drew said and Carew did.

And we realised if Carew was awake, he went into a trance and would recite the message on the parchments.

'So we have to spend all day tomorrow in this cave, but won't it be dangerous to travel by night?'

'The dark is not our worry,' Soltain said. 'The Evil is. We Dwarfs are more adapted to the dark than you, so we will lead the way. Also, don't forget this road was built by Dwarfs.'

'So does that mean we can rest all tonight and tomorrow?' asked Rocco.

'I suppose so,' said Drew. 'That's if we are to take heed of the parchment, and it has not let us down so far.'

'Great,' said Rocco. 'I can sleep and eat all day.'

'Sleep you may,' Drew replied, 'but eat—that is another question. We only have a small amount of provisions left, and they must be rationed equally among the company.'

'What about the magic Elvan cake?' Rocco asked quite sarcastically.

'Will you shut up?' Peto said angrily. 'I'm sick of listening to your complaints about food, how much further is it, when are we stopping for lunch, and so on.'

You should have seen the faces on the rest of the company, as Peto's words echoed their sentiments.

Rocco was also aware of the company's reaction and felt wounded to the core. He walked off to one of the other rooms in the cave to sulk.

'I know we are all on edge,' said Tarew, 'but there was no call for that, Peto.'

'I'm so sick of his whinging,' said Peto.

'Aren't we all?' laughed Jula. 'But now is not the time to add to our tension.'

'Excuse me,' said Peto. 'That's a bit the pot calling the kettle black.'

Jula ignored him. 'I will go and talk to him,' she said then walked into the other room and over to the corner where Rocco was seated.

He looked up. 'Why do they all pick on me?' he asked.

Jula sat down next to him. 'Please, Rocco, we are all under pressure at the moment, what with the capture of Mecco and this dangerous journey to meet our other friends. We are all afraid. And you are always asking those annoying questions.'

'That's right,' said Rocco, 'now you too. None of you really like me. Anyway, you're an Aldation, what would you know?'

'Well, you're a Kab,' Jula abruptly replied, 'and we all know about their greed and ability to use other people.'

Jarew had walked into the room and overheard the conversation. 'You are all stupid anyway,' he said. 'It doesn't matter what creed you are.'

Wecco, who had followed Jarew and overheard his comment, pushed Jarew and said, 'Don't you talk to Jula like that.'

Suddenly the whole company had joined in the altercation. But then Carew stood up and began to speak loudly.

'The Evil power has you in his sight
And is causing tension so that you fight.
So be very careful what you say.
You must not let him turn you that way.
So reject the evil thoughts that invade your psyche,
And use your powers of good that will be your key.'

'Stop this,' Drew shouted. 'Did you lot not hear what Carew just said? This is exactly what the Evil wants us to do, fight among ourselves.'

Drew's words slowly brought them to their senses, and you could feel that they were rather embarrassed about their behaviour.

Rocco stood and apologised to Jula and to the rest of the company for his selfish behaviour. 'I will try not to be so annoying in the future,' he said.

They all hugged each other and patted each other on their backs.

'Now that's more like it. Now we must get some rest,' said Drew.

It was a restless sleep for them all that night, thinking about what had happened. It was also a cold night so they all huddled into the room where Rocco had settled. But the warmth of the wool jackets that Mecco had bought for them didn't bring them the comfort they expected as they could not stop thinking about what might be happening to him.

57
CHAPTER

The Escape from Malfarcus

Yobtowoy stood over his prisoners gloating, 'Think you're smart, getting away from us once, but from here, you have no chance. As you can see, we don't even need to put bars on the windows. Even an Elf could not vanish from this height!'

Yobtowoy and his company snickered and sneered at us. What an ugly sight it was. El Masrew and I lay there as if we were helpless.

Yobtowoy remarked, 'The master will be very pleased. You will soon get to meet him first-hand. He will be arriving tomorrow morning.'

I could sense a groan from Sebcon whenever the Evil's name was mentioned, although I was sure he could not hear it from where he was.

Yobtowoy and his companions slammed the door and walked off, talking and laughing, their voices growing faint the further they went from the cell.

Then Lord Sebcon appeared. 'We have no time to waste,' he said. 'The Evil has underestimated your power, Mecco. He is not aware you have the ability to vanish and thinks that El Masrew by himself will not be able to travel far. That's to our advantage. Now I want you to look out the window from left to right very slowly and project to me what you see.'

I did this, and then Sebcon said, 'Now, I have an escape route for you. It will be difficult but I sense your magic power is strong enough to get you past this obstacle.'

El Masrew and I looked at each other, and he shrugged his shoulders.

'Yes,' said Sebcon, 'I know you cannot see an escape, but there is one.'

'Do you have Elvan rope?' he asked El Masrew.

'Yes.'

'Good,' said Sebcon. 'That will help you to climb up the north face of the mountain and down to the northern road that will lead you back to the bridge of Malfarcus.'

I looked at the size of the mountain and shuddered. 'But it is hundreds of paces high,' I said.

'You will have Elvan rope,' Sebcon said. 'That will help you climb the mountain, and you can use it to get you down the other side. From there it should be easy. You may have to use the vanishing as you climb the mountain, but make sure you do not doubt yourselves.'

The first thing El Masrew did was to look at me with an element of doubt.

'No, El Masrew, do not doubt him,' said Sebcon. 'He has more power than you and me combined. Doubt yourself long before you doubt Mecco.'

I was about to ask Lord Sebcon how he was to escape, but before I could open my mouth, he replied.

'I will not be escaping,' he said. 'I can be more helpful here distracting the Evil.'

'How can you be of more help', asked El Masrew, 'if you are still captured?'

The image of Lord Sebcon was of him standing with head held high.

'My mortal body is finished,' he said. 'My only escape is to know that you are back with your friends. That is where the defeat of the Evil lies, and with that will be my release. He will be extremely angry and will know that I had a hand in your escape. He will try to get me to talk and I will let him think he is succeeding, but I will tell him that you are heading for the gate. He will think it will be simple to recapture you.'

I was not too pleased with this outcome and could sense El Masrew felt the same.

'Sometimes,' said Sebcon angrily, 'things do not go the way we would like, and choices must be made, hard as they may be. It is better for two to escape than to have three in the Evil's clutches. I have no way of escaping from these restraints and my power is weak now. Besides, they were placed here by the Evil himself, and if the restraints are removed, he will know immediately and return on his evil steed. Sometimes we may not like the cards we are dealt, but play them we must and to the best of our ability. So there are no choices here. Fate has made it for us.'

His image quivered. We knew he was growing weak, but he continued, 'We all have a rendezvous with death. It is the final adventure. But we do not have time for this discussion. I must outline the escape route to you.'

He explained to us what he had in mind, and we listened carefully.

The sun had now set, and Sebcon said, 'Eat some of the food they placed under the door.'

El Masrew and I turned up our noses.

'Yes,' he laughed, 'I know it does not look very appetising, but it is nutritious and you will need the energy. They will make another round just before midnight, so rest and be ready to go as soon as they leave your cell.'

We ate and rested as best we could. Midnight approached, and just before the guards were to make their rounds, I sensed the Evil enter the room. I projected my feelings outwards and lay there thinking of pain, agony, and rope burns around my wrists. I acted as if I could not see him. He scrutinised each cell and at times moved up very close to our faces. In one instance, I thought I had given it away for as he began to fade and move away, he suddenly flinched and turned back quickly to look at me. Luckily, I felt that he thought he was being deceived, so I turned to face El Masrew and asked him in a frightened voice, 'What do you think will happen to us now?'

And that was enough to convince him. In an instant, he disappeared.

The guards arrived and looked us over. We lay there groaning, and that seemed to make them happy. They then left with their usual sneering and jeering.

As soon as they were out of hearing, Sebcon appeared.

'I suggest you tie the Elvan rope around your waists in case of a mishap. Now go,' he ordered, 'and please do not feel bad about me. It is my fate, and you two can only help me by finishing the quest.'

His image trembled, and he brought his right palm up to his left chest slapping it with his left hand, opening his arms and bowing to signify Elvan luck. We responded likewise, although unhappily, thinking of his fate. El Masrew and I walked towards the open window and tied the rope around our waists, stepped on to the sill, looked at each other and then to our place of destination, and disappeared.

I materialised on the level section of a roof of a large building to the right of the jail. I glanced around and could not see El Masrew. Then I heard a gasp and there I saw him, in a daze, hovering on the edge where the roof sloped and swinging his arms desperately to stop himself from falling backwards. It all seemed to be happening in slow motion. I ran in the opposite direction while pulling on the Elvan rope. As he fell, I slipped, and his weight dragged me towards the edge and over and down the sloping part of the roof. As I slid, I spotted a pipe that was protruding out of the roof and grabbed for it. I stopped the fall, nearly pulling my arms out of their sockets and holding on to the pipe with all my strength.

'Are you okay?' I screamed out.

'Yes, I'm fine. Now pull me up,' he called. There was no way I could pull him up with the angle I was at, and if I let go of the pipe, we would both go off into the air!

'Is there anywhere down there where you could take your weight off?' I asked.

He looked around then swung himself over onto a small windowsill. When the rope went slack, I dragged myself up and placed one leg on either side of the pipe then began pulling him up. Once he reached the guttering, he grabbed hold of it, taking the tension off and I moved back on to the level part of the roof. I slowly walked over to the opposite edge while pulling on the rope to keep it taut. Eventually, I dragged him up on to the level part of the roof, and he lay there clinging to it as white as a sheet. He eventually sat up, and I sat down next to him and put my arm around him as Drew used to do for me when I was scared.

'Thank you, Mecco,' he said. 'I'm ready to continue now.'

We moved again, this time not towards the city gate but towards the mountain to our west that backed on to the city. We could have taken a shorter route, but after our first mishap, we decided to take our time. In the beginning, we travelled slowly from rooftop to rooftop, but with each attempt, we improved. Finally, we reached the city's edge. The mountain was in front of us, and we were only a few hundred paces from its base. It looked much steeper than we had first imagined. We moved silently, glancing at each other occasionally, both aware of the other's thoughts.

We stood on the last building and decided that El Masrew should go first. I attached the rope to a chimney, and El Masrew kept the other end around his waist. We looked at each other, then in a split second, I helped project him on to a ledge about thirty paces up the cliff. I sighed with relief when he materialised on it, and I sensed his relief as well. I untied the rope and hitched it around my waist. Then we both projected me up to the same position.

We stood on this narrow ledge, trying to find a secure object to attach the Elvan rope to. About twenty paces directly above us was an old withered tree, so we threw up the Elvan rope. Now Elvan rope is not like any old rope. It can be told what to do, and this rope did exactly what El Masrew asked of it. It tied itself to the old tree and dangled down for us to use as a safety harness in case the next ledge was not wide enough to hold us. This gave us the opportunity to swing down and try again on another.

We both focused hard to find another ledge, but it was very dark. We made two attempts. On the first, El Masrew disappeared, and all was silent when suddenly he came swinging back down out of the dark, knocking me flying off the ledge. As I fell, I desperately grabbed for him, and the two of us went swinging like a pendulum. We slowly came to a stop and steadied ourselves then dropped to the ledge. We both stood shaking.

'I don't think we can make it,' said El Masrew. 'It is too dark.'

'We don't have much choice,' I declared. 'We must keep trying. We have to get away from this place tonight.'

I then tried with no luck, but El Masrew was prepared when I came swinging back and he grabbed and steadied me.

'I can't do it,' he announced. 'This is madness. If we fall from this height, even our magic will not save us.'

'Look,' I said, 'I know this may seem difficult coming for a mere mortal, but I know we can make it. Please trust me.'

'I can't,' he repeated. 'The evil in this place has drained me.'

'I shall tell you something, El Masrew,' I said, 'but it must be our secret. Promise me.'

He looked at me strangely. 'I promise,' he swore, 'but what possible help would you telling me a secret do for us now?'

As we stood on the edge of the ledge, I informed him of my Elvan heritage. He stared at me intently for ages, without saying a word.

'I have only known you for a few days,' I added, 'but I feel the power and magic within you. Please don't let the Evil drain your confidence. I also see much better, even in this light, and I will do my best to guide us in the right direction.'

'Thank you, Mecco,' he said. 'I do trust you, and I'm ready to leave this evil place.'

I focused really hard and made the next attempt and found another ledge. This one was only about a foot wide, but there was a large rock that I attached the rope to and then gave him the go-ahead. El Masrew then untied the magic rope from the tree and tied it around his waist then vanished from the ledge below, materialising next to me.

'Thank you again, Mecco,' he said as he steadied himself.

As we continued from ledge to ledge, our confidence grew till we were halfway up the mountain. We calculated that at this pace, we should be at the top well before sunrise. There was a wide ledge about thirty paces up, and this one was easy to get to, as were the next three. Now, we were only about a hundred paces from the top, but morning was breaking with a fog rolling in. But this could be in our favour as the Evil scouts would not be able to see us.

Then we came to another wide ledge, but we could not find anywhere to attach the rope. There was still another ledge a little higher to our left, and there was another old tree stump there we could use. But from here, we had no harness to support us, and the rope was a few paces too short to reach the tree stump. However, we had no choice.

We decided that El Masrew should go first so that I could use all my powers to help propel him to the next ledge. He took hold of one end of the rope, and off he went. He landed on the edge of the cliff, but it began to crumble. He was about to fall, but the Elvan rope attached itself to the old tree just as El Masrew fell. He slipped down the rope, finally grabbing it a few feet from the end. He came flying right past my head. When he swung back the other way, I grabbed him and pulled him on to the ledge. We looked at each other. That was a close one! But at least now we had the rope attached to the old tree. We then had to jump up a few feet to get hold of the rope. Then one at a time, we vanished to the next ledge, then up again to another one only thirty paces from the top. We regathered our confidence, and El Masrew was about to project himself when the fog rolled in with great speed.

'I can't see the top of the cliff,' he said. 'I don't think I can do it.'

The fog was so thick that we could hardly see each other.

'It will be fine,' I reassured him. 'I shall go first and take the rope with me and attach it to something. Then you can come up.'

'But how can you see where you are going to project yourself?' he asked.

'I don't know how,' I said, 'but I can sense where the edge of the cliff is.'

Without further discussion, I took the rope, and off I went into the fog, landing about two paces past the edge.

'I'm here and fine!' I screamed. 'Now take the end of the rope and tie it to you and don't worry. I have the other end attached to a large boulder.' I waited, but there was still no sign of El Masrew.

'What is the matter?' I called. 'It is safe, and we must get away before the fog lifts.'

Suddenly there was a whoosh, and he materialised, stumbling on the very edge just as the sun rose. I grabbed him and dragged him away from the cliff.

'What luck!' I said, trying to distract El Masrew from his close call. 'I think the fog will hang around for a while longer and hide us from the Evil.'

58
CHAPTER

Kotovin and Silvertail

Dawn came slowly; in fact, they never saw the sun that day as a heavy fog had covered the mountains and the ravine. This was in the company's favour as Jula and Wecco were friends again and could now light a fire and cook all the provisions for a hearty breakfast. They made a healthy stew with the leftovers to sustain them for breakfast and dinner that day and for the next day's breakfast.

The day dragged on, and after they did their exercises, they became rather bored. Then finally, Peto and Ricco asked Drew if there was anything else we needed to know about the quest.

'All has been revealed as far as I know,' he said, 'and that which will be revealed by the parchments will be revealed to all of us in time. But Carew could tell you some more Elvan history.'

So on and off for the rest of the day, Carew related more Elvan history. The mist began to dim, and they knew the day was drawing to a close and it was time to eat some of the stew. They ate in silence, still a little upset with their behaviour the previous night.

'Please put it behind you,' said Drew, sensing their unease. 'It was because we are so close to the Evil's abode and his Evil power permeates this area. The most important thing is to be aware and fight it and remember if you think good together, good you will be.'

This cheered them up, although there was something wrong with Jarew as he was looking rather strange. Just as night fell, Jula, who was sitting near the entrance of the cave, saw seven glowing shapes hovering in the air in front of her. She pointed out at the mist.

'Look,' she said. 'Can you see that?' But before any of the company could turn around to look, they disappeared. She insisted they were flying men or women with wings. She wouldn't stop talking about them, and the company, in the end, agreed for peace and quiet to let her think she saw them, although they really thought she had imagined it.

There were still a few hours to go before their departure, and Peto and Ricco asked Carew to tell them a story about the Elves. 'But no more history!' they requested, and Jula and Wecco echoed their sentiments. 'Yes, please, tell us a story.'

Carew looked at Drew. 'Is it fine to tell them a story?' he asked.

'Yes,' Drew said. 'Of course, you may.'

'Then please', Jula requested, 'tell us the dragon story you have mentioned before.'

Carew looked at Drew and said, 'May I tell them about your grandfather Kotovin and his playmate Silvertail?'

There was a crescendo of yes from the whole company, even the other Elves. Drew had no choice but to say yes.

Carew began, 'Many, many years ago, there were two great dragons that lived in our forest, and they were good dragons. They were never any trouble; in fact, they kept to themselves and were rarely sighted by either Elf or Man. For hundreds of years, they lived in the forest until about three hundred years ago when the female fell pregnant and delivered nine eggs. The news travelled fast through the forest and even as far as the city of Man, who then passed the news on to the Evil, who at that time was in the process of building his fort of Malfarcus.

'He sent spies out to travel through the forest and to find out where the dragon lair was. It took him ten years to eventually discover it. I suppose none of you are aware that it takes a dragon fifteen years to hatch a brood of eggs.' He then went on. 'The Evil sent men who had been seduced by the dark power to steal the eggs and kill the dragons.'

'Did not the Elves try to stop them?' asked Jula.

'We had a pact with the dragons to always stay away from their lair,' said Carew, 'and this we always respected. The men had entered from the far western side of the forest, and we had no warning until it was too late and they had killed the dragons and slipped away with their eggs, except one.

'It was winter when they sneaked up on the two sleeping dragons in their brooding hibernation. Before the dragons could reawaken to defend their unhatched young, they were set upon. In the confusion that followed while the men were slaughtering the dragons, one of the eggs was knocked away. It rolled out of the lair and down into a small hollow where it lay hidden from the poachers.

'The Elves heard the cry of the dying dragons as the disciples of Evil did their depraved deed. Archers were dispatched immediately to find out what had transpired at the dragons' lair. By the time the archers arrived, the men had finished their miserable, murderous mission.'

The company sat with their mouths agape, anticipating the rest of the story. Even Drew sat quietly listening, though he had heard it many times before. Carew loved storytelling. He was savouring the moment by hesitating before continuing.

Jula called out what the rest of the company was feeling. 'Come on, what happened next?'

He continued, 'The men had escaped from the forest with eight of the eggs, long before the Elves had arrived at the lair. It was a sad sight to see the battered, bent bodies lying there with blood splattered everywhere. The archers stood staring in shock at the sinister sight, their heads bowed, with silver tears rolling down their cheeks. From the tears that fell on the ground that day, saplings sprang of silverbark trees that now cover where the dragons' lair used to be. Whenever you see a silverbark tree, remember they came from tears of tragedy.'

'So what happened to the eggs?' asked Jula.

'They were taken back to the fort of Malfarcus, and the Evil hatched them and fed them a vile potion that the young dragons became addicted to. This was how the Evil seduced them to do his depraved deeds. Seven young conscripts from one of the towns were also brought up with the dragons. They were also fed the vile potion, and they became symbiotic with the dragons. If only the young men and dragons knew. They could give up that vile potion and think positive thoughts, and in a few months, they would be cured of their addiction.'

'And what of the egg that rolled into the hollow?' asked Peto.

'This is where the story gets a little less serious. Drew's grandfather Kotovin was one of the archers and could not stand the sight of the slaughtered dragons. He walked down the hill to sit by himself with silver tears in his eyes. He sat there for ages. Then out of the corner of his misty eye, he saw something shiny lying in a small hollow under a bush and went to investigate. And to his surprise, it was one of the dragons' eggs. He removed his cape and hood and placed the egg gently in his hood, rolling his cape around it to protect it from the cold.

'He showed his companions his find and then marched back to the lake by the waterfall. Kotovin laid the egg at the feet of the elders, and they decided the egg must be protected at all cost from the Evil. Kotovin took it to a secret part of the lake which was magic. His task was to look after the egg till it hatched. For five years, he tended the egg. In the winter months, he lay with his body curled around it with Elvan blankets over them both. In the summer, he placed it on the warm sand by the lake. His friends would visit him often to swim and dive from the cliff above the falls, but he never once let the egg out of his sight.

'Then in the spring of the fifth year on a warm morning, a crack appeared on the egg. Kotovin waited all day for something to happen, but the egg lay perfectly still. Kotovin would not leave the egg for a second. He waited and waited, then late on the afternoon of the third day, the crack split open, and a smiling face appeared. It looked up at Kotovin and squawked. The tiny dragon pushed and squeezed himself around till he finally broke completely out of the shell. He ran over to Kotovin and licked his face and wagged his silver tail. A great friendship was born on that day, and for the next twenty years, they were never apart. Kotovin taught the young dragon, whom he called Silvertail, to swim in the lake and dive from the clifftop.

'Both of these feats were quite uncommon for dragons, but he trusted Kotovin. They also slept together in a cave by the lake. The thing about dragons is that once they are hatched, they grow at an incredible rate. Soon he was too large for the cave, and they had to find a larger one.'

Carew stopped the story and asked for a drink of water. Jula rushed over and grabbed a mug of water and handed it to him, then sat down and waited for him to restart. He coughed and cleared his throat.

'Come on, we will have to leave soon,' said Peto.

Carew was really savouring the moment now, and after his friends' demands, he began again. 'Now where was I? Yes, I remember the two companions went on many adventures but we only have time for one, and I think it should be Silvertail's winging.'

Jula interrupted and asked, 'What is winging?'

'Winging for a dragon', Carew replied, 'is like teething for you humans.' And then he continued with the story. 'Silvertail had not yet grown his wings, but there were small bumps on his back where they were trying to push through. Winging is a very painful experience for a dragon. In fact, it can go on for months. The story goes that Kotovin used to rub special cream on the bumps every day to ease the pain while Silvertail lay there making loud groans and roars that the other Elves could hear from across the lake. One day, he had just finished rubbing in the cream and was standing in front of Silvertail patting his nose and talking about what they should do that day. As they talked, a large crane flew down and landed very hard on his bumps. Silvertail got such a fright that he breathed out his first shot of fire from his nostrils. Poor Kotovin was standing directly in front of it and was hit full force. His clothes and hair were all burnt. He had to run and dive into the lake to put himself out. Then just as he was emerging from the water, all his friends arrived and there he was: pitch black with only half his clothes hanging from him and his hair all sticking up and burnt.

'You can imagine the laughter that followed. Kotovin was very upset and wouldn't speak to Silvertail for hours after that. Poor Silvertail followed him around all day, trying to apologise, but he was also very excited about being able to snort fire. Eventually, Kotovin forgave him, and their friendship grew and grew. Silvertail would warm water in the lake in the winter with his fiery breath just so Kotovin could bathe. When his wings grew and he could fly, he would take Kotovin on great adventures.'

At this point, Drew interrupted. 'We must stop now,' he said. 'It is time to depart on our quest.'

Well, you can imagine the groans of disappointment from the company.

Carew teasingly said, 'They went on so many more amazing adventures.'

'At our next opportunity,' Drew said, 'Carew can tell you more stories, but now we have a job to do.' The company reluctantly started to pack up the rest of the gear.

59
CHAPTER

A Flying Finish

'Okay,' said Drew, 'it is now time to depart on our night walk to the Rope Bridge.'

The air was still heavy with mist, and they could see no more than a few paces in front of them, so Soltain suggested they tie the Elvan rope around each other, just in case of an accident.

'What kind of accident?' Rocco asked nervously.

'Don't worry,' Drew said. 'It is only a precaution.'

Rocco still looked a little worried, but Soltain assured him it would be fine and requested that they tie the rope tight around their waists. Once they were all connected, they set off through the fog.

Dolark led the way followed by Soltain, the children with the Elves bringing up the rear. It was not a very nice experience. They had to feel their way along the rough cliff face and had no idea what might be living in the cracks and crevasses. In some sections, the ledge was very narrow; at times, they could feel the edge of the precipitous path. For hours, they walked up and up the mountain. All the company could hear was Rocco's heavy breathing. Then at about midnight, the ledge started to level off, and they continued for another hour. Rocco's breathing settled down, much to the company's delight.

Then slowly the path began to decline and they all thought this would make Rocco happy, and they were correct. For the next few hours, all went well until they heard a loud squawking of what seemed like crows nearby. Poor Rocco screamed, jumped with fright, then slipped and fell into the ravine. If the crows of Malfarcus up till now had no idea where they were, they certainly were aware now after Rocco's screams penetrated the silence.

Wecco, who was closest to him, yelled, 'Rocco, shut up! We will pull you up. Don't struggle.'

They all pulled on the rope and up he came, lying on the ledge, gasping for air. If it had not been such a serious moment, they all would have laughed themselves hoarse, which they did in future retellings of the story, much to Rocco's displeasure.

Now that their whereabouts were probably known, they would have to take even more precautions and try to be at the Rope Bridge before sunrise.

'We must not dally,' said Drew. 'Keep moving.'

Rocco was going so slowly that the rest of the company had to practically drag him along. A slight glow in the eastern sky signalled sunrise was only a half an hour away. They had still not reached the bridge. Drew was becoming anxious, and the rest of the company were starting to sense his anxiety.

'Look, there through the mist,' cried Dolark. They strained to see what Dolark was pointing at, and there above them, they could see rope supports that were anchoring the bridge to the cliff face. They now felt certain they would make it, so off they hastened and their anxiety turned to delight.

On the other side of the bridge stood the wizard, lords, and the three Elves, and they sensed the jubilation of Drew and his companions.

'The quest seekers are nearby,' said the wizard Naroof. 'They are on the other side of the Rope Bridge, but I also sense danger.'

He was correct. The Evil had received news from the crows of their location on the track and had sent three Pernicious, who were now hovering in the fog above the bridge.

Drew also sensed the dangers. 'Carew,' he said, 'you should go first with three of the children, then Tarew with the other two.' He looked at the two Dwarfs and added, 'You go last with Jarew. When you are all safely on the other side, I will join you.'

However, Drew sensed another source of Evil coming down the track alongside the gorge. But he said nothing to the others.

The fog was starting to dissipate and they could now see ten or twelve paces ahead, so the first four departed and disappeared into the mist.

There, watching on the other side was the second company anticipating what would come out of the mist that surrounded the bridge. Carew, Jula, Wecco, and Rocco had passed halfway but were moving very slowly as the bridge had begun to sway. The fog was lifting quickly and the second company could now see all of the bridge, but so could the Pernicious. The wizard summoned the Elvan archers to line up along either side of their end of the bridge. If the Evil creatures made any movement, they were to send a hail of arrows at them, making sure their friends were not in the line of fire. As it became clear, they could see there were only four friends emerging from the mist.

The wizard Naroof told the rest of his company to stay, and he walked out to greet them, ushering them to safety. The wizard continued walking out to meet the next three who were following in hot pursuit. He greeted them and urged them to get off the bridge as fast as possible.

The second company welcomed the first four quest seekers with great enthusiasm as they did for the next three as they stepped off the bridge. Jarew and the Dwarfs had now reached the wizard, who was halfway across, and he ushered them past him. As they made their way to safety at the end of the bridge, the wizard asked where Drew was.

'He should be behind us,' said Jarew.

As they stepped off the rope bridge, the wizard looked back across it as the last of the fog was blown out of the gorge by a fresh wind. The Pernicious had manoeuvred themselves across to the far side of the bridge, one above and one on either side. They were now only a few paces away from Drew. The wizard pointed his staff at the Evil creature hovering above Drew and told the Elvan archers to aim at the other two and to release their arrows on his mark. From where Drew stood, the rope supports protected him, but if he tried to run across, he would be vulnerable to attack.

The second company and the quest seekers stood watching the drama unfold, feeling quite helpless and annoyed that they had left Drew by himself. Then the evil that Drew had sensed earlier materialised. Marching down the old road along the gorge that led from Malfarcus was a company of Menlins and Goblins. Things looked bad for Drew. If he stayed put, the Evil army would capture him, but if he made a move to get across the bridge, he would leave himself exposed to the three Pernicious. Drew could not use the vanishing as the bridge was still swinging and he could not be sure if he would rematerialise on it. The Pernicious hovering above him moved to the centre of the bridge and landed on it, blocking Drew's escape route. The Evil's men were now only a few hundred paces from the bridge and advancing fast, aware of the position their prize was in.

Drew had removed his Elvan sword from its sheath as the creature began to advance on him. The army of Good stood watching as the drama unfolded, not knowing what they could do. Suddenly, the wizard aimed his staff at the Pernicious on the bridge and told the archers to fire. The arrows headed for each creature on either side of the bridge, and the wizard fired his staff. At the same instant, Drew cut through the rope supports on the left side of the bridge with one almighty swing from his magic Elvan sword.

As the side of the bridge fell away, it threw the Pernicious off balance just as the fireball from Naroof hit its target, and the creature tumbled screaming horribly into the ravine. The rain of arrows hit their targets, forcing the two remaining creatures to fly off to a safe distance. With the soldiers of the Evil now only twenty paces away, Drew held tight to one side of the rope bridge, his friends watching as he hung on by one hand.

Then just as the soldiers of Evil were only a few paces away, he swung his sword again, cutting the last support. For a few seconds, he seemed to hover in the air, and then the bridge fell away towards the opposite cliff below the road where his friends were waiting.

Drew swung about like a rag doll as the bridge crashed into the cliff. His companions stood watching and wondering whether or not he could keep a grip on the swinging bridge. The Pernicious that had been hit by Naroof's blast had regained his balance and pulled himself out of his dive. As he did, he became aware of the Elf swinging on the end of the dangling bridge. He made a deafening, dreadful noise that echoed over the mountain and sent chills through all the company standing on the cliff road.

The other two Pernicious turned and dived towards Drew while the other came from below. The archers had reloaded and were waiting for the right opportunity. As they watched, their end of the bridge had somehow started to move with Drew ascending with it. The company turned around to see that Peto and Rocco had attached two horses to their end of the bridge. They had sliced through the ropes that had connected the bridge to the cliff and started the horses walking away along the road. The Pernicious were getting closer and closer, but Drew kept moving up the cliff.

Naroof aimed his staff then looked at the archers and said, 'Now.' A hail of arrows and the fireball went flying through the sky towards the three evil creatures. Drew was now only five paces away from safety, but one of the Pernicious had flown back and was about to grab him when suddenly it bounced off a haze of light surrounding Drew. As he dangled there precariously, he realised his friends had moved to the edge and projected the force field around him, protecting him from the Pernicious. As he was dragged on to the road, they could all see the look of relief on his face. He stood and brushed himself down as his excited friends gathered around, hugging him.

The two companies stood watching as the three Pernicious swung around and flew off in the direction of Malfarcus. The Evil's foot soldiers standing on the opposite side of the ravine also turned and marched back up the road from where they had come. The two companies greeted each other, and each side began with a flurry of questions from each other.

Naroof walked over to Drew. 'Please come here and tell us about Mecco's capture.'

Drew stood among his friends, relating the story. After the excitement had settled down, Naroof addressed the quest seekers, his company, and the leaders of the armies of Good. 'The Evil now has a lord, a child, and an Elf. This will give him great confidence, although I must add that I have some strange feelings that I cannot decipher exactly. But I think it is in our favour. For now, we must continue until we reach the bridge of Malfarcus.' He turned to the Elves of the quest seekers and asked, 'Have you received any more messages from the ancient parchment?'

They shrugged their shoulders and looked at Carew, so he opened his leather satchel, which held the parchments.

'I did have a strange moment', said Carew, 'as we were standing here watching the Pernicious attack, Drew. And I think it may have been a message.' He stood up and looked at the parchments and said, 'Yes, there is one.'

He started to read:

'Two of your friends have escaped the fort.
At the bridge you should be, or they will be recaught.
So be on your way to that evil place,
Pack up your supplies and make haste,
And together with the powers you possess,
The evil in this world you can regress.'

'That has reaffirmed exactly what I was sensing,' Naroof said as he turned to the newly arrived quest seekers. 'Are you in condition to continue the march?'

They stood proudly with their chins in the air. 'Lead on,' said Peto. 'We are fine, and we must be there for Mecco.'

The company mounted. Drew and Peto rode El Masrew's horse while the rest of the quest seekers doubled up on the horses of the second company. They set off on what they thought was the last leg of their journey, with the sun breaking through the clouds. The morning was looking good for travelling as there had been no more snow. The road had dried up, and there was a sense of confidence in the air.

60
CHAPTER

The Mutated Spiders of Cadabar

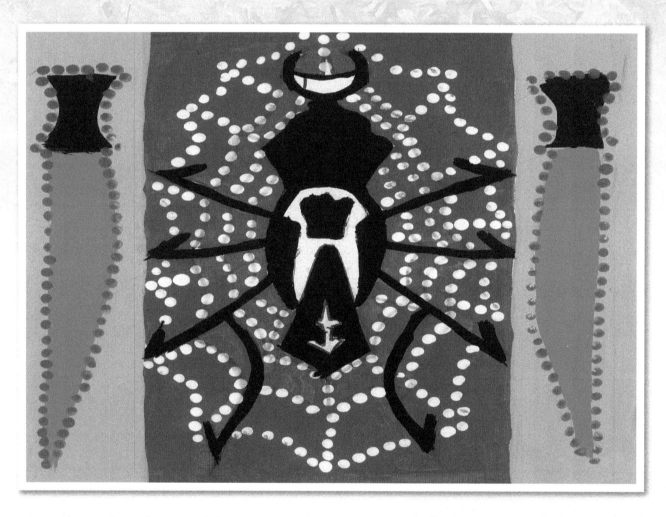

We stood on the top of the mountain and looked back towards the evil fort, thinking about poor Sebcon and what was to become of him. We turned around to see how hard our descent would be. To our surprise, it was not a sheer cliff but a gentle snow-covered slope that went all the way down to the edge of the woods. And we could see where the road cut through the forest by the indent winding its way through the trees.

'This should be easy,' I said, but El Masrew shook his head.

'Maybe,' he said, 'but we will be completely exposed to the Evil. Let us hope they are not looking for us here.' As we discussed the situation, the fog descended from the mountain and crept over the valley.

'Now that's what I call luck,' I said. 'The fog will hide us from the evil scouts.'

'Perhaps, as long as it stays,' replied El Masrew, 'but how will we know which way we are going?'

'We should just continue down,' I said, 'and eventually, we will reach the forest and then hopefully the road.'

So off we went, trudging through the deep snow, which was heavy work after climbing up the mountain all night. After an hour, the fog lifted, exposing the mountain. El Masrew was worried about the Evil finding us, but luck was on our side. There in front of us was a clump of trees with rainbow bark, similar to the red bark trees of the forest of Gundy. We hid under their canopy for hours and tried to devise a plan. As we sat there, I realised the answer was right in front of me.

'Our problem is solved,' I said to El Masrew, and I pulled off a section of bark from one of the trees.

He looked at me strangely. 'So how is that going to help us?'

'Peto and I used to use the bark of similar trees back in the forest of Gundi to slide down the Dunes of Croll. We can do the same on this mountain of snow. We will be in the forest in no time at all.'

I searched around the trees for a larger piece of bark that the two of us could use. I found one and ripped it off and fashioned it with a curve at the front that one of us could hold. The other would sit behind with his legs wrapped around the one in front. As I was preparing it, we heard the sound of crows squawking, and we hid ourselves under the thickest canopy of one of the trees till they departed.

It was now reaching midday and the clouds had cleared, the wind had died, and the day was as still as it could be. At another time, I would have called it a perfect winter day, but we didn't have time to appreciate it.

As I looked back over the mountain, I could see our tracks through the snow and realised that was why the crows went away so quickly. They knew our location and were flying back to inform their master. I estimated it to be about six kilopaces to the edge of the forest, so we positioned ourselves with El Masrew at the front and me behind and off we went. I had not anticipated the speed we were going to reach or the surprise awaiting us three quarters of the way down the slope.

It grew steeper as we descended, and the bark on these trees had such a smooth surface it made our sled pick up speed faster than I had anticipated. It was not long before I realised we were going way too fast, but by now, there was nothing we could do. Sliding on snow is a lot faster than sand; that is one thing I learnt on this day. I was panicking but could not let El Masrew sense the state I was in.

'This is fun,' he screamed as we went flying over a small mound and were airborne for a few moments. As we landed, the slope grew steeper, and our makeshift transport increased its speed.

El Masrew was now sensing my concern at our speed. 'How can we slow this thing down?' he shouted.

'We used to put out our feet out on the sand hills, but it won't work at this speed. We will just have to hold on and hope for the best.'

As we slid across the snow, I wondered why the Evil had no lookouts stationed on the mountain. In the next few seconds, we would know why. He never needed them. A kilopace ahead of us was a massive ravine about two hundred paces wide and six hundred deep that stretched the length of the mountain. We were not aware of it as the snow that had fallen had camouflaged it from our view.

We were now controlling our sled quite well and could see the forest looming up ahead of us. We were starting to believe we would make it when we noticed a dark line in the snow ahead. As we rapidly drew closer to it, the dark line widened and we instantly realised what it was.

At that moment, a flock of crows dived down towards us, but we were moving much too fast for them to attack us. They followed in our track, making hideous cries. The edge of the ravine nearest to us was two hundred paces higher than the far side, so hopefully we would have built up enough speed to carry us across. We now used our senses to communicate and realised we had no choice but to continue. We decided when we flew off the snow into the air over the gorge that we would take hold of the bark, and if it looked as if we would not reach the other side, we would use the vanishing. Hopefully this would help us to reach our objective.

The slope now became even steeper, which luckily gave us more speed and, hopefully, the momentum to cross the chasm. The crows were still following but at a distance. The ravine was approaching, so we grabbed hold tightly of the bark and braced ourselves for takeoff.

And take off we did! As we left the snow, all we could hear was the sound of the wind flying past us and the occasional cry of a crow.

We glided silently over the ravine, hoping to reach the other side, but when we were probably no more than twenty paces away, our momentum started to slow and we knew we would not make it. We synchronised our timing, took a tight hold of the bark, and used the vanishing. We had no idea whether we would make it or crash into the cliff face and fall to our deaths. But no, we materialised, landing with a thud and losing none of our speed. And as I looked around, I could see the crows hovering around the ravine's edge, with no idea where we had disappeared to. The slope was beginning to level off, but hopefully, our momentum would take us right up to the forest. No luck. We came to a stop a hundred paces from the edge then continued running on foot. Our legs were shaking, and for some reason, I picked up the bark and took it with us. The snow here was much harder, and we made our way to the forest just in time as the crows descended towards us with three Pernicious in their wake. We talked later of the experience and our doubts that we would make it, but also the exhilaration.

We ran like mad into the deep undergrowth. I realised I still had the bark and was about to drop it, when I remembered that we needed to conceal our scent. I knew the odour from the oil in the bark would be our best bet. We stopped and rubbed the bark all over us. We could hear the Pernicious flying above the forest and knew we should keep well clear of the road.

Thankfully, the crows were not keen on following us into the forest, although at the time, we didn't know the reason. We travelled south as fast as our legs could carry us, now and again using the vanishing. Then on one of the vanishings, we realised why the crows never entered the forest. My Elvan armband began to glow just before we initiated the vanishing. As we materialised, we found ourselves caught in a large web hanging between the trees that crossed our path.

'Stay perfectly still,' said El Masrew. 'I think we are in a web of the infamous spiders of Cadabar, but I don't understand how they got into this forest so far south.'

This was the strangest time to think of this, but as I looked across at El Masrew, I could not help but think of Drew and whether he was safe.

'You are a strange human,' said El Masrew. 'You are hanging from a giant Cadabar web, and you are worried about whether your friends are safe. Now stay perfectly still.' He surveyed the web only to find that there was no spider anywhere to be seen. 'We must be very careful as I have heard they hide themselves to keep out of the cold. But they have a line of web attached to where they are and will be out of their hiding place and on to their prey in no time.'

'That's great,' I said. 'So what now? We just hang around here waiting till he comes back?'

'No, smarty,' said El Masrew. 'I have an idea. Your hand is close to your Elvan knife, so reach down very slowly, retrieve it, and cut around my arm so I can also get to my sword.'

This I began to do and eventually El Masrew fell to the ground and was now free. As he fell from the web, the vibration activated the spider's line that connected his web to his cave. As I was bouncing back and forth in the web, El Masrew started to slash around me.

'Well,' I said, 'if he didn't know we were here before, he sure knows now.' And sure enough, within seconds, this strange thing was at the side of the web.

'What is it?' I asked El Masrew. It was terrifying; it must have had a body about two paces long with each leg also two paces long.

'This is not a Cadabarian spider,' said El Masrew. 'I have never seen one like this. It looks half man, half spider.'

We later discovered that the Evil had captured some young Cadabarian spiders and crossbred them with men to create this hideous creature. Then he let them loose in the forest many years ago. These strange creatures eventually came to be known as Aracmen. Thankfully, they were quite deaf and had very bad eyesight, although their other senses were extremely responsive. The creature pulled on the web with one leg to start me swinging and, I assume, to judge my weight. There were only about five strands now to cut, but El Masrew had stopped. The creature had seen the glow of the Elvan sword, and its instincts told it beware. It hovered, waiting for the Elf to make a move. They stared at each other as if mesmerised.

I started to continue to cut myself free with my knife. As I cut one of the last five strands, the Aracman's eyes turned quickly to me. I cut another, but it had had enough and started to move towards me. I cut one more and was now only hanging by two strands. El Masrew had now regained his train of thought and swung at one of the last strands. I fell to the ground with the last fibre of web still attached to my right leg. The strange spider had reached across and grabbed my foot with two of his legs and was dragging me towards him.

'No, you don't!' screamed El Masrew, swinging his sword at the spider's leg that had a hold of me and slicing right through it. But the spider had dragged my leg towards his fangs. As El Masrew plunged his sword into its side, the spider's fangs pierced my leg. It made a strange sound then fell from the web, screaming in pain. El Masrew cut the last strand, and my leg fell to the ground next to the spider. He bent down to help me up and asked how I felt.

'I feel fine,' I replied, 'but let's get out of this place.'

We started to run and could now sense our friends and knew they were near. But I started to feel quite strange, then the next thing I knew, I awoke and found myself lying under a pile of dead leaves. The creature's venom had reached my nervous system, and I had fallen unconscious to the ground.

El Masrew could not carry me, so he hid me from the Pernicious under some leaves and went to get help. I think I was very lucky as the spider's fangs had not penetrated too far. Only a small amount of venom had reached my bloodstream. I regained consciousness rather quickly but had the most hideous headache. It was worse than that hangover I had in the tavern at Gamba.

I shook my head and sat up, regained my thoughts, and then stood up, my head still shaking. I was starting to feel a little better and decided to make my own way out of this evil place and continued to run towards the edge of the forest. I could see the sun hitting the snow around the edge of the road, and I knew I was very close. I was now only a few hundred paces from the edge of the forest. Through the trees, I could see the stone bridge of Malfarcus only four or five hundred paces away. I ran like mad towards it.

61
CHAPTER

All But One Together

The two companies were leading the army of Good up the road to the bridge of Malfarcus. They marched non-stop till midday when they could see the great stone bridge looming up ahead. The bridge was a magnificent construction of dark-grey granite with two towers, each one hundred and fifty paces high, at either end. Facing away from the bridge were two statues fifty paces high, of men of some noble race also in grey granite.

The history of this race has been lost in the past, but it is said they are the ancients who lived here long before the arrival of the immigrants from the Old World. The bridge was built by the old race, and the Evil fashioned his fort on their design.

As they approached the bridge, the two companies and the army stood in wonder at the craftsmanship of this masterpiece of construction. The company was advancing on the bridge when the wizard Naroof held out his arms.

'We must not cross,' he said. 'I sense there may be a trap.'

The army halted along the road, and the two companies dismounted and stood waiting to see what the next move was. Naroof walked up to the end of the bridge and stood staring into the crevasse and across the bridge.

'There is something unusual about this bridge,' he said. 'I cannot put my finger on it, and I'm not sure what we should do.' The company grew restless, waiting for a decision.

Naroof suddenly turned around and said, 'I sense the Evil very close to the other side of the bridge, but I also sense hope from Mecco and El Masrew.'

As the wizard stood addressing his friends, Peto pointed across the bridge. 'Look!' he shouted. 'There, running along the road is an Elf.'

The wizard turned to the direction Peto was pointing. And sure enough, running as fast as he could along the road was El Masrew. Bayrew and Carawarew were about to run across the bridge to meet their friend, but Naroof's hand went out to stop them. He was halfway across the bridge when a flock of crows came up from behind and dived towards him.

Naroof lifted up his staff, pointed it towards the crows, and fired. A fireball went flying past El Masrew, exploding directly among the crows and scattering them in all directions. As he got closer to the far end of the bridge, the company could see the distress on his face. *Where was Mecco?* they wondered. Had he been recaptured?

El Masrew staggered to the end of the bridge, collapsing exhausted into the arms of the two Elves who grabbed him by each arm and helped him to a granite bench.

The group gathered around, waiting to hear what he had to say. His breathing was deep and heavy, and it took him a few moments to regain his breath and speak. It seemed like ages till he finally relayed what had taken place in the forest.

'We must cross the bridge and help Mecco,' he said to the quest seekers. 'He may be in great danger.'

Naroof stood between the friends and the bridge and stretched out his hands. 'No,' he said, 'you must not cross. It is what the Evil wants. When you cross into his territory, he has ways of harnessing your powers against you.'

'Then what must we do?' asked Jula. 'If Mecco is unconscious, then it will be easier for the Evil to recapture him.'

'If El Masrew has covered him in leaves', said Naroof, 'and he still has the odour of the bark on his body, he should be safe from the Pernicious.'

'As long as he stays still,' El Masrew added, 'he should be safe from the strange spiders of Cadabar.' But then he asked, 'But he was bitten, and what if the venom kills him?'

Naroof assured his friends that the venom of the Cadabar spiders would only put him to sleep for a few hours. 'The spiders like to eat their prey alive,' Naroof said. The thought of this put shudders up their spines.

Dolark and Soltain stepped forward. 'We have dealt with giant spiders in the west,' they said. 'We will cross the bridge and bring him back.' They turned to El Masrew and asked, 'How far along the road and how far in the forest is he?'

'These are no ordinary spiders,' said El Masrew. 'They are bizarre creatures, half man, half spider, and I don't know what they are capable of.'

Naroof was starting to get angry and stamped his staff upon the granite stones under their feet. 'No one is going anywhere', he said, 'till I say so. We must wait here till I can think of a solution.'

62
CHAPTER

A Bridge to Cross

I continued running and was just about out of the forest when two of those strange spiders jumped out in front of me, blocking my way. I stopped instantly, standing perfectly still while I analysed the situation. As I looked around, I noticed under my feet were strands of web travelling along the ground in all directions. I realised I could not make the slightest move.

After a few minutes, the spiders began pulling on the web to find out where I was, but this gave me time to focus on where to project myself. I jumped up and down on the web to let them know where I was. When they made their move, I used the vanishing to project myself out on to the road.

As I materialised, I could sense my friends close by but, alas, also the Evil. I began running towards the bridge. It was still a fair distance away, and as I drew closer, I glanced to my left. There, marching from the fort of Malfarcus was the Evil with his Six Pernicious and his forces. I could feel his power surrounding me and draining my energy. My legs and arms felt heavy. It was such a strain to even walk. I could hear in the distance my friends calling for me to run, but I couldn't.

I concentrated with all my energy and slowly dragged myself to the edge of the great Granite Bridge. The Evil was walking towards me at a distance of a hundred paces with his army and there on the other side stood my friends with the forces of Good.

I looked at the Evil, who beckoned me to join him. I remembered what Naroof had said about thinking hatred, so I thought forgiveness towards him so that his power would not overcome me and make me unable to defend myself. I could feel his Evil power drawing me towards him.

I started to drag myself towards the side of Good. I was a third of the way across the bridge when there, in front of me, a crack appeared and it slowly began to widen. I could sense his power trying to destroy the bridge. I stopped and looked at my friends, who were beckoning me to run.

As the crack grew wider, I stepped back in the direction of the Evil. I then sensed the power of my friends working to stop the crack. But so did the Evil! He summoned the Six Pernicious to attack them. The Six passed overhead and dived with their claws outstretched, accompanied by the evillest screeches. The six would have been no match for the side of Good, but I realised the Evil was using them to distract my friends from stopping his destruction of the bridge.

His ploy had worked, as suddenly the middle of the bridge started to collapse. A crack appeared five steps in front of me. I started to move back, but then another crack appeared right under my feet. The more I stepped back, the more the cracks appeared. I was now back at the Evil's side of the ravine with the bridge slowly disintegrating in front of me and falling into the deep crevasse.

His power had grown stronger. I was now alone, and the Good had no way of crossing. The Evil was no more than fifty paces from me. He looked at me with great intensity. 'Embrace what you know is the way!' he screamed.

I could feel the hate in me towards him for what he had created in our world. I knew I had to fight it. I concentrated on the good of my friends, knowing I could not let them down.

The Evil was now only twenty paces away. 'Child, you cannot fight. This is your destiny,' he said. 'You are what you have been created by your creed, and this will never change.'

I looked back across the void, where the bridge stood no more than a few minutes ago. It was too far to try the vanishing, and I could feel the power of the Evil draining all the strength from me. Standing nearby with no way of helping me were my friends and the allies, their eyes staring at the scene taking place. Did the future of the world hang on this outcome?

The Evil's armies and his captains were standing behind him, with the Six gliding down to land, one after the other, next to him. As he continued to walk towards me, I could feel his power and had no idea how to combat it.

He stopped and held out his hands towards me. 'Embrace it,' he said. 'It is your fate, Mecco. There will be a great reward waiting for you in paradise.'

How stupid did he think I was? I looked at him and yelled, 'If I join you, I sell out all that I know is good, for nothing more than a promise that any sensible person would know is a lie. The paradise we go to is only made from the mortal deeds we perform.'

He looked with piercing hatred towards me, even though I could not see his eyes. 'If you do not join me,' he said, 'one of the other creeds will take over and force you to become one of them.'

I fought his evil power and answered, 'I know where my future lies, and it is to fight the hatred and evil forces projected on Man.'

'You have no choice,' he bellowed. 'Your friends are on the other side of the gorge, with no way of helping you.'

He started to move towards me, and I could feel myself growing weaker the closer he came. *What evil power does he possess?* He reached out his hands, and the power was draining from me. Suddenly, I sensed the power of my company of friends. I looked across the ravine, and I could see my five friends, the Elves, the lords, the Dwarfs, and the wizard all holding hands and looking at me. I could see a row of seven beams of light being projected to a single point where they converged into one beam that was aimed at me, and I realised what they were doing.

I looked back at the Evil. He sensed he had to move now. He rushed towards me, but I did a backflip into the ravine, knowing I would be safe as the power of my friends helped me up and across the gaping hole where the bridge stood only moments before. It was the jumping trick we'd practised in the magic clearing all those months ago. I spun around and around then up, landing safely on the other side. My friends looking in wonder as the armies of Good and Evil faced each other with no way of ending the conflict.

The Evil screamed out across the ravine, 'This is not the end! You are not safe yet. You may have won the first move, but we will regroup and eventually the Six and what they possess will be mine.'

63
CHAPTER

Epilogue

My friends and allies gazed at me in wonder. They hesitated before coming over to hug and congratulate me.

'Thankfully you made it across the ravine,' said Drew. 'I had doubts, I must admit.' He then threw his arms around me and hugged me really tight.

'So did I,' added Carew, 'but you are here. You may not be one of us, but you are like us.' And he also embraced me like a long-lost brother.

El Mazrew also hugged me and whispered in my ear, 'Your secret is safe with me, Mecco.'

My friends were all hugging me and slapping me on the back. The lords and Naroof had held back and, after all the commotion had died down, walked over and patted me on the back.

'Well done, Mecco,' said Lord Arcon. 'I knew that you had great powers but never expected that.'

As the compliments flowed, I could see the wizard Naroof staring at me strangely. I began to feel quite embarrassed that they were giving me all the credit.

'Please,' I said, 'enough with all the compliments. I have to thank all of *you*. I would never have made it without you helping to project me across the ravine.'

The company stopped talking, and they also stared at me peculiarly.

'But, Mecco,' said Jula, 'we didn't help you. We tried, but the Evil was somehow stopping our powers from passing over the chasm.'

'But I could sense you all,' I said.

'Yes, that was our plan,' said Lord Arcon. 'But with the Evil blocking our powers, we had no way of getting you to our side of the bridge.'

My knees suddenly went weak. I started trembling and could feel myself falling into aftershock, thinking of what could have been. As I was falling, Drew grabbed me and laid me gently on the ground. I lay there thinking, *If my friends didn't help me, what were those beams of light?*

Lord Devcon looked down at me and said, 'We thought that all would be lost with the Evil capturing you, and with him stopping us from crossing the bridge, we had no way to help you. But your powers are much stronger than ever we imagined.'

I looked up at my friends as they stared back at me with concern upon their faces. 'But I saw you all holding hands,' I said, 'and seven lights converging to a single beam and then straight down upon me.'

Naroof, who had not said a word until now, repeated what Jula had said. 'We didn't help you, Mecco. It was not us.'

Tarvin and Drew looked at each other. 'Did you say seven beams of light?' asked Drew.

'Yes, it looked seven, maybe six, but I can't be sure,' I responded.

Tarvin looked at me, then Drew, then the rest of the company. 'There is something you all must know,' he announced. 'When we get back to the outpost of Malfarcus, we must talk.'

As we looked across the gorge, I saw that the bridge was still there, and the evil forces were nowhere to be seen. All looked peaceful.

'The bridge is there,' I said. 'How could it be? The Evil destroyed it and it fell into the ravine.'

'The bridge was not destroyed,' said Naroof. 'It was a trick of the Evil. He mesmerised you into thinking it had collapsed. There is nothing we can do here now,' he continued. 'The Evil has retreated into his fort, and those gates cannot be penetrated. We must retreat and devise a plan for the future, which must involve returning with a larger army and breaching the city of Malfarcus.'

We marched back to the outpost at the start of the gorge. I rode down with Drew, my arms wrapped round his waist. I felt safe now, and it was good to be back with my friends. El Masrew was riding with Tarvin, and they rode alongside us. I knew exactly what he was going to say.

'Yes, El Masrew,' I said, 'I feel such guilt as well for leaving Lord Sebcon. But as I said this, he interrupted me.

'We all have a rendezvous with death. It is our final adventure.' He reached out his hand to mine and grabbed it. 'You are a good lad,' he said, 'and may the luck of the Elves be with you always.'

On the trip down the gorge, the company bombarded me, one after the other, with questions. I lost count of how many times I told them of our escape from Malfarcus.

The sun had set, but the wizard Naroof said, 'We must ride on and prepare for the troops so when they reach the outpost of Malfarcus, there will be food and lodgings ready for them.'

When we arrived, the Dwarfs that had been left at the fort helped us with the preparations. The wizard Naroof ushered the two companies into a large room where Bayrew and Wayrew were lighting a massive log fire. We made ourselves comfortable, sitting and silently staring at the crackling fire, waiting for the others to arrive. Then Naroof, Tarvin, and Drew entered.

'Now,' commanded Naroof, 'explain the mystery of the beams of light to the rest of the company.'

The two Elves sat down, and Naroof gestured to Tarvin. 'We have angels helping us,' he announced.

The room fell silent except for the crackling of the fire as we sat with our mouths agape. I thought, *Angels? Angels? Beams of light.* I then remembered all those strange experiences of seeing lights and Jula saying she saw glowing, flying people only a few days ago. Seconds passed though it seemed like ages, then all at once, there was a crescendo of questions.

'Please, quiet,' shouted Tarvin, then he went on. 'The old parchments we brought from the Old World had a line at the end of the prophecies in ancient Elvan. This line when we translated said,

When times are rough and the world is in despair,
Seven angels in the sky they will appear,
To help balance the power of the Evil force.
Their light will help to change the course.

Knowing nothing of angels and not being sure of our translation, we never mentioned it. Now we must assume the translation was correct all the time and we can continue the quest, knowing we have powerful protectors.'

'But who are these angels,' asked Lord Arcon, 'and why help us now?'

'Even among Elves,' replied Tarvin, 'angels are only a myth, and your guess as to why they should help us now is as good as mine.'

'It can't be!' said Jarew. 'There are no such things as angels.'

'The strange thing about angels', declared Arcon, 'is that they are said to be only real for those who believe in them, so you shall never see one.'

Naroof sat, not saying a word, just listening to the discussion.

'I don't think we should worry', said Drew, 'why or for whatever reason they have decided to help us, but the fact is they are helping us.'

Jula piped up, saying, 'I hope we get to meet them. I would love to meet an angel.'

Naroof finally stood up to address the meeting and exclaimed, 'If we have need of angels to balance the power, then the Evil must be growing stronger somehow. I think we should head back to Basscala and spend the rest of winter there and try to find out whatever we can about the Evil, his weaknesses, and how to breach the city of Malfarcus. We must also send spies into the three cities of the Evil. If the angels appear again, we will worry about them when it happens. So rest tonight, and tomorrow, we march back to Basscala before the heavy snows arrive.'

The Six of Croll moved off into an adjoining room where there was another log fire raging and made themselves comfortable.

Jula and Wecco asked, 'Are any of you hungry?'

The company shook their heads except yes, you guessed it, Rocco. So Jula went out and got some supplies and made up a board of cheeses, speck, olives, and chopped apples. It looked so appetising that in the end, everyone decided to have some, much to Rocco's annoyance. We sat there discussing what had happened to us during the past year and what was to come. Then Drew, Carew, Tarew, and Jarew asked if they could join us.

'Of course, please make yourselves comfortable,' said Jula, and she added, 'We thought you were still in discussion, and we didn't want to disturb you.'

I think they were a little disappointed we didn't invite them to join us. So not to cause any more problems, I asked if any of the others wished to join us. The three Elves of the north—El Masrew, Bayrew, and Wayrew—jumped at the invitation, as did the Dwarfs Dolark and Soltain. The wizard Naroof, Tarvin, Master Baylib, and the three lords stayed talking.

After a half an hour, Lord Arcon told us all to get some rest, as tomorrow would be a big day. We all settled around the fire, snuggled up in the sheepskin jackets I had bought in the valley of Prill. I had Peto on one side of me, resting his head on my shoulder, and Drew on the other side, with his hand resting on my arm. I dozed off realising how much I loved my friends and how safe I felt with them all nearby.

The End

THE ELVAN CALENDAR

There are thirteen years with names, and each elf born in a particular year has the year affixed to the end of their name; for example, the first four Elves in the story were all born in the year of Rew: Drew, Carew, Tarew, and Jarew. In this history, you will come across other Elves born in different years, and their names will have that year affixed at the end of their name.

The years are

Vin	Way	Wing
Ruth	Mort	Gong
Say	Rad	Rew
Ven	Young	
Rong	Matta	

THE DWARF CALENDAR

The Dwarf calendar consists of fourteen months of twenty-six days, and every four years, another day is added to the months of Mac. The Dwarfs also have the month they were born as a suffix to the end of their name.

Para, Lib, Lark
Tain, Hillock, Pid
Look, Bain, Prac
Cholas, Brack
Main, Mac, Lain

PLACES

The four provinces of the New World are

North: New Callisto

East: Bossintia

West: Sardaroof

South: Mardascon.

The Dunes of Croll

The river Condoor

The village of Malla

The forest of Gundi

The forest of Gong

The tree of Golla

The village of Woodchisel

The village of Guy

The falls of Nebbia Circum

The city of Basscala, home of Revcon and Devcon

The caves of Mooloo

The lake of the black swans

The forest of Woolinbar

The valley of Kassob

The city and castle of Kassob, home of the wizard Naroof

The evil city of Bossak, the home of the wizard Drascar

The river Underhill

The fallen city of Blarak

The fallen city of Howyard

The village of Gamba

The village of Bassmont

The city and fort of Malfarcus

The gorge and River Malfarcus

The River Hawk

The port of Hawksfort

The town of Garlarbi

The River Kutta

The triple lakes of Bulla

The river and lake Bacca

The lakes of Eople

Mount Gatta

The valley of Prill

The village of Dissident

The great forest of Barrington

The gorge of Malfarcus

The Valley of Dead Fig Trees

The River Malfarcus

INDEX

P

R

S

CPSIA information can be obtained
at www.ICGtesting.com
Printed in the USA
BVHW022054070722
641565BV00019B/259